A SIMPLE
TWIST
OF FATE

A SIMPLE TWIST OF FATE

APRIL ASHER

ST. MARTIN'S GRIFFIN
NEW YORK

First published in the United States by St. Martin's Griffin, an imprint of St. Martin's Publishing Group

A SIMPLE TWIST OF FATE. Copyright © 2025 by April Schwartz. All rights reserved. Printed in the United States of America. For information, address St. Martin's Publishing Group, 120 Broadway, New York, NY 10271.

www.stmartins.com

Library of Congress Cataloging-in-Publication Data (TK)

ISBN 978-1-250-35785-4 (trade paperback)
ISBN 978-1-250-35786-1 (ebook)

Our books may be purchased in bulk for promotional, educational, or business use. Please contact your local bookseller or the Macmillan Corporate and Premium Sales Department at 1-800-221-7945, extension 5442, or by email at MacmillanSpecialMarkets@macmillan.com.

First Edition: 2025

10 9 8 7 6 5 4 3 2 1

Mom.
You taught me that there is strength beyond muscles,
bravery beyond epic battles, and courage that far
outweighs measurable actions. And most importantly,
that *Fate* is what we make it.

A SIMPLE
TWIST
OF FATE

I

Teenagers Are Velociraptors

Harlow "Harry" Pierce caught a hex, and not one of the insignificant varieties where you reached for Clearasil pimple patches and hoped your new concealer really did *cover it all*. No, luck and Harry were not best friends nor acquaintances. At this point she'd take frenemies with benefits over the cold, hard reality.

This curse wielder meant business, throwing her off-kilter by messing with her commutes all week and then knocking her to the ground with a double whammy—getting fired from the company *she'd* built and surviving a horrific case of food poisoning. You'd think being sacked while puking your guts out would've delighted any ill-wisher, but nope.

Lulled into a false sense of security, she didn't see the third clobbering until, after a quick sprint to the mailroom, she stood—dressed in her Wolf Girl Gone Wild summer PJs—in the hall outside her locked apartment door and realized the teenager supposed to be serving a grounding sentence in her bedroom was MIA.

But not for long.

Harry turned the corner of Lafayette Street and headed up Broome, her thick-soled wolf slippers protecting her from both the hot New York City summer sidewalk and its questionable puddles. Even in the SoHo neighborhood, no one balked at her choice of evening wear or the magical compass lighting her palm as she used her descry magics to track down a soon-to-be even *more* grounded sixteen-year-old.

Descry abilities didn't come in handy often. Lost necklace here. Misplaced vibrator there. In the case of her professional organization business, her meager magics helped turn over-crowded and nonfunctional rooms into blissfully efficient spaces. But that was before she'd gotten the board boot that afternoon. Now, most of her magical usage would come from being the guardian of a surly teenager whose life goal was tripling Harry's gray hair count before she hit thirty-five.

Harry's palm flared brightly a second before the light flickered and petered out. Unease twisted her stomach into knots as she glanced up at a nondescript redbrick building. Blackened windows that hadn't seen a squeegee's damp side in goddess knows how long made it impossible to peer inside, and a precariously dangling sign hung over an aged green door, the only indication that the place hadn't been abandoned eons ago.

A Demon's Promise. Brokering Agency.

"Oh, I don't think so." She yanked open the door to the demon-brokering company, her earlier unease morphing into angry determination as she drilled the demon behind the counter with a hard glare. "Back away from the kid. Right now."

Two heads swiveled her way.

"You've got to be kidding me." Grace released her signature annoyed huff, shoulders slumping.

"Can I help you?" The Quell demon's reptilian eyes flickered as he studied Harry with wary interest.

"No, but I can help you by giving you five seconds to throw away that contract before I call the Supernatural authorities. She won't be needing it," Harry snapped.

Grace glared at her, the teen's staple facial expression right up there with the exaggerated eye roll and snort of derision. "What are you doing here?"

"Preventing you from doing something that you can't take back. Making a Demon's Promise will bring nothing but problems."

"So, in other words nothing will have changed."

The supernatural behind the counter cleared his throat. "If I may interrupt . . ."

"You may not," Harry and Grace said in unison.

Harry summoned her best mom glare, which was admittedly pretty damn weak, considering she'd only had a year's worth of practice, and propped her hands on her ample hips. "I don't know what kind of shifty operation you're running here, buddy, but—"

"I operate a legitimate business." He puffed out his barrel chest, the move thinning his nearly see-through shirt. "I don't need to resort to shifty operations."

"What's so legitimate about signing a minor to a Demon's Promise? Because the last time I checked, it was punishable by a lifetime sentence in the sulfur pits of Hell."

The older demon's red-scaled face paled to a dark pink. "I—I didn't know."

"And now you do. So, what will it be?" She held up her phone, careful not to show the blank screen. She'd gotten a low-battery warning the second she'd left the subway station, and the damn thing was as dead as her dating life, but that was on a need-to-know basis. "Am I calling the authorities, or will you be warming up your shredder?"

The demon snatched the contract laid out in front of Grace and, with a parting stink eye, hustled through a beaded curtain and into a back room. Harry waited for the following door slam before she turned to a feral teen.

"I can't believe you just did that!" Grace accused angrily.

"And I can't believe you even entertained this as an option! What the hell were you thinking . . . or were you even thinking at all?"

"He said he could help."

"He'd say anything if it got your signature on that paper, Gracie, and Supernatural Law or not, once it was there, there wouldn't have been anything we could've done to remove it."

"How many times do I have to tell you that it's *Grace*? Not Gracie. Or Gracie Lou. G-R-A-C-E."

Twelve dozen. Fifty. Truthfully, it didn't matter how many reminders she got, Grace would always be the three-year-old toddler Harry had met when she answered an ad for a roommate thirteen years ago.

Harry pointed to the door. "Let's go. We'll talk about this more when we get home."

Grace flicked her gaze over her outfit, landing last on her wolf-paw-clad feet. "I am *not* walking next to you when you're wearing that."

"Why? Embarrassing? Good. Then I'll stick real close to your side so there's not a doubt in people's minds that we're together. After all, if you'd been in your room, where you were supposed to be, then I wouldn't have trekked across town wearing my PJs." She pointed to the door again. "Now move it before I decide that belting out 'Hungry Like the Wolf' is a good way to pass time on our commute home."

Grace's dark eyes narrowed. "Even you wouldn't be that embarrassing."

"Oh yeah? Move it, kiddo. Or I'll make sure we take the long way home for shits and giggles." Harry rose to the challenge, mentally apologizing to the poor people about to suffer through her singing voice.

This time, on their commute back to Brooklyn Heights, she got a few looks and led two different sing-alongs, one on the R train, where Grace looked prepped to hurl herself out the nearest emergency window. Through it all, Harry mentally formulated a plan and a speech, and hoped like hell she didn't say something stupid.

In all reality, she didn't need to be hexed to put her wolf-slippered foot in her mouth. Unlike parenting, *that* came naturally, even more so when dealing with a teenager whose inner supernatural decided it was no longer content remaining confined in its human skin suit. Mystery genetics aside, her best friend, Cassie, made the parenting thing look so damn easy, which was one reason why Harry agreed to becoming Grace's temporary guardian while Cassie attempted to track down her one and only one-night stand and demand answers.

They'd hoped for it to take a month, and then one month turned into two, then two morphed into six. Now at over a year, Harry mourned the loss of her Cool Aunt Harry title and warily accepted the hostile attitude, frequent eye rolls, and annoyed snorts that came with her new one . . .

Teenage fun-killer.

Never show weakness. Cassie's parting words echoed in her head. *Teenagers are like velociraptors. When they smell blood, they go in the for the kill.*

Harry stopped singing Duran Duran while Grace keyed them into their apartment, and the second they stepped into their cozy two bedroom and closed the door, the teenager bee-lined to her room.

"We need to talk about what happened." Harry firmed her voice and crossed her fingers it didn't waver.

Grace pointed to her ears. "Can't hear you. I'm listening to music. Something recorded this century."

Harry called on her magic—and the green earbud—and magically plucked the device from Grace's left ear. "Pink will still be around a few minutes from now and then you can go back to ignoring me. But first, we talk and have an actual conversation."

Goddess. Her mother's words somehow transported through time and space—and from her parents' archaeological dig six thousand miles away—and flew out her mouth. She'd be so damn proud.

A soft, golden spark flickered in the teen's usually dark brown eyes, a sign her inner supernatural was rising close to the surface. "Pink is more *your* speed. And I'm listening to music so I don't *have* to carry on a conversation with you."

"First, do not use my love for Pink as a negative personality trait. It's uncalled for and downright rude. Not to mention a bit hurtful."

"And second?" Grace cocked her hip. "If there's a first, that means there's a second."

Smart teenage smart-ass. "I'm still thinking one up."

Harry's gaze drifted over to today's mail sitting on the

kitchen table and the very distinct manila envelope on top . . . and not where she'd left it.

Things slowly clicked into place.

She'd received notification from Grace's school that afternoon, the principal officially extending her suspension indefinitely. Accidentally set fire to *one* chem lab and they got their knickers in a twist . . . but add that infraction to the list of others and they had a tiny leg on which to stand. A thin flamingo leg, but a leg nonetheless.

Ignoring the pit of uncertainty churning in her stomach, Harry lifted her chin. "We're not giving up, Grace. And maybe homeschooling isn't such a bad idea while—"

"I'm lighting things on fire?" The teenager lifted a dark eyebrow, her tone laced heavily with sarcasm.

"While we consider all our options."

"We have no more options, Harry. Especially now that my name is probably blacklisted by every Promise broker in the tristate area."

"*That* was never an option and it never will be." Harry pushed a hopeful smile onto her face. "I requested a meeting with Alpha Cho, from the Salem, Massachusetts, pack, and once I get word, we can—"

"Go on another road trip for no reason. Great." Grace rolled her eyes, plucking her earbud from Harry's hand. "What makes you think they can help when all the others before them couldn't? Or the covens before them? We've road-tripped to dozens of supernatural groups all over the Eastern Seaboard, and they've all shrugged their shoulders and sent us on our merry way."

"Not *all*. The coven out of Vermont gave us our third verification that we *are* dealing with an inner shifter. There's someone out there who can help. We just haven't found them yet," Harry stated adamantly.

"Well, it's their turn to seek, because I'm getting damn tired of it." Grace turned to the short hall that led to her room, each step stealing another ounce of moisture from Harry's mouth.

Time was up, and it fucking hurt Harry to swallow the fully formed lump in her throat. "My aunt Nora invited us to come live with her . . . and I think we need to go."

Grace spun, her dark eyes wide. "The aunt Nora who lives in Bumblefuck, Colorado?"

Harry shot her an unamused look. "That would be *Fates Haven*, Colorado, and you may want to curb that sailor mouth around Nora."

"So you've already decided that we're going? No 'conversation' about it? No making a pro and con list? Harry makes the decision and that's how it is? What about your job? And Mom?"

"My job is no longer an issue and your mom and I talked about the possibility of Colorado the last time she checked in." Which was almost a month ago . . . not that Harry was counting.

It turned out finding Taylor Swift tickets was easier for Cassie than tracking an almost-nameless supernatural with a love for old rock music and living off-grid.

Grace snortled. "Great. Then it was just me left in the dark. Even better."

"Look, I didn't tell Aunt Nora yes for certain, but I think it's something we should seriously consider."

Tiny embers sparked from Grace's fingertips, quickly turning to a steady blue and pink pulsing flame. Grace and Harry had learned a while back that her fire didn't hurt Grace, but the toll it took on her surroundings was an entirely different story.

"Ugh. Why does this keep *happening*?" Grace growled.

Harry kept her voice soft and calm. "Remember the breathing exercises that the Savannah Coven taught you. In for four. Hold. Out for six."

"It's not working." Grace glanced at her fully-fire-encompassed hands with panicked, golden-speckled eyes. "It's growing. It keeps getting bigger!"

"Look at me, not your hands," Harry demanded gently, stepping forward. "Breathe."

"Stay back. I don't want to hurt you." Grace took a hasty step toward the window, her chest heaving with quick, heavy breaths. "See. *This* is why I went to Demon's Promise. I need them to take this away before I hurt someone . . . or worse."

"Honey, they can't take this away. You need to breathe, and let me help you." Harry reached for her, but the teen snapped back, her fire-laden hands getting too close to the nearby curtain.

A single fiery ember danced through the short space and landed on the thick cotton material. Harry watched in horrified fascination as that one spark transformed into a full-fledged flame, lighting the entire window treatment faster than any witch could say hocus-pocus.

Grace's startled cry jolted Harry into action seconds before the smoke alarm wailed overhead. By the time she dug through the kitchen's under the sink cabinet and returned with the fire extinguisher, the fire had jumped from one window drape to the next.

"Stay back." She pulled a frightened—and now flameless—teenager away from the growing fire, and tugged the pin.

In less than ten seconds, a thick white mist coated their entire apartment, but Harry used every last bit of it, making it look like it had snowed indoors before calling it quits.

Five minutes later, and holding an eviction notice to prove her landlord hadn't issued an empty threat when he'd spewed "third strike—or fire in your case—in a week, and you're out," she plugged her dead cell phone into a charger and had her first call connecting.

"Hey, Aunt Nora." Keeping one eye on the too-quiet sixteen-year-old three feet away, Harry let out a resigned sigh at the older woman's gentle greeting. "Is that offer to come home still good?"

"That offer never expires, dear." The older witch's familiar, melodic voice brought tears to Harry's eyes. "Bring yourself and my new niece to mix one cup of water, one cup of mayonnaise, and a teaspoon of vanilla."

Harry blinked, trying to connect the nonsensical words when she realized . . .

The Witch's Oath.

The one she'd had Nora swear before Harry had left Fates Haven. The one that prevented Nora from sharing anything about Fates Haven or its inhabitants with Harry, instead, belting out random recipes.

Nora sighed, her frustration with the oath palpable even over the phone. "If you're coming home to chocolate mayonnaise cake, maybe we can reevaluate this little oath thing, yeah?"

Harry grimaced. "Maybe."

"There's healing to be had, Harlow Pierce, and the blending of the cocoa and sugar will be here to help."

"We'll see you in a few days." Harry swallowed her forming ball of emotions. "And, Nora?"

"Yes, dear?"

"Let's keep this low-key, okay? No one-page ads in the *Haven Herald*. No streamers."

"Fine, but a parade is still an option, right?"

"Uh, no."

Nora went a bit too quiet.

"Aunt Nora?" Harry prodded.

"Hm?"

"I mean it. No fanfare."

"Yes, dear. I understand . . . but you realize that chocolate mayonnaise cake is still chocolate mayonnaise cake, yes?"

Harry sighed. There was no way she could forget. "I know."

Nora didn't need an ad in the town paper, to hit up a party supply store, or organize a parade for Fates Haven citizens to find out the Runaway Pierce Witch was back in town. The shifters would quickly sniff her out. The witches, sense her magic. And the vampires, see her miles before she crossed the borders into the supernatural Denver suburb.

And that was if the seers didn't already see her coming.

2

Sugar Tits & Treats

Jaxon Atwood put out so many fires this morning, adding firefighter to his résumé wouldn't be much of an exaggeration. First, a *literal* fire, created by teenage shifters curious about what type of fireworks generated the biggest wow factor when tossed in a bonfire, and then a long line of metaphorical ones of adults lacking the ability to settle their own squabbles.

He'd once thought his mother overly dramatic when she'd complained about being a glorified babysitter to the country's largest shifter pack. Hell, he'd even scoffed, sure she'd been exaggerating, but now he bore the Alpha title and his mother never missed an opportunity to tell him *I told you so*. Not that he'd admit it to her, but she'd downplayed the pain-in-the-ass level on such a deep scale.

Having averted yet another crisis that could've waited until morning, Jax hung up his latest call and shoved his cell in his pocket. He should've finished handling Rocky Mountain

Pack stuff hours ago and already completed a half-day's work at Pierce House, but he'd been forced to call Nora and reschedule yet again.

Not that the older witch minded, but *he* did. He'd looked forward to demo day on her gazebo all damn week and not only because it meant working out his frustrations with a heavy mallet and a crowbar. It also meant bringing the existing structure back to life and as owner of Restoration & Renewal, he could make it happen.

To Nora Pierce, those currently rotten wood planks meant the world. Restoring her gazebo to its former glory was the least he could do for the woman who supported him through his teenage asshole years.

Hell, she put up with him through his adult asshole years, too, one of the few people in town who never obeyed the fuck-off stamp etched on his forehead. Jax wasn't good with words, or feelings, but he sure as hell knew his way around plank beams and buzz saws.

Jax parked his R & R pickup along the curb in front of Howlin' Good Time, his hands twitching on the steering wheel as he contemplated pulling right back onto Fates Boulevard and heading home to his cozy—and isolated—cabin. He wasn't in the right headspace to "people." Not that he ever was, according to his friends.

A back-out story formed in his head, but as he glanced at the local watering hole, it paused. Loud, pulsing music and laughter normally spilled out from the front door, the town hot spot pushing the fire-code rigidity on a nightly basis. But not only was the pub atypically quiet and dark, but empty.

Jax glanced up the boulevard to see each storefront looked

the same, dark window after dark window. The faint, faraway sound of music combined with the entire town already packed up for the night meant one thing.

If he moved quickly enough, he could get home before anyone spotted him.

As if sensing his looming departure, his cell rang.

Jax contemplated letting it go straight to voicemail, but instead, answered with a growl. "What?"

"Get your fucking, scowling ass over here, Atwood," Silas McCloud's low baritone rumbled from the other end of the line.

"Asses don't scowl, jackass."

"Huh. Then that must be your face. Maybe one of these days I won't confuse the two."

Jax shut off the ignition and climbed out his truck. "And where exactly should I be hauling my scowling ass because it looks like everyone has already packed up for the night."

"Glance to your left, man. Follow the sound of the music."

Jax glanced across the street toward Havenhood Park, the Haven's micro version of New York City's famous Central Park, and sure enough . . .

People walked the grassy knoll while others relaxed on picnic blankets spread over the ground. The town's iconic Starlight Gazebo was ablaze in little white fairy lights; and further to the left, the sound of music drifted from the direction of Pixie Pavilion.

"And what's the occasion tonight?" Jax pocketed his keys and jogged across the street.

"Do the people of Fates need a reason to let down their hair and dance under the moonlight?" Silas snarked.

No truer words were ever uttered. The Full Moon Frolic.

Movie Monday Under the Moonlight. If the day of the week ended in a *y*, the citizens of Fates found inspiration for a community gathering.

"Move it faster, man. If you're not warming a stool in five seconds or less, Maddox and I are dragging you over by your tail. I bet even Gavin will risk wrinkling his suit to help, too."

Low laughter and echoed agreements went off in the background.

Jax crossed the knoll and headed toward the pavilion, giving a few hello nods on his way. "You know, three-on-one odds don't bother me. It's not like I won't come out on top."

Silas chuckled. "You're really pushing it, Atwood."

Jax chuckled, and his inner cougar practically purred at the idea of taking on his friends.

Although the demon no longer worked as an assassin for hire, and Silas had cut ties with the Angelic Academy where he'd had a brief stint as an instructor, neither his skills nor his reflexes suffered. Opening Beast Mode, the gym and workout spot a few storefronts down from Howlin', he stayed both sharp and lethal, even hosting MMA nights—or what he called organized ass kicking—that brought people from all over.

Maddox King, although technically human, could also hold his own in a brawl . . . especially if it was to protect someone in his tight circle. Jax had wondered on more than one occasion if the tattoo artist didn't have at least a little supernatural in him.

But it was Gavin Bishop, one of Fates Haven's newest residents, who was the real wild card in any potential three-on-one scuffle. A friend of Mad's from their college days, the reserved vampire sported a British accent and played the bookish librarian part for the Fates Haven Public Library extremely well. But instincts—and seeing the vampire wail on the heavy bag at Beast Mode—told Jax that the quiet guy hid a hell of a lot behind his pressed suits and perfectly kempt hair.

The four of them were all different. All assholes in their own ways. And the bastards were probably the only people who could talk him into something he didn't want to do—or out of something he did.

"Just get over here." Silas hung up with a warning growl as Jax reached the Pixie Pavilion, Howlin' Good Times' pop-up spot for Fates Haven outdoor events.

Slow-moving ceiling fans kept the air circulating beneath the structure's copper roof, but despite the slight breeze, it was still hot as hell, Jax's T-shirt practically suctioning to his back.

It didn't take long to find his friends. They'd be hard to miss even if his inner mountain lion didn't pick up their distinct scents quickly. They sat at the bar, each grinning at him from over half-empty beer mugs. A low-key sense of dread formed in the pit of his stomach because smirks usually spelled trouble.

The majority of people stared openly as Jax wove his way through the crowd, a few skittering from his path and quickly averting their eyes as they dipped their heads to whisper to one another.

Although a Denver suburb, Fates Haven maintained its small-town feel with its quaint cobblestoned sidewalks and magically glowing lanterns that lit up Fates Boulevard every sunset. And then there was the robust gossip mill. Newsworthy or not, nothing remained secret in Fates for long, whether it was from pure nosiness or in someone's best interest.

Judging by the rise in blatant murmurs as he crossed the pavilion, this round of gossip consisted of the former.

He ignored the curious stares as he grabbed the empty seat

next to Silas and nodded to Howlin's new owner. "Hey there, Kailani."

"Alpha At—"

"Kai," Jax growled in warning. He shot her a hard look that tipped her mouth into a knowing smirk.

"You know that to get used to the title, you eventually have to use it, right?" Kai teased.

"Eventually isn't right now, and definitely not after spending all day listening to people kiss Alpha Atwood's ass."

She slid him his usual without him asking. "Point made. Let me know if you need something with more kick."

"An ice water is perfect, Kai. Thanks." With a parting nod, she turned toward the next waiting customer.

"Glad you decided to join us," Silas's baritone voice teased.

"You made the invitation sound so inviting. How could I refuse?"

The demon snorted. "Relax, you'll have plenty of time to embrace your inner furmit and hibernate in your bear cave until the morning, or whatever you shifters do."

"Mountain lions don't hibernate and they sure as hell don't live in bear dens. You'd think a former bigwig assassin to the Powers That Be would know his shifter traits. And what the hell is a furmit?"

"A hermit who sprouts fur." Silas sent him a pointed look. "Look in the mirror and you'll see Exhibit A. And I do know shifter traits. I'm an expert on all supe entities."

Maddox, sitting on Silas's other side, snorted. "Except if that supernatural is a curvy-bodied angel whose favorite accessory happens to be a three-foot-long celestial blade."

Silas drilled an elbow into the other guy's rib cage. Mad

nearly toppled from his seat, the bulky tattoo artist clutching his midsection and sucking in a wheezy breath. "Fuck, man. I think you bruised a rib."

"Humans. So fragile," the demon quipped as Gavin, a grip on the back of Maddox's shirt, effectively lifted him back into position. "Maybe you should put your mouth on a leash. Jax probably has one you can borrow."

Maddox released a pained laugh, chuckling harder as his attention slid over their shoulders. "I couldn't have asked for better timing than this."

Jax didn't ask what he was talking about because the demon stiffened, instantly alert. Only one person got that kind—or any kind—of reaction from the levelheaded Silas.

Elodie Quinn approached, her gaze flicking from Gavin to Maddox, pointedly skipping Silas, and then landed on Jax. "Can we talk for a second?"

The warrior angel may look the picture of petite innocence, but he knew firsthand the redhead didn't intimidate easily and she possessed the ass-kicking ability to back up her snarky attitude. It was a necessary skill when ridding the world of rogue demonic entities hell-bent on bringing hell to earth.

Although she hadn't been doing much ass kicking lately. Jax hadn't asked for particulars, but he didn't think her return to Fates Haven a few months ago was entirely her own idea.

The angel nibbled her thumbnail, a telltale sign something was on her mind.

"Depends." He eyed her warily.

She cocked an auburn eyebrow. "On?"

"Is it about whatever put that look on your face? Because I hit my quota for headache-inducing issues a few hours ago.

Best try your luck tomorrow." She shot him a hard glare, making him sigh. "Or now. What's up?"

"Have you heard? The entire town is practically buzzing about it."

Jax glanced around the pavilion; and sure enough, at least a dozen people brazenly stared their way, one vampire in the corner watching so raptly he spilled his blood shake over the front of his white polo shirt.

A bad feeling settled low in Jax's stomach. "You know I don't care shit-all about the Fates Haven gossip mill. People's business is *their* business, not mine."

"She's coming back, Jax," Elodie whispered.

He chose that exact moment to take a swig of water; and at her words, the liquid traveled the wrong way. He choked. Tears sprang to his eyes as he attempted sucking in a dose of oxygen.

"Are you attempting to kill the man?" Silas glowered at the angel, slamming his broad hand against Jax's back. "You can't drop that kind of a bomb on someone and not expect a volatile reaction."

El's eyes narrowed on the demon. "I must have missed class the day you covered that at the academy."

"Not like you would've listened even if you had been there," Silas volleyed. "I've never met anyone more averse to following directions than you. It really is amazing that you lasted in the Warrior Guard as long as you did."

"I follow the directions that make sense, and my leave of absence is only temporary."

By the time Jax took easy, unobstructed breaths, the two former colleagues looked ready to pummel each other.

He coughed, gaining the angel's attention. Pretending he didn't know who *she* was insulted them both.

Harlow Pierce.

Harry.

Once upon a time, Nora's great-niece had been the center of their teenage friend group, and the heart of his entire world. To anyone on the outside, they made no sense. She'd been the calm to his storm, the soft, smooth edges to his hard, jagged ones. They'd been opposites in every way, and yet it hadn't mattered a damn bit.

Until suddenly it did.

Until that Fates Festival when she left him standing in the middle of Havenhood Park with love on his mind and heartbreak ripping apart his fucking chest.

"She's not coming back, El." His voice came out harsher than he'd meant it to. "It's like those celebrity death hoaxes that circulate every year."

"Yeah, but this time it's—"

"People attempting to cure their boredom by stirring up the past. That's all it is."

"But—"

"Harry is *not* coming back to Fates, Elodie!" Jax immediately regretted his outburst as dozens of heads, which had all been previously side-eyeing him, now stared blatantly.

All the looks now made sense.

Scrubbing a hand over his face, Jax battled his inner cougar for control, the cat practically clawing apart his insides. "Harry made it clear on multiple occasions that she has no intention of ever setting foot back in town. And in case you somehow missed it, we sure as hell didn't miss the anti-tracking spell she dropped on her way out."

He sure as hell didn't. Not the first time he'd attempted to track her and ended up standing in front of the country's

"Largest Adult Sex Shop," nor the second time when he could've posed with the Guinness World Records largest feline hairball. Every attempt to find the Runaway Witch ended in some off-the-wall, obscure location.

With no Harry in sight.

"Don't do this to yourself each time this rumor resurfaces, El. You need to get over it. Get over *her*."

She glared at him. "Oh? Like you?"

"I don't know what you're talking about." He gripped his glass a little tighter than necessary, jaw clenched.

"Sure you don't, Mr. Happy and Carefree."

"I'm perfectly happy."

"And full of bullshit, apparently. Tell me, how many relationships have you had over the last thirteen years?" She pointed a finger at him in warning when he opened his mouth. "I'm not talking about your one-night sexual distractions. I'm talking about an actual give-and-take relationship with emotions on the line."

He returned her glare with one of his own and answered with a blatant non answer.

She snorted. "My point exactly . . . so pardon me for holding out a little hope. I've been waiting for years for the chance to apologize—"

"Apologize for what?" Jax's cougar growled low in his throat. "We did *nothing* wrong, Elodie. That ceremony fucked us over as much as it did everyone else in this town."

"But the two of you—"

"El, do you feel like we're Fated Mates?" Next to Jax, a strangled sound came from somewhere in the direction of a certain silent demon.

"Fuck, no." Her lip curled up in disgust.

"And what would you do if I laid a kiss on you right now?"

"I'd send a palm thrust into your *nose*, and then follow it with a knee to the *gut*. Maybe top it off with an elbow to the *ear*. A typical NGE." Her lips twitched into a small, knowing grin.

"Exactly. No Fate Match. No feelings. No need for a fucking apology." Fuck, he wished the knot in his chest would loosen. "I get your need to hold on to a little hope, but sometimes hope leads to disappointment and we've all experienced enough of that to last us a lifetime. I sure as hell have. Why add to it unnecessarily?"

"Something feels different about it this time. I can't really explain it."

"Are your angel senses tingling? There's probably a cream or something you can get for that."

Chuckling, she shoved his shoulder. "Fuck you, very much, Atwood. I'm serious."

"So am I. Trust me. All this Harry-is-coming-to-town gossip will die by morning . . . or I'll buy you that yearly subscription you keep yapping on and on about."

Her eyes rounded eagerly. "The Sugar Tits & Treats monthly subscription box?"

"That would be the one."

A small smile blossomed on her face. "Well, I guess a girl wins either way. You're on."

She flashed him a wink and left as abruptly as she'd arrived, disappearing into the growing crowd. All three of his friends openly stared at him with mixed looks of what the fuck?

"What?" Jax questioned.

Silas lifted a dark eyebrow and broke the silence first. "Did you seriously offer to buy Elodie the subscription box from my grandma's bakery?"

"Yeah. Why?"

"You have no idea what's in one of those things, do you?" Maddox grinned.

"I would assume whatever their monthly treat is. It's not like it matters, because I'm not wrong. No way is Harlow Pierce showing her face back in Fates Haven."

"You better hope so . . . or you'll have to come to grips with the fact you're building your friend's sex toy stash one subscription box at time."

The guys laughed at his expense while he digested the new information. A taste *and* a treat . . . at Sugar Tits Bakery.

Well, fuck.

His friends' laughter grew louder as he swallowed a groan. Elodie would have to buy her own Sugar Tits box because he wasn't wrong. The day Harlow Pierce rolled back into town was the day one of her aunt's garden gnomes became something other than a nuisance.

3

Cinna-Boob Buns & Erection Éclairs

Steam poured out from beneath Harry's hastily bought station wagon, the literal bubble gum Band-Aid she applied to the faulty hose connection a few dozen miles ago doing next to nothing to hold it all together. Buying the thing from a guy nicknamed Bargain Ben was the embodiment of a risky move, but time constraints and monetary funds necessitated desperate measures.

The hunk of junk only needed to survive a few more miles.

Literally. Less than one mile away from the outskirts of Fates Haven, and then another two until they reached Pierce House, they'd made over sixteen hundred miles on hope, tears, and gas station junk food.

A lot of gas station junk food.

Her earbuds as firmly implanted as they'd been since leaving New York, Grace scowled from the back seat. "Are we ever getting back on the road? My sweat stains have sweat stains."

"This should last us until with get to Aunt Nora's. If it doesn't, the search and rescue team can use it to track us down." Harry let the hood drop and climbed behind the steering wheel.

She turned on the ignition and held her breath until the engine coughed back to life. "Practically purrs like a kitten."

A sickly rattle shuddered through the car, backfiring out the tailpipe.

Harry winced, catching Grace's eye in the rearview mirror. "So it purrs like a geriatric kitten. It's still a purr."

Eye roll one billion and twenty-three was sent her way as Harry pulled back onto the road, this time with the AC turned off for fear of overheating her bubble gum patch up.

A flock of prehistoric pterodactyls attacked Harry's stomach the closer Fates Haven loomed in the distance. Located along Denver's outskirts and nestled at the base of the Rocky Mountains, the cozy supernatural community announced its presence—and its long-standing position as the global record holder for the highest FMP (Fated Mates Percentage)—with a massive age-ravaged welcome sign.

Become Fated in Fates Haven
Population: 8,584 Living
2,163 Undead and/or Undead Adjacent

"Wow. You take me to all the nicest places, Harry," Grace deadpanned from the back seat. "We should revisit the 'conversation' about how dragging me here isn't a punishment."

"It's not a punishment. It's—"

"The last hope for the lost cause?" A dark eyebrow lifted toward her hairline. "Got it."

Harry snapped her gaze toward the rearview mirror. "You

are *not* a lost cause. And Fates Haven isn't a punishment. It's a great place to grow up. Why do you think I picked the Haven when my parents gave me the option of growing up here with Aunt Nora, or at one archaeological dig after another?"

"If it's so great then why did you run away from here as if your ass was on fire?"

"How did you—"

The teenager snorted. "Please. You and Mom are never as quiet as you think you are when you talk . . . especially on Margarita Mondays."

"If we aren't quiet, then you should already know why I left Fates." She shot the teenager a pointed look and got silence in return, counting that a temporary win.

The truth was even Cassie only knew the CliffsNotes version why she'd left Fates Haven thirteen years ago. *Heartbreak.*

Much more convoluted, the slightly less abridged version consisted of attending the annual Fates Festival Finding Ceremony 100 percent certain that the Blue Willow Wisp would guide her to her Fated, and watching that glowing bastard steer her best friend there instead.

She didn't blame Elodie, or even Jax. Fate answered to no one but itself; and by participating in the Finding Ceremony, you risked discovering your perfect soul match was your mortal enemy since childhood . . . or worse. That it *wasn't* the one you loved with your whole heart.

Knowing—and accepting—the risk didn't prevent Harry's heart from breaking or her feet from moving when she watched Elodie's flame come to a flickering stop right in front of Jaxon.

College, New York City, and her friendship with Cassie helped her heal over time, but sputtering down Fates Boulevard toward Pierce House, her wounds reopened and sent an aching throb through her chest.

Or maybe they'd never healed, her time away having been nothing but a shoddy bubble gum patch job.

The town looked the same except entirely different. Lined with small white lights, Havenhood Park's garden paths blinked like a fairy wonderland, prepped to indulge the fantasies of the Haven's youngest residents or the adults simply looking for a momentary escape.

Since it was nearly eleven o'clock, not much remained open, but in the morning, Ezra Carmichael and his husband, Ali, would be sitting outside the barber shop at their usual table, with large cups of untouched coffee; and Genevieve Michaels, with a broom in hand, would sweep the sidewalk in front of her antique store, Timeless Treasures. But there were definitely a few business additions to the boulevard that hadn't been there when she'd left.

Taking a deep breath to work through the heavy anvil pressing against her chest, Harry stole a glance toward Grace. For the first time during the entire trip, the teen's face wasn't buried in her phone as she watched the passing scenery with wary hesitance.

"It's not New York—" Harry began.

"You think?" Grace snorted. "The sun practically went down a few seconds ago and everything is already closed. What do people do around here for the rest of the night?"

"Sleep?" Her joke earned her a glare. "Seriously, it's not as bad as you're thinking. The boulevard shops usually close early when there's some kind of community event happening."

"Like what? Bingo?"

"Maybe." Her lips twitched. "Or there could be a movie night at Havenhood Park or a bonfire at Mystic Lake. Fates Haven isn't individual people all sharing the same space. It's one big—and sometime dysfunctional—family. It's . . . home."

Folding her slender arms over her chest, Grace slumped back in her seat. "It's not *my* home, and they're certainly not my family. Mine is currently on some pointless quest to find some rando sperm donor that most definitely does not want to be found."

The teen's icy words sent another sliver of pain slicing through Harry's heart. "All I ask is that you try, Grace. Just . . . try. Please."

Harry's gaze flickered to the back seat; and in that split second, she didn't see the snarly teenager but a scared girl doing her best to hide how much she was truly freaked out. Pushing her right now or dare mention anything about *emotions*, and she'd shut down quicker than the Fates Boulevard businesses on community bingo night.

With every block they passed, more smoke plumes billowed out from beneath the car's hood. By the time the wagon rolled to a gradual—and permanent—stop down Nora's long driveway, the engine released one final, ear-piercing death rattle and tuckered out.

Harry felt like the damn car.

Impatient for a shower, food, and to collapse face-first on a soft mattress, she slipped out from the driver's side and soaked in the sight of Pierce House.

Decorated with colorfully bursting flower boxes that would magically bloom all-year thanks to Nora's magical green thumb, the two-story captain-style house stood at the end of the street like a massive bookend, basked in a moony, ethereal glow.

Its large, wraparound porch had hosted more than its fair share of Teddy Bear Tea Parties and welcomed countless trick-or-treaters on Halloween nights. Harry had experienced second base for the first time on that very porch swing. It all seemed like yesterday, but the sagging swing and weathered porch's aged wood planks said otherwise. The slightest weight could probably cave the entire structure.

"Why didn't you tell me, Aunt Nora?" Harry murmured to herself, a weighty sadness settling in her throat.

"Wow." Grace stopped next to her, the look on her face unimpressed. "Guess I can check 'Living in a Horror House' off my bucket list."

"Gracie," Harry warned.

Grace rolled her eyes as Harry tested her weight on the porch's first step. The second her heel hit the aged wood, Nora's welcome chimes, hanging from the front stoop, tinkled in a nonexistent breeze.

"You're invited!" Her aunt's voice filtered in with the music. "Come join us at Havenhood Park or risk boredom! And if you're Harlow, know that I canceled the parade."

Harry groaned. Havenhood Park this late meant one of two things. Either the entire town was present, or it was her aunt's Craft Coven meeting. The former meant her low-key arrival wasn't happening, and the latter meant potentially scarring the teenager at her side because her aunt's crafting buddies were as fond of moonlight skinny-dipping as they were of plaster of paris sculpting.

Unwilling to chance either scenario and willing to do a little breaking and entering, Harry took another step and was met with both an ominous groan of wood and another musical chime.

"Before you go any further," Nora's magical voice warned, "you should know that the house is magically booby-trapped. Another step may lead to trapped boobies."

Behind Harry, Grace snorted. "Is she serious?"

"Unfortunately." Harry retreated down the steps, glowering at the offending chimes. "We'll have to find Aunt Nora at Havenhood and get the bypass phrase."

"Can't you guess it or something? Or—I don't know—use a physical key? All I want to do is eat and sleep—even if it is in the horror house."

"No physical key. And the last person who tried guessing one of Nora's bypass phrases walked away with a permanently enflamed pimple on the tip of their nose. It's not worth all the magical treatments." At least that's what she told herself on a repetitive loop.

"I'll stay here." Grace slid onto the station wagon's smoking hood. "Make sure no one steals the car."

"I'm not that lucky." Harry slipped an arm through the teen's and brought her back to her feet. "But you're coming with me."

"Seriously? I'm sixteen! You don't trust me to stay by myself in Bumblefuck, Colorado?"

"No, I don't trust *myself* alone in Fates Haven, Colorado. If this is one of Nora's attempts to *Nora*, you'll be my voluntary sacrifice. You'll jump into the crowd so I can make my escape. You don't mind a little cheek pinching, right?"

"Actually, yes, I do. And why do you need escape route if this community is *family*?" Grace tossed her words back at her like the smart-ass she was.

"Dysfunctional family," Harry corrected. "And if I hadn't just spent a gazillion hours inhaling car fumes with a surly teenager in the back seat, then I'd be more prepared for dealing with said dysfunction. Don't question. Just walk."

They strode arm in arm down the sidewalk the few blocks toward Havenhood Park, the music echoing in the distance getting louder with each step. Hopefully that meant there wouldn't be any Craft Coven skinny-dipping; and while that should make her happy, it also turned her recently consumed gas station burrito into a small boulder in the pit of her stomach.

Calling on her descry magic, Harry followed the low, warm pulse of Nora's energy to the open area next to Pixie Pavilion.

Find the witch. Get the bypass phrase. Get gone.

That was the plan and for once it appeared she and the teenager next to her shared the same one. Unfortunately, the citizens of Fates Haven didn't have the same mindset. Although not as crowded as the knoll by Starlight Gazebo, the outer fringe of the park wasn't without well-meaning people.

While most old neighbors smiled and nodded in greeting as she and Grace passed, a few more outspoken townspeople stopped her for hugs and small talk. Even more gawked and dipped their heads, whispering behind their screen hands."

Grace let out an irritated huff. "Not exactly subtle, are they? Or quiet." She tossed a mini growl at a pair of teen vampires, who quickly dispersed and scurried in the opposite direction. "I didn't realize the Runaway Witch was my guardian. And here I thought your name was Harry all these years."

Harry barely stifled a groan at the nickname. "Please don't tell me what they're saying. I'd rather not know. Just . . . turn off your shifter hearing."

She snortled. "We wouldn't be here if I could."

"Point made. Let's find Nora, get the pass phrase, and get back to Pierce House where we can—"

"Hide? Wallow? Hunker down?" Grace lifted a dark eyebrow. "Maybe we should perform an exorcism on the place before we close our eyes. Is there a supply store around here for that kind of thing?"

"I was going to say sleep for two days straight, but those first three suggestions work, too." Harry slid her gaze over to the pavilion and toward the abutting tree line where a long line of card tables had been set up with mounds of food.

It looked like every Fates Haven citizen brought something to the table, but Harry's gaze landed on the bright pink-and-black-decorated section and the equally colorful older woman standing behind it.

Nora Pierce, her white hair pulled into an immaculate, curly updo and wearing an eye-catching geometric dress, piled a dessert stack as high as the Statue of Liberty on a young demon's plate before sending him on his way. His large eyes focused on his newly acquired sugary treats as he hustled to catch up with his waiting friends.

Despite being well past the older witch's bedtime, Nora's eyes glittered brightly, a soft, knowing grin tilting up the corners of her mouth. Harry and Nora talked often and did the halfway meet for vacations and get-togethers, but it had been close to a year and a half since they'd had their last one.

Tears welled in Harry's eyes. "Hey, Aunt Nora."

Nora's head snapped toward her and her smile was instant, stretching ear to ear as she navigated around the table much faster than an eighty-eight-year-old woman should be able. "Don't you *hey* me, kiddo. Get your ass over here . . . both of you."

She pulled Harry into tight a hug.

Nothing surpassed a Nora hug. Harry lost her battle against

forming tears as she returned the older witch's embrace; and then in true Nora Pierce fashion, her aunt refused to let Grace skulk in the background and tugged the teenager into her arms, too.

Grace stiffened, but as Nora quietly whispered something in her ear, the young shifter melted into the hug and even half-heartedly returned the gesture with a few awkward back pats.

Harry quickly wiped away an errant tear. The magic of Fates Haven already at work . . .

She hoped.

Her smile still solidly in place as she grasped the teen's hand, Nora gestured to the park. "Welcome to Fates Haven, Grace. Ah, it felt good saying Fates Haven and not chocolate mayonnaise cake or broccoli brownie bites. Fates Haven, Fates Haven, Fates Haven."

Harry smirked. "Taking advantage of the oath's caveat, are we?"

"Smartest fail-safe ever created. Now that the two of you are now here, I won't have to talk about mayonnaise cake ever again." The older witch smiled, unfazed, as she turned toward Grace. "I know it couldn't have been easy leaving behind everything you know, but if there's one thing the Haven hasn't done, is meet a stranger. We'll get this straightened out."

Nora shot a meaningful look at Harry over Grace's head. "For both of you."

Harry swallowed a ball of emotions. "I think what we both need right now is a shower and a week-long nap. If you give me the bypass phrase—"

"Oh, that old thing?" Nora waved her hand. "There is no bypass."

"But—"

"It's just a deterrent system to keep people off those rickety old stairs. Well, and to keep Chuck Nolton away. I swear that man needs to learn what it means when a woman ghosts him after a good time."

Grace seemingly choked on her own spit, but Harry couldn't help but chuckle as the teen's face went pink. "If there's no by-pass, I think Grace and I are heading back to the house and—"

"Eat," Nora interjected, hauling them toward the pink-and-black polka-dot table. "Or your empty stomachs will keep you both up all night grumbling, and I just happen to be manning Marie's table while she hits the loo."

"Marie? Even in New York, there's no one that comes close to Marie's sweets." Harry's mouth practically watered as she eyed the very pink table and the elegant, retro-looking sign. "Wait. Does that say . . . ?"

"Sugar Tits." Nora beamed proudly as she put glazed rolls in Harry's and Grace's hands. "Marie rebranded and had a grand reopening about a year or so ago. You can imagine the starched shirted old crones on the town council getting hit with a case of the vapors over it, but it's been a fountain of fun."

Grace's eyes fastened on the sugary treat in her hands, and what most definitely looked like a centered—and erect—nipple. "Is this a boob?"

Nora nodded. "It's a Cinna-Boob Bun. Try it. You'll love it. It practically melts on your tongue . . . or if you don't want something glazed, we have a few Erection Éclairs, too. The cream inside them practically bursts with—"

"No," Harry and Grace said simultaneously, Harry adding, "The Cinna-Boobs are just fine. Thank you."

Grace dug into her bun, failing to mask a snort-laugh behind a fake cough. They really were mouth-melting good, and before she realized, Harry devoured the entire boob. Grace did, too, for once too distracted to scowl.

"Once your stomachs are settled, I'll go sign us up for the karaoke—"

"Uh, no," Harry interjected, horrified at the idea of singing in public. Again. "No parade. No karaoke. It's been a really long few days. Gracie and I just need to head back to the house and get some sleep."

"You're right." Nora smiled understandingly, squeezing each of their arms. "Of course. Rest up tonight and start fresh tomorrow. I already set up your rooms. Harry, you're in the blue guest room at the end of the upstairs hall, and Grace, honey, yours is the second door on the right. It has its own bathroom, so no sharing counterspace. I tried refreshing the atmosphere a bit, but whatever you don't like, we can change. I'll take any reason to go shopping."

"My own bathroom?" Grace's eyes lit up. "Sweet."

"You're giving her my old room?" Harry's stomach twisted as she fought a fresh wave of panic.

"May as well as it's already suited for a teenager with the walk-in closet and the bay window." Nora grinned knowingly. "If you're worried about the Great Escape Oak you used to sneak out for your shifter boy shenanigans, I had that thing removed years ago. It would've toppled onto my roof with the first snowfall in the state it was in."

Mischief danced in the teenager's eyes as her gaze volleyed between Harry and Nora. "*Harry?* Sneaking out to meet a boy?"

Nora chuckled. "Oh, sweetheart. The things I could tell you."

"Please don't," Harry interjected. "Ever."

Both Nora and Grace chuckled, and the sight and sound

of the teen's small grin brought a flutter to Harry's heart. She reined in her brewing emotions so she didn't spook Grace into shutting down.

"Grace, honey, why don't you grab one of those pink boxes, fill it up to the brim, and take it back to the house. We'll have a sugary breakfast of champions in the morning." Nora waited as Grace got busy, shoving a bunch of Cinna-Boobs and Erection Éclairs into the bakery box.

With Grace distracted, Nora returned her assessing gaze to Harry. The older witch always saw so much more than she ever said aloud. Time melted away and Harry's sixteen-year-old self stood in the Pierce House living room after a bonfire party, trying to convince her aunt she hadn't downed half a bottle of peach schnapps.

"Not that you're not always gorgeous, but you're a tired gorgeous, sweetheart. You look like you could sleep for a year," Nora admitted.

"Then I look exactly how I feel. It's been . . . rough. The last few months especially." She snuck a look at Grace, making sure she was still occupied. "Just when we think we may be close to answers, something comes along and knocks it away. And it happens often enough that it's hard not to get discouraged. Especially for Gracie."

"And for you."

"I'm an adult. It's different for Gracie . . . and with Cassie gone right now trying to find the most elusive of shifters? Things have been tense."

"She's no closer to finding the father?"

Harry sighed. "Two steps forward and about twelve back. He hadn't been kidding when he told her that he kept a low profile. *No profile* would be more accurate."

During their eight-hour night stand at a music festival, "Luke" and Cassie exchanged first names and nothing else. Well, except body fluids. But they'd parted and her friend had been left with great memories, a warm glow, and a little bun in the oven.

Nora squeezed her hand. "I know it's been hard with Cassie gone, but that girl has you looking out for her, too. That counts for something."

"Not so sure she sees it that way. Everything I say or do is wrong. Cassie checks in when she can, but the check-ins are getting more and more infrequent. I can feel Gracie pulling further away. Tonight was the first time I saw her lips twitch into something that wasn't a snarl in months."

"We'll figure all of it out, but the important thing is that you're not alone anymore. The people of Fates Haven are nothing if not resourceful."

Harry eyed the Sugar Tits table and smirked. "Is that why Marie now makes Cinna-Boob Buns and Erection Éclairs instead of blueberry scones?"

Nora lifted what Harry guessed to be an éclair from a plate. "Oh, she still makes those, too, but they're called Blueberry Ball-Busters."

"An erotic bakery in quaint little Fates Haven . . . who would've thought."

"I did. Who did you think gave Marie the idea when she said she needed to find a fresh spin to put on the bakery?" Nora winked and they both laughed. "You made the right decision in coming back to the Haven, sweetheart. This is exactly where both you and Grace are meant to be."

"I just hope the Rocky Mountain Pack can help give us some answers. She hides it behind a wall of snark and attitude, but Gracie's scared. Hell, I am, too. I don't know what we'll do if Alpha Atwood can't help. It's a miracle the last sparkage only singed our curtains and didn't burn down the entire apartment building."

Something glittered in Nora's eyes as she patted Harry's hand. "There's no doubt in my mind that Alpha Atwood can help."

"But *that* is a task for tomorrow morning. Ringing Patty right now definitely won't put me in her good graces." They'd always gotten along, Patricia acting as a stand-in mother when her own moved from one archaeological dig to the next.

But that was before Harry left town without saying good-bye to anyone.

Before she'd placed the anti-tracking spell so no one could follow.

Most people in the Haven would probably welcome her back with open arms and curious questions, but there was at least one who definitely wouldn't.

A severe bolt of pain ripped through her chest as she conjured the mental image of Jaxon Atwood. Once upon a time, Jax had been her world; and in the blink of an eye and a flash of a flame, he'd ended up her one and only heartbreak.

As Harry's mental image of Jax slowly melted away, so did the heartburn from hell, leaving behind a heated tingle that had her rubbing her sternum. Out of habit, she released a small thread of descry magic and instructed it to seek its source.

It didn't take long to find it standing next to Pixie Pavilion.

Wearing faded jeans and a soft, muscle-hugging T-shirt, the brooding figure was broader and much harder than in her memory. More than a few days' worth of stubble peppered his angular jaw, not quite thick enough to hide the wild tick of his jaw muscle as he clenched his teeth.

And his eyes . . .

Silver eyes were lasered on her, a metallic shimmer signaling that his inner mountain lion wasn't far from the surface. He stood still as a statue, a predator waiting to make that final pounce. Unmoving. Unblinking.

He was the one person who definitely wouldn't welcome her return with smiles and fanfare.

Jaxon Atwood.

The Alpha's son.

And her not-so-fated after all.

4

Mental Math

Harry pinched the bridge of her nose so hard her eyes teared. Three hours, eight on holds, and five misconnections later and she was no closer to getting an appointment with Patricia Atwood than when she started. They'd now transferred her to someone named Sunny, and Harry quickly learned it wasn't a name given to her for possessing a sunny disposition.

"Look"—Harry took the kind of deep, cleansing breath for which she always directed at Grace when she went sparks up— "you don't understand the full scope of the situation. We must see Alpha Atwood."

"Oh, you *must*? Well, in that case, I'll put you down for to-morrow."

The fake sugary voice grated on Harry's last nerve. "Now you're not even disguising your disdain."

"Because I've told you numerous times that the Alpha is simply too busy for drop-ins."

"Which is why I'm trying to make an appointment."

"Yeah. At the last minute . . . for this *dire* situation. The Alpha has appointments filled up—quite literally—for the next few months. And you think you'll get one this afternoon simply because you feel you need it?"

Pacing her room, Harry smashed her phone harder to her ear. It was a damn good thing she didn't possess Grace's inner shifter because she probably would've already sent something up in flames by now or at the very least created a smoke show.

Harry loathed everything to do with nepotism, but she'd stoop to even lower for Grace. "Actually, Sunny, yes, I do. Alpha Atwood and I go way back and I'm sure if you mention my name, the Alpha will have you find a spot for me this afternoon. Five minutes. That's all I'm asking for."

Sunny snorted. "I'm a shifter, not a witch. I can't magic an opening, and at this point in time, I don't see that happening until tutu-wearing piglets take to the sky. Hold, please."

Murmured voices volleyed back and forth from the other end of the line, one a muffled Sunny's and one distinctly lower and more rumbly. The schedule keeper did not sound happy, her tone short and clipped, voice rising to unsafe decibel levels.

The phone shifted before Sunny came back on the line, her voice strained. "I'll squeeze you in today at one thirty. Not one thirty and thirty seconds or one thirty-one. *One thirty.* Arrive late and you're a witch without luck."

Harry air punched in victory, careful to keep her voice the same fake polite as the woman on the other end of the line. "I completely understand. Thank you so much for your understanding and for doing everything you could to make this happen, Sunny."

Harry tossed her cell on the bed and let out a relieved sigh. *Watch out, airline pilots, because there are dapperly dressed*

Babes flying crop dusters. Maybe she should buy a lottery ticket or something.

That thought quickly soured, as did the minuscule breakfast she'd choked down a few hours ago.

She'd gotten that appointment with Patty . . . *yay*!

That appointment was at the pack ranch . . . *less* yay.

Stepping foot on pack land increased her chances of a run-in of the Jaxon Atwood variety . . . the *furthest* from yay as one could get. Especially since every time she thought about the last unexpected collision, she felt seconds away from hurling.

They'd been nearly a fraction of a football field apart and yet walking headfirst into a brick wall would have left her less disoriented. Twelve hours after the encounter and her heart still skipped a beat whenever she replayed the scene in her head.

Which meant her heart basically danced an entire Broadway show all throughout the night until she finally called sleep a lost cause and got ready for the day.

"But that was yesterday. Today is a new day." Harry turned to the antique dressing mirror and stared at her nauseated reflection. "You got this, Harlow Pierce. You're gonna slide into your big witch panties, stuff your boobs into your armored bra, and you're gonna get shit done, Pierce witch style."

Sealing the deal with a final nod, she turned to grab her I-mean-business dress laid out on the comforter, but where she'd put her lucky undergarments, there was no favorite bra.

She glanced beneath the polka-dot sundress and searched under the bed, but the bra was nowhere to be found. "Backup armored bra it is."

She turned toward the dresser when a breeze rustled the gauzy curtain. "I didn't open that window. . . ."

A shadow shifted as a female gnome jumped onto the windowsill, Harry's favorite gravity-defying bra clenched in her stone-gray hands.

"Son of a—" Harry leaped for the hellion, but with even quicker reflexes, it hurtled itself through the open window and skied down the sloped tin roof with a happy-making squeal. "One cup could fit your entire body, so good luck getting it to stay up!"

Sanjay Sharma, one of Nora's closest neighbors, chose that moment to walk past with his little Yorkie. With an internal groan, Harry waved and immediately closed the window.

She refused to let this dampen her positive can-do attitude, but it also didn't stop her from grumbling as she finished getting ready, heading downstairs right as Nora and Grace stepped inside from the back porch.

Grace's smile flattened the second she laid eyes on her. "Is that your bra I saw on the garden statue outside?"

Harry sighed. "Because of course they used it to decorate the fountain. Nora, we really need to do something about those gnomes."

Her great-aunt chuckled. "Oh, I know. Jax has been on me about that for a while, but you have to admit that the little stony buggers keep things lively around here."

"Yeah, it's a regular ole house party." Harry grumbled, before shooting an expectant look to Grace. "Achievement unlocked. We got the appointment with Alpha Atwood, so we should head out. I don't want to be late and give them a reason to want to reschedule."

It was the teen's turn to grumble. "Can't have that."

Nora reached out, giving Harry a hand squeeze before she shuffled to her purse and pulled out her car keys. "Take Hilda.

Driving that station wagon despite its . . . experience . . . is a high-risk life choice."

"Your little hatchback? What if you need to go somewhere?" Harry took the keys.

"Honey, I have a phone and I can bring up the Ryde app like anyone else."

Grace snorted. "Everyone except Harry."

"I can operate the app," she defended herself half-heartedly. "I'd just prefer to put my life in my own hands when I get behind the wheel of a car. Not someone with an unknown track record seconds from being dropped by their insurance carrier."

"Is that why I don't have my driver's license? Because you don't trust me behind the wheel of a car?"

Yes. *Maybe.* "No, you don't have your driver's license because in New York, it wasn't necessary. Everything is a train or bus or Ryde ride away."

"And now everything is at least a thirty-minute drive."

She had her there. "We'll talk about lessons."

"Really?"

"Absolutely. Just as soon as I find someone with nerves of steel willing to teach you."

Grace rolled her eyes but didn't argue as she headed out to Nora's yellow hatchback, Harry following. Five minutes later, she drummed her fingers against the steering wheel column and fought the desire to make a U-turn.

Hightailing it back to Pierce House after her fifteen-yard run-in with Jax hadn't been her finest moment. Definitely not the bravest. With Fates being Fates, a face-to-face encounter was inevitable, but she'd preferred to be mentally and physically ready for it instead of whatever the hell happened last night.

If they ran into Jax a second time, she'd be prepared. Maybe even say hello. Definitely no running away.

Again.

But once she survived the encounter, all bets were off, and she'd commandeer the nearest dark corner or hall closet for a cathartic hyperventilation session. Because holy hexes in a baked bread basket . . . thirteen years had sure done Jax Atwood good. She'd been an embarrassing few seconds away from drooling on her shoes.

But she'd been there, done that—and him—and refused to take a return trip to Heartbreak Land. Grace constantly harped on her seesaw decision-making. Dinner. Outfits. Movies. Harry blamed the back-and-forth on the structured rigidity of her—former—day job.

But one thing on which she stood firm?

Harry didn't trespass on someone else's Fated Mate.

Jax Atwood was never meant to be hers. Her future was still out there; and whether it included a Fated or not, she sure as hell knew it included Grace and that's what mattered right now.

Sitting in the passenger seat, the teen in question slid her a coy smirk. "So, Sir Stare-a-Lot from last night is Shifter Boy, huh? The one you snuck out your window to meet?"

Harry tightened her grip on the steering wheel. "I don't know what you're talking about."

Grace's lips twitched knowingly. "Sure you don't. That's why you're simultaneously going pale and red in the face. I didn't even know that was possible."

"It's the rosacea. It doesn't mean anything except that it's time to change my skin-care regimen. It sure as hell doesn't mean that Jax is Shifter Boy." She winced the second she said his name, and Grace, being the astute teenager she was, quickly caught on.

"Jax, huh?" Grinning, she dramatically tapped her finger to her lips. "Now why does that name sound familiar? Could it be that Jax and the 'Jaxon' I heard you and Mom talk about are one and the same? Which would most definitely make him the ex, and if he's *the* ex, I assume that means he's Shifter Boy. Unless you snuck out of Nora's to meet up with multiple different guys. If that's the case, I applaud your former horny teenage self."

"I preferred it when you were a toddler and didn't hear anything except *ice cream* and *playground*." Harry sighed. "And, yes, Jax is Jaxon, and the ex . . . and Shifter Boy."

Grace grinned. "Thought so. He seemed to have that broody shifter thing down pat. So you and him were a thing?"

"A *long*, long time ago. Practically before your lifetime." She shifted in her seat, the already small car shrinking a few more sizes. She cranked the AC, but the sweat dotting her forehead didn't go away.

"So what happened?" Grace drilled further. "Without telling me disgusting details that will traumatize me for life."

"What makes you think something happened?"

"Exes don't become exes unless something happens."

"Why are you suddenly the one with all the questions?"

"Why are you evading?" Grace folded her arms over her chest. "People evade when they're dancing around the truth—or so you taught me."

Harry shot her a frustrated glance. "My words of wisdom are meant to be weapons against other people. Not against me." At the teen's pointed look, she sighed. "Fine. Yes. When we were barely older than you, Jax and I had a . . . thing. But we grew up and realized we were meant for other people."

Technically, *Jax* found out he was meant for someone else.

"Yeah, I'm not buying that." Way more perceptive than she should be for someone so young, Grace asked, "Will he be at this meeting since he's a shifter?"

Goddess, she hoped not. "You don't need to buy it. Just rent it, and then accept that's all the information you're getting. As for the meeting, while I don't expect him to be involved, we may see him at the ranch. Alpha Atwood is his mother."

The sixteen-year-old's eyes widened. "Seriously? A female alpha? That's pretty badass."

"Patricia Atwood is the definition of badass, which is why you need to be on your best behavior. Don't—"

"Piss off the people who could *maybe* help me?"

"Exactly. Patty has always been fair and honest, but she doesn't tolerate any crap. So press pause on the sarcasm."

"That's like asking me not to breathe."

"Gracie . . ."

"Fine," she agreed with a hefty sigh. "But you need to chill out because your twitches are making me twitchy and we both know what happens when my twitches get twitching. I'm pretty sure the alpha lady wouldn't appreciate me setting her house on fire."

"No twitches," Harry agreed, and that was like *her* not breathing. Her entire body buzzed, the sensation strengthening as they approached pack lands.

Spanning several hundred miles, the Rocky Mountain pack's territory was the largest in the country with multiple outposts and compounds, the most centrally located—the one outside of Fates Haven—hosting the Alpha House.

Once upon a time, she'd spent almost as much time there as she did at Pierce House. Bonfires. Pack runs. A small hot spring—thoroughly surrounded by trees and rocky formations and about a three-mile hike up the mountain—once served as her and Jax's getaway from prying eyes . . . and clothes.

Harry kicked up the AC another notch as she rolled Nora's little yellow car up to the ranch's outside gate. A young guy, close to Grace's age, stepped out from the guard shack and dipped his head to look through the open window.

"You're not Nora Pierce, but you're driving Ms. Pierce's car." He leaned an arm casually against the hatchback's hood, his smile broadening as his attention shifted from Harry to Grace. "And you're not Nora either."

Unimpressed, Harry leaned forward to cut off his ogle fest. "Pretty astute of you. Harry Pierce. *Harlow.* To see Alpha Atwood. We have an appointment."

"Someone mentioned you'd be stopping by." He glanced back to Grace. "But we keep a thorough detailing of who comes and goes off the compound, so I'll need both your names to enter into the log."

"Harlow Pierce and Grace Taylor. We're kinda on a time crunch, so . . ." Harry fought the urge to growl.

"Sure. Of course. You two have good visit. Maybe I'll see you around." He flashed a smile toward the passenger seat and buzzed open the gate before ushering them forward.

Grace glanced at the kid as they passed, something akin to interest shining in her eyes.

Thank goddess Aunt Nora cut down that damn tree.

They bounced over the dirt and gravel lane, passing the large fields dotted with both steers and horses. Grace soaked it all in as they approached the Alpha House, an oversized two-story log and stone building that served as both the pack meeting house and offices, as well as Patty Atwood's family home.

Jax's family home.

People littered the grounds of the compound, some sending curious looks their way as she pulled to a stop near the house. She no sooner stepped out from the car when she heard her name called.

A tall, broad-shouldered figure jogged over, a baseball hat obscuring his face until he got within a few feet.

An automatic smile slid over her face as she forgot all about her time constraint. "Maddox."

"Get your ass over here, girl." Mad picked her up in a bone-crushing hug and spun her until she cried for mercy. "Fuck, it's good to see you. Who would've thought that the Fates Haven rumor mill was right for the first time in forever?"

"It's good to see you, too, Mads . . . and all your tattoos." Harry grinned as he put her back on her feet and allowed her to get another good look at her old friend.

The baby face he'd possessed at eighteen had transformed to angled cheekbones and a strong, square jaw that was blanketed in a well-trimmed beard. His black T-shirt hugged a broad, well-built chest and emphasized the colorful tattoos decorating the entire lengths of both arms. He looked a far cry from the young boy she'd once called friend, and yet that beaming smile was exactly the same.

"Are you still working here at the ranch?" Harry felt guilty that she didn't already know. That was something a friend should know about another.

"Fuck no. My shit-shoveling days are over. I board my horse here and came by for a quick ride. Lenny and I opened our own tattoo studio in town. Once Upon a Tattoo. You should swing by and check it out . . . get a little ink and a Reading."

"She's still doing them?" Thinking of one of her best friends—and Mad's sister—Lennox, she smiled.

He chuckled. "Even earned herself a nickname: Fortune-telling Tattooist. She hates it, but it's great and it brings in the business. Who wouldn't want their fortune told via their own personal tattoo? Well, except for Bryce at the bowling alley. He's still pissed his fortune—and tattoo—involved a rabid opossum. But seriously, Lenny will be thrilled to see you."

"Really?" Harry asked warily.

"Sure. After she gets done yelling at you. And she's been a little moody lately with her seer abilities on the fritz so there's always the possibility of a thrown punch, but overall? Thrilled."

He winked, letting her know he joked, but she wasn't so sure that wasn't exactly what would happen. Lennox, Elodie, and she had been quite the trio growing up, keeping all the adults in town on their toes. The Trouble Trio. The epitome of what happened when a witch, a seer, and an angel with anger management issues walked into a room.

And then she'd turned the trio into a duo when she left.

Harry conjured a smile she hoped didn't showcase her nerves. "I'll make sure to stop by the shop once things have settled a bit."

As if realizing she didn't stand there alone, Maddox's gaze strayed to an atypically quiet Grace. "And who do we have here?"

"This is Grace. Grace, this is Maddox King. One of my dearest and oldest friends."

"It's nice to meet you, Grace. Harry and I used to skinny-dip together."

Harry snortled. "We were like two years old, and only because those fancy swim diapers were hard to come by back then."

"Still. It happened." He shrugged, grinning, as about a hundred questions shone through his eyes as his gaze bounced between Grace and her.

Noting her friend's hands loosely stuffed into his jeans pockets and his casual ease, Harry quickly put two and two together. "You knew we were coming here today, didn't you? Were you the grumbly voice on the other end of the phone, talking to Sunny?"

He smirked unapologetically. "I may have been . . . hanging out . . . with the Alpha's secretary when your appointment request came in."

"You're the reason I finally got the appointment." She pulled him into a quick, hard hug. "Thank you, Mads. Thank you so much."

"No thanks necessary." He gave her another squeeze before allowing her to pull away. "I figured you wouldn't have requested one if it weren't important."

"It is. There's no way we could've waited months to get an audience. Alpha Atwood would be seeing us even if I had to tie myself to the front guard shack. I mean, it worked once, right?" She smiled wanly, remembering that they'd done something similar when the town council threatened to paint Starlight Gazebo some ghastly shade of neon green.

Her joke didn't quite land with Maddox, his smile melting away. "Is everything okay? Who do I have to bury?"

"No body to bury, and hopefully things will be on the road to okay once we speak to Patty. Luck is on our side so far, right? She's actually here in Fates Haven and not visiting one of the other compounds."

"Patty." Maddox blinked twice, his gaze hesitant to meet her eyes as he scratched the scruff on his jaw. "Yeah. She . . . uh . . . does get bitten by the travel bug quite a lot these days. Let's get you two up to the main house."

"I don't want to keep you from something you need to be doing. I know the way."

He waved it off. "Nowhere I'd rather be than right here. Plus, Sunny isn't always the warmest ray of sunshine and I need to make sure my skinny-dipping partner gets treated right."

"Why do you *hang out* with someone when they're an asshole a majority of the time?" Grace asked in her direct way.

Maddox stared at the teenager with panicked eyes before shooting a worried look to Harry. "What do I do here? Do I lie? Ignore? Divert? Cue a fella in here."

She chuckled. "If you figure out the best tactic, let me know."

"It's . . . uh." Mad's shifted awkwardly on his feet. "Adult reasons."

Grace wisely remained silent.

"So . . . let's get you to that meeting."

More than a few people stared as the three of them walked through the massive kitchen and toward the back end of the house that held the pack office. All seemed familiar—and quiet—until they reached the small waiting room. Behind the Alpha's closed office door, loud voices volleyed back and forth, each rising by the second until one sounded like a near growl.

One that was Jaxon's.

"You're back for more already?" A gorgeous blonde gave Maddox a sultry smile as she stepped around a desk. "I'm not sure I can swing another break so soon after the other."

Behind Harry, Grace faux gagged, the sound shifting the woman's attention their way. "Who are you?"

"Sunny, these lovely ladies are Alpha Atwood's one thirty appointment," Maddox addressed the blonde. "Right on time."

"I've been directed to cancel all meetings for the rest of the day." Scowling, she sent a disgusted look toward Harry's simple sundress. "Sorry. You'll have to reschedule it for another time. We might be able to squeeze you in in about a month or so."

Harry scoffed, sensing how unsorry Sunny actually was. "That's not happening. My appointment was for today, and we'll be meeting the Alpha today."

"I'm not sure who you think you are to make such demands, but Alpha Atwood will see you when Alpha Atwood can see you, and that's in a month. Maybe two."

A low growl rumbled through the room, and the other woman's eyes widened as they snapped to Grace.

"Don't talk to her like that," Grace warned. Her hands, clenched at her sides, vibrated.

"Oh, shit." Harry grabbed the teen's shoulders and turned her attention away from the rude secretary and toward herself. "Hey. No. Don't listen to her. It's okay."

"She shouldn't talk to you like that." Grace's voice lowered, taking on a slightly husky rasp. "It doesn't like her attitude . . . or her smell. She . . . stinks."

"Excuse the hell out of me," Sunny interjected, her voice a high-pitched squawk. "I bathe regularly, and the perfume I use costs more than your entire wardrobe."

"Will you shut the hell up?" Harry snapped. "Can you see I'm trying to prevent her from lighting your chemically bleached hair on fire?"

The woman snapped her mouth shut and folded her arms over her chest.

"Gracie. Please." Cupping the teen's face, Harry searched the now purely golden depths of her eyes for some sign of the sarcastic but good-hearted girl she knew to be in there. "Neither she, nor her opinions, matter. Keep it together. Breathe."

"Fuck breathing," Jaxon's deep voice contradicted. "That won't do shit. At least not on its own."

He stood in the open doorway, his broad shoulders taking up the entire space. Last night's fifty-yard stare down had absolutely nothing on this six-foot-long jump. Jax's dark eyes pinned Harry to the spot, making it difficult for *her* to breathe.

Heat crept up her cheeks, dotting a new sweat line across her forehead the longer his gaze held hers. It wasn't until someone's shocked gasp ripped her attention away that she realized the reason for the sudden increase in temperature were Grace's flame-engulfed hands.

"Double shit."

* * *

FUCK IF JAX knew what the hell was happening. One second he was bitching out the ranch manager for mucking up the animals' feed schedules again, and in the next, an unfamiliar shifter energy slid against his cougar's, making his inner cat hiss in alert.

Stepping out of his office to find a spritely teenaged shifter prepped to blow—or Harry seconds away from becoming the first casualty—definitely hadn't been on his day's bingo card.

"Step back, Harry." Jax remained fixed in one spot, commandeering the teen shifter's attention with a swell of his cougar's power. It wasn't something he liked to do often, but desperate measures . . .

Her gold eyes swung his way, and a low, animalistic growl

slipped from her lips. "No. I won't let you talk to her like that either."

Jax kicked up a single eyebrow. He couldn't remember the last time he'd been challenged by another shifter, and there wasn't a doubt that was what this little spritely thing of a teen was primed to do.

"I have it under control, Jax," Harry interjected, her tone stiff. "We've been handling things just fine for a while now."

He let out a humorless laugh. "Yeah? And is that why you're here? Because you're doing just fine handling things on your own?"

"Look, we—"

"What do you need, kid?" Jax swung his focus back to the girl, slowly closing the distance until he stood between Grace and Harry, a protective wall for them both. "Do you need to breathe? Or do you need to let something out?"

"I don't know." The girl whimpered, but her fists tightened as little embers sparked around her hands. "I don't know what I need."

He directed her with a firm but soft "With me," and led the way outside.

Harry protested to Maddox the entire way as they all followed, but teen remained hot on Jax's heels until he guided her to a gentle stop and pointed to an abandoned wheelbarrow six feet away.

"Whatever you feel itching below the surface? Let it out and light it up. Direct it toward the hay in that wheelbarrow." He stood calmly at her side.

Eyes wide and panicked, she shook her head so hard she made him dizzy. "I'll lose control like I did at school. I could hurt someone."

"Does it look like anyone is around right now?" He glanced around the open space, glad to see most of the workers keeping their distance. "The closest thing to you right now is that wheelbarrow."

"And *you*. How do you like having eyebrows? My chem teacher claims she was rather fond of hers until I accidentally melted them away," she quipped dryly.

"A human?"

She nodded.

"I'm a shifter. Anything that's melted off, stabbed through, or broken, will mend itself before I even finish reciting the alphabet." He nudged his chin to the waiting wheelbarrow. "No more excuses. Light. It. Up."

She threw a confused look to Harry, as if asking for permission.

"If you think it'll help, do what he says, Gracie." She gave the teen an encouraging nod. "It's okay, sweetheart."

Her narrow shoulders tensing, the teen glared at the hay as if it insulted her favorite music group. Two seconds into the stare fest, her heated sparks transformed into small flames, and soon enough, her arms were completely engulfed from the elbow to her fingertips like a human torch.

"Holy fuck, Harry," Maddox whispered behind them. "I get why you're here now."

"We don't know what to do," Harry admitted softly. "I'm hoping Patty can steer us in the right direction."

Maddox flashed Jax a concerned look, but a massive blast of heat yanked their attention to Grace, who flung her hands out in front of her. With a heart-wrenching scream, she hurled thick, twin beams of flames at the hay. The wheelbarrow's entire contents went up in a flash, leaving nothing behind but smoke, ash, and a pile of melted, gnarly steel.

Next to Jax, Grace panted heavily, her knees knocking together. But she no longer sparked and her eyes were back to a warm, rich brown.

He studied her carefully, looking for any sign he'd pushed her too hard. "How do you feel now?"

"How did you know that would work?"

"I didn't."

"You didn't?!" Harry stepped forward, her eyes glittering with that temper he'd once found sexy as hell. Still did, if he was honest with himself. "You treated her like a fucking guinea pig? Do you have any idea how badly that could've turned out?"

"Yeah, but it worked." He remained in position, arms crossed over his chest, as she got the closest she'd been to him in thirteen years.

She drilled a finger into his chest, sending a little magical zing down his spine. "You pompous, reckless *jackass*! Who the hell do you think you are to risk something like that?"

"I'm not so sure why're you're huffing when everyone is standing perfectly healthy and in one piece . . . except for my wheelbarrow."

"That stunt could've backfired in ten different ways, but you didn't give a damn, did you? We came here hoping the Alpha could help Grace. We didn't come so her son could put her in even more danger."

Jax pushed through his amused annoyance and registered her words. "You're here to see the Alpha."

Maddox cleared his throat. "Harry and Grace are your one thirty."

Well, fuck . . .

Harry looked from Maddox to Jax and back. "No, we had an appointment with Alpha Atwood. With *Patricia*."

Jax slowly twisted his lips into a sardonic grin. "Thirteen years is a lot of time for things to change, sweet pea. Except that temper of yours, apparently."

He hadn't meant for the old nickname to slip out; but her eyes narrowed as if prepping to hurl daggers, obviously seeing it as a dig. He went with it. "Mom stepped down from her post about a year ago and is currently living the retired life and traveling all over the globe."

"No."

"Yes."

Her anger-pinked cheeks visibly paled. "You mean that you're . . ."

"The new Alpha Atwood . . . and we should chat about why you're bringing an unidentified, uncontrolled shifter onto my pack lands without proper authorization."

A low, now familiar growl came from the teenager's direction. He returned it with a warning growl of his own when an errant thought had it coming out more like a squeak.

Dark hair. Dark eyes. A certifiable overflow of shifter stubbornness.

Grace was definitely in her teens, but how *far* in her teens? Seventeen? Fifteen?

Or . . . *fuck*. She was pretty damn petite. Could she be a bit younger?

The girl's lips twitched into a small smirk as if she dared him to vocalize his thoughts. Finally, she chuckled, her laughs ending in faint snorts. "Don't give yourself a heart attack, *Alpha* Jax. I am *so* not your daughter."

"Gracie!" Harry exclaimed at the same time Jax questioned with a, "How did you know what was going through my head?"

"Please. It was written all over your panicked face as you started doing mental math. I'm sixteen, and Harry isn't my mom. She's my guardian while my actual mom is off playing hide-and-seek with a shifter with no intention of ever being found."

Jax couldn't articulate words or fully form major thoughts as a million of them whipped through his head, each more confusing than the next. "Mads, why don't you give Grace a tour of the ranch while Harry and I head to my office and . . . catch up?"

"I think I'd rather stick around for the conversation about me, thank you very much," Grace smarted back, her glare almost matching Harry's.

Jax transferred his attention to her and let his cougar inch slowly to the surface, close enough for the young shifter to sense the power rippling in the air. "Not all our conversation will be about you, Sparks. Take a tour with Maddox and we'll find you when we're done."

The teenager's gaze bounced back from him to Harry a few times before she reluctantly followed Maddox to the barn. Maddox sent Jax a silently mouthed *behave* directive he had no intention of following.

He headed back to the Alpha House and sensed Harry's glare on the back of his neck the entire way. Good thing she didn't have the fire gift like the kid or else she'd have burned a hole straight through his spinal column.

In the small foyer outside his office, Jax excused Sunny for the day and as expected, she put up a fuss while she gathered her things. But he didn't want more ears around for this "talk" than there needed to be.

Once it was him and Harry in the suddenly small confines of his office, the tension in the room could've been cut by a putty knife.

Harry broke the looming silence with a heavy sigh. "A shift in power or not, unless Patty retired to Fiji or somewhere equally remote, maybe this conversation should wait until she's available."

"She's not in Fiji."

"Good. Then—"

"But she also no longer handles Rocky Mountain Pack issues . . . and it appears as though you brought a doozy of one to my doorstep."

Harry's lavender eyes darkened, signaling he'd stoked that temper. Again. "Grace is not an issue. She's a child."

"A *shifter* child. And one you're finding difficulty controlling . . . unless I'm reading the reason for your 'appointment' wrong and it really was just to reminisce on the good ole days."

"This was a bad idea. I don't know what Nora was thinking even suggesting this." She stood to leave, her hand on the doorknob.

Jax sighed. "Harlow, wait."

She spun around, her dark hair rippling over her shoulders. "For what? To sit here while you continue to call my ward an issue and berate me for trying to find someone who can help her? You obviously know why we're here, Jax, and you're playing fucking games."

"The woman I remember didn't used to be such a quitter."

Anger sparked and so did her magic—literally. Its slow rise

thickened the air and lifted the hair on his arms. A few loose pieces of paper fluttered on his desk before settling down.

She took a daring step closer to him. "A quitter? You have no idea what the two of us have been through over the last few years, so you can take your smug attitude and tuck it in your overfilled litter box."

"So why don't you tell me."

She still looked prepped to run; and even though it would probably be for the best, he forced himself to chill and gestured to the vacant chair. "I can't help either of you if I don't know what I'm working with. It's obviously challenging enough that it brought you back to Fates Haven after thirteen years of self-imposed exile."

So he couldn't chill completely.

Point for Harry that she didn't rise to the bait. Clenching her jaw, she refused to sit and leaned back against the wall by the door. "Grace is obviously a shifter, but my friend Cassie, Grace's mom, doesn't know anything about her father other than his name. Luke."

"Luke. And . . . that's all?"

She glared at him. "Stow your judgment, Mr. Judgy McJudgerson. They met. They felt a connection. They had an eight-hour romance. All she knew about him was his first name and that he was just 'passing through' town."

"So I take this to mean that Grace has never shifted?"

Harry took a slow, deep breath. "No. When she showed no signs of shifting around her twelfth birthday, her pediatrician said her shifter side was most likely too dormant to ever make a transition. They said her father probably wasn't a full shifter either. Muted shifter genetics, they said."

He snorted. "That girl that just lit a wheelbarrow on fire does not have muted genetics."

"Tell me about it. Two years ago, she started having problems with some kids at school and then, bam. Switch flipped."

Jax added knowingly, "Her shifter decided it didn't want to remain dormant anymore."

"You can say that again. Quick temper. Up and down mood. *All* the attitude. At first, we mostly blamed it on teenage hormones—and a large part may have been just that—but then the sparks happened. They don't harm her, but the rest of her surroundings aren't immune. I'm pretty sure we're on our seventy-fifth Target comforter by now."

Jax slowly digested all the info. "Can she control it *any* better than when it first started?"

"About ten times better, which should say how out of control it was in the beginning. Cassie's been trying to track down her mystery shifter all of the past year to get answers, but every time she gets close, there's a roadblock. While she's doing that, I've taken Gracie to every shifter pack along the Eastern Seaboard and worked with nearly every coven, but no one can get a handle on Grace's shifter lineage. And other than the breathing, which only works about fifty percent of the time, absolutely nothing has worked to rein in her abilities."

For the first time, Jax truly let himself see how tired she appeared. Yeah, she possessed the same fight and temper of the girl he remembered, but she also had a lot of something else.

Resignation.

The Harlow Pierce he'd once fallen in love with didn't resign herself to anything. If she didn't like something, she changed it. The fact this was out of her power was most likely eating her alive.

He cocked an eyebrow and leaned his ass against his desk. "So you thought I could do something that dozens of others couldn't?"

Her gaze snapped to his. "Actually, I'd hoped your mother could."

"She's not here, so you're stuck with me."

"Obviously," she retorted dryly.

He debated on how to play this. Not helping the young shifter wasn't an option, but everything else that came along with it he could do without.

"I'll help Grace, but there will be ground rules," he heard himself say.

"She'll do whatever you ask her."

"The rules aren't for her. They're for you."

"Me? Like what?" Harry's expression went from hopeful to wary.

"Keep your distance. Support Grace and cheer her on however you like, but if you don't agree with one of my methods, you either suck it up and soldier onward, or you pull me aside and express it in private. *Never* in front of Grace."

She shifted uncomfortably on her feet, looking as though she wanted to argue. "I guess I can do that . . . as long as you promise to listen to my concerns."

"I'll listen, but just to prepare you, your concerns won't change my tactics. You came here looking for help from a shifter, and I won't reach that by catering to the whims of a witch. And so you're aware, my tactics sure as hell don't involve meditation and breathing exercises."

Actually, neither was a completely horrific idea, but he wasn't about to admit it.

Her eyes narrowed on him as he purposefully pushed each

and every one of her buttons. "Fine. I'll trust you until you give me a reason not to, but I won't hand her welfare over to you with no questions asked. So that distance you want will only reach so far."

"Do you want Grace back to being a regular, mouthy teenager?"

"I'll probably regret it later, but, yes. I do."

"Then those are the rules. Take them or leave them and try your luck somewhere else."

But he sure as hell hoped she didn't.

He wasn't so arrogant to think he could help the girl after so many failed, but he also knew quitting wasn't in his DNA. Despite his earlier button pushing, it wasn't in Harry's either. It was one of the things he'd admired most about her.

She nibbled the left corner of her bottom lip. "I'll take them. But you best be prepared for me taking you to the side a lot."

Jax grinned. "You wouldn't be you if you didn't."

While Harry's previous tension had somewhat melted away, his had ratcheted up another million degrees. He didn't doubt his ability to help Grace, or to find someone who could . . . but he was less certain about his ability to maintain his distance from her guardian.

"I'll be down at the stables at seven tomorrow. Have her here and ready to work."

She cocked a gorgeous eyebrow. "You're training tactic is manual labor?"

"I'm nothing if not a multitasker."

With a snort, she nodded and turned to leave, stopping as she gazed around the room. "I know I don't really have a right to ask, but she's okay? Elodie is doing well?"

It took him a second to read into her hesitantly asked question.

She thought they'd Mated.

His immediate, bursting desire to clear up her assumption startled him into silence. He'd never once considered El an option, and vice versa. But telling Harry that the only woman he'd ever pictured himself with in a happily-forever-after way left him thirteen years ago would only set him up for another epic disappointment.

Harlow Pierce already proved once she didn't believe in what they had. No way would he give her a clear path back into his life and into his heart for her to shatter it a second time.

He purposefully avoided her unspoken question. "She's doing well. With this being Fates and all, I'm sure you'll be running into her sooner or later."

With a nervous smile, she nodded and left his office.

Feeling as though he'd gone eight rounds with a heavyweight boxing champion instead of one petite Pierce witch, he fell into his seat with a heavy groan. "Fuck me."

Maddox chose that moment to appear, a knowing grin on his face as he plopped in the chair across from Jax and kicked his boots onto the desk. "And to think I nearly turned down Sunny's offer for a backroom hookup today."

Jax growled at his friend and pushed his feet off his desk, the move making the human laugh harder. "This isn't a game, Mads."

"I know. It's a fucking Broadway show . . . and I personally cannot wait to get to final act."

Jax wasn't so sure he'd survive until intermission, much less curtain call. Harlow Pierce possessed the ability to knock his feet out from under him without even trying, and it was clear that in her time away from Fates Haven—and him—that skill had grown more potent.

If he didn't play this carefully, he'd be sprawled flat on his ass and he wasn't so sure he'd have the fortitude to climb back to his feet.

5

Stealth Is My Middle Name

In Harry's experience, morning-after regret usually came on the heels of a few empty tequila bottles and the disappearance of a favorite pair of panties. This time, it was due entirely to the previous morning's run-in with Jax.

No naked shenanigans. No alcohol. Just a simple agreement that would potentially put them in close proximity again and again. Day after day.

The odometer of Nora's hatchback's rolled, and so did her stomach, a repetitive sensation since being back in Fates Haven, and one she wished she could shake off.

"It would be understandable if you want a few days to adjust to all these recent changes before diving right into things," Harry heard herself say. "Nora mentioned picking up some stuff to make your room feel more like yours. We could go shopping . . . or something."

Silence from the passenger seat had her glancing right.

"What?"

"Wasn't the entire point of this cross-country relocation to work with the Rocky Mountain Pack to see if they can help me find answers? That won't happen while shopping for a blue comforter."

Of course she chose *that* moment to break out the maturity.

Grace studied her carefully. "Do you not trust Alpha Atwood? Or do you not trust *this* Alpha Atwood?"

"That's not a simple answer."

"Actually, it kinda is."

Did Harry trust Jaxon?

With Grace's physical safety? Yes. There wasn't anything Jax wouldn't do to keep the people under his care safe. Being a protector was engrained in his DNA. But did she trust him with Grace's heart?

That was the trickier answer to give.

Heartbreak happened—intentionally or not—with *any* formed attachment. And there would be an attachment. To Jax. To Nora. To Fates Haven itself. Though Grace was now overwhelmed by all the unknowns, the town's magic and its inhabitants would work their way into her heart until they became an integral, invaluable part of her very existence.

It's how the magic worked.

It's how the *town* worked.

Harry mistakenly thought thirteen years and nearly two thousand miles were enough time and distance to work Fates Haven out of her system, but that idea had been nothing but stubborn denial, a flaw in her thinking that became more evident with each passing day.

She carefully considered her words. "Jax wasn't the Alpha Atwood I pictured helping us, but there's a reason his mother left him in charge. He'll do whatever he can to help you, even if that's helping us find someone who might be able to do it better."

"Then what's with bribing me with a shopping excursion?"

Harry kept her eyes on the road as she navigated the pebbled lane leading up to the RMP front gate. "Because the last few days have been a lot, and I wouldn't fault you for needing time to get your legs underneath you and feeling a bit solid again."

Grace snorted. "My legs are just fine . . . but something tells me yours are little wobbly."

Harry slid the teen a look. "You're hanging out with Aunt Nora too much. She likes seeing things that aren't there, too."

"So you're not hiding at Pierce House to avoid running into anyone?"

"I'm not hiding. Am I not taking you to the pack ranch right now?"

"Yeah. And what are you doing right after?" Harry opened her mouth answer, but Grace beat her to it. "You're going straight back to the house."

"Have you seen the state of that place? My descry magic is practically itching to be let out and get everything organized and in its place."

"That's probably the well water or something."

Harry rolled her eyes at the teen's obvious sarcasm. "Aunt Nora is doing us a favor by putting us up like this. The least I can do is help bring Pierce House back to its former glory."

"So you're returning a favor and not actually hiding?"

"Exactly."

"Alpha Atwood is doing us a favor, but I don't see you offering to organize his junk drawers." Harry threw her an unamused look that had the teenager chuckling. "Just pointing out the obvious."

"It's rude to point," Harry volleyed back, this time unable to help chuckling along with the teen as she slowly brought Nora's car to a stop. "Call me *any*time and I'll pick you up. If you feel overwhelmed, or you feel like it's not working. One ring and I'm here . . . unless you want me to stick around and—"

"I'll be fine. You don't need to stay." Grace hopped from car so fast she was almost a blur as she rounded the hood to come to a stop next to a waiting Jax.

His looming presence powered down any additional attempts to backtrack. With a few days' stubble and wearing worn, faded jeans and a T-shirt molded to his upper body, he exuded every quintessential bad boy fantasy she'd ever had. The only thing missing was his black leather jacket, but considering he never went anywhere without it, it couldn't be far.

With a knowing smirk tilting up his mouth, Jax propped a forearm against the car hood and leaned toward her open window. "You're almost late."

"*Almost* is not late. It's *on time*," she quipped.

"This time, but the Harlow I knew was notoriously late to everything, so I'm just giving you a gentle reminder. My days are jam-packed and scheduled to the minute."

She shot him a glare. "Well, I'm not the Harlow you once knew because, as you've pointed out before, that was thirteen years ago."

"But she still occasionally runs late," Grace chirped, rocking in her sneakers, "that's why she sets three different alarms. The alarm. The backup. And the backup to the backup, which is all the way across the room and doesn't turn off until you physically get up and shut it off."

Jax cocked up a sexy eyebrow, his gaze never wavering from Harry's. "Guess some things never change."

Some things didn't, namely the ridiculous urge she had to grab his hair and climb him like a redwood tree. To restrain it, she grasped for the nearest change of topic. "I'm leaving you with precious cargo, Jaxon. And I hope I don't have to remind you that she's only sixteen."

"Then I guess taking her to Howlin' for a beer afterward is out, then? Damn." With a smirk, he tapped the car's hood, officially dismissing her. "I'll bring her by Nora's when we're through, so there's no *sticking around* necessary."

Damn shifter hearing.

She opened her mouth to counter, but he beat her to it . . . again. "Remember the rules, Harry. No interference. If you stay, there's no way you'll keep your gorgeous mouth shut. I'll bring her home when we're done for the day."

Her heart skipped hearing him call her mouth gorgeous, but it was quickly dampened by annoyance. "Fine. But she better be dropped off without a hair on her head singed, cut, or missing entirely . . . and I will count them if I have to."

Harry caught sight of Grace's eye roll, and with one parting glare at Jax, she turned the car toward the main road, keeping her eyes on the duo in the rearview mirror until they were little more than two specks on the horizon.

He wasn't wrong. Grace needed concentration, and much as Harry hated to admit it, that wouldn't happen if she were underfoot. Grace needed to fly solo.

Or have the illusion of it . . .

That little devil and angel sitting on Harry's sunburned shoulders whispered, *Do I stay, or do I go?*

Harry debated on the long, bouncy trek toward the main road, and before she took the final right turn that would lead her into town, she'd won the deliberation and didn't lament over its questionable end result as she executed an abrupt U-turn.

Neither Jax nor Grace needed to know she was there, and she wouldn't stay long. Just long enough to ensure Grace was safe and comfortable, and then she'd slip silently away with no one the wiser.

No harm. No foul. No interference. And no breaking Jax's rules.

Stealth was practically her middle name.

* * *

STARING AT GRACE, Jax tried drumming up something wise to say. Or, hell, anything that wouldn't slap him with a raging case of foot in mouth. Limited kid experience—and personal encounters—taught him that he couldn't count on having once being a teen not to make an ass of himself.

Grace shot him a coy, smart-assy smirk. "So are we meditating or something, Master Yoda? I'm not sure what this silent staring thing is if not meditation."

"Fuck. Sorry." Wincing, he ran his hand through his hair. "Shit. I probably shouldn't swear around you, should I?"

Her eyebrow lifted higher. "I'm sixteen, not six. And you do know I've been living with *Harry* since before I spoke actual, full-on sentences, right? Sometimes the things that come out of her mouth would make a grumpy sailor blush."

Actually, he hadn't known that. That meant Grace had been part of Harry's life since the second she'd kicked him out from it. Her Mama Bear protectiveness made so much more sense.

"Still doesn't have much of a filter, huh?" Jax asked as evasively as he could.

"We live—well, *lived*—in New York City where no one has much of a filter."

New York City. And that answered the thirteen-year-old question of Where in the World Is Harlow "Harry" Pierce? She'd always loved the idea of bright lights, a 24–7 cupcake delivery, and an endless sea of possibilities. It made sense.

"Point made . . . and no meditation." He nudged his chin toward the barn in a silent direction to follow, and she did, keeping stride with him easily.

He watched from his peripheral vision as she openly gaped at the horses, her lips twitching into what could be loosely classified as a grin.

"You spend a lot of time around horses and other animals?" Jax asked conversationally.

Her attention slid to him. "We did just talk about me living in New York my entire life, right? Its only wildlife other than man-sized cockroaches and swarms of winged rats, are the actual rats themselves."

"*Winged* rats?"

"Studies have been done on New York City pigeons." She shivered in mock revulsion. "I'd rather cuddle a rat fresh out of the toilet than one of those flying petri dishes."

He chuckled. "So not used to animals. Got it. Then I guess we'll ease you into this." He stopped in front of Mamoa's empty stall and grabbed the two shovels propped against the wall, handing her one.

"What am I supposed to do with this?"

"Did they not have shovels in New York, either?" he joked wryly.

"Hardy har-har." She looked at the dirty hay and back to him. "But seriously? You must be joking."

"You'll eventually realize that I don't joke often." Stepping into the stall, he demonstrated. "Body mechanics is important when shit shoveling. Bend at the knees, drop the blade with a shove and a tilt, and then lift with your legs. Do anything else and you'll be in for a world of hurt in the morning."

"How the hell does shoveling horse crap help me figure out what the hell I am, or how to control it?"

"It doesn't." Ignoring her curses, he answered truthfully. "But it does give me insight into your work ethic because, as you've probably guessed, this won't be a walk in Central Park."

"Trust me. Nothing about this has been easy," Grace muttered, but got to work, shoveling the dirty hay and tossing it into a waiting wheelbarrow.

"I hate to break it to you, Sparks, but it'll get harder before it gets easier. And I'm not even talking about gaining enough control and easing you into your first shift. It's what comes afterward that will be the biggest hurdle."

"Afterward?"

Jax paused to study the teen. "How much time have you spent around shifters?"

She shrugged. "I went to public school in a big city. Supernaturals were everywhere."

"Sitting next to a shifter in class is a hell of a lot different from *spending time*."

"My best friend is a shifter," Grace said quietly. "Or at least, they were."

"They *were* a shifter? As in, they're not anymore?"

She refused to meet his gaze as she continued shoveling. "They're still a shifter. They're just not my best friend anymore. When everything started happening, things changed. It became too much for them, and I can't really blame them. I was a dumpster fire. Almost literally."

Something tugged in his chest at the way she played off something—and someone—that had obviously meant a great deal. "I'm sorry that happened, Sparks."

She shrugged.

Jax slowly got back to work. "Do you know what occurs when a shifter suppresses their animal side for too long?"

"My guess would be not good things."

"That guess would be correct. Regardless if your inner shifter spent most of its life locked up by choice or not, it was imprisoned in tight quarters. It won't be shitting sunshine from its ass when it makes it first appearance. It's gonna be angrier than Harlow without her morning coffee."

"Harry doesn't drink coffee," Grace volleyed, her eyes flickering gold as they snapped to him. "And you think I locked it away on *purpose*?"

Jax blinked. *Harry doesn't drink coffee?* Once upon a time and pre–final exams, she seriously contemplated the pros and cons of begging Doc Johnson to insert an intravenous line and injecting the stuff directly into her veins.

Not wanting his barn burned, he pulled his focus back to the bristling teen in front of him and continued carefully but honestly. "Locked it away on purpose? Probably not. But when shifters sense a threat—of any kind—things happen. A shifter's first instinct is always to defend. It's very possible that in a threatening moment, it chose flight instead of fight and locked itself away. To protect *you*."

She scoffed, her temper waning. "Great. So I'm a groundhog shifter. Case closed. Puzzle solved. Everyone can get back to their regularly scheduled lives."

Jax chuckled. "I've yet to meet a groundhog that can fling flames, so I think it's a pretty safe bet that that's not what we're dealing with here."

Although Grace formed a small pack with her mother and Harry, as the lone shifter, it wasn't the same as belonging to a *pack*. Way before young shifters sprouted their first fur—or feathers, young shifters learned the way a pack interacts. Family did not always mean blood, and unfortunately sometimes the opposite was true.

To be comfortable in a pack, Grace first needed to be comfortable around him. He'd sugarcoated it when he said her shifter—once freed—wouldn't be sporting a shining disposition. Making sure there were no casualties was his top priority, and that meant there'd be times he needed to push her, and push hard. That couldn't happen if he didn't have her trust.

Working side by side, they cleaned out the rest of the stall in silence, Grace never once complaining. They replaced the last of the dirty hay when a very unmistakable scent hung in the air, and it didn't belong to any of the animals.

Harry.

"Hey there, boss." Devon, one of the pack's trackers in training, stepped up to the stall, Mamoa on a rein behind him. Devon's typical smile increased by ten thousand watts when he laid eyes on Grace. "Not—Nora's back! Grace, right?"

"Hi." Grace's cheeks pinked.

"Devon. Is me. I'm Devon." The kid chuckled awkwardly.

"Smooth, kid. Really smooth." Jax smirked before getting an idea. "You know what, Dev? Could you do me a favor and show Grace how to get Mamoa comfortable in the stall and set up with his feed buckets? There's something I have to check out."

"You got it, boss."

"Thanks." He clapped the kid on the shoulder and gave Grace a supportive nod. "You'll be in good hands with Devon until I get back. He was practically born on a horse."

Jax followed his nose and the tingle down his spine. The flowery scent intensified when he turned right, so he headed left, going out the front of the barn until the odor all but disappeared. He hung another left, and rounded the back. Midway around the barn, he let his nose and tingles guide him the rest of the way.

He silently vaulted over the back fence and stepped around the corner . . . and there she was.

Or more accurately, her backside.

Chest plastered to the barn as she peered through a crack in the back door, Harry listened to Devon explain to Grace how to ensure the stallion got the exact amount of prescribed grain.

Whether Jax was good at stalking, or she was too invested in whatever was happening in the barn, she didn't hear him approach, mumbling something about horny teenage shifters under her breath.

Hands shoved casually in his pockets, Jax stopped less than a foot away. The two oblivious teens inside the barn had no clue to anything outside their four-foot-radius world.

Jax leaned close to—but not touching—Harry's ear, and whispered, "This doesn't look like keeping distance, sweet pea."

"Shitholes and cum buckets." With a startled yelp, Harry spun around, the quick move kidnapping her balance and windmilling her arms.

Jax lurched forward to prevent her from falling on her ass.

"I'm fine." She batted his hands away and stepped back. "I—"

"I wouldn't step back again if I were you." He eyed the wheelbarrow behind her knees.

She shot him an annoyed look as she regained her balance. "You know what most people wouldn't do? Creepily stalk up behind someone and then try to send them into cardiac arrest."

"Says the witch who's creepily stalking around corners and listening to people's conversations." He tucked his hands back into his pockets and waited for what no doubt would be an interesting retort . . . and she didn't disappoint.

"I wasn't stalking. I was *observing*."

"From around a corner. When you were explicitly told to go home."

A fire lit in her lavender eyes. "I guess it's a good thing that I'm allergic to being told what to do because this doesn't look like training. This looks like enabling teenage flirting."

His lips twitched. "Come on. Did you forget what it was like to be their age?"

"No! I most certainly did not! Which is why I know that, while this all looks sweet and innocent on the outside, it's just a glamour for what's lurking beneath the surface."

"They're kids, not a dormant volcano primed to blow."

Jax nearly smacked himself for the offhanded comment because they both knew they'd done a hell of a lot more than innocent flirting at Devon and Grace's age, and judging the redness rising to Harry's cheeks, he didn't stroll down memory lane alone.

"They will definitely not be a repeat of us." Harry took a small, half-measured step back, and then a second.

He didn't have enough time to warn her.

The back of her knees hit the wheelbarrow and this time, there was no regaining her balance. With a small squeak and wet squish, she plummeted into an overfilled and very fresh mound of manure.

He covered his mouth to hold back laughter, but it didn't do a damn thing, a rolling chuckle quickly turning into a full-blown chortle.

"I'm glad you find this funny." A disgusted look on her face, Harry alternated between silent gags and soft curses. "This cannot be happening right now."

"Oh, it definitely is." He laughed harder, tears springing to his eyes as she squirmed to shimmy her way back to her feet and only succeeded in drilling herself deeper into the muck.

"Do you think you could help me out a little?" She growled in frustration, almost sounding like a shifter instead of a witch. "Or would you like to keep standing there laughing?"

"If you remember, I did try to warn you—and help you. But you waved me off, stating that you were 'just fine.'" He chuckled.

"What the hell . . ." Grace's shocked voice joined the melee. She and Devon stood in the now open barn doorway, twin looks of horror on their faces. "Why are you sprawled in a pile of horse crap?"

Harry sighed helplessly. "Whatever do you mean? This looks as good a place as any to put my feet up for a spell." She reached a hand out to the teen. "Can you help me out?"

"Yeah, no. Hard pass on that." Grace stepped back as if her guardian's hand would stretch and latch on to her from six feet away. "I'm not touching you with a ten-foot pole until you've showered at least twenty times, and then it'll take another twenty for actual skin on skin contact."

Jax snorted, earning himself a glare.

"Stop laughing," Harry demanded.

"I don't think I could if I tried." Hooking his fingers through her belt loops, he smirked. "I'm gonna pull you up and out . . . just try not to touch me."

"Please hurry. It's starting to seep through my jeans and to my under . . ." She gagged. "Just hurry."

"On the count of three . . ."

"Three already. It's already three, Jaxon. Pull me out. Now."

He yanked, and the heavy, wet *squelch* as she returned to her feet produced a few gags from the teenagers' direction.

Hands still propped on her belt loops, Jax couldn't help but tease, "It's almost like karma was telling you that you should've left when you were supposed to."

"I'm not getting in the car with you smelling like that." Grace wrinkled her nose and stepped farther back.

Harry glanced at her clothes with a groan. "I can't get in Nora's car with me like this either."

Realizing his hands were still on her body, Jax quickly dropped his hold and diverted. "The way I see it, we have a few options. You can use the shower up at the Alpha House, we can hose you off right out here, or we can end things short today and I'll take the two of you back to Nora's in the pickup."

Harry bit her lip, considering her choices. "I don't think one shower is going to cut it, and I'm not exactly relishing the idea of an ice bath, so third option it is."

"Works for me." Jax nodded. "Devon will drop off your car later. But I'm telling you right now, Grace is riding shotgun."

"Where am I supposed to sit? The roof?"

He dropped the truck's tailgate and pointed to the bed. "Do you need a boost or can you take a running jump?"

Falling on old habits like teasing Harlow Pierce wasn't the smartest move, but, hell, if he couldn't help himself . . .

especially as she stubbornly attempted to hoist herself into the back of his truck.

"I cannot wait to tell Mom about this." Grace chuckled as she slipped into the passenger seat, her fingers already flying over a text screen.

"All comfy?" Jax waited for Harry to get situated in the corner until closing the tailgate.

"What are the chances you won't breathe a word of this to anyone?" She shot him a pleading look.

"This is Fates Haven. We both know I don't have to say anything for word to get around."

Harry groaned and Jax chuckled as he got behind the wheel, shooting a wink at Grace in the process. She giggled and his grin broadened.

For the first time in a while, he looked forward to the town's gossip mill doing its thing.

6

Frosting Cums in All Flavors . . .

Q: How many showers does it take to feel clean
    after falling into a wheelbarrow full of horse
    poop?
A: More than twenty.

After getting home from the Atwood ranch the previous day, Harry scrubbed her skin raw and used every ounce of soap in her possession plus everything beneath the sink, but it wasn't until Nora brewed up one of her magical bath bombs that the manure stench finally dissipated and the older witch deemed her appropriate for public inhalation.

Ten minutes into Nora's shopping errands, Harry wished the stink back and longed for the cozy confines of her bedroom back at Pierce House.

The customary smile and wave that came with living in a community like Fates Haven was exhausting. Her cheeks ached from contorting her face into one smile after another, and her right wrist tingled with a carpal tunnel flare. In New York, it was walk and dodge, and absolutely no eye contact. On the other hand, watching Grace's amazement as Nora stopped and chatted with person after person, addressing them each by name, was amusing as hell and brought a smirk to Harry's lips.

"What?" Grace turned her attention toward her.

"Just watching you watch Nora. I'm used to this, but it's fun seeing someone experiencing it for the first time."

"When she said shopping excursion, I thought we'd actually be shopping. You know, receiving goods with the exchange of money." She glanced at her single bag from the indie bookstore, Judge a Book By Its Cover. "When do we reach the shopping part of this excursion?"

"Oh, my dear, sweet, ill-informed Grace. Nora's shopping is a full-fledged social event sprinkled with a few purchases here and there. She's only getting started," Harry teased.

Nora said her goodbyes to yet another neighbor and turned to them expectantly. "After all this shopping, I think we deserve a sweet treat. What do you two think?"

A pair of speed walkers zipped by, each nodding their hellos as they raced by at vampiric speed, pints of O-negative energy slushies sloshing in their tumblers.

"I think I'm in a Stepford Twilight Zone," Grace joked dryly.

Nora chuckled, looping her arm through the teen's. "Nope. You're just in Fates Haven."

"Are people always so . . . weird?"

The older witch looked confused. "Weird?"

Harry bit her lower lip to keep from laughing. "I think she means *friendly*."

"Are people not friendly in New York?"

"Not like this," Grace admitted. "We only acknowledge our neighbor once or twice a year when their mail accidentally gets stuck in our box. Except for that Halloween rager they held one time. Harry body-slammed their door in her PJs and flipped her witch switch. If they ever held a party again, they invited mimes."

Nora tsked, leading them down the boulevard. "That is a crying shame. Fates Haven isn't without its issues, especially in the last decade or so, but for the most part, the people of the Haven are well-intentioned, well-mannered, and well-meaning."

"What's been happening in the last decade?" Grace asked curiously.

Harry studied her aunt carefully, curious about the answer herself. When she'd left Fates Haven, the older witch made a Witch's Oath to keep Fates business—and news about anyone from it—in Fates. All the not-knowing had been ridiculously difficult in the beginning, but the clean break was necessary. If Harry had been regaled with story after story about home, there would have been no way she would've been able to keep her distance—much less her heart—intact.

"I suppose you could say that the town's been a little down on its luck," Nora answered thoughtfully. "Thirteen years ago, especially at this time of year, these streets were crammed with tourists shoulder to shoulder, both supernaturals and humans, soaking in the magical atmosphere and gearing up for the Fates Festival. Now? Not so much."

"Why did people stop coming?" Grace asked.

Nora shrugged her narrow shoulders. "Unfortunately, they haven't felt the need, but between you, me, and my tarot cards? Something is shifting in the air. I'm not sure what yet, but change is on the periphery, and it won't stay there for much longer. Ah! Here we go. The perfect place for a pick-me-up."

She held open a very pink door and ushered them into

Sugar Tits & Treats Bakery. New paint and counters had given Marie's sweet shop a cosmetic facelift, but the small boutique tables and mismatched chairs sprinkled throughout the space helped maintain its cozy, inviting charm.

"There you go, Hal." Marie handed the older gentleman at the counter a wink and a bright pink box. "I'm sure Lydia will be tickled pink with this month's Taste & Treat. Just make sure she reads the directions this time. We wouldn't want a repeat of last month, now would we?"

Hal, a vampire approaching his early fifties, blushed as he nodded and thanked her before slipping out the door.

Harry hadn't seen the demon baker for thirteen years, but she hadn't changed a bit, her dark hair peppered finely with the same amount of gray and slicked back into a bun on top of her head. A dress, this one black with white polka dots, emphasized every plentiful curve; and her apron, probably one of dozens she owned, was splattered with flour and sugar and read *Frosting Cums In All Flavors & Consistencies*

"Mix me, bake me, and glaze me up! Harlow Pierce, get your sweet little ass over here and give Marie some sugar!" The woman quickly rounded her counter despite her short legs and yanked Harry into a fierce embrace. "If it weren't for my arthritis, I would've kicked myself in the ass for having to go to the bathroom the other night when I did."

Harry hugged the older woman back. "It's good to see you, Marie."

She stepped back and swatted her gently. "Don't you dare stay away from Fates that long again." She turned toward Grace and stuck out a hand for the teen to shake, obviously reading her discomfort. "And you must be Grace. I've heard so much about you from Nora that I feel like I already know you."

"I liked your Cinna-Boobs," Grace said politely.

Marie's eyes lit up. "Then you'll have some on the house! Let me get those on plates."

"Actually," Nora interjected, "we have another stop to make and I can't be late, so can we get them to go?"

"Oh! That's right! The *meeting*! Let me box up a few for you, and I'll give you a second sampler box to sweeten up the crowd." Marie busied, readying their treats, and threw a hell of a lot more than Cinna-Boobs in the box.

Not longer after, they were walking back down Fates Boulevard armed with a whole host of Erection Éclairs and what Harry assumed to be the Blueberry Ball-Busters. They went a half block when Grace's posture stiffened, the teen nervously tucking a loose strand of hair behind her ear.

"Hey there, Grace!" A familiar voice called out a few seconds before the teen from the ranch came jogging over from across the street. "Ms. Pierce . . . and Ms. Pierce."

Harry frowned at the kid. "Devon, right?"

"That's me." His smile bounced between her and Grace before settling on the teen. "I'm not sure what you're all up to right now, but a few friends and I are heading over to Swirlie's Soft Serve for some ice cream. If you want to join us. They have some pretty off-the-wall flavors that you won't find anywhere else."

Harry prepped to decline for Grace, "Actually, we were about to—"

"That sounds like fun," Nora interjected. She turned to Grace. "You'd probably be bored where Harlow and I are going. We can swing by Swirlie's on our way back and pick you up."

Grace grinned, nodding, her cheeks pinkening. "I'd like that. Count me in."

Harry frowned. "I don't—"

"Oh, it'll be fine." Nora shooed the teens away and took Harry's arm. "There's not a lot of trouble for kids to get into around here."

She snorted. "Teens can always find trouble. I know. I sure as hell did when I was that age."

"Yeah, but the fun kind of trouble. Not the jail room and bail money kind . . . although I do recall that *one* time. But that's neither here nor there. Devon's a good kid. He'll watch over Grace. I really do have someplace to be and I can't be late. Not with so many lives on the line."

Harry shot her aunt a worried look, sobering quickly. "What's wrong?"

"It would be a quicker and shorter list to name what isn't wrong." Nora glanced at her watch and cursed, picking up the pace and leading the way farther down Fates Boulevard. "It's moments like this where I wish that whole witch's broom thing wasn't a social media gimmick. Pick up the pace, girl . . . or there may be nothing but a rubble pile by the time we get there."

* * *

THE WAY NORA spoke about the next errand, Harry expected an underground death match or at the very least, one of those unsanctioned MMA fights she'd heard about through the Fates Haven rumor mill. Maybe even mortal combat, although that yet remained to be seen, because she wouldn't be shocked if a few of these people hid crossbows beneath their clothes.

Heightened tensions thickened the air in the Fates Haven Town Hall, exacerbating the fact that the AC was most definitely on the fritz. Sweat glued Harry's sundress uncomfortably to her upper body as she pictured snowy mountainsides and icicle smoothies in a last-ditch attempt in pretending it was cool.

"This definitely isn't what I pictured when you said lives were on the line," Harry whispered to her aunt. "From what I remember, these meetings are mostly about who's bringing what food dish to the next Midnight Movie in Havenhood Park."

"Oh, that's on the docket as well, but we have much more pressing concerns to discuss this time around." Nora nudged her into an empty seat in the last row. "This looks like a good spot to soak in the entire room. I'll be back in a jiffy."

In true Nora fashion, the older woman's social butterfly skills kicked in as she maneuvered around the room, leaving Harry to gaze around the meeting space that doubled as the Fates Haven community theater.

Seven seats sat behind a long table on the stage, reserved for the council itself, with two microphone stands on each side of the room for the audience to voice concerns and questions.

So far she hadn't spotted anything different from the last council meeting she'd been dragged to. Then Sanjay Sharma, the owner of Yummy Delights on the far end of Fates Boulevard, stepped up to the podium and called for everyone to take their seats.

Harry fully expected Nora to rejoin her, but instead, her aunt headed toward the front and, while taking the end seat at the council table, flashed her a wink.

Nora was on the council.

Harry was equal parts curious and concerned. The woman never had one good thing to say about the town council. *They couldn't find their way out of paper bag with a GPS and a flashlight much less dig themselves out of a budget hole.* That she remembered, one of the less colorful admonishments Harry had heard through the years.

She scanned the room to see if anyone else was as surprised to see Nora up there, but everyone took her presence in stride, which meant Nora hadn't hijacked someone's seat after stuffing the real member into a coat closet and was now an official member.

"What in the Twilight World?" Harry mumbled, gazing over the crowd.

A familiar heated tingle turned her attention to the far left where Jax stood, propping up the wall with his broad back, his legs spread and massive arms crossed over his chest. The only thing needed to complete his bodyguard look were mirrored sunglasses and an earpiece.

Her humored snort caught in her throat when she slid her gaze back to the front of the room and stumbled over another familiar face.

Despite having not seen her in thirteen years, Harry immediately recognized the petite, curvy redhead standing in the first row; and judging by the fishlike opening and closing of her mouth, she recognized Harry, too.

Elodie Quinn. Her once upon a time literal wing woman, best friend, and angelic ass kicker extraordinaire.

And Jax's Fated Mate.

Harry summoned her emotional battle armor and quickly superglued it in place, but she wasn't quick enough. That mass of muscle behind her sternum quivered, the severe ache making it near impossible to breathe without conscious effort and focus.

El looked as if she'd stepped out of a photograph from

thirteen years ago. She wore a pretty pink sundress that worked with her curves and flared out at her hips. Anyone who didn't know the angel would think her flirty and twirly, when in reality, the only time she twirled was to put someone in a headlock and make them scream for mercy.

Next to her, and staring openly with a whole slew of emotions fluttering over her timeless face, was Lennox. Her pink hair was done in a retro-forties pinup style, and she wore what looked to be snug brown leather pants and a torso-hugging tank top that fully displayed her seer's tattoos—quite a few more had been added to her collection through the years.

Harry offered a shy, awkward wave as Sanjay called for everyone's attention.

Lenny and Elodie reluctantly turned to the front, their heads bent toward each other as they whispered. Harry couldn't help herself. As if her neck possessed some kind of magnet, her head turned back toward a stoic Jax.

Except he didn't look exceptionally stoic, and he no longer looked toward the front of the room but right at her, his gaze more potent than a supersonic seat warmer. Heat flooded her body, so intense she forced her gaze away and focused it on the fire alarm over Nora's right shoulder.

Why weren't Jax and Elodie sitting beside each other? The seat on the angel's right was open, but he made no move to join his Mate or her friend.

Harry scolded herself for letting her mind wander places it had no business side tripping. Fate made it obvious that Jax was not meant to be hers. It wasn't her concern or right to ask questions about his relationship with Elodie. Even if Harry asked those questions silently to herself.

Sanjay quickly brought the town council around to to-day's agenda, which did include mention of next week's meal sign-ups for the Midnight Movie. For the next fifteen minutes, Harry's mind wandered to anything and everything except the two people on opposite sides of the room; but the more she avoided, the more aware she became, catching Elodie glancing over her shoulder a handful of times.

As the meeting wound down, Harry contemplated exit strategies that would get her out of the building quickly and with as little human interaction as possible. She prepped to move when from the end of the table, Nora cleared her throat, gaining everyone's attention.

"I do believe we're forgetting the last topic on today's agenda." Nora smiled innocently, but Harry knew that look. It was the one that appeared right before trouble followed.

"Shit," Harry mumbled quietly, replanting her ass in her seat. *What was that witch up to?*

"If Sonia would kindly read back the minutes from our last meeting? I do believe we agreed to discuss the plans to reinstitute the Fates Festival."

Harry's mind blanked as her head snapped toward her aunt.

Sonia, the board's meeting secretary, glanced through her notebook and nodded. "Yes, we did agree to tack it on to this week's meeting."

Sanjay's lips tightened into a thin line. "Are we absolutely certain that bringing back the festival is a good idea?"

"What could possibly be bad about it?" Nora questioned.

"Using town funds to throw something so extravagant that might not even do what we hope seems like a risky endeavor."

"A risky endeavor would be not to attempt it." Nora glanced

over the crowd of citizens. "Fates Haven has slowly been getting new breath into its lungs, and I know I'm not alone when I say that there's been something *extra* in the air as of late."

"Wonky magics . . ." someone shouted.

"Unusual weather patterns," another chimed.

A slew of murmured agreements trailed over the room.

"Yes. Yes, all of that, but we also have new businesses popping up. Our population has seen a slight increase for the first time in thirteen years. There's no time like the present to make something that was once old, new again."

"And what are your thoughts about the Finding Ceremony, Nora?" Sanjay asked. "We can't exactly have a Finding Ceremony without a Fate Witch, and as far as I'm aware, Remus Chardonnay is still missing in action since botching up the last one."

Nora waved away the man's concern. "While I'm not entirely giving up on the idea of a Ceremony, it's not required to have one at a festival. Food. Drink. Entertainment and games. What Fates Haven and its residents need most right now is to remember that we are one community. A family."

"And our Midnight Movies don't do that?"

"Sanjay, you know there's always been something different about the Fates Festival. I say at the very least, we continue with our plans for the Festival itself and incorporate a few of the newer entertainment events that were pitched to the council last meeting. I don't know about you, but I loved the idea Elodie proposed about the Mud Runner."

Sanjay sighed when nearly the entire audience nodded their agreements. "Fine. We'll continue with plans to bring back the Fates Festival, but instead of the usual monthlong festivities, let's give it a trail run at two weeks. I'll leave the event-choosing in your capable hands."

Nora smiled happily. "Wonderful! I'll choose seven and will post the sign-ups on the council website by the end of the day."

Sanjay looked less cheerful. "And if that's all?" He glanced around the quiet room before nodding. "Until next time, that's a wrap for today."

Overwhelmed with the idea Nora had been planning to bring back the Fates Festival—and possibly the Finding Ceremony itself—Harry forgot all about her quick exit until it was too late.

Elodie and Lenny stood in front of her, the former looking awkward and as uncomfortable as she did, and the latter looking especially pissed, her arms across her chest and scowl firmly in place.

Maddox's warning blared in her head.

"Do you think it's really her?" Lenny stared but spoke pointedly to Elodie. "It could be a glamour like they use at that fae club in Denver. It's barely been—what? Thirteen years? Do you think that's enough 'time' that Harry said she needed in her goodbye text?"

Elodie shot Lenny a stern look that drew the seer's attention. "Really?"

"What? It's a genuine question."

"Do you think now's the right time for that question?"

Lenny shrugged. "If not now, I wouldn't know when."

Elodie rolled her eyes and turned a small, reassuring smile Harry's way. "Ignore her. She's been snitting about for a few weeks now."

"She's good at ignoring," Lenny murmured under her breath, only slightly loud enough for Harry to catch the gist.

She let it roll off her back, knowing it wasn't anything she didn't deserve. She did leave Fates Haven with vague, unhelpful texts, and then she'd spelled herself so no one could track her down. If the roles were reversed, she would've led the convo with that ass kicking Maddox mentioned.

Elodie, moving way too quickly for Harry's eyes to register, yanked her into a bone-crushing hug. "You're so lucky that I'm a lover and not a fighter, bitch."

"Says the girl who wanted to start an underground fight ring in the ninth grade." Tears welled in Harry's eyes as she battled back a rush of emotions. "Breathing is starting to become an issue, El."

"Shit. Sorry." Elodie eased her hold but didn't pull back for another few seconds. "And I still think the freshman fight club was a missed opportunity. Tell me you wouldn't have loved an opportunity to kick Karen Pardon's ass without any repercussions."

Harry chuckled. "I guess it's safe to say you've kept up with your training?"

"Youngest member of the Angelic Warrior Guard." Her smile slowly dimmed. "I'm taking a bit of a break right now, though. Came back home to recharge and rejuvenate."

Something told her there was a lot more to that story, but Harry kept the questions to herself. They'd been reunited for less than five minutes. She didn't deserve to have all her questions answered after going AWOL on everyone thirteen years ago.

She snuck a look at a frowning Lennox. "Missed you, too, Lenny. I heard you're doing well. Maddox told me about your tattoo shop and it sounds amazing. Can't say I had you and him being business partners on my bingo card though."

"We haven't killed each other yet, so that's a plus," Lenny retorted.

"We should have a girls' night," Elodie said, taking Harry by surprise. "We're all over twenty-one now, so we can do more than drive down Fates Boulevard whistling at the hot people playing flag football in the park. Hell, we can get into Howlin' Good Time without being carded."

"Oh. I . . ." Harry struggled to come up with a logical-sounding excuse. "Uh . . ."

A safe chat in the middle of town hall was an entirely different beast from a girls' night, which would no doubt include alcohol if they dropped in at Howlin'. Alcohol did more than lower inhibitions. It loosened lips and she needed to keep hers locked up tight.

"I'm not sure that—"

"Oh, a GNO! That sounds like a splendid idea!" Nora popped up on her left.

"It does sound like fun"—Harry's mental wheels spun wildly—"but I'm not sure it's a good idea to leave Gracie alone. She hasn't really acclimated to the new surroundings yet and I should stick close."

"Oh, pish. Grace and I will do just fine. I'll make us some virgin margaritas—well, I'll make hers virgin—and we'll watch whatever bingeable show happens to pop up on one of the streaming services." Nora patted Harry's arm and smiled at Lenny and Elodie. "Harry will be there. Goddess knows she needs to get out and let loose a bit."

"You make it sound like I'm a shut-in or something," Harry grumbled.

Nora chuckled. "I don't think I'd use those exact words, but you have become a bit of a hoverer, my dear. Go out. Have fun. I think the little break will do you and Grace some good."

Elodie shot Harry a genuine, happy smile. "That's great.

How does tomorrow sound? Howlin' runs a ladies' night special on umbrella drinks and, I don't know about anyone else, but I could definitely use the pick-me-up."

"Tomorrow. Sure." Harry pushed a smile on her face and hoped it masked her sudden desire to throw up. "I'll meet you both at Howlin?"

"At nine?"

She sucked in a whimper. That was an hour past her new bedtime . . .

"Nine sounds good."

Elodie leaned in for another hug, this one not nearly as painful. "I can't wait to get to talk some more, Har. I missed you."

Those balls of emotions came back, clogging her throat. "I missed you, too, El. I'll see you tomorrow."

With another round of hugs and goodbyes done and she and Nora alone, Harry turned toward her aunt, hands on her hips.

"What's that pursed look for? Should we stop by the grocery and pick up some prunes? You look a bit backed up, my dear."

"Do not give me that sweet and innocent look, Nora Pierce. I don't need you making play dates for me," Harry said sternly.

"You're welcome." The older witch flashed her a wink. "Now let's go get Grace and make one last stop before we head back home. All this excitement has made me ready for a date with my pillow."

"And here I thought it was all the meddling," Harry muttered following her aunt.

Nora chuckled. "Oh, sweetheart, I'm only getting started."

And that was exactly what Harry was afraid of.

7

The Red Devil Dress

Each throb of Jax's head was synchronized with the steady beat of his heart rate and there didn't appear to be an end in sight. Even max doses of ibuprofen didn't dim the persistent ache, the med nothing more than a damn Tic Tac at this point.

It started the second his alarm blared and progressed through each meeting, and there'd been a hell of a lot of them. Meetings with the heads of the other Rocky Mountain Pack communities. Meetings with neighboring pack alphas. Meetings with . . . hell if he could remember. Halfway through the lineup, he did more passive listening than active, a coping mechanism that was more beneficial for the other involved parties. He was one *But, Alpha Atwood* away from snapping at someone.

Literally.

His inner mountain lion bristled, agitated and on edge as he'd been for the last fifty-seven hours and forty-seven minutes . . . not so roughly around the exact time they'd first laid eyes on a certain curvy witch.

Keeping his distance wasn't working. Not that he thought it would be a piece of cake in a town like Fates Haven, and that was before he agreed to help Grace piece together her shifter puzzle.

The landline phone rang in the outer room and a second later, Sunny's voice pierced his temporary quiet. "Line two, Alpha Atwood."

"Whoever it is, I'm busy."

A few seconds later, his cell vibrated on his desk with an incoming text.

> Answer my phone call or
> I'll be forced to take drastic
> measures.

"Just what today needed," Jax grumbled to himself just as the phone in his hands rang. "And to what do I owe this pleasure? Bored already? Because if you're calling to tell me that you made a mistake in retiring, I'll start cleaning out my desk now. It's all yours."

Not that he'd added a whole lot to it. Or anything. He glanced around the top, the only thing on it stacks and stacks of paperwork.

"Bored?" Patricia Atwood chuckled, her voice light and breezy and extremely happy sounding. "Not in the least. I just returned from swimming with the sharks, and can I just say that it was life-changing."

"What a coincidence . . . I just got off a virtual meeting with about six of them, but I don't feel all that changed. Except if you count the increased pounding in my head," Jax muttered.

His mother chuckled. "Oh, my sharks were certifiable teddy bears to *that* lot. I even fed one. From my hand."

"So what I'm hearing is that you're not ending your retirement?" He sat back in his chair and kicked his boots up on the desk, something his mother would've been horrified to see. "You sure there's nothing I can say or do to lure you back?"

"Don't take this the wrong way, sweetheart, but I'm perfectly content—ecstatic even—to not see your face for quite a while."

"Gee. That's not difficult to take the wrong way or anything." But he totally got it.

His mother had lived and breathed Rocky Mountain Pack business since before he could even walk, the job costing her more than her time and energy. It had also fueled the fires of his parents' subsequent divorce.

"From what I hear, you're doing great," his mother stated approvingly. "Just keep doing what you're doing and follow your gut. It'll never steer you wrong."

"Considering how far away you are, I'm surprised you're hearing anything."

His mother chuckled at his blatant attempt to figure out her mystery location. "I'm close enough to hear that a certain saucy witch with periwinkle eyes has come back to Fates Haven."

"I'm not talking about her, Ma." That damn pulse in his head worked overtime at the mention of Harry.

"Jaxon . . ."

"I'm a little old for you to *Jaxon* me, don't you think? Besides, it's not like she's here permanently, or even of her own volition. She's back because she needs something. Ironically, from you . . . who is now me."

"Did she say she's here temporarily?" Patricia asked innocently.

"Honestly? I have no idea. And it's none of my business either. What *is* my concern is this pack, my business, and evidently Nora's brilliant new idea to resurrect the Fates Festival." A sharp flare of pain throbbed behind his eyes. He pinched the bridge of his nose, willing the orbs to stay in his head.

"And a teenage shifter of unknown origin," his mom added.

"Seriously. How *are* you getting Fates Haven gossip where you are? Is there some kind of newsletter that goes out weekly or something?"

She chuckled. "Oh, I have my ways and, no, I will never tell. But now that you brought up your teenage mystery, how is that going? Any progress in identifying her shifter potential?"

"I didn't bring Grace up. You did." Jax smirked, practically seeing his mother's cogs turning. "And she hasn't burned anything down since she set fire to my wheelbarrow, so I suppose you can count that as progress."

"So she really does have fire capabilities?" Patricia hummed. "Interesting. Other than phoenixes, I'm not aware of any other shifter types that possess fire."

"Not so sure we're dealing with a phoenix. They're typically about calm and peace and I guess it could be her age, but Grace is all snark, bite, and—"

"And fire," his mom finished.

"And fire," Jax agreed. "I've been meaning to talk to Harry about the possibility that the fire abilities aren't coming from the father at all. She said Grace's mother is human, but it wouldn't be the first time that latent supernatural abilities manifest after sleeping a few generations."

"Hm. I guess that's another possibility. But I feel as if Harry—or Nora—would sense if Grace were developing some kind of elemental witchling powers. It's definitely a mystery.

Keep me posted, and if you need to bounce any ideas off someone, you know where I am."

"Actually, I'm not entirely sure where you are right now, but I get what you're saying, Ma. Thank you. Hope you keep having a good time."

"Oh, I will, sweetheart. I definitely will." She smooched the phone. "Love you. Miss you. And, Jaxon?"

"Yeah?"

"She's extremely lucky to have you in her life."

"Pretty sure after I made her shovel horse shit, she's not feeling the same way." Jax chuckled. "But I hope I can help her out. If she can't trust herself, she can't fully trust others, and whether or not her shifter identity is a pack animal, she'll need a community."

"Absolutely . . . but that wasn't who I was talking about."

"Mom . . ."

"Love you! Don't forget to play nice! Kisses!"

She hung up, leaving him with an abrupt silence and an even bigger headache.

"Let's go!" Maddox burst into his office, a determined look on his face. "Come on. Chop-chop. The darts won't fly themselves. Actually, in Fates Haven that's kinda possible, but the beer won't drink itself, so pack up and let's go."

"I told you I wasn't up for tonight. I'm gonna go home and—"

"Sulk. Yeah, I got the message that you had *Sunny* deliver. Silas and I are in agreement. That reasoning sucks and we're not accepting it." Mads stood solidly, his beefy arms folded across his chest, ink on full display. "You're in brood mode. And there is no place more dangerous to be when you're in brood mode than alone with your thoughts."

"I'm not in brood mode," Jax denied half-heartedly.

Mads cocked up a pierced eyebrow. "A lot of shit has rained down on you over the last few months, and then throw in everything this past week? No one denies you have a good reason to brood. But we both know—whether you want to admit it or not—that holing up in that sad shack you call a cabin will only make it ten times worse."

"Beer won't magically make it all go away either."

"No. But you wiping Silas's ass at darts with one eye closed and one hand tied behind your back might make it all a little easier to deal with." Sensing Jax's resolve weakening, Maddox added with a smirk, "Seriously. Think about the pout when he loses. Again."

"Fine. But I'm only sticking around for one beer and one dart game. Then I'm getting my brood on back at my sad little cabin."

"That's what I'm talking about!"

Jax grudgingly followed, regretting his choice before he even exited his office.

* * *

HARRY STEPPED INTO her room, her comb stuck halfway through her hair, and came a dead stop as she tried rationalizing what she was seeing. Through her exhaustion, she couldn't really put it all together.

"You know what? I don't have the energy for this," Harry announced to the one-foot gnome currently playing dress-up with yet another set of her undergarments. She waved the creature off. "Take them. I don't care. Have yourself a little fashion show with all your little gnome friends."

It twittered insensibly before climbing onto the windowsill.

With a final wave of its bra-clenching hand, it disappeared into the night. Harry closed the window behind it and contemplated diving into her bed and dealing with the aftermath later—both the wet bed head fallout and being a no-show for girl' night out.

She almost talked herself into it when her phone rang.

Seeing the caller ID, she picked the cell up immediately. "Please tell me you found him, got answers, and you're coming home."

Cassie's tired sigh didn't give her much hope. "That would be a big no, bigger no, and unfortunately no. I followed a promising lead to Alaska, but when I got here the trail went cold."

"Gee, a cold trail in Alaska. Who would've thought?" Harry joked dryly.

"I was hoping you two were having better luck than I was."

"That is yet to be determined." Harry flung herself back on the mattress. "I've seen Gracie smile more since we've been in Fates Haven than I have in the last year, so that's something. It's been at my expense, but I'll take it when I can get it. Moving her out here to Colorado definitely didn't win me any popularity points, that's for sure."

"Smiles are good," Cassie reassured. "I wish I was there with you two. If I don't catch a lead soon, I guess I could—"

"Come back and then leave again when you catch another whiff that could be Mr. Mysterio?" Harry smiled wanly. "That didn't go over too well the last time we tried that."

"I know, but I feel bad knowing everything you're going through and not being there to help with it."

"Like Aunt Nora always says, we've got the entire town of Fates Haven behind us, so we're not without help."

"And you have a certain Alpha Hotwood behind you, too."

Cassie's low voice dripped with mischief. "Or maybe he's on top. Or behind. Or—"

"Does Gracie *really* need a phone? It might do her some good to unplug for a bit."

Cassie chuckled. "So it's true? The Alpha helping figure things out is the same one who snuck you from your childhood bedroom for midnight rendezvous and a little hanky-panky in the witchy's panty?"

"Please never say that again," Harry begged. "But, yes. You'll be unsurprised that my sucktastic luck continues and he is one and the same. And, no, there is no hanky-panky happening in this witch's panties."

"I didn't say anything."

"You're thinking it."

"Your descry magics have expanded to telepathy now?"

"No, but they have been a little wonky since we got here."

"That's probably because of Alpha Hotwood."

"Seriously, Cass. No. I don't fuck with Fate, and Fate already made it clear that Jax is meant for someone else."

Cassie growled. "You're a fucking kick-ass witch, an incredible best friend—when you're properly caffeinated—and you're a phenomenal aunt to my daughter. Not to mention loyal and dedicated and—"

"You make me sound like a service dog."

"You know what I mean. Fuck Fate. Make your own. *You* tell *it* how things will be; and if Fate ends up being right in the end, at least you'll have taken *your* path to get there. Not that I've ever been—except on this Alaskan excursion—but I hear off roading can be pretty fun."

Harry wished it were that simple, but Cass had a point. "I'm going out tonight with my childhood best friends. Or at least I was in the middle of convincing myself not to bail."

"Do not bail."

"But it'll be awkward and—"

"Did you bring the red dress?" Cassie asked.

"It's a girls' night out, Cass. I'm not fishing for a bed partner tonight."

"Why the hell not? The endorphins released with great sex have been proven to improve a person's overall outlook and mindset. Not to mention blood pressure."

"My outlook and mindset are just fine, and my blood pressure was normal until about five seconds ago."

"FaceTime. Now," Cassie ordered, the request popping up on Harry's phone a second later. The instant she connected, her best friend's face filled the screen, looking so much like her daughter with twenty additional years. "Look into my eyes."

Harry snortled. "Are you trying to hypnotize me?"

"I love that you're helping me take care of Gracie, Harry. I do. I hate to think where the two of us would be without you, but you have to take care of yourself, too." Her friend studied her through the phone and smiled wanly. "Something tells me that Grace isn't the only one who will benefit from being in Fates Hollow."

"Fates Haven."

"That's what I said." Cassie's smile looked so much like her daughter's. "Love you. Now take me to my crotch goblin and then go put on the red devil dress."

"Fine." Harry sighed, knowing she was beaten.

"And I'll find out if you bail, both on the girls' night and the dress."

"Yeah, I know." Harry shuffled down the hall and knocked on the teen's door once, then twice. On the third rap, it flung open and there stood an annoyed sixteen-year-old. Harry held out the cell. "For you."

"Is it Mom?" Grace looked hopeful.

"Unless your mom is some weird lady who likes giving out unsolicited relationship advice and ultimatums—Oh wait. Yeah, it's her."

Grace grabbed the phone and disappeared back into the teenage abyss that was her room.

With a heavy sigh, Harry returned to hers and yanked open her closet. With a plunging neckline, snug waistline, and short, flirty skirt, the aforementioned red dress had earned its own nickname after conjuring a record number of free drink offers as well as one-night-stand invitations.

She wasn't looking for either of those things tonight, but the smallest bit of luck couldn't hurt, right?

8

The Pointy End of a Demon

Harry'd been in her fair share of bars and clubs, bumping and grinding against random sweaty strangers there was no chance she'd see again the next day. As a twenty-something in New York City, those experiences were basically a rite of passage.

Howlin' Good Time was more dive bar than trendy hot spot, its ancient jukebox tucked in the corner next to a small stage that was occasionally used for live entertainment or karaoke nights. But gone were the peanut dust and shells that once littered the floor; and while the tables and chairs were mismatched and well used, the corner booths and tables boasted lush, padded benches and high-backed antique chairs that would've looked chic and trendy in a city poetry club.

Someone had given the place a facelift with fresh paint and a retro-antique style right down to the elaborate crystal chandeliers and dimmed, ambience-creating lighting. This was the type of place that Cassie would absolutely adore.

Harry smoothed her dress's skirt and glanced around the

familiar unfamiliar place, sending a tentative smile to the shifter bartender.

"Hey, Kailani." Harry tried ignoring her awkwardness and the nearly dozen people staring at her as she approached the counter with a small wave. "It's good to see you!"

"Look what the cat dragged in." Kai paused in her glass cleaning and smiled warmly. "Or should I say the angel and the seer . . . because I'm assuming you're the reason those two have been watching the door for the last fifteen minutes."

She nudged her chin to a corner table, one with the elaborate high-backed chairs, where Elodie and Lennox sat, waving Harry over. She returned the gesture, letting them know she saw them.

"It's girls' night out. The first in a long time." Harry's mouth went dry as she fought to keep a confident smile on her face and not give in to the nausea rolling around in her stomach.

"Say no more. I got you covered." Kai slipped a shot glass filled with a pink foamy liquid toward her. "A shot of Liquid Courage. On the house."

"A little bit of that definitely wouldn't hurt." Harry downed it after a quick sniff, realizing it wouldn't have mattered if it smelled like battery acid if it helped her get through this night a bit easier. The sweet liquid slid down her throat, tickling her nose in the process. "Wow. That's really good."

"And packs a pretty big wallop if you consume more than one, but it does the trick."

"Thanks, but I don't want to get you in trouble. I'll pay for it." She reached into her purse, but the shifter waved it off.

"Owner's perk. I don't have to answer to anyone except me."

"I was wondering about the new ambience. Charlie was

allergic to change of any kind . . . which surprises me that he willingly sold the place."

Kai chuckled. "No one was more surprised than me when he offered me the deal. Technically, he's still a silent partner, but he's very, very silent and living the retirement life right now, hopping from one cruise ship to another."

"Good for him. And good for you, too. Congrats." Harry slid a look toward Elodie and Lenny, their heads bowed close together as they spoke to each other. "I guess I should get this night started, huh? Do me a favor and if it looks like I need another dose of Courage, send one my way. Wallop packing or not."

"Will do." Kai chuckled and gave her a little salute as she turned to help her next customer.

Harry made her way across the room and was given twin smiles . . . well, a smile and a slight grimace.

"I have to admit, I thought you'd bail," Lennox admitted. She filled up three empty glasses from what looked to be a pitcher of frozen margaritas.

Harry chuckled awkwardly. "I had to make sure Nora and Grace were set up with streaming access. Nora said something about watching the *Halloweentown* series . . . to give Grace an idea of what she had to look forward to being in Fates Haven."

Elodie snorted. "Hopefully minus the evil warlocks."

"Maybe Nora's gnomes can be considered the evil entity of the Haven story. If they keep up their current rate of underwear snatching, I'll be going braless and commando in another week. I haven't gone without a bra since I was in the third grade."

They all chuckled, some of the awkward tension melting away.

"Grace is your friend's daughter? The one who's having difficulty reining in her shifter?" Lenny asked.

Harry couldn't even be surprised news traveled the way it did. She nodded. "She's more like a niece to me, but, yeah. We're dividing and trying to conquer, so while I stick with Gracie and try to find answers in the supernatural community, Cassie is trying to find them direct from the source. I hope being here in Fates Haven will break our unlucky streak."

Elodie added, "You heard Nora at the town council meeting. There's been something stirring in the air."

"Pollution?" Lenny joked, earning her an eye roll from the angel.

"Something . . . *other*. If you ever meditated with me, you'd probably feel the difference, too."

"No way in hell will I make that mistake again. Any benefits gained from the meditation would immediately fly out the window with all that . . . other stuff."

"It's called training," El said wryly.

"It's called not ever happening. I'll leave all that 'training' to you. I'm perfectly happy with my life of leisure at the tattoo shop."

Harry chuckled. She missed this back-and-forth banter.

Suddenly, she felt silly for being so worried. Like Cassie, Elodie and Lennox were her ride or dies. If one of them ever texted wear a disguise, bring a shovel, and don't ask questions, she'd don a blow-up unicorn costume, raid Nora's garden shed, and seal her lips shut with Gorilla Glue.

They both would do the same, although Lenny would probably forgo the unicorn costume for something a bit more on-brand for her. Like a velociraptor.

Seeing her inner struggle, Lenny paused with her drink halfway to her mouth. "What's wrong?"

Harry swallowed the lump forming in her throat. Len may be pissed, but she still cared. "I really missed this . . . and the two of you. I'm sorry for being such a—"

"Nope." Elodie cut her off with an adamant head shake. "No apologies. No guilt. We wasted enough time without one another to be bogged down by all that other nonsense."

Lenny lifted a pierced eyebrow. "Speak for yourself. I wouldn't mind an apology or twelve. And a little groveling to go along with the guilt isn't exactly unappealing either."

Elodie shot their friend a warning glare, but Harry intervened with an emphatic "I'm sorry, Lenny. Those words are so inadequate, but they're true. There's no excusing the way I cut away from everyone."

"There's really not."

"I know."

"It was pretty shitty."

Harry nodded. "It was totally shitty. I can't even count the times I thought about coming back, or picking up a phone, but by the time I'd pieced myself back together, I was sure everyone here had moved on. What was the point in ripping open old wounds?"

Elodie glanced from Harry to Lennox as the seer contemplated. "I won't forget."

"I wouldn't expect you to. Hell, I wouldn't want you to either. It happened. It's part of our history."

Lennox looked deep in thought before giving Harry a slight nod. "I guess we could see where this thing goes. But another fuckup and I'll be the first to call you out."

"I wouldn't expect anything else." Harry smiled tentatively, a heavy weight sliding off her shoulders.

Elodie whooped loudly, lifting her glass in the air. "Let's hear it for the official reinstatement of the Trouble Trio's GNO."

Chuckling, they all clanked their drinks before taking long drafts through their straws.

Elodie hiccupped and giggled. "Fates Haven thought we were menaces when we were sweet, innocent teenagers. Can you imagine the havoc we can create now that we're adults?"

"I can't, but I'm kinda looking forward to finding out." Harry grinned wide.

"Wait," Lenny interjected, "when were we sweet and innocent?"

Harry's worries melted away with each joke and laugh—and the flowing drinks didn't hurt either. Kai kept the margaritas coming, swapping out different fruit flavors each time they went up for refills. Harry sashayed back to the table, a mango peach margarita pitcher in her hand, when the bar's door opened.

She didn't need to feel the temporary rush of outdoor sauna to know who'd arrived.

The air shifted, knocking her off-balance the second her eyes locked on Jax. She stumbled, catching herself on a nearby table before she ended up wearing their next round of drinks.

It should be illegal to look that damn good wearing jeans and a T-shirt, and yet Jax looked edible. Sex on two well-toned and muscular legs. Sex with a scruffy, angular jaw. Sex with flashing, silver eyes that lasered in on her the second he glanced her way.

Maddox was on his left, and although she didn't know the man-bun blond in the suit, the third guy on the right had such a striking resemblance to Marie that he couldn't be anyone other than her grandson, Silas. The last time she'd laid eyes on him, he'd been baby faced and awkward, and sported a mouth full of braces.

It took everything in Harry to pull her gaze away from the four hot guys, or if she were honest, the one in the center. She quickly headed back to the Trouble Trio table and took her seat, her legs a little unsteady.

Jax being here with his friends didn't need to be a thing. They were all adults, albeit she was a slightly tipsy one who now regretted that last round.

"And there goes the neighborhood." Shoulders deflating, Elodie locked her pink glossy lips around her straw and sucked down her replenished drink as if it were a milkshake. "I swear sometimes I think I'm cursed."

Lenny chuckled. "You really ought to be used to this by now. This is, after all, Fates Haven. It's not like there are a whole lot of places to unwind."

The angel shot Lenny a dark scowl. "How does one get used to pure evil?"

Harry's gaze bounced from friend to friend. "This could be the margaritas making my brain a little fuzzy, but I'm lost. Who is pure evil?"

"Silas McCloud." Elodie threw a disdainful glance toward the new arrivals. "Look up *narcissistic demon hole* and you'll see a picture of his smug mug right there . . . beady eyes, sharp fangs, and all."

Harry slid a look to Marie's grandson, now sitting at the end of the bar. Dark hair that was shorn on the sides and longer on top flopped over twin pools of piercing, oceanic blue. He laughed at something Maddox said, his head tossed back.

"Maybe I need a new contact prescription, but I don't see beady eyes or sharp fangs."

"He disguises them well. Trust me. They're there."

Harry shot another look toward the bar, and mentally cursed when her gaze collided with Jax's. Turned halfway on his stool, he didn't bother hiding the fact he stared. Harry shifted uncomfortably in her seat, her cheeks heating.

Why the hell did he have to look at her like that? And with Elodie sitting right across from her?

Harry ripped her gaze away and made a futile attempt to ignore the physical response Jax's attention conjured. She peppered Lenny with a pleading look. "You'll have to help a witch out here because my Elodie-ese is a little rusty. What's the deal with Marie's grandson? I know he only visited during the summer, but I don't remember him being—"

"Evil incarnate," Elodie finished.

"Would Jax and Maddox really be friends with him if that were the case?"

She scoffed. "He's a good actor, and not that I don't adore Jax and Maddox, but they're easily duped. Trust me. The demon practically had the entire Angel Academy staff and student body fawning all over him when he was the guest instructor my last year before graduation. It was nauseating."

Lenny chuckled. "I'm sure it had nothing to do with the fact that he gave you your very first 'needs improvement' score ever."

Elodie's face reddened. "Because I didn't execute the drill his preferred way. I did it better, and faster, *my* way. He's so lucky all his underhanded tricks didn't cost me my first Guard assignment selection. If it had, he would've found himself on the pointy end of my celestial blade."

"And yet here we are years later and you're still pining over the fact you didn't end up on the receiving side of his pointy end," Lenny murmured. "Then or now."

Harry choked on her drink, having chosen that moment to take a sip. She coughed, tears leaking from her eyes as she wheezed. "Excuse me?"

Elodie glared at the seer. "That is not what this is about."

"I think the angel doth protest too much. Honestly, I think you two should just have a naked battle already and call it a day. Fantasy fulfilled."

"I do not fantasize about sex with Silas McCloud."

"Would you like me to play the recording of you sleep-talking that weekend we went to the T-Swift concert? Because those moans of 'Oh, Silas' say otherwise."

Harry's head spun as she tried to wrap her head around all the information being tossed around. "Okay, pause, rewind, and press play again, but this time, in slow motion. You used to have a thing for your old academy instructor—"

"Guest instructor," Elodie corrected. "It thankfully only lasted a semester, and I did not have a thing."

"Correct," Lenny agreed, "because it's not past tense."

The redheaded angel shot Lenny a look that would've frozen her into an ice sculpture if she'd had elemental magic, but Lennox didn't back down, lifting a pierced eyebrow. "I dare you to tell me I'm dead wrong."

El opened and closed her mouth, looking like a fish out of water. "Stop using your seer gifts on me. It's rude and not to mention against the girl code."

Lennox chuckled. "You know I'd have to tattoo you to experience a Sight. Plus, I don't need to use my gift to see what's staring all of us right in the face. Except, of course, you and Silas."

"But what about Jax?" Harry heard herself blurt.

Her friends' heads swiveled her way, both wearing twin looks of confusion. It only fueled her own, which was worsened by the damn margaritas.

"What about Jax?" Elodie asked cautiously.

"I mean . . . the Fates Festival. The Finding Ceremony." Harry's throat nearly swelled closed. "The Blue Willow Wisp." Her gaze bounced from friend to friend before landing and staying on the angel. "Your wisp guided you to Jax at the Finding Ceremony. The two of you are . . . Fated."

Understanding slowly dawned on her friend's face as she reached across the table and took her hand. "No. We're not."

"But you are. We all saw. . . . I don't understand."

"The Blue Willow Wisp was wrong, Harry. So, so wrong."

"The Wisp is never wrong," Harry whispered, the words sending a searing ache through her chest.

"It was that year, and it fucked up so badly that no one has seen a Wisp since. Or the Fate Witch, but that's beside the point." Elodie paused. "Wait . . . did Jax tell you that we're Fated? Because if he did, I'll go over there and kick his ass so hard my boot'll tickle his tonsils."

"No. He . . ." He didn't say *anything*.

He had to have known what she thought, and he'd chosen not to correct her.

"So there hasn't been a Finding Ceremony in . . ."

"Thirteen years," Lennox finished. "Nora didn't tell you? It's kinda a big deal that she finally convinced the town council to give the festival another go. Even without an actual Fate Witch and Finding Ceremony, it's a big accomplishment."

Harry grimaced. "When I left, I bound Nora to a Witch's Oath. She couldn't talk about anything Fates Haven related unless we were in Fates Haven. If I kept hearing about everyone back home, there was no way I would've been able to stay away, and I couldn't come back because . . ."

Because she thought Elodie and Jax had Mated. That like other couples led together by the Blue Willow Wisp, they'd found their happily ever after and did exactly what the Fates Haven welcome sign instructed and Became Fated in Fates.

She looked to Elodie. "Are you sure you're not Fated to Jax?"

"Would I secretly want to be on the pointy end of an insufferable demon narcissist if that were the case?" She snapped a warning finger toward Lennox. "Do not say a damn word or I'll personally show you what all that meditation has done for my training regimen."

Lennox mimed zipped lips. "Not saying a word."

Elodie squeezed Harry's hand. "I'm not Fated to Jax, Harry. No one in Fates—tourist or citizen—has found their Fated since the Finding Ceremony the year you left. The town is at risk of losing its Highest-FMP-in-the-world designation."

"*No one* has found their Fated?" Shock struck Harry still.

"Not a person. And the more time that passes, the more the magical ley lines diminish. At least, that's what Nora says is the reason behind all these wonky power surges and dead spots."

Harry shot Lenny a grim look. "Your Sight? Maddox said something about it being on the fritz? Is it because of the ley lines?"

She shrugged. "Your guess is as good as mine, but that's the working theory."

"Well shit."

"Pretty much sums it up."

"I don't know about you two, but I'm suddenly really

freaking thirsty." Elodie grabbed the empty margarita pitcher and hightailed it toward Kailani.

Harry let everything sink in deep and still had difficulty processing.

Fates Haven was losing its mojo. *Literally.*

Both the Blue Willow Wisps *and* the Fate Witch were AWOL.

And Elodie and Jax weren't Fated—to each other or to anyone else.

* * *

JAX TOOK A sip of his beer and realized too late that he'd been nursing the same one for the last hour and it was about as cold as fresh piss. He pushed it away with a grimace so he didn't make the same mistake again and realized there was no point in pretending he wasn't distracted by the Trouble Trio reunion happening in the corner of the room.

Good things never happened when those three got together, and judging by the occasional furtive glances they kept shooting his way, tonight wouldn't be an exception.

"Looks like you owe Elodie that Sugar Tits subscription box, huh?" Silas teased coyly from over the rim of his beer. "Guess the Fates Haven gossip mill wasn't so hoaxy this time around after all."

Jax threw him a glare. "You have a point to the commentary?"

"Just a few observational facts."

"And are you sharing the rest of them with the class?"

"Nope." Silas popped the *P* with a smirk on his face. "Gonna keep them to myself and release them in one dramatic wave. It's more entertaining that way."

"You and I have different definitions of entertaining," Jax grumbled.

Maddox chuckled. "I may be a party of one, but I can't wait to see what those three get into."

"You're definitely a party of one, and I can already tell you exactly what they'll get into: mayhem, mischief, and—"

"Margaritas," Silas interjected. "Looks like a lot of margaritas have made their way into them, too."

Fuck. He wasn't wrong. As they spoke, Elodie unsteadily sauntered from the bar to her table with another pitcher of frozen something in her hands. The girls each took large swigs before getting up from their seats, Lenny manually hauling Harry from her plush chair with a yank. They laughed their way to the back pool table.

Jax nearly swallowed his tongue. Harry selected her cue and got into position to break the balls apart, her dress hem rising to reveal a tantalizing amount of bare thigh. The sleek, red fabric tightened around her ass with every movement.

He'd always been an ass man and she had a spectacular one. Then and now. He couldn't help but watch her glide around the table, biting her lower lip as she contemplated every shot as if about to take a calculus exam.

"This is fucking painful to watch." Silas's groan ripped Jax's attention away from Harry's legs. "Put yourself out of both our misery and go over there already, man."

"And what exactly would that accomplish?" Jax demanded.

"Hell if I know, but at least I wouldn't have to bear witness to that fucking sad-sap pining look on your face."

"I do not have a pining look."

Maddox grunted. "It's a little bit pining."

"Fuck you both. It's not." His gaze reflexively veered to

the pool table; and at the sight of Elodie and Harry teasingly bumping into each other, something stirred deep in his chest. "Fuck."

Pining.

"He sees it now," Gavin declared correctly.

Chuckling, Maddox knocked his beer glass into Silas's. "Job well done, my friend. I applaud you and your insight."

"And I bow with my ass planted on this stool." Silas smirked.

"Even if you were right—which you're not," Jax lied, "there's no way in hell I'd go there again."

"To the pool table over there or into the gorgeous brunette currently shooting daggers your way?" Silas asked.

Jax took a quick glance at the pool table. Sure enough, as subtle as she tried to play it, Harry snuck them a quick look, and her eyes, even from the distance, practically lit up with an increasing swell of undecipherable emotions, none of them too happy looking.

"Both," he answered. "Getting involved with Harlow Pierce is like attending a county fair. The food's delicious—while you're scarfing it down. The game's fun—when you win the human-size unicorn prize. But then the fair packs up and heads to the next town and you're left behind with nothing more than memories, food poisoning, and a house with a new bedbug infestation."

"That's the story you're sticking to?" Silas snorted.

Kailani whistled, the sound piercing through the already loud bar, bringing everything to a low hum as she held up a paper stack before slamming it down on the bar. "The town council dropped off interest forms for the Fates Festival events! Choose wisely and place your forms in the box at the end of the bar."

People swarmed the stack. Even Maddox leaned over on his stool and grabbed a form.

"What?" He shrugged. "There's no harm in seeing what they're offering."

Silas chuffed and took a sip of his beer. "No way are they offering anything I'd be caught dead doing."

"You mean you're not participating?" Elodie's voice oozed false sweetness as she stepped up next to Silas, flanked by Lenny and Harry, all looking a bit tipsy. "However will the rest of us recover from that devastating disappointment? Scared of the humiliation when people realize you all aren't the big bads that you pretend to be?"

The demon swung around to face the angel, his signature cocky smirk firmly in place. "Oh, angel eyes, I'm the absolute baddest. It just wouldn't be fair to the other participants. If we entered, the highest rank anyone else could get would be second."

A challenge hung in the air.

It didn't need to be a physical thing for people to see it. Hell, the entire bar went silent, holding their collective breaths, gazes volleying back and forth between the two. Jax knew firsthand how quickly this could get out of control.

He cleared his throat. "I think what Silas means is that our gifts would make it too easy for us to win these kinds of events. It wouldn't be fair for those who didn't have the same talents."

Harry snortled, earning his attention.

"You have something to say, sweet pea?" Jax challenged.

"Not so sure I'd consider egotism a talent for"—she picked up the list of scheduled festival events and tromboned it in front of her face, attempting to put it into focus—"Paintball Pandemonium. Or Dud Runner."

"I think you mean Mud Runner."

The witch waved her hand, the move wreaking havoc with her balance as she swayed. "Dud Runner. Mud Runner. It doesn't matter. Egotism still won't help you."

"It's not egotism when it's true."

"It's not true unless it's proven."

Elodie and Lenny nodded their agreements, instantly becoming Harry's cheerleaders.

"And how do you suggest we do that?" Jax rose to the bait, doing exactly what he'd mentally warned his friend against.

The Trouble Trio shared a few looks before Harry folded her arms over her chest, matching his pose. "I would think a firsthand demonstration would do the trick. Your group . . . the Big Bads . . . against our group—"

"The Trouble Trio," Elodie interjected, looking smug.

Harry nodded supportively.

"There's four of us and only three of you. We wouldn't want you to cry foul at the end of the Festival when you don't win a single event."

"Then we'll find a fourth. We'll call ourselves the Fearsome Four."

Jax shot a look to Silas and was met with a coy, interested smirk. Maddox shrugged. And Gavin was doing Gavin things and didn't have a damn thing to say, his nose buried in his book.

This was a fucking bad idea.

Everything in Jax told him to abort and abort quickly. Instead, he met Harry's gaze head-on. "Three events. The Fearsome Four against the Big Bads. Winner gets what?"

"I think it should be a matter of what the loser has to do."

"And what's that?"

She shrugged. "Maybe we should let the good citizens of Fates Haven decide that . . . unless that's a little too high stakes for you guys."

A small round of whoops and cheers sounded around the bar at the gauntlet that Harry just thrown down.

He gladly picked it up. "You're on, sweet pea. And why don't we go one step further and let these loyal patrons vote on what three Fates Festival events will be part of the showdown?"

"Sounds good to me."

After another round of cheers, Kai went into action, setting up a makeshift voting station for people to put their selections. There was no way this wouldn't come back to bite him on the ass in a need-stitches-and-a-tetanus-shot kind of way, but so far, Silas and Maddox were too busy attempting to rile up an already flustered Elodie and Lennox to share his sentiments.

Jax smirked at his friends' antics. Some things never changed.

An overexcited voter brushed past Harry, knocking her off-balance and straight into him. His arms shot out and wrapped around her waist, preventing her from spilling to the floor.

Sucking in a groan, he closed his eyes and tried ignoring her sweet, lilac scent. He failed miserably, every inch of his body humming as if brushing up against a live wire. It took a few seconds to realize that the sensation came from him.

Or more accurately, his mountain lion.

The bastard was purring, the vibration pushing his chest further against Harry's back.

"Is the ground moving, or . . ." Harry's voice trailed.

Jax quickly shut off the damn purr and, with great difficulty, took a half step back but kept his hands braced on the swell of her hips. "You okay?"

Her cheeks pinked, whether from the alcohol in her system

or something else. "Yeah. Thanks. Guess I went a little over-board with the margaritas. It's been a while since I've been off duty."

His lips twitched. "Plus, you've never been able to hold your liquor. Let's not forget the homecoming incident junior year."

Harry shot him a look over her shoulder that put her back once again firmly against his chest. "That night was to remain buried in a deep, dark vault never to be spoken about again."

"Afraid what Lenny would say if she found out it was really you and not Maddox that threw up in her little purse thing?"

She spun in his arms, putting them chest to chest as she drilled a fingertip into his sternum. "Deep. Dark. Vault. And you'd be smart to remember that I know a few secrets of yours, too, Jaxon Atwood."

His smile slowly dimmed as he reflexively glanced at her mouth mere inches away. "Don't I know it."

She swallowed, the move more prominent with their close proximity.

He couldn't tear his eyes off her, and when her own gaze dropped to his lips, he released a small groan. "You're killing me here, sweet pea."

Her mouth opened and closed a few times before her knees gave way. He caught her before she hit the floor. A commotion sounded around them as her friends hightailed it to her side.

"Is she okay? What happened?" Elodie brushed the back of her hand over Harry's forehead.

"Pretty sure it was margaritas on what was probably an empty stomach," Jax said dryly.

"No, no. I'm okay." Harry's face was white as a sheet. "What was the vote?"

"I think you'll have to find out the results tomorrow. We should get you home."

"No, no. Really. I'm fine." She swayed.

"Yeah, I don't think so." Catching her body with his shoulder, he dipped down and picked her up in a fireman's carry. "I think it's way past your bedtime. Kai? Hit me with a bottle of water?"

"Sure thing." She tossed him one which he caught with the hand that wasn't currently planted just below Harry's round ass cheeks.

"Put me down," Harry ordered, squirming on his shoulder. "Jax! Seriously! This is not the view I expected when I came back to Colorado. I'm not impressed."

Elodie and Lennox chuckled, watching the show.

"Wow. It's like no time has passed." Elodie smirked.

"If only," Jax murmured, glancing to his friends. "You got those two?"

Maddox nodded. "Yeah, I'll dump them off at Lenny's place. You sure you got her? I don't mind taking her home, too."

"Nah. You're heading to the other side of town and I have to pass Pierce House on my way."

Harry braced her hands on the small of his back as he walked toward his truck in the back parking lot. It was just the two of them and the twinkling stars overhead. "I'm sorry, Jax."

"Yeah? You're sorry about what?" He dug his keys out one-handed and, standing at the passenger door, unlocked the pickup.

"I lied."

"About?"

"I am impressed with the view back here. Thirteen years

ago, I didn't think your ass could look any better than it did then, but I was woefully mistaken. I'd take this view over the one from the Mount Evans summit any day of the week."

"Ditto, babe. Ditto." He swallowed a chuckle and, after opening the passenger door, gently deposited her on the end of the seat. Her eyelids, half-mast and quickly dropping, fluttered open as she gripped the front of his shirt.

"I can't go back to Nora's," she claimed adamantly. "Not like this. Not . . ."

"Twelve sheets to the wind?" Jax smirked.

"Teenagers are harsh, Jax," Harry yell whispered. "I don't remember ever being so . . . moody. But if I come back home like this, I will never hear the end of it. She'll use it to extort something out of me. Please."

He couldn't even ask her please what because her eyes drifted closed. Jax sighed and got her settled in the seat, putting on her seat belt and making sure she was fastened in tight. By the time he came around to the driver's side and started the truck, she'd pushed her forehead against the cool glass and was already fast asleep.

This entire night was one bad mistake after another.

Letting Maddox talk him into going out. The Big Bads versus Fearsome Four challenge. Not letting Mads take Harry the fuck home.

And he was making another one, driving past Pierce House and heading away from town. He badged through the ranch's front gate and toward his cabin. He had no neighbors. Just his four walls and nature, and the bubbling creek feet off his back deck that made for some great morning fishing.

Jax didn't bring people here.

Ever.

And damn if he would think about why that was changing right then and there.

Pulling up to the front porch, he cut the engine and glanced at the woman at his side, her soft snores filling the small space.

He'd settle her in his bed and sleep on the couch, or better yet, head outside to sleep on the hammock hanging on his back porch. No fuss. No muss. And no intoxicating Harlow Pierce sweet scent tempting him to do something stupid.

He jogged up the steps and unlocked and opened the front door before heading back to a sleeping Harry. "Up we go . . ."

She stirred when he opened her door, eyes fluttering open as he settled his hands on her hips. He wasn't prepared for the intensity of her gorgeous periwinkle eyes and froze, his body inches away from hers.

"Why didn't you tell me, Jax?" Her gaze roamed his face, unfocused but searching.

"Why didn't I tell you what?"

"That you and Elodie never followed through with the Fated Ceremony."

His throat dried as he forced himself to meet her confused gaze. "What would that have accomplished?"

"I dunno. Everything. Nothing." She peered up at him through her lush lashes. "Weren't you even a little tempted to go through with it? I mean, the Wisp led her to you."

"I wasn't tempted in the least, sweet pea," he said honestly.

"Why?" Her question was barely a whisper.

He propped his forehead gently on hers, and answered equally as softly, "Because she's not my Fated."

Harry was. He felt it to his soul. In his blood. With every

heart pound. But hell if he'd let himself act on it right then. Or ever. No matter how tempting the woman in front of him may be.

Eyes wide and blinking, Harry slowly and subconsciously wet her bottom lip, her gaze dropping to his mouth seconds before she leaned within kissing distance. Jax reflexively shifted closer, his mind foggy with need.

A split second before contact, his hand shot out, gently cupping her cheek and halting the forward momentum. His inner mountain lion hissed at him for stopping something they both wanted more than their next breath.

"I'm sorry, Harry . . . but I can't." He released a slow, staggering breath. "It's really not a good idea."

The look on her face nearly ripped his insides into shreds, worse than his cougar could've ever done. She nodded and pulled back, the move loosening something in her body because she paled instantly, hand clapping over her mouth.

"I don't feel so—" She lurched forward, her forehead hitting his chest as she evacuated every ounce of margarita she'd consumed in the last eight hours. Possibly her lifetime.

Jax grimaced at the heavy fruit scent hanging in the air . . . and all over him.

Yep.

One bad decision after another. Tomorrow he was determined not to have any repeats.

9

Crap. Sh!T. F*Ck.

Someone shoved her on a twirling hell ride and put the control stick into full throttle and, in case that wasn't misery-inducing enough, drilled her with a spotlight that seared through her eyelids like light sabers.

Harry groaned, the vibration scouring her throat like rusted nails dipped in battery acid as she slowly convinced herself to move. An inch. Two. Aches rippled through her body, their severity more intense as she brought a hand to her still spinning head.

Nope. Her head wasn't spinning. The room was.

She pried her eyes open a fraction of an inch at a time and realized the room wasn't one she recognized. A fireplace was angled in the corner, and colorful accent rugs blanketed pristine, but aged, hardwood floors. Exposed wood beams on the ceiling and gray stone walls gave the place rustic, natural vibes consistent with a lot of Colorado mountain homes.

If she'd been kidnapped, she was probably still in the state. So . . . good news.

She fought her way into a sitting position at the edge of the bed and spotted bottled water and ibuprofen.

"And they're Florence Nightingale kidnappers." She chased two pills with nearly half the water and grimaced at the severe cotton mouth and her tongue's attempt to stick to her teeth.

Brief snippets from the previous night trickled their way into her consciousness, from her nerves prior to the meetup with Elodie and Lenny, to the wide variety of fruit margarita pitchers. Ah, the margaritas. Some people thought hard liquor the most dangerous of alcohol, when in reality it was drinks like mango peach daiquiris and strawberry kiwi margs. When people didn't readily taste the harsh alcohol burn, it was way too easy to overindulge and fall into a steaming wheelbarrow of bad decisions.

She'd definitely done both. Literally. Figuratively. So many bad decisions she didn't know which one made her head throb more.

So far, the one where she volunteered herself and her friends to possible public humiliation was in the lead, but the one where she mortified herself in the privacy of Jax's truck came in a really close second. Only time and the ibuprofen kicking in to chase away the brain fog will tell if they might swap places.

She'd performed her best drunken come-hither look and sent him an engraved invitation for him to kiss her, and he'd returned that invite damn quick. No RSVP. Not even an envelope marked *Return to sender*.

Just not quick enough to avoid the great margarita purge.

Harry rubbed her pounding head as her brain mentally

replayed the horrified look on Jax's face as she vomited all over his well-toned chest. And pants. And shoes. Thank goddess he hadn't been wearing his favorite leather jacket or she'd have to enter the Witness Relocation Program.

"Guess we're amnesia-ing," Harry murmured to herself, already wiping the image from her mind as she puttered barefoot out of the bedroom to inspect the rest of the cabin.

It only took a few seconds of inspection to realize the place belonged to Jax. Everything was clean, clutter free, and a stylish mixture of rustic charm and modern delights. There was an open-plan kitchen with a simple table and two chairs. A worn leather couch sat across from another fireplace, this one taking up nearly the entire wall and sporting a natural wood mantel she had no doubt that Jax crafted himself.

Harry peeked through the front window and saw Nora's little hatchback sitting out front. At least someone had the foresight to gift her a getaway car, and she couldn't even be upset about it.

Watch enough rom-coms and you quickly understood that sticking around after a major faux pas was not the way to reestablish your dignity. She quickly found her purse and keys on the kitchen table, and drove as if the memories from twenty hours ago were hellhounds nipping at her heels.

She'd nearly lost them by the time she turned on Fates Boulevard, but the second she pulled up to Pierce House, they clawed their way back.

Three people sat on the bottom porch steps, two who looked nearly as miserable as she felt.

"There goes hoping it was all a figment of my imagination." Harry climbed from the car and prepped to face the music.

Lenny, face pale and nearly fully obstructed by the large

sunglasses perched on her nose, leaned heavily against the porch frame. Elodie, always vibrant and well put together, sported a just-rolled-out-of-bed look—a tattered rock band T-shirt and grungy sweats, her hair in two lose braids on either side of her head.

The only one who looked rested, relaxed, and downright gleeful was the sixteen-year-old currently lounging back on her hands, her legs kicked out in front of her and a beaming smile aimed Harry's way.

"Well, well, well. Look what the little hatchback drove home." Grace's lips twitched with a growing smirk. "And where have you been, young lady? Or should I just say lady?"

Fuck. Cassie would hear about this before the end of the day, Harry was sure.

"I'm not gracing that with a response." Harry winced as her words reverberated in her head.

"Which part?"

"Any of it." She precariously sat on the bottom step next to the pillar and prayed the entire structure didn't go down with all their combined weight.

"I'm sure I'm not the only one who's curious about the answer."

"You're not," Lenny supported.

"Definitely not." Elodie mumbled her agreement, her chin propped on her hand as if her head weighed the equivalent of a freight truck. "But we'll round back to that later."

Grace sighed. "Fine."

Harry shot them all glares. "Is it Harry-versus-everyone-else day? And how the hell have you three become *everyone else*? I haven't introduced you yet."

Grace still looked smug. "I don't know what you mean. We

go way back . . . at least an hour or more. They came here looking for you this morning, and much to all of our surprise—except Nora's—you weren't here."

"Rounding back to that, remember?" Sitting up a little straighter, Elodie added, "First, let's talk about this Big-Bads-versus-the-Trouble-Trio thing."

Harry let her head fall back against the rail with a groan. "I was really hoping I'd remembered that wrong."

"Actually, it was the Big Bads versus the Fearsome Four," Lenny corrected.

They all shot her looks.

"What? Don't look at me like that! I was the innocent bystander in that epic gauntlet toss. The two of you did all the heavy lifting."

"What are the chances that we can back out of it with a 'jinx' and move about our day?" Harry asked hopefully.

Elodie snorted. "With Silas? Zero percent. The demon thrives on competition like a competition-eating incubus. No, we only have one option."

"A time-reversal spell?" She looked at her friend pleadingly. "Because I'd really like to do over the last twelve hours entirely. Every. Single. Second."

"Our only option is to suck it up, ramp it up, and dish it out."

"Is that warrior angel lingo, because one at a time those words make sense to me, but linked together? Not so much."

Elodie straightened to her full five-foot-two-inch height, her head lifted and her green eyes blazing as she slid her gaze from Harry to Lenny to Grace. "Fearsome Four . . . it's time to squeeze into those sports bras, hit the training field, and show those *not so* big bads who they're messing with."

"Three hungover and full-of-regret supernaturals?" Harry answered.

Lenny lowered her glasses to glare at the angel. "When you say training field . . ."

"Wait. Four?" Grace fidgeted, looking uneasy as she fully digested Elodie's speech. "Why are you looking at *me*? I'm underage, remember? I was nowhere near that bar when you all threw this gauntlet or whatever. I don't even know what the hell a gauntlet is!"

Elodie shrugged unapologetically. "Sorry, kid. We need a quad, and since your guardian is the one who issued the challenge, you're the fourth by default."

"How the hell does that work?"

Harry's stomach twisted. "Can we get back to this training-field mention. Would this be a literal field or . . ."

"Leave the particulars to me. I'll get everything situated."

"That's kinda what I'm afraid to let happen." Another thought pushed its way through Harry's fog. "Wait. Do we know what we're training for? What events did everyone at the bar pick?"

Elodie dug her cell phone out from her pocket and shoved the text message from Kai in front of their faces.

Event 1: Paintball
Pandemonium
Event 2: The Night Drop
Event 3: Mud Runner Royale
Loser: Provides backup vocals
and dancing to the Gargoyle
Girls' Fates Festival reunion
appearance
Winner: Gloating rights

"Crap," Grace muttered simultaneously with Lenny's "Shit" and Harry's "Fuck."

Harry didn't need to possess Lenny's seer abilities to sense that this wouldn't end well, and the trip there wouldn't be all that pleasant either.

* * *

JAX DUCKED AND wove left, whipping his hands up a split second before a clenched fist slammed against his palm. Another duck, weave, and smack! The punch landed, ricocheting vibrations up his arm straight to his shoulder.

"You pulled that one, Bishop." Silas, arms propped on the top rope of the boxing ring, studied each move with a critical eye. "Stop half-assing it and go in for the kill."

"I'd rather he didn't, considering I'm the one on the receiving end of the killing." Jax cleared his throat, countering Gavin's every step as he held the sparring gloves in place.

Gavin landed a right hook that would no doubt leave a vampire fist imprint in Jax's palm.

"Not the kill but better." Silas nodded in approval. "Still holding back, though."

Jax shot the demon a glare. "Seriously? What did I do to piss you off?"

"Nothing. But when you use my gym to hide from whatever put that look on your face when you walked through the door this morning, this is the risk you run. It's all on the sign, man." Silas nudged his chin to the hanging sign over Beast Mode's entrance:

Leave Your Shit at the Door . . . or Else.

Jax ducked, feeling the rush of air whip past his left cheek with Gavin's next jab. "I'm not hiding, and I didn't bring any shit here."

"Then why are you here on a weekday morning and not at the ranch Alpha-ing, or at R and R. Or, hell, at Pierce House knocking shit down."

At the mention of Harry's family home, Jax dodged when he should've ducked.

Gavin's meaty fist landed with a sharp crack on Jax's lower jaw, the vampire's force knocking him clean off his feet and onto his ass.

Temporarily stunned and seeing stars, he rubbed his jaw. His face would've broke with that one if he'd been anything but a shifter.

Gavin grunted and extended a hand to help him up. "Guess we got the answer to Si's question."

Jax wouldn't deny it, but he also wouldn't admit it, heading over to the water station. Gavin followed while Silas hung back to set up another pair of fighters in the sparring ring.

The quiet vampire took a long gulp of his water despite not having broken a sweat and studied Jax like a bug under a microscope. He didn't question, badger, or goad, unlike the other bastards Jax called friends, but sometimes the silence was worse than the heckling.

"Okay, yes," Jax growled, giving in to the silent weight of Gavin's stare. "There's a mountain of RMP shit I could be excavating right now, and while my foremen have everything covered at the restoration sites, today would've been a good day to demo the Pierce gazebo. Hell, it had been on my calendar until . . ."

Gavin cocked a golden eyebrow. "Until . . . ?"

Until he took Harry back to his sanctum of solace and

nearly kissed her fucking senseless. And then to add to the night of bad decisions, until he'd taken way too much pleasure in the sight of her sleeping in his bed, wrapped up in his blankets, her silky hair fanned out across his pillow.

Harlow Pierce was pure temptation, the only person on the planet who could make him forget his name, his responsibilities, or any number of shifter survival instincts. When she'd blatantly asked why he hadn't told her that he and Elodie never Fate matched, he'd nearly told her the damn truth.

And *that* would've been the ultimate bad decision.

Fool him once, shame on him. Fool him twice, call him an ass for letting his guard down. Again. Distance from the woman he left sleeping in his bed was the only way to ensure he didn't do something stupid, like fall back on old habits.

It was worth the sore jaw.

"You're a man of quiet contemplation, right?" Jax searched for any topic that would steer him away from thoughts of Harry. "You meditate?"

"I'm a vampire who's surrounded by walking blood buffets all day and night. What do you think?" Gavin joked dryly. "Yes. I meditate. Why?"

"I'm helping a moody, smart-mouthed teenage shifter of unknown origin who lacks a filter and who tends to light things up when her temper hits its roof. Add in the fact that she's never shifted before, and I'm a bit out of my element here," Jax admitted. "I've helped shifters shift for the first time. That's not an issue. It's . . . everything else."

"Are you asking if meditation would help with that everything else?"

"Would it?"

"Definitely. If done right, there really isn't anything that meditation can't help with. I'm not saying it's a cure by any stretch, but it can sure as hell work as a mood stabilizer and help improve focus and concentration."

"All things needed to survive through a successful first shift."

"It definitely wouldn't hurt. Once you've laid the foundation for good meditation practices, it'll—theoretically—make it ten times easier for your young shifter to communicate with her shifter entity."

"Theoretically."

Gavin nodded. "It's nature based. Some animals find it easier to keep an open communication than others. Bear shifters, for example, usually prefer a 'show' more than 'tell' approach to communication, while avian shifters are typically a bit more emotion driven. Wolves and the feline groups are pretty close to the middle. For them, it often varies by their human side."

"Therein lies the problem. We don't know which way the shifter blows."

"We have a pretty extensive supernatural studies section in the library. Feel free to use it while you're perfecting that meditation. Hell, I'll even do you one better and offer my research help."

Silas snorted, joining them. "I love how he makes that sound like he'd be the one doing you a favor when in reality, doing research is like going to an amusement park for him."

Gavin shrugged, not denying it.

"Now that the two of you have that settled, we need some serious shoptalk." Silas slammed his hands down on both their shoulders.

"About?" Jax asked warily.

"Paintball Pandemonium, the Night Drop, and the Mud

Runner. Personally, I don't see how we could lose any of those events, much less two, but I wouldn't put it past Elodie Quinn to play dirty. We need to talk strategy."

If only developing a strategy solved all Jax's problems.

But if it temporarily distracted him from them, he was all-in.

10

Awaken the Kraken

Pierce House's once lush gardens had long succumbed to knee-high weeds and mischievous gnomes, and its full wrap-around porch looked a far stretch from grand—or up to code. The damn thing looked ready to cave if so much as a pebble fell on it at the right spot.

Once Jax unloaded the supplies into the backyard, he'd pivoted his plan, leaving the gazebo for another day. The safety of those in the house came first, which was why he'd begun ripping away the rotted planks before the sun came up.

It wasn't like he slept much lately.

A certain curvy witch invaded not only his awake-time thoughts but his dreaming ones, too. The end result left him hot, bothered, and hard, none of which had been rectified with a cold shower and a strong tugging session. He needed to tear things apart with his bare hands and knock shit down.

If only those little gnome bastards wouldn't keep absconding with his damn tools.

Nora's soft heart and love for the beastly little miscreants who treated the unkempt grounds like a Weed Wonderland, made his job ten times more difficult. He had no such fondness for the little thieves. As he tossed another rotten board, about a half dozen of them scattered, the sound of their non-sensible stone-rubbing twittering fading in the distance.

Most of the rear porch had to go, either rotted or warped from time, weather, and wear, but any salvageable wood would be saved for work elsewhere on the house. This timber held too much history to toss away without another thought.

He bent to grab his crowbar from his bag and found it empty. "What the . . . ? Hey!"

A shirtless gnome with red pants and white suspenders froze, his beefy hands wrapped around the end of the crowbar as he dragged it behind him. Realizing he'd been caught red-handed, he redoubled its efforts, dragging the iron against the slate.

"This is not yours." Annoyed more than angry, Jax grabbed the other end and tugged. "Release."

Red Pants yanked back, his wrinkled face distorting as he unleashed a high-pitched snarl.

"You sure you want to play this game, buddy? Fine. I'll play."

Jax handed his inner cougar the reins. The mountain lion surged forward, enough to subtly lengthen his canines and release a low, rumbling growl that nearly shook the ground beneath his feet. It did the trick, the gnome dropping the crowbar with a frightened squeal and hustling his stony ass toward the weeds. Before he lost himself in the foliage, a momentary burst of bravery turned him back around, flipping Jax what constituted as his middle finger.

"That wasn't very nice," came a sassy reprimand. "Maybe he was just trying to help you."

"Your conscience is supposed to be floating in the middle of a wildflower field or on a beach somewhere. It's not supposed to be in this garden and focused on my manners or lack thereof." Jax shot the teenager a look, but with her eyes closed, she didn't see his disapproving frown. "And he was definitely not trying to help."

Much to his surprise, Grace had been the first person he'd laid eyes on this morning, coming out to help him unload his tools and supplies. And then she'd stuck around. His first instinct was to give her a mallet and tell her get smashing, but he remembered his conversation with Gavin and changed tactics.

He wasn't certain she was getting anything out of it, but Nora's gnomes sure were, climbing her like a jungle gym before diving off and doing it all over again. She let them play, occasionally reaching up and freeing one if it got tangled in her hair, and then went back to her silent meditation.

"It's kind of difficult to go to a beach when there's a grumpy kraken nearby," Grace joked.

"I'm not a kraken. I'm annoyed. Damn pests already stole half the tools I came here with. They keep it up and I'll have to hammer in the nails with my head."

"At least we both know it's probably hard enough to do so."

The attempted crowbar thief returned and climbed in the crisscross of the teen's lap. Using it like a hammock, he kicked back and, after sticking out his little stone tongue at Jax, closed his eyes.

"Gnomes get a bad rap. They're not so bad." She patted the snoozing gnome in her lap. "Just like my little buddy here. He's just misunderstood."

"He's also stealing your necklace. Five more seconds and the little bastard will have it stuffed down his pants."

Sure enough, Red Pants held the unclasped gold chain in his hand, and Grace, with a raspy growl, snapped out of her meditation pose and quickly evicted him from her lap, taking her necklace back. "See if I ever share my breakfast with you again, Emmett. Bad boy."

The gnome stormed off, waving his hands, and disappeared behind an oversized tree stump.

"That thing has a name?" Jax asked, dumfounded and confused.

She shrugged. "I don't know. He looked like an Emmett to me, so that's what I named him. He seemed to like it well enough."

The teen put her necklace back into place, her gaze wary as she watched Jax pull a few planks and then replace them with fresh timber. "Did you hear I've been roped into whatever gauntlet thing that you and Harry have happening? There was talk about a fearsome foursome or something. All I know is that somehow, even though I wasn't present, I'm expected to participate."

He shot up an eyebrow and yanked at another plank, tossing it onto the pile with the others. "You're their fourth?"

"Apparently . . . unless my shifter mentor thinks it would be too strenuous and too much pressure to put on a young shifter during my training. I'll gladly back out . . . for progress's sake." Her broad, hopeful smile took him by such surprise that he paused before laughing. The longer he laughed, the more her smile dimmed. "Guess that's a no."

"Sorry, Sparks. But I actually think it might be a good idea."

"Yeah? How do you figure that?"

"Well, you'll be meditating three times a day, really rein in that focus, and by the time the first event rolls around, you can use that new blissful control of yours to focus on those heightened gifts."

She cocked a dark eyebrow. "How exactly will burning hay in a wheelbarrow help me aim a paintball gun?"

"It won't, but your heightened eyesight will. Not to mention that during the Night Drop, you'll get to use all six senses."

"You mean five."

He shook his head. "Not when you've got supernatural DNA. There's always a little extra in there. Some people call it intuition. Others call it the Sense."

"What do you call it?" Grace stood and brushed off her jeans.

"I call it my gut."

"At your age, it could also be called an ulcer." Grace's lips twitched at the snarky joke.

He fought off a smirk, distracted for long enough that the back door opened before he realized.

"Gracie, I'm—" Harry lifted her foot to step onto the non-existent back porch, and Jax leaped over the bare frame, catching not only her squeal but her body as she tumbled into his arms.

Her ponytail swept across her face, her chest heaved, and her heart beat wildly at the base of her throat. "What the hell just happened?"

"Morning." His voice turned to gravel as she pushed her hair from her face, her periwinkle eyes drilling him right to the core. His own heart lurched before she turned her gaze away and looked around.

"Where did the porch go?" Harry asked. "Did those little stone hooligans steal that, too?"

"They kleptoed things from you, too? Glad I'm not the only one."

"Where do you think the angel in the fountain got all the lingerie?" Grace chuckled.

His gaze slid to the dancing angel taking center stage in the overrun garden maze. A good quarter football field away, he hadn't noticed until now that the angel did indeed sport what looked to be a push-up bra and, god help him, a matching corset.

His imagination kicked in instantly, replacing the angel statue with a mental image of Harry. Full-on curves. Luscious breasts spilling from the delicate fabric, fabric that could probably be easily torn away by his hands, teeth . . . or claws.

Jax's cock twitched.

"You can put me down now." Harry looked up at him expectantly, totally unaware that she'd unintentionally awoken the beast—both the one in pants and the cougar itching to get closer to the surface.

"Oh. Yeah. Sorry." He released her legs and held her torso, the move brushing her entire lower body against his in the process.

Fuck and him. He swallowed a groan.

She glanced at what remained of the back porch. "So . . . you're doing work today?"

"Sorry. I told Nora, but I guess you didn't get the memo. Yeah. The entire thing all around needs to be torn down and replaced, but I wanted to start here before someone—"

"Fell to their demise?" Her lips twitched. "Too late for that apparently."

"Apparently." Jax chuckled.

A small chortle turned both their attentions to the teen. Grace's nose wrinkled. "Older people flirt so . . . weird. It's almost painful to watch."

"What?" Jax and Harry questioned simultaneously.

"Uh, no." Harry shook her head adamantly. "No flirting happening here."

"Not in the least," Jax agreed, quickly dropping his hands and taking a small step back.

The teen didn't look convinced, and, hell, he wasn't, either.

Harry fixed her ponytail and turned, a pretty pink blossoming on her cheeks. "I'm heading into town to meet Elodie and Lenny. I got an SOS text and that could mean an actual SOS or—"

"Or she's found a way to get under Silas's skin," Jax added, smirking.

"Yeah, I noticed that seems to be a goal of hers on the daily. I got the CliffsNotes version from Lenny, but I have a feeling there's a lot more to it. It's weird, because when he used to come visit Marie during those summers in high school, I thought they'd actually had a thing for each other."

"Pretty sure they still do and that's the problem—but you didn't hear it from me."

"Got it." She mimed zipping her lips. "Well, I guess I'm off to see an angel about the mayday call." She glanced at Grace. "You want to come with me?"

"Nah. I think I'll stay here and work more on this meditation. Maybe if Alpha Jax can go without awakening his kraken for longer than ten minutes, I might make it to an actual beach."

"Not sure what you're talking about, but it's good to have a plan. Hope it works out." With a wave, Harry headed toward the side gate, her hips swaying like a sexy pendulum.

Jax's gaze fixed on the movement and the curve of her ass. Her jean-encased thighs. The messy ponytail that left that special spot on her neck exposed, the one that when nibbled, kissed, or licked, turned her into a moaning puddle of need.

A dry heave turned his attention back to the teenager. "What?"

Grace was already reclaiming her spot on the grass, her legs folded beneath her as she shut her eyes. "There isn't a beach far enough away to get that image out of my head."

"What are you talking about?"

She popped one eye open wide enough to glare at him. "You know what I'm talking about, and that's all I'm saying on the matter because even though Harry's not my mother by blood, watching you watch her ass has the same ick factor as if she were."

Denying it was pointless, so he turned back to his task with a grunt. Maybe he needed to take up some meditation, too. But something told him that focusing on a beach wouldn't be far enough to get Harlow Pierce out of his head . . . because his imagination and rampant libido would just bring her along for the journey and end up marooning them both on a deserted island.

* * *

HARRY GLANCED AROUND Fates Boulevard, looking for the source of Elodie's SOS call. Cars motored up and down the street and people roamed the park, some alone and others in groups. No car accidents. No ambulances. No blaring, obvious distress beacons.

She glanced at the text again and verified she was at the right address.

"Oh, good. You're confused, too." Lenny sauntered up, glancing around before her gaze landed on the gym across the street. Beast Mode. "Now I'm confused and really fucking concerned."

Harry followed her gaze across the street. The place looked busy with a crowd inside as well as a steady flow of people heading in and out. "Fill me in, please."

"That's Silas's gym." Lenny glanced back at the abandoned storefront they now stood in front of. "And something tells me that we weren't given this address by chance or coincidence."

"Oh, good! You're both here! Man, you two know how to hustle. That's great, and just what we need to get this ship sailing." Elodie took a sip of the ice coffee in her hand and glanced around. "Where's Grace? I thought you'd bring her, considering she rounds out a Fearsome Four."

"Grace is meditating with Jax."

Her friends shot her twin curious looks.

"Let me rephrase . . . she's meditating while Jax broods a few feet away," Harry corrected and her friends nodded, now understanding. "Plus, I didn't know exactly what this mayday text was about, so I decided she was best finding her focus."

"Absolutely no worries. Actually, she's probably better off than any of us, considering she's fresh out of PE class and all. This is mostly for us." Elodie palmed a set of keys and opened the creaky door to the old storefront.

The place looked as if it had been abandoned for years and used as a Halloween horror house each October since. Random holes littered the walls, and an eclectic array of shelving units and garbage lay scattered over the floor.

"Isn't it great?" Elodie beamed, scanning the open space.

"For . . . ?" Lenny prodded.

The angel stood in the center of the room, narrowly avoiding a mysterious puddle of brown goo, and opened her arms in an inviting ta-da moment. "You're looking at the future home of Winged Warrior Self-Defense . . . and the current training ground for the soon-to-be ass-kicking Fearsome Four."

"Say what now?" Harry asked, confused.

Elodie looked around the room, her pupils practically transforming into little throbbing hearts. "People keep asking me for one-on-one self-defense lessons; and, while that's fine and all, I thought, how much better would it be for it to happen at the same time?"

Harry and Lenny shared a look, neither knowing what to say.

"That's great, El." Harry finally took the leap. "But isn't your ideal plan to get back into active service?"

"Yeah, but I'm not going lie. It'll probably take some time to get my fighting wings back, and running Winged Warrior will not only fill some of that time but also help keep me on my toes. And we can use this space to get our shit together before the Fates Festival games begin. It's a win-win for everyone!"

Lenny studied their friend through judgy eyes. "And this has nothing to do with the fact that Silas's place is literally right across the street? I love you, El, but that seems a little sus."

The angel shrugged. "I didn't notice the location until I already signed the lease, but I think it's perfect. People who want to focus more on mindless brute force can keep going to Beast Mode, but now there will be a second option for those who want a more thought-out approach to self-defense. More Bruce Banner than the Hulk."

Harry didn't believe that one damn bit and neither would anyone else.

"Wow. Well . . . congratulations." She gave her friend a hug, and shrugged in Lenny's direction. "If anyone can make something like this work, it's you."

"Thanks. I know it needs a little love, but I think with a little TLC times three we should be able to dust off the cobwebs and make it workable for the meantime."

Lenny perked. "Say what now? How is it that you buy a heaping pile of questionable asbestos and Harry and I become 'volunteered' into manual labor?"

Elodie cocked an eyebrow. "Too busy with your exceptionally busy dating life to help out your best friend fulfill her ultimate dream?"

"First, that's a low blow. Second, your ultimate dream was to be the youngest member of the Angel Guard. You already achieved that."

"Okay, so this is my second ultimate dream."

"I thought that was to make Silas McCloud 'rue the day he was hatched.'"

Elodie tucked her hands on her hips. "A woman can have multiple dreams, Lenny. This is one of mine. Why are you trying to yuck my yum?"

Harry chuckled. "No one's trying to yuck your yum. I think she's just concerned because Lenny knows how hard it is to run your own business . . . and she has Maddox helping her out."

Lenny nodded, folding her arms. "Yeah. That. Especially in Fates Haven now of all times. In case you haven't noticed, people aren't exactly flocking here with U-Hauls and movie trucks. I can't remember the last time our population sign went up."

"Technically it went up by two not that long ago."

"Harry and Grace don't count. They're here out of duress, and probably not for the long-term."

Both friends looked at her and she couldn't breathe, much less talk.

Long-term or short-term? She hadn't let herself think much past getting help for Grace. Nothing really waited for them back in New York anymore. No apartment. No job. Cassie was still a wandering woman until she found Mr. Mysterio. But it was too big a question for her to contemplate right then, and definitely not with the weight of a thousand question marks hanging over her head.

Harry cleared her throat. "Didn't I hear something about Maddox's college friend moving to town not that long ago. That's another person."

Point for Harlow . . .

Lenny's cheeks pinked. "Gavin. Yeah. That's true."

Harry stared as her tattooed best friend suddenly avoided all eye contact and looked uncomfortable in her own tattoo-decorated skin.

"I think Nora's right," Elodie piped up. "Things are shifting in Fates. We can all feel it, but even if forced to sell Winged Warrior when I head back to the Angel Guard, at least I'll have done something worthwhile while I've been here."

Now that sounded like the Elodie everyone knew and loved.

Harry smiled supportively. "And you get bonus points for pissing Silas off in the meantime."

"Exactly! It's an everyone-wins situation."

They all laughed. Harry clapped her hands and, tossing her purse on a small table that had seen better days, glanced around the empty front room, her magic already rolling off her fingertips. "We should probably get cleaning and organizing if this place is about to be ground zero for the demise of the Big Bads."

Elodie nodded in approval. "Now you're talking my language. Silas McCloud won't know what hit him. Let's do this!"

The angel immediately burst into action, pulling out what looked to be brooms and mops from a small closet tucked into the corner.

"You're enabling her behavior—you know that, right?" Lenny, a smirk in place, bumped her shoulder into Harry's. "You won't have anyone but yourself to blame when this comes back to bite us all on the ass."

"Maybe. But look how happy she is, Len." Harry grinned. "Tell me how you can yuck the yum on someone wearing a smile that big. Potential bite on the ass or not."

The seer rolled her eyes, but chuckled, already reaching for a broom and a dustpan. "I'll remind you that you said that when we're taking you to the clinic for your rabies shot."

II

Duck & Weave

Unable to tear her eyes away from the macabre crime scene in front of her, Harry gaped. Tape on the ground. The ominously flickering overhead fluorescent lights. A villain humanoid tightly holding what looked to be indestructible rope while grinning sinisterly, an expression she'd only seen in one of Grace's horror movies.

Whether it was a commuter wearing a business suit and a horse head mask on the subway, a coffee shop celeb sighting, or a hairy-assed streaker running down the middle of Broadway, New York quickly taught its residents to graze and go.

Graze your gaze over the sight, and then keep on motoring.

But Harry was frozen to the spot, unable to look away.

"Here's what we're going to do." Lenny barely moved her lips as she leaned toward Harry and Grace. "On the count of three, we're scattering like cockroaches. Angel kick-assery or not, she can't go after all three of us at the same time."

"I thought you weren't supposed to run from most big wildlife," Grace asked, innocently curious. "At least that's what I read in that Colorado nature magazine on Nora's coffee table."

"This is scarier than a bear waking up after a long hibernation, kiddo."

Harry nodded. "This is Elodie the Eliminator."

She shivered, assaulted with Fates Haven High senior week flashbacks and memories of the persistent rash she developed after diving into the Big Bates Hot Spring because Elodie—the Eliminator—was insistent that the clue to the next scavenger hunt spot floated on top of the filmy water.

Not only had it not been a clue, but she'd been right to question the water quality and ended up with conjunctivitis, a stomach "'infestation," and two rounds of antibiotics. Elodie had shrugged, stating, "Better safe than in last place."

Harry begged to differ. No one's stomach should be "infested" with anything except Pizza Suprema pizza and gelato.

But that was El. Competitive. Committed. And iron willed.

"I don't think running will work," Harry admitted reluctantly. "She's got that look in her eye."

Elodie planted her hands on her curvy hips. "You realize I'm standing right here and can hear every word out of your mouths, right?"

"We know." Lennox nodded. "That's why we're debating our chances of making a run for it. I'm a little on the fence about our odds."

"I feel pretty good about mine," Grace interjected. "I helped my middle school track team make it to the state championships two years in a row. I've seen Harry run. I think your odds are at least seventy–thirty of making a clean break. She has a finicky left knee . . . especially if she eats any of those inflammatory foods, and we ordered in Italian the other night."

"Hey!" Harry protested before they all burst into laughter. "But not wrong."

When the laughter died down, she finally addressed the elephant in the room. "Okay, El. What is all this?"

Elodie smile broadly. "This is Watch Your Step."

"This looks like there's a six-year-old somewhere with an empty toy chest." Harry glanced at the wild array of LEGO pieces and action figures spread out all over the floor.

"I will not confirm nor deny that statement. This"—Elodie swept her hand over the soon to be Winged Warrior Self-Defense space—"is our first step to becoming one cohesive team."

"This looks worse than when you showed us this place a few days ago and that's saying a lot," Lenny quipped.

"Also, why did we spend hours cleaning if this was your endgame?" Harry asked.

Elodie tossed them each a glare. "Would you rather I drag in some treadmills and have you all run for five miles?"

"No, no." Harry battled to remain upbeat as she eyed both the rope and the blindfolds in the angel's hands. "Let's . . . Watch Our Step."

An hour later, with a plastic samurai sword implanted into the vulnerable arch of her left foot, she regretted all that enabling and cheerleading she'd done to keep Elodie smiling.

"Step right." Grace's instruction came from somewhere across the room. "No, no, Lenny. You go left. *Harry* has to go right."

"I can't go left if Harry is going right. We're kinda tied back-to-back!" Lenny released a frustrated growl that had Harry chuckling. "Seriously? Now is not the time to lose it, Pierce. Focus. Shit. My head is getting woozy. I think I've lost too much blood from stepping on that last LEGO block."

Harry's chuckle grew to full-blown laughter, her tears automatically dried by the blindfold.

"I'm glad you find this funny," the seer grumbled.

"Come on. You have to admit this is a slight bit ridiculous."

"What's ridiculous is thinking that this will do a damn bit of good in prepping us for paintball."

Elodie's amused voice echoed from a few feet away. "Paintball is all about teamwork . . . and right now I'm not seeing a whole lot of it."

"That's because you're not the one working here."

"Someone has to keep you all on track. Besides, Grace and I just went through the course, and I do have to say, we did so in record time. You just have to stay on track and focus."

"Right now, the only thing we're on track for is needing a tetanus shot. Remind me why Harry and I are being navigated, barefoot and blindfolded, through a toy minefield by someone who doesn't know the difference between their left and right. Little clue: spread out the hands and left makes the L."

"This isn't as easy as it looks, you know," Grace defended.

Elodie tsked. "You can swap navigators just as soon as you make it across the room."

"I won't have any blood in my veins by then," Lenny retorted.

A brilliant idea struck Harry. Or maybe the blood loss made it seem better than it was. "Len, follow my lead, okay?"

"We're literally ass to ass. Do I have much of a choice?"

Harry closed her eyes despite the blindfold, and called on her descry magics. The tingling sensation built in her veins, flowing from her core and out to all her extremities until it slowly seeped into the air. Her hair brushed her cheeks in a magically created breeze . . . and she guided them to a slight step right.

She grimaced, prepped to step on another superhero, but when her foot came back feeling nothing but cool, smooth floor, she smiled.

Step by step, she led the way across the room, hearing Elodie's softly muttered, "About damn time."

In less than five minutes, they reached the other side. Grace laughed and Lenny ripped off her blindfold, demanding to be immediately untied. They all enjoyed a brief victorious moment.

"Easy peasy." Harry wiped her hands on her pants, a satisfied grin on her face.

A magical gust whipped through the room, knocking Grace sideways. Elodie caught her before they both toppled to the floor.

"I think you can turn off the magics now, Harry," the angel quipped.

Harry closed her eyes and called back her magic, demanding its return, but it didn't listen. Instead, the power intensified. Papers left over from the original state of the gym soared through the air, creating a little papernado, and a flying stuffed pig with wings pegged Harry in the side of the head.

"It's not listening to me." She grimaced, breaking a sweat from attempting to corral the out-of-control magic. More and more toys whipped through the air like plastic projectiles. "It's like it—"

"Your magic is all wonky just like everything else in town," Lenny pointed out. A remote-control car flew across the bridge of her nose, narrowly missing. "Shit. This is worse than the toy minefield."

"We've got to get out of here," Elodie added.

Harry took Grace's hand and led the charge across the room. They ducked and weaved, the trek more precarious than when they'd done it blindfolded. They each got pegged by no less than three or four airborne toys by the time they barreled through the front door, toppling over one another and spilling in a four-person wreck on the sidewalk, Elodie on top.

Grace's laughter from the bottom of the pile ignited Harry's, then Lenny's. Soon enough, they all lay on the ground in various states of hilarity, the people of Fates Haven walking past them with curious looks.

Mrs. Muhammad from the post office stuck her head out only to shake it and mutter something about the Trouble Trio.

"It's the Fearsome Four," Harry corrected her, eliciting another round of fresh laughter. "Shit. I have to stop laughing or I'm going to pee my pants."

"Ew. Get off me before that happens, please." Grace shoved her leg, which was still somehow draped on top of hers.

"Here's what I want to know . . ." Harry sighed, glancing at her fellow troublemakers.

"What?" Lenny asked curiously.

"Since we had to duck and weave and hurdle and stuff to get out of the toy storm, does that mean we can count that as training for the Mud Runner?"

A small smile tilted up the seer's lips. "Sounds good to me."

"You wish." Elodie stood up first, brushing her hands over her pants before helping everyone else up one at a time. "I have a special training exercise for that one. You'll love it. Or at least you won't hate it as much as you did this one."

"Somehow, I sincerely and very highly doubt that." Harry's cheeks ached from smiling. "But bring it. With training like this, nothing will take down the Fearsome Four."

Except maybe LEGO pieces.

* * *

JAX HEARD GIGGLES from around the front corner of Pierce House, and a second later, Harry and Grace turned the corner. The young shifter was the first to sense him, her body momentarily stiffening until she glanced up and looked directly at him as if she'd known exactly where he stood.

"Hey, Jax." She glanced to the back of the house. "Wow. You tore down a lot more of the porch."

"Had a mostly free day today so I figured I'd try and get as much done as I could." He nodded toward the temporary staircase he'd put up that led to the back door. "Now you all can get safely in and out. I'll start building the real thing once I have my guys clear out all the excess junk boards."

"Cool. Well . . ." Grace glanced from Harry to him and back. "I'm heading in and taking a shower. Maybe try to call Mom."

She disappeared into the house, but Harry stayed, looking unsure whether she wanted to follow or not. He grabbed the T-shirt he'd draped on the old railing and shrugged back into it. As he pulled it over his head, Harry's eyes dropped to the tattoo on his torso, a scenic view of Mystic Lake during a full moon.

It wasn't any regular view. It was *their* view, the one they'd escape to on countless nights when they'd been young and in love. He wasn't sure if she recognized it or not, and he wasn't about to ask.

He nudged his chin to where Grace had disappeared into the house. "She seems to be smiling a little more these days."

"She still has a lot stacked against her, but she seems to be taking it in stride." A small smile formed on her lips. "And today was definitely interesting, to say the least."

"Interesting in Fates. Imagine that." His gaze scanned her face, memorizing every line and delicate curve.

The girl he'd once fallen in love with was definitely still there, but mixed with someone new. Someone with a host of memories and emotions he couldn't quite pinpoint.

And a slight shadow.

He'd thought it a metaphorical one until she shifted on her feet and realized that it wasn't metaphorical at all, and it wasn't an actual shadow.

"What the hell happened?" Cupping her chin, he gently tilted her face so the moonlight kissed her skin and spotlighted the forming bruise. "Who the fuck do I have to bury?"

Jax's eyesight sharpened, his cougar riding him hard and demanding he find answers. Harry's purple eyes locked on him, unblinking, a deer caught in a predator's line of sight.

"Sweet pea, you better answer me right now." His voice dropped, sounding gravely even to his own ears. "*Harlow.*"

She took a slow, stuttered breath, but didn't pull away. "It was a flying Babe. No one to bury."

A coy smirk drew his attention to her mouth. "A what?"

"There was a magical wonky windstorm during our 'training' and I got nailed with a flying pig wearing a studded collar. It doesn't hurt. I actually forgot it was there."

It wasn't until her soft hand touched his arm that he realized he still cupped her face and stood way too close.

He dropped his hand and apologized. "Sounds like training is going well then, huh?"

She snortled. "About as well as can be expected with Elodie

leading the charge. She really wants to beat Silas. You all might want to warm up your vocals and brush up those dancing skills. Maybe watch some videos. Take up stretching. Because she is determined to win."

"Silas is pretty determined to win this thing, too."

"Yeah, but does he have you dodging toys while blindfolded and tied to each other? Because if he doesn't, then he's not taking this training thing seriously enough." Harry paused a beat before breaking into laughter.

"You got me there." He joined in her laughter until they naturally sobered, leaving them in loud, awkward silence.

They took turns looking at each other and then away. Twice, they started talking at the same time, then stopped, chuckling at their ridiculousness.

"My friend Gavin is Fates Haven researcher extraordinaire and the town librarian, and I've been telling him about Grace. Filling him in a bit on what's been going on, and he tracked down a few books that he thinks might help us out," Jax said.

"Really?" She looked up at him, eyes wide and hopeful.

"I didn't want to say anything to Grace because I didn't want to get her hopes up, but it's pretty damn obvious that whatever we're looking for, we won't find it in any regular old texts that just anyone can pick up and read. In order to answer difficult questions, we need to find the hard-to-reach answers."

"That makes sense, I guess."

"I could let you know when the books come in and we can make it a research party. Or something. I mean, it's no flying toys, but . . ."

She smirked. "Yeah. I definitely want to help with that. Thank you."

He nodded, shoving his hands in his pockets.

"Well, good night, Jax." She stopped at the base of the temporary stairs. "And thank you for helping Nora with getting Pierce House back up and running. She doesn't say anything, but I know it's difficult for her to see it like this."

"It's not a problem. Nora has done a lot for not only me but for the whole town. She's long overdue a little payback."

She smiled and climbed the stairs, stopping at the top and glancing his way as if contemplating saying something else, but Grace flung open the door, phone in hand.

The teen's mischievous smirk didn't mean anything good. "Mom wants to know why you let someone tie me up with rope and put a blindfold on me. I told her it was to encourage me to listen to directions, but I'm not sure she believes me and she wants to talk to you."

Harry's string of soft curses had Jax chuckling as he turned to clean up his things. For one flicker of a split second, it had felt like time had rewound thirteen years.

12

Spitting Llamas

Four hours, ten stores, and a full back seat later, and the "short" errand run Harry offered to do for Nora was finally coming to a close. Not that she minded. An attempt to use her descry magic to tidy up and organize the cluttered attic ended up doing the opposite.

Like what happened at Elodie's gym space, things had started fine, and then wham, bam, kapow. Shit flew, dropped, and exploded. Frustrated and in desperate need of a breather, Harry had volunteered her errand services after dropping Grace off at the pack ranch for more manure shoveling meditation.

She'd learned a long time ago not to ask questions of Nora when it came to her shopping lists, and as such, Harry had been on a mission to acquire everything from breadcrumbs to a climbing harness. In the bottom of her reusable bag, she now toted around a subscription box from Marie's bakery. Something in the older demon's eyes told her that it wasn't filled with

Cinna-Boobs or Erection Éclairs and no way in hell was she brave enough to open the box and find out.

Harry now opened the door to Once Upon a Tattoo, and was immediately regaled with memories of the space once being an old bank. Brick and stone complemented the industrial, antique feel, and yet somehow made the large waiting room cozy and inviting in shades of steel, blacks, and reds. Leather sofas and glass tables gave off a coffeehouse vibe, along with the framed artwork decorating each wall.

Harry recognized Lenny's signature style every place she looked. Funky. Chic. And fun.

Maddox, standing behind the lone counter, glanced up and threw her a smile when she approached. "My day just got infinitely better. What brings you to this end of the boulevard?"

"Errands." She glanced around. "I've been back for how long now and haven't stopped by yet. This place is amazing."

"Yeah, it's working out really well. With my business sense and Lenny's talent, it's a match made in tattoo heaven."

Loud arguing sounded from the back rooms a second before a furious-looking vampire stormed out, cutting a hard glare to Maddox. "I'm not paying for this shit."

Maddox didn't seemed phased. "Actually, my friend, you are. You did. Two days ago when you got the tattoo placed. Sorry to be the bearer of bad news."

"Why the fuck should I pay for this?" He ripped open his buttoned shirt, displaying what looked to be a spitting llama with wild eyes and flaring nostrils. "What the fuck does this mean? Not only is it there at all, but your seer can't seem to tell me *why*! Now you're telling me I can't have a refund?"

"Dude, you signed the disclaimer. Did you read the thing at all?"

Lenny slowly stepped out from the back, giving Harry a faint wave before lasering her glare on the supernatural practically blowing steam from his ears. "Byron, not only did you sign the waiver, but I gave you *two* outs before we got started. You knew the very high likelihood that this would happen."

"Not this." He once again opened his shirt and smacked the spitting llama on the snout. "Not once did you say a fucking llama."

"Yes, this. And I even told you about the last guy's rabid raccoon! And if my memory serves me correct you said, 'That's a risk I'm willing to take.' Well, Byron, meet your risk."

The vampire blustered before letting out a toothy hiss and speeding from the tattoo shop, the door slamming behind him.

Harry waited a few heartbeats before releasing a throaty chuckle. "Pretty sure you can expect a glowing Yelp review right there."

They all laughed, even Lenny, although she looked a significant degree more tired. The phone rang and Maddox answered, turning to talk to the person on the line.

"Want a tour?" Lennox surprised her by asking.

"Yes, please!" Leaving her shopping bag on the counter, Harry followed her through to the back and was surprised at how big the place really was.

There were a lot more workrooms than she'd thought, a few of them occupied by other tattooists, but Lenny brought her toward the Vault, which turned out to be her main creative area with an elaborate chair and table set up in the center and an art studio tucked into the back corner. An open sketchbook lay open on the desk and loose works in progress littered the surface.

"This is amazing, Lenny." Harry couldn't stop her eyes from

feasting on every inch of the place. "I'm really glad you stuck with the art thing."

She shrugged. "It's tattoos."

"Uh, no." Harry pointed to at the wall to a beautiful watercolor that there was no denying was Starlight Gazebo surrounded by vivid flowers. "This is artwork on skin rather than a stretched canvas. Never undersell yourself or your talent."

"Not all that talented lately." Lenny dropped into her desk chair with a heavy sigh.

Harry sat in the one on the other side. "I don't know, that llama on Byron out there looked pretty damn realistic."

They stared at each other before cracking up, Lenny so hard tears sprang to her eyes. When they could finally breathe, the seer groaned. "I'm not sure how much longer I can take this broken feeling. People sit in my chair and the Sight comes. It works right alongside my hands as I place the tattoo . . . and then it stops. Disappears. No more Sight. No Reading. Clients end up with a spitting llama on their chest but with no freaking idea as to why."

"Hence the waiver?" Harry guessed.

"Hence the waiver. And the multiple verbal warnings. We spent years trying to get the studio seen in the ink world, and it was finally starting to happen. Now?" Lenny shook her head, visibly frustrated. "We have enough regular clients coming in for ink that we can keep the doors open and lights on, but it's nowhere near the volume it once was."

"You mean when you got named the Fortune-telling Tattooist?" Harry teased.

"Please never utter that name again." Lenny groaned. "Although he denies it, I'm pretty sure Maddox came up with, because I woke up one day and suddenly it was plastered all over our social media accounts."

"Oh, he totally came up with it, but it's sweet. He's proud of you. You should have heard him boasting about you when I first returned to Fates." Harry loved this back-and-forth, finally feeling like things were slowly leveling into a new kind of norm. "Do you have any clients coming anytime soon?"

Len glanced at her table calendar. "Not for another two hours. Why?"

"I've been running around for Nora all day and I think I should treat myself for surviving her list."

"What did you have in mind? Lunch?"

"A tattoo. A *regular* one. Not that I don't love and trust you, but I'm not sure I can pull off a llama."

Lenny's pierced eyebrow twitched. "You seriously want a tattoo? Do you already have one?"

"Nope. Virgin skin." Harry smirked mischievously. "Does that excite you?"

"Pretty sure that's every tattoo artist's dream." Lenny laughed. "Do you have an idea of what you want?"

"Not a damn clue. I've been thinking about it for years, stalked countless Pinterest boards, and I can never make a final decision."

"Okay, well . . . we have some books out front if you need some inspir—"

"Nope. I want you to decide."

"Me?" Lenny's eyes rounded. "Decide what I should tattoo on you? In permanent ink?"

"Do you use temporary ink?"

"No. No, I do not."

"Then, yeah. Permanent ink. I mean, there are a few stipulations." She ticked them off on her fingers. "One: it has to be a Lenny original. I don't want something I'll be able to find anywhere else. Two: no time like the literal present in which to get it done. Also, it prevents me from chickening out yet again. And three." She stood and turned around, pointing to the upper swell of her left butt cheek. "I want it placed right here."

"You want me to tattoo anything I want on your ass?"

"Not on my ass *proper . . . north* of my ass."

"Regular ass-adjacent placed tattoo or not, that's a whole lot of trust you're putting in me."

"I know, and I do." And she meant it.

Harry needed to repair the damage she created when she left Fates Haven the way she did, and first up was showing the people she loved that she had all the faith in the world in them. It was herself she was a little less sure about.

Lenny flipped through a few papers on her desk, searching for something. "I do have something I've been working on for a while. Let me show you—"

"Nope. Don't show me. Just tattoo."

Lenny bit her lip nervously. "You know this is highly irregular and not the least bit recommended, right?"

"Yep and yep. Now, where do you want me?"

With a nervous laugh, Lenny pointed to the nearby table. "Go ahead and lie face down and I'll get everything set up."

Harry swallowed the lump in her throat. The smile on her friend's face told her that she made the right decision and she got into position, rolling the top of her pants down.

Lenny was in artist mode, prepping her table with meticulous care and double-and triple-checking that she had everything she needed before she wheeled a chair over to Harry's side. "Last chance to back out. I wouldn't hold it against you."

"But I'd hold it against me." Harry gave her a small smile. "I'm ready. Give me my Lenny Original."

The machine hummed to life, and she held her breath. She'd known it wouldn't tickle, but at first touch of the needle she hissed. Lenny turned on some music, the old-school stuff they used to belt out in the car as they drove to Mystic Lake on hot summer nights. Soon enough, Harry was distracted enough to fumble her way through the lyrics.

Only a minute or two into the design, both Lenny and her tattoo gun froze.

"You okay? Why'd you stop?" Harry peeked over her shoulder. The rapid rise and fall of Lenny's chest, along with the occasional blink, was the only sign of life. "Len? You're starting to freak me out. Did your hand slip? Did you cut a butt artery or something?"

"I feel it," Lenny murmured.

"You feel . . . it? Tired? Inspired? Horny?" Realization hit Harry between the eyes. "Oh, you feel the Sight?"

Lenny slowly nodded. "It feels different."

"Different how?"

"I don't know." Lenny finally unfroze her fingers, her tense muscles easing a fraction as she stretched them. "I should probably stop."

"Stop? You just started! You don't have to Call it toward you, right?" Harry knew her friend typically had to invite her ability into action, much like she did her descry abilities. "As long as you don't Call it, we should be good to keep going."

"That would normally be fine with me, but I'm not Calling

right now and it's getting stronger. It's like the Sight wants to be in the driver's seat and I'm having a difficult time not sliding over and letting it have the spot."

"Has that ever happened before?"

Lenny shook her head. Unease turned her nerves into a cold sweat across her brow.

"Maybe you should go with it," Harry heard herself say after a prolonged silence.

The seer's head whipped her way. "What?"

"Let it take over. See what happens. You said it's never happened before. It could turn out to be a good thing. Maybe your Sight fixed its glitch."

"Or it could be a catastrophic failure and is the first new step to a downward spiral. And you, as my canvas, would literally live with that failure etched on your ass."

"When you put it like that . . ."

Lenny nodded.

"I want you to keep going even more."

Her friend looked at her as if she'd sprouted two heads. "You cannot be serious. If this is some twisted way to get me to not be mad at you for leaving like you did . . ."

"It's not all that," Harry said truthfully. "I just think that there's a reason why it feels different and you should follow the direction it wants you to go."

Looking ready to bolt, Lenny glanced from her tattoo gun and back to the unfinished design hovering just above Harry's butt. "Fine. I'll keep going. But if you end up with a laughing donkey flying over your ass, don't come crying to me."

Harry chuckled. "An ass on an ass. That would be fun. Definitely a conversation starter. Any other directives?"

"You can't look at it once it's done. Sight tats are a little different from regular. The ink needs a little time to grab hold. We'll have to cover it for at least twenty-four to forty-eight hours before I attempt to get a Reading off it."

"Grab hold of what?"

"You. Or to be more accurate, your future. Your Fate. Whatever the hell it thinks needs to be Read."

Harry shifted, trying—and failing—to keep her nerves off her face. Feigning courage she no longer felt, she nodded, getting back into position on the table. "Then you should probably get started."

13

On the Prowl

Harry shifted on the bench and sucked in a whimper as a searing, throbbing pain heated her left butt cheek. Letting Lenny give her her first tattoo a day before Paintball Pandemonium hadn't been one of her brightest moments. Neither had lighting Elodie's competitive fires by laying down that bet at Jax's feet.

The angel was in full throttle, pacing back and forth as they listened to the crowd cheer in the stadium. You'd have thought paintball an Olympic event with world-record-breaking potential for how many people sat in the stands at the Fates Haven High football stadium, watching the spectacle and rooting for their favorite team.

They'd run the game tournament style, pitting team against team in a bracket system, the winner progressing to face off with the winner from an earlier matchup. So far, team Fearsome Four was undefeated and, believe it or not, advancing to the final round.

Against the Big Bads.

No one was more surprised than Harry.

Or sore.

They waited along the tunnel wall as a player from Jax's previous opponent's team was brought through on a stretcher, his ankle twisted at an odd angle. The young warlock had freaked out when caught in the crosshairs of both a vampire and a demon and during a runaway attempt, barreled over one of the low walls. The live-action replay on the jumbotron still had Harry wincing.

"Having second thoughts?" Jax's warm breath brushed against her cheek as he leaned deliciously into her personal space. "It's not too late to withdraw."

She shot him a look, her lips nearly brushing his he was so close. "That's not happening."

"No one would hold it against you. We are pretty intimidating. It seems like we're eliminating our opponents faster and faster with each round. By my calculations, ours should be over in about ten seconds . . . and ten only because we'd drag it out a bit. To get the audience's hearts pumping. I mean, they came out all this way to be entertained, right? Can't have it all over in five seconds or less."

She refused to look at the gorgeous tilt of his twisted smirk, and folded her arms over her chest. They didn't quite make it all the way, her body covered in protective padding and a helmet that made her head feel like it weighed twenty pounds by itself.

"Is this you trying to psych out your competition?" Harry questioned knowingly. "Because that makes you seem a bit nervous about your odds. If you were that sure of yourself and your team's quick ten-second win, why bother with intimidation tactics?"

"Not intimidation . . . just doing you a favor by letting you know what you'll be up against. We'll try not to make it too embarrassing for you." He winked, and damn it if the sight of it didn't dampen her panties. "It's the least we can do."

"Push him out of your head, Pierce." Elodie's sharp bark snapped her to attention and away from the sight of Jax's black camo–clad ass as he joined his team on the other side of the tunnel.

"He's not in my head," Harry lied.

El's look told her she hadn't been very convincing. "Pants. Head. Wherever he is currently taking up space, evict him. Now. We have some egotists to crush into a fine, shimmery powder and we can't get distracted by some hot ass. Speaking of . . . what the hell's wrong with yours? You've been squirming around like you sat on an anthill since you got here."

Harry's gaze locked with Lenny's before she turned it back to the anxious angel. "Nothing. Just . . . adrenaline."

And the tattoo given to her by the Fortune-telling Tattooist that she can't look at until one more night at the earliest.

"She doesn't mean that literally, right?" Grace asked from her right as Elodie checked Lenny's protective gear one more time. "I'm pretty sure you'd be failing at this guardian thing if you dragged me into a competition that was to the death."

"I'd like to think she's kidding, but I've seen that look before and it never leads to anything good . . . but I think we're okay."

"You don't sound too positive."

"I'm positive this will be an interesting experience." Harry pushed a smile on her face.

"And we've officially made it to our final two teams," Nora's voice echoed over the loudspeaker.

As the Paintball Pandemonium's official MC, the witch

stood on a small stage near the lower entrance to the high school football stadium, her sequined T-shirt loudly proclaiming her team Fearsome Four's top fan.

"Let's hear it for your Paintball Pandemonium finalists," Nora announced to the roar of the crowd. "First up and out of the tunnel . . . they're big . . . they'd bad . . . and they are not the least bit horrible to look at with all that muscle . . . it's team Big Bads!"

The crowd's roar grew, feet stomping in the stands as Jax and the others pushed off the wall.

"Ready to get your ass handed to you, angel eyes?" Silas taunted Elodie. "I'll try to do it gently, but no promises."

"And I'll be feeding you your horns and tail . . . and I *won't* be doing it gently," the angel volleyed back, her voice deceptively sweet.

Jax shot Harry another coy wink and followed in a jog behind Maddox, Gavin, and Silas as they exited the tunnel and entered the field.

"We got this." Elodie turned to their team. "They may have brawn, but they don't have two brain cells between the lot of them."

Grace fidgeted nervously. "I don't know. Isn't that one guy some kind of bookish research wonder or something. I'd think you'd have to be pretty smart to—"

Elodie shot her a glare that snapped her mouth shut.

"Never mind."

"Thanks to the other rounds, we now know what works and what doesn't," Elodie pointed out. "Be quick. Be efficient. Be lethal. They won't be pulling any punches and neither should we."

"And now, for our last team, but certainly not least"—Nora's voice echoed from the speakers—"they're fearsome . . . they're a foursome . . . and they are sugar and spice and both naughty and nice . . . they're the Fearsome Four!"

The crowd roared again, and Harry and the others headed out to the field.

She sucked in a breath, and next to her, Grace groaned. "Did the population of Fates Haven triple overnight or something?"

"Pretty sure it's more than triple." Wincing, Harry sent an awkward wave into the stands.

There'd been a lot of people watching this morning's first matches, but nothing compared to this. The Fates Haven citizens brought some friends, and the friends brought some friends and maybe a few dozen long-lost relatives.

Photographers standing on the sidelines took picture after picture, cameras flashing wildly as Harry and the girls took their spot next to the already waiting Big Bads.

Harry stopped next to Jax, the shifter sending her a small lip twitch. "That's a lot of people to lose in front of, huh?"

"Yep. You'll have to tell me how that feels later. I'm guessing not too good," Harry shot back, pasting another smile and giving another wave to the crowd as Jax chuckled.

It took Nora a few attempts to get the crowd to settle, and then she picked up her microphone and turned to the teams. "I'm sure this is old hat by now, but let's cross our i's and dot our t's, shall we?"

The teams both nodded.

"This is not a game out of that survivor book the kids love. Hence, no bloodshed." Nora shot a look between Silas and Elodie that made Harry chuckle. "However, this is a Fates Festival event and any and all talents are welcome to be used. Got speed? Sprint away. A keen sense of smell? Get sniffing. Any special gifts get a thumbs-up. Your job is to protect the flag in your end zone while attempting to steal the other. Does anyone have any questions before you're each magic-dropped to your respective parts of the field?"

Everyone shook their heads.

"Good." Nora nodded. "Oh, and one more added caveat for this final competition . . ."

The older witch paused for dramatic effect, and it worked. Harry stood stiff, wondering what the hell caveat her aunt could have added.

"This time"—Nora smirked mischievously—"you won't be magic-dropped with the rest of your team. Good luck, and play nice, kids."

With a dramatic hand wave, a warm magical breeze made of pure gold and glitter washed over the eight of them, and before Harry had a chance to protest, the cloud disappeared and her vision slowly cleared.

She sneezed, the magic getting into her nose and making her eyes tear. When she finally blinked the moisture away and her vision cleared, she cursed. "Well, crapology."

Nora hadn't been bluffing.

Harry stood alone near a hollowed school bus. From what she remembered of the field's layout, there'd been two, one near her team's flag and one somewhere around the forty-five yard line. She didn't see her team's flag which meant she was nowhere near the one she'd been charged to protect and about halfway to the one belonging to the Big Bads.

A rolling animalistic roar echoed from nearby.

Jax. He'd forgone his battle gear and paintball weapon to be either their team's protector, or worse . . . their tracker. As another roar erupted from her left, this time a hell of a lot closer than before, she realized . . . *tracker*. Definitely tracker.

Harry took off in the direction she hoped was the right one.

She'd erroneously thought Elodie too meticulous when she'd gone over a possible scenario in which they got split up. Being at least halfway to Jax's team flag meant she'd graduated from defense to offense. She had a flag to find and procure and evidently a cougar to outmaneuver.

Harry sprinted to the stacked-barrel wall, quick and as silent as possible, which turned out to be not much of either. She kicked a stone as she ducked behind the barrels, wincing as it bounced against something metallic in the distance. Probably the bus.

Shit. She hoped Jax wasn't too close.

Harry crossed everything as she ducked from cover spot to cover spot. *Keep moving.* That had been Elodie's advice if they found themselves on the offensive line. They couldn't do anything about Gavin's vampiric speed, Silas's brute strength, or all Jax's super shifter senses, which meant it was best to keep moving and hope one if not all of them became preoccupied with someone else.

Harry crouched behind a flock of pink flamingo yard decorations and scanned for her next cover spot, finding it nearly fifteen yards away in the form of a small brick retaining wall.

Another yowl—this one close enough to raise the hair on the back of her neck—pierced the air. Cougar Jax had gotten a whiff, and he was on the hunt. Movement on her left snapped her head in that direction, and then to the right. The time for carefulness was done and it was now time to hope and haul ass.

Securing her paint gun on her back, Harry took a deep breath and ran toward the retaining wall as if hell itself was hot on her sneakered feet. Cursing the entire way, she held her boobs in place and booked it. Something whizzed by her right shoulder and slammed into the ground at her feet.

A spray of blue paint.

"Found you, Harry!" Maddox taunted, releasing another barrage of paint pellets. "You can run, but you can't hide . . . at least not from my very own hunting cougar."

Another spray of paint came as she zigzagged and dove for the retaining wall. Everything jarred on impact, rattling every bone in her body.

"You know you can't get very far"—Mads chuckled—"not without a miracle. You're all by your lonesome out here. Silas already outed Elodie, and Lenny never saw Gavin coming he was so fast."

"That still leaves me and Grace, so I wouldn't count us out just yet," Harry called. If what Maddox even said was true and not a very tired method of faking her out.

Closing her eyes, she let her descry magic flow through her veins. The air moved, shifting her hair away from her face as she called it to her . . . their flag . . . and a route to it.

"You think that's going to help you, babe?" Mads asked, obviously sensing the magic rising in the air. "If you surrender now, maybe we'll go a little easier on you in the next event. What do you say?"

She ignored him, her magic locating Maddox crouched behind the barrels from which she'd just run.

Harry shifted her paintball gun into her hands and checked the mechanism, making sure it was prepped to fire. "Keep dreaming, King."

She leaned to the far left and fired off a series of shots. Maddox's low curse had her grinning ear to ear until he retaliated, each fired shot making her temporary safe spot sway precariously.

She wouldn't be covered for too much longer. She needed to fire and run.

She laid down a series of shots toward Lenny's brother, making him duck or risk being ousted in the event, and spun right toward a large, snarling mountain lion.

Less than three feet away and obviously using her distraction to sneak up on her from behind, Jax growled, his fur standing on end as his gold eyes locked on her.

Sure, she could shoot him. It was Jax. In his cougar form, the paintball would likely feel like a tickle, but the animal lover in her still couldn't do it.

His upper body lowered to the ground, hindquarters and tail twitching as if prepping to leap. Harry backed up a step. He wouldn't hurt her, but she sure as hell wasn't letting him pin her to the ground so Maddox could walk right up and smack a blue paintball on her chest protector either.

Hands raised as if trying to placate a regular animal and not the man who'd been taunting her with a smirk less than fifteen minutes ago, she took another step back. Cougar Jax took one forward. This wasn't getting them anywhere.

His hind quarters wiggled and Cougar Jax pounced. A blurry streak whipped past Harry and rammed into Jax with a loud crash of grunts and limbs. Grace, with her arms and legs locked around the large cat's middle, wrestled a dazed Cougar Jax off his feet.

"Go!" Grace threw at Harry, ripping through her shock. "Their flag is unprotected right now! Go, Harry!"

Maddox popped up out of nowhere and laid down blue fire. Harry booked it around the second bus and saw the swinging flag in the end zone. With victory within her sight, she didn't process the sudden thunderous roar of the crowd or the game-ending buzzer until something hard slammed against her ass.

A bolt of pain zapped from her tattoo and through her tailbone, trickling down her legs as she dropped face-first into a muddy section of the football field. She didn't need to look to know she'd been pegged with a Big Bad paintball.

Game over . . . and it wasn't the Fearsome Four who'd won.

Elodie was going to be so fucking pissed.

* * *

VICTORY SMELLED A lot like s'mores, or it could be the scent of toasted marshmallows hanging in the air, the roaring bonfire large enough for at least two dozen Fates Haven citizens to get their campfire fix at one time.

That was Fates Haven. Celebrate one activity with another, and with the first Fates Festival event entered in the logbook, excitement for the festival's return had grown exponentially. People had shown up en masse to watch Paintball Pandemonium, signaling to a very thrilled Nora Pierce that she'd been right to bring the festival back.

The bonfire at Mystic Lake was not only to celebrate the festival's return but the bang with which it did. Jax maneuvered through the crowd, accepting congratulations on a game well played, as he tried not lingering too long in one spot. He told himself it was because he didn't people well.

And then he told himself he was a big ole liar.

He'd spent the better part of the last forty-five minutes looking for a particular brunette he couldn't evict from his headspace. He found her sitting on a piece of driftwood a good distance from the fire, her bare toes stretched out as the lake's water ebbed and flowed. She shot an occasional glare off to her left and when he followed it, he saw Grace talking to Devon, both teens' faces practically lit up by their smiles.

Jax swallowed a chuckle. "Good thing you don't have the ability to freeze shit with that glare or poor Dev would be an ice pop by now."

Harry startled, glancing up at him with a guilty expression before focusing way too hard on what looked to be her iced Fruity Freeze. "I don't know. My magic has been a little wonky lately. I could probably pull off a freeze glare if I were really lucky."

"Is this seat taken?" He surprised not only himself but her by asking.

"It's a public beach and a public piece of wood, so go for it."

He sat, making sure to keep a foot between them. His willpower may be strong but not when it came to the woman next to him. "He's a good kid, you know."

Harry shot him a questioning look.

"Devon. Don't get me wrong. He's a teenager, through and through, but he's a good kid. He's respectful. He knows the importance of boundaries. Grace could do a hell of lot worse than crushing on him."

"Who said she has a crush?" Harry tossed him a glare before sneaking another look at them and cursing. "Fuck. Yeah, she has a crush. I just hope she doesn't end up crushed."

"You can protect her from a lot, but you can't protect her from that."

"Have a lot of experience raising teenagers, do you?" Harry teased lightly.

"I've been raising an entire pack for the last few months

and, let me tell you, I wish they had mature heads on their shoulders like Devon. He sure as hell has a better one than I did at his age."

And when he'd been Dev's age, he and Harry had already been in deep. The good girl and the bad boy. The witch and the shifter. At least he thought they'd been in it together. Turns out, it had been a one-man diving expedition, and no one told him until he watched his heart walk away without so much as a single glance.

The past became a third person sitting between him and Harry on the log.

She stood and brushed off the seat of her jean shorts. "I should go find Nora."

"That's it?" Irritation bubbled to the surface and he slowly got his feet, too, watching her retreating backside. "One brief mention about back then and you run away just like you did that day? You haven't changed at all in thirteen years, huh?"

She spun around, hair flying around her shoulders. "You have no idea who I am right now."

"Yeah? And whose fault is that, Harlow?" He used her full name on purpose, knowing it would piss her off even more. It worked.

Periwinkle eyes narrowing on him, she held her ground as he slowly approached, diminishing the distance between them.

"I'll tell you whose fault it is," Jax growled, years of agitation and anger bubbling to the surface. "It's the fault of the person who left without so much as a 'see you never.' It's the fault of the person who enabled that damn anti-tracking spell."

At the widening of her eyes, a small sense of victory zipped through him.

"Yeah, that's right, sweet pea. After the fourth attempt, I lost track of all the different places your spell landed me, places where you were definitely not living."

"I . . . didn't know."

"And nor did you want to, or else you wouldn't have cast the damn thing. Or sworn Nora to a Witch's Oath." He stopped less than an inch away, the soft glow of Harry's eyes nearly drowning him right there on the rocky Mystic Lake beach. "So you're right. I don't know the woman you are right now, and it appears that I never really knew the girl I thought you were back then either, because *my* Harry, the one both me and my cougar practically claimed as our own, would've never shut us out and walked away. She would've never let us go without putting up a damn fucking fight."

"I don't know what to say, Jax," Harry murmured, her shoulders deflating along with some of her anger.

"I don't expect you to say anything. Just know that although I'm glad Lenny, Elodie, and the rest of Fates Haven seems to have adopted a selective memory when it comes to the details of your departure, I sure as hell haven't. I *can't*. I remember it all as if it were yesterday, and I sure as hell won't be forgetting it anytime soon."

The sound of a throat clearing signaled they weren't alone, but Jax didn't need it to know Grace had joined them, and not far behind stood Devon.

The teenager's gaze shifted from him to her guardian, cautiously wary. "Is everything okay over here?"

"Everything's fine." Harry pushed a small smile to her lips and stepped back. "Just a long-overdue talk."

Grace didn't look as if she believed it, drilling her gaze on Jax.

"What she said." Jax played along. He'd said his piece. Now

the ball was in Harry's court. "And speaking of a talk, I wanted to congratulate you on that takedown at the end of match. I have to admit, I didn't sense you coming until my paws left the ground."

A small smile twitched on Grace's face. "Yeah, I was a little proud of myself for that one. I'm honestly not sure what happened. At first, I could hear Gavin tracking me through the course, and used it to keep my distance. And then I scented Harry and followed the trail."

"You honed in on us using your shifter senses. That's a good thing."

"It's good that it was that close to the surface that I could use my senses that easily?"

"And that you used them while maintaining control." Jax nodded. "You could've very easily used that sparkage of yours to light my tail on fire, and yet you didn't. You used your speed and strength to take me by surprise."

Devon chuckled. "And there's not many who can lay claim to that ability. Many shifters have tried, which makes you the ultimate badass."

The kid looked at Grace with little hearts in his eyes.

"He's not wrong." Jax chuckled. "Which reminds me that Gavin texted me a bit ago. Those rare texts came in earlier today while everyone was at the event, and it turns out the collection is a bit more vast than what he'd thought. He asked if anyone wanted to help."

"Absolutely!" Grace turned toward Harry. "I mean, if that's okay?"

"A research party sounds fun. Count me in." Harry nodded her support.

"I'll touch base with Gavin and we'll set up a time. Just fair warning, though, he's extremely particular about book handling," Jax added. "If he even catches wind of someone dog-earing a book, he may take a bite out of you."

Grace chuckled, but at his serious face, the laughter slowly died away. "Wait. Are you serious?"

He shrugged. "I wouldn't suggest trying it to find out, Sparks."

14

Ass Reading

Harry paced her bedroom, second-guessing the smartness of this plan. In her defense, she'd been replaying her conversation with Jax over and over in her head and didn't really hear Elodie's "brilliant" idea until she heard herself agree and it was too late to take back.

"Are they there yet?" Cassie leaned closer to her own phone screen as if she could see around her.

"Trust me, you'd know if Elodie walked into the room, but they should be here soon. Even if there's a traffic jam, it only takes five minutes to get from one end of Fates Haven to the other." Harry nibbled on the corner of her thumbnail.

"I still can't believe you got a tattoo without me, you witch. All that begging I did and one excuse after another. Not the right shop. Lax safety regs. Not finding a design that calls to you. And then you end up letting someone choose your tattoo for you."

"Not just anyone, Lenny. And, yeah, I'm having a serious

case of regrets right now." Harry paused in her pacing. "Shit. What if it really is a rabid raccoon or a laughing donkey?"

Harry heard Lenny and Elodie before they burst into the room.

"Told you you'd hear them." Harry smirked, waving her phone in the others' directions. "Cassie, meet Lenny and Elodie. Len and El, meet Cass."

Elodie lurched forward and stole the phone. "Can I just say that you raised a kick-ass daughter? I know we technically lost Paintball Pandemonium, but she was lethal. Took Cougar Jax straight off his feet and I seriously cannot remember that ever happening before."

Cassie laughed. "Thanks, but I didn't raise an ass kicker alone. Harry had a huge hand it, too."

Elodie slid Harry a wink. "Yeah, I can definitely see that. So . . . are we ready to have ourselves an ass Reading or what?"

Harry groaned. "For the last time, it's not *on* my ass."

"Well . . ." Lenny added, chuckling.

"So it's a bit north of my butt cheek proper and a smidge south of the waistline." She turned to Lenny. "So how do we do this Reading? Do I moon you and the meaning smacks you like a spitball on the forehead or what?"

"First, I want to preface by saying that this may all be for nothing," Lenny warned. "You know what my track record has been like lately."

"I do."

"And you can't be mad at me if you end up with a design you don't like."

"I won't. Promise . . . unless it's something gross like a leech."

Lenny looked more apprehensive than even Harry. "Then let's get set up."

With Elodie holding Cassie on the phone, Harry helped Lenny dim the lights and set up the pillar candles, and then with more than a few nervous chuckles from everyone in the room, Lenny sat cross-legged on the floor, a few scant inches away from a standing Harry's rear end.

There was a shift in the air moments before a warm sensation tingled across her butt.

Lenny nodded slowly. "It's time."

Holding her breath, Lenny slowly peeled away the bandage. Twin gasps erupted from both Elodie and Cassie while Lenny remained still. The pillar candles flickered as the seer then closed her eyes, sweat dotting her forehead.

"What's happening?" Cassie whispered.

"Len is trying to Read the tattoo," Elodie answered in a soft murmur.

"Len would like some quiet please," she retorted.

"Are you okay?" Harry watched her friend sway in the tall mirror. "You're looking a little pale . . . and nauseous."

A low groan rolled from Lenny's throat before all her tension melted away. Her body sagged heavily, as if weighted with bricks, and teetered forward.

Harry caught her a second before she face-planted on the floor and broke her nose. "Shit. Lenny. Are you all right?"

"I'm okay." She shot her an apologetic look. "I'm sorry, Harry. The Sight was practically within touching distance, but it just wouldn't take hold. I can't Read it."

"It's okay." Harry hid her disappointment with a small smile.

"No. It's not." Lenny released a frustrated sigh as she got to her feet. "Gah. It feels like I'm freaking cursed."

"Not just you. The whole town. So chin up, babe," Elodie quipped.

Please don't be a raccoon. Please don't be a raccoon. Closing her eyes and trying not to grimace, Harry turned her ass toward the mirror and counted down from five. At one, she peeled her eyes open one at a time and instantly locked on the fresh tattoo. . . .

"You've got to be fucking kidding me."

"Well, it's not a raccoon," Cassie chirped. "It's actually really pretty with all the shades of blue and purple."

"Seriously, Cass?" Harry shot her friend a glare to the phone Elodie still held.

"Don't give me that look. You're the one with a blue flame lighting up your rear end. I mean, it's a pretty flame. Oh, my goddess! You have a fire in your pants." Cassie chuckled. "Ooh! Maybe it's telling you that you're about to come into some smoking hot sex . . . or an uncomfortable yeast infection."

"It's not any regular flame," Lenny added.

"No, it's not." Harry turned to look at her ass one more time and grudgingly admitted that Fate really had it out for her.

There was no other reason to have her tattoo be the spitting image of a Blue Willow Wisp that caused the derailment of her life thirteen years ago. Now, instead of the memory permanently etched into her memory vault, it was also forever memorialized on her ass cheek.

* * *

JAX TURNED YET another page, scanned its contents, and flipped again. Gavin's promising book arrivals had been more bookish and less promising, not really telling them anything they didn't know. Except that the rare unicorn shifter shit rainbows and was prone to constipation that only a fiber high in glitter could cure. That was info that could've stayed dead and buried, but now held a prominent spot in his knowledge bank.

He flipped another page, only to be met with more of the same.

"What the hell did that book ever do to you?" Gavin glared at him from across the table.

"Not tell me what we're looking for, that's for damn sure." Jax sighed, sneaking a glance two tables over where Harry and Grace poured over another book stack.

He'd been surprised she'd shown up after their discussion on the beach; and while she'd acted civilized and even smiled at Gavin when they talked, she'd steered clear of Jax. No smiles. No jokes. Nothing.

And he fucking hated it.

"Oh, for fuck's sake. Either go over there and apologize or shake it off and move on." Gavin kept his gaze locked on the book in front of him.

"I have absolutely nothing to apologize for. I'm not the one who left the people they claimed to care about most, and then returned expecting to drop back into Fates Haven life as if nothing changed. Asking for favors no less."

"And yet you're sitting here in the library—for the first time since I've known you—and treating my extremely rare new additions as if they've just insulted your cougar's alpha nature."

Jax shot him a stern glare that the bastard batted away with a faint brow lift. "Maybe I'm doing it in the hopes that the sooner we solve Grace's shifter issue, the sooner they can get on with their lives . . . outside Fates Haven."

Gavin snorted, obviously not believing him any more than he believed himself.

Jax scanned another page until movement pulled his attention toward Harry. She patted Grace's shoulder and headed toward the coffee station Gavin set up on the counter. She fumbled with the controls, opening and closing the top a few times before frowning at it like a complicated calculus problem.

"I'll be back." Receiving a grunt from the vampire, he headed toward Harry. "You have to turn it on before you put the pod inside and then wait until it flashes."

He reached over her shoulder, removing her chai packet from the chamber, and reflexively settled his spare hand on her hip. Harry startled, but kept her place as he showed her how to work Gavin's fancy coffee machine. It hummed to life as it prepped.

"Still not much of a coffee drinker?" he asked.

"It has its time and place, neither of which is right now." She stared intently as the tea drained into her waiting mug.

He sighed. "Harry, about the other night, I—"

"You weren't wrong." She turned toward him, the move putting them chest to chest as her gaze lifted to his. "But I can't change what happened, and I know that I can apologize for the way everything played out over and over again, but it won't make a difference to you."

Jax opened his mouth to hopefully say something not stupid when Grace called out, her brows furrowed as she ran her finger over the page in front of her.

"What's up? What did you find?" Gavin got to her first, peering over her shoulder.

"I'm not really sure. Probably nothing," Grace moved the book his way and his eyes scanned the page.

Harry and Jax headed toward them.

Gavin rubbed his trimmed beard, telling him he was deep in thought. "Or maybe something."

"What something?" Harry asked eagerly.

Gavin handed her the open book and Jax leaned closer for a peek. She shifted it so he could see, too.

"This just mentions shifters of folklore." Harry glanced up, confused. "How is this something?"

"Because a lot of this realm's folklore is based in another realm's reality—or supposed reality."

"This realm and another realm?" Grace asked, confused. "How many realms are there?"

"Honestly? It's anyone's guess." Gavin nudged his chin to all the books they'd spent hours poring over. "These only talk about shifters from this realm. We've been overlooking the possibility that maybe the shifter we're looking for is not from *this* realm but one of the others."

Grace's eyes widened as big as dinner plates. "Are you saying I'm a freaking alien?"

Gavin chuckled. "No. Well . . . no. At least not the Mars kind."

"What other kinds are there?" Sparks drifted up from the teenager's hands and Harry, quick to move, shoved the book in Jax's hands.

"Hey. It's okay. This is a good thing." Harry crouched in front of her, slipping her hands over Grace's.

"How is being an alien a good thing? We watched *War of the Worlds* together. You saw what happened."

"Yes, and we also saw *E.T.*" Harry smiled soothingly. "We've spent this whole time focused on thinking one way and it's hasn't led us closer to answers. Maybe we need to change that mode of thinking."

The sparks died away as Grace calmed, slowly nodding. She glanced at Gavin. "Okay . . . so not a Mars alien. So what are we talking about here?"

"I think we should consider the fact that we might be looking for a fae shifter."

Silence hung in the air, more potent than moonshine.

Grace shifted awkwardly in her seat. "I thought that there aren't many fae here anymore."

"There's not," Jax added. "With the weakening of the fae portals fifty years ago, most fae returned home, not many wanting to risk being stuck here permanently. It's also why there isn't a whole hell of a lot of written history about them. They took most of it with them."

"So in theory, if there isn't a big fae population that stayed behind, finding information on this Luke guy should be a hell of a lot easier." Harry squeezed Grace's hand. "We just have to find ourselves a popular fae who claims to know everyone and everything and start asking questions."

Gavin grimaced. "That's easier said than done. The fae—as a whole—are not very chatty when it comes to their way of life."

"Then we need to what? Get them drunk so they loosen their lips?" Harry joked. "But first, we need to find a fae."

Gavin was back to stroking his beard.

"Gav?" Jax watched his friend.

The vampire sighed. "I know a guy, but I'm warning you right now, he's not the chatty type . . . alcohol or not."

"Maybe if we make our case, it will appeal to his softer side." Harry's tone was hopeful and Jax couldn't blame her.

"He doesn't have one of those . . . but I agree that I think it's our best chance to find out anything about this Luke. Or anything related to fae shifters at all."

"So you'll make the introduction?"

Gavin laughed. "You don't want me introducing you to him. Trust me."

"Why not?"

"Because he vowed to put a stake through my heart the next time he laid eyes on me."

Jax lifted an eyebrow. "What the fuck did you do to piss him off? Sleep with his girlfriend or something?"

"Asked to borrow a book he has."

Grace made a small squeaking noise.

"It doesn't matter." Determination glinted in Harry's eyes. "Tell me where to find him. I've been told I can be really persuasive."

Jax growled, his cougar rising to the surface. "Did you not hear what Gavin said? He threatened to kill him just for asking to borrow a copy of Nancy Drew mysteries or something."

"I don't care. This is the closest thing to a lead that we've had in *ever*. I'm not letting it slip through my fingers because the guy has an anger management problem. It's a risk I'm willing to take."

"Well, it's not one I'm willing to let you take."

"Good thing that you're not the boss of me, Jaxon Atwood. Or my Alpha." She glared daggers at him, daring him to argue.

Fuck.

He pinched the bridge of his nose, trying to tell his cougar to calm down as he clawed him from the inside, itching to get out and let his displeasure be known, too.

"Fine." He growled. "But you're sure as hell not meeting him alone. I'm going with you."

"And me," Grace chimed.

"Hell no," Jax said at the same time Harry snorted. "No way."

Harry turned her gaze on him. "Fine. You can come . . . but so help me, if you growl even one time and this guy threatens to put you in a cone of shame or something, I'm not stepping in to help you."

"I think I can contain myself," Jax said.

Gavin snorted. "Can you really? The fae are all about manners. If my contact feels disrespected in the least, he'll send you on a wild-goose chase just because it would amuse him."

"I can be a goddamned respectful delight."

Three sets of snorts went off around him.

"What?" Jax drilled them all with a glare. "I can."

Gavin clapped him hard on the shoulder, a smirk playing on his lips. "Sure you can . . . but maybe we should go over some basic do's and don'ts when it comes to dealing with fae. And then let's talk about what you're each going to wear."

"Wear? Why does it matter what we wear?"

"He owns Glamour, a club in downtown Denver, and if you hope to have even half a chance of getting an audience with him, you need to stand out from the crowd."

Jax didn't like the sound of that one damn bit, but he knew that he'd end up liking the reality of it even less.

15

Glamour

The second Gavin mentioned Glamour, the fae-owned club, Harry mentally pictured some pretty horrific images. Cramped, crowded spaces. Loud, pulsing music. People grinding against each other in ways usually reserved for naked bedroom activities.

This was a hundred times worse.

She didn't do clubs like this even when she'd been in her clubbing phase, much preferring to dance in her and Cass's living room, their remote-control mirror ball flickering from the ceiling and creating an entertaining light show for the squealing little one hanging on their legs.

Not to mention, the comfy clothes.

Goddess, she missed her comfy clothes right now.

A warm hand settled low on her exposed back and she tried—and failed—not to startle despite knowing to whom it belonged. Jax's warm heat wrapped around her as he guided them through the sea of bodies.

"You okay?" His mouth brushed the shell of her ear, close enough to be heard over the pulsing music.

"Just peachy. We're here to ask a favor of an old fae who evidently likes breaking his boredom by requesting his guests perform like puppets for his entertainment, and I get to do it while feeling I'm about to expose a butt or a boob if I make any abrupt movements."

Not to mention this was really the first time they'd spoken more than a simple greeting since he picked her up an hour ago. While Lenny, Elodie, and Grace had primped, plucked, and perfumed her as if this was a real date despite her protests, she'd felt like an anvil hung over her head, prepping for the awkward silence to come. And she hadn't been wrong. They'd shared not more than a few sneaking glances . . . until now.

"So in other words, you've never been better," Jax joked dryly. "Great. Me, too. I just absolutely fucking love putting myself in the center of attention."

Harry snorted. "If Gavin's friend hates him as much as he claims, then maybe he should've been the one to come and get his attention." She glanced through the sea of gyrating bodies. "Because I'm not so sure we'd get it even if we got naked and actually did what these people are mimicking."

Jax's heated gaze warmed a path right to the thong Elodie had strong-armed her into because "You absolutely cannot have panty lines with this dress." Maybe mentioning sex around the man she'd been picturing naked since returning to Fates Haven wasn't the brightest move . . . but she couldn't help wondering.

Thirteen years to change.

To harden.

To . . .

Jax's low chuckle rumbled through her body as he leaned close, lips brushing her ear. "Keep thinking whatever you're thinking, sweet pea, and I don't think it'll take much for us to get our host's attention."

Her head snapped toward him. A big mistake. His mouth, less than an inch away from hers, twitched knowingly. "It's not polite to go around sniffing people."

"I'm not sniffing, baby. I'm just breathing normally. It's not my fault that your arousal is like damn catnip to my mountain lion."

Choosing to ignore both her dampening pseudo underwear and her now racing heart, she glanced around the crowded club and mentally cursed. There was no way they'd get the owner's attention in this madhouse.

Large overhead strobe lights flickered and beamed throughout the otherwise dark open dance floor; and on one end, a DJ took center stage, a wide screen at her back as she head bobbed to the music. People were packed shoulder to shoulder on the main floor, and the second-floor behind its railing didn't look any less cramped.

Harry didn't know this many people lived in freaking Denver.

"Over there." Jax ran his hand up her arm and nudged her chin to the third-floor wall of mirrors artfully slanted toward the crowd and up to the high vaulted ceiling. "Gavin said this guy likes to be entertained, right? No better place to do it than behind one-way mirrors where you can see out but no one can see in. How much do you want to bet that our fae is hiding in his office up there?"

"Nothing because you're probably right. But that will make it that much more difficult to get his attention. I honestly think we could both strip and he probably wouldn't bat an eye."

Feeling Jax's gaze on her, she added, "And, no, I'm not willing to test that theory."

Lips twitching, he shrugged. "Just an idea."

"A bad one, so let's start thinking a bit more out of the box."

"Well, we're definitely sticking out a bit right now by the fact we're not dancing," Jax said dryly.

Harry scanned the room, and he was right. A few people nearby glanced their way, giving them up-and-down perusals. When she looked back to Jax, he held his hand out for her.

Bad idea after bad idea . . .

She took it, sliding her hand over his callus-roughened palm. His fingers wrapped around hers snuggly, his other hand dropping to her lower hip as he guided her close. All moisture in Harry's mouth dried instantly.

This was a necessary evil. The only lead they had that could possibly get answers for Grace. For that kid, she'd do anything, even if that meant subjecting herself and her body to the sweet, sweet torture of being pressed up against Jaxon Atwood.

Jax sighed softly, the sound pulling her gaze to his. "What?"

"Could you look a little less like someone is ripping off your fingernails with a rusty pliers?" Jax's light tone contrasted with his tense expression.

She relaxed her shoulders with a sigh. "Sorry. There's just a lot riding on this. Grace was practically beaming hope from every orifice earlier today, and I really want this to give us something to work with. Anything. And then there's . . ."

"There's what?" His gaze roved over her face as he watched her intently.

Him. This. *Us.*

"This isn't the time for that discussion," Harry murmured, forcing her gaze away from his. A chicken tactic? For sure.

Also needed if she had any hope of this harebrained plan working.

The hand on her hip slowly slid its way around her back, leaving a goose bump trail in its wake. Jax gently flexed his fingers on her bare skin while the hand holding hers did the same, silently asking a question and awaiting her answer.

Her gaze found his and everything else fell away. All her hesitancy. All her reservations. Every single reason why this wasn't a good idea. Harry shifted deeper into his arms and was quickly enveloped by the heat radiating off his body. She let out a contented hum as it blanketed her, sending an inviting warmth from her toes to her nose.

Jax guided their bodies into a slow sway, one much slower than the gyrating bodies around them but a hell of a lot more intimate. She slid her hand over his broad shoulder and behind his neck, fingers playing with the soft hair at his nape. Jax released a faint noise before he slowly dragged her even closer, both arms now wrapped around her waist.

Not even a piece of paper could fit between them, their bodies flush, and Jax's leg finding its way between her feet to fit her even closer. She fixed her gaze at the base of his throat and willed her breathing to slow, but it didn't work, doing the opposite the second his palm cupped her cheek and tilted her face toward his.

The gold-flecked gaze of his inner mountain lion looked back at her, the color flickering from its typical stormy gray. There was a lot of emotion swimming in that look, way too much for her to interpret without assistance.

Jax brushed his thumb over her bottom lip, his gaze dropping to watch the action. "You have no fucking clue what you're doing to me right now, sweet pea."

"I think I have a little bit of an idea." With every sway of their bodies, the telltale hardness of an erection brushed against her stomach. Goddess knew her little scrap of underwear was already beyond saving.

Fingers flexing around his nape, she slowly lifted to her toes. Jax took the silent hint and dropped his head until their lips were mere inches apart. She wanted his mouth on hers more than she wanted her next breath.

"Jax . . ."

An annoyed cough interrupted the moment. "The two of you need to come with me."

Jax pulled back with a growl, swallowing it when he recognized one of the bouncers from the entrance. The guy was dressed in all black with mirrored sunglasses and could've doubled as a Secret Service agent on his off time.

"And why is it that? In case you didn't realize, I'm having a moment with my girl here," Jax ground out, playing the annoyed club patron.

Hearing him use the term "my girl," despite this being their game plan, sent a little zip through Harry, but she quickly toned it down. This was what they'd hoped to happen. They'd been singled out, and they hadn't even had to resort to a striptease on a tabletop.

"Relax, babe." She amped up her smile, leaning fully into his arms as she turned toward the bouncer. "Do you mind telling me why? We haven't done anything wrong, have we? We've just been enjoying our time at one of our favorite clubs."

"Actually, I do mind. With me. Now." Not bothering to clarify or make sure they followed, he turned, his large body parting the crowd without even trying.

"I think we found someone even less personable than you," Harry joked. She stepped to follow, but Jax's hand caught hers.

"I'm not so sure about this."

"What's not to be sure about? This is what we wanted."

He shot a conflicted glance to the departing security. "I know, but—"

"No buts. This guy has potential answers to questions about Grace, or at least where we might be able to find them. I'm not *not* following. You can stay here if you'd like."

Jax growled, his grip tightening. "You are not going up there alone."

She smiled sweetly. "I am if you don't follow."

Summoning a small magical gust, she broke his hold easily and followed the bouncer through the massive crowd. Jax caught up to her just as agent bouncer pointed to an elevator tucked in the far corner. The elevator screamed rich elegance with upholstered walls and gold fixtures that would've looked expensive even on baroque furniture.

Agent Bouncer gestured them inside and after hitting the button on the wall, stepped out and left them alone for the ride up.

The tension in the small space rose as they did; and when the doors opened, Harry sucked in a breath. "Holy crap."

Jax's arm was back around her waist. "Gavin said the fae love nature. Guess he wasn't wrong."

Nothing was natural about the magical scene in front of them, an ethereal garden in the heart of a Denver club. There wasn't a single sign of the industrial hot spot, no walls or the steel accents of the downstairs decor. Only a clear, dark purple sky with twinkling stars and an entire parade of flowers.

So many vividly colored flowers.

A butterfly flapped across Harry's face to land on a golden sky-reaching oak, and the moment it did, all its butterfly friends followed, covering the tree until it looked to be one rippling entity. Every color was bold and eye-popping, and so damn bright it almost hurt to look at any one thing for longer than a few seconds.

"Come in. Come in. Pull up a mossy pad and have a seat," a deep voice urged. "I don't bite . . . unless asked."

Jax's hand tightened on her hip as they stepped into the garden wonderland. A faint shimmer melted across the sky. It took a moment to realize that was the window peering down into the club. A man, who couldn't have been older than his early twenties, lay back on what looked to be a hovering cloud lounger.

Everything about him sparkled from his diamond-encrusted skin to the musical ballad of his voice. His long dark intricately braided hair fell far past his shoulders, hitting close to his waist if he'd been standing.

He smiled as they approached, taking equal time to eye them each up and down before fixing his gaze on her.

"I haven't come across one of you in a long time." He vibrant smile was almost blinding.

"Um . . . a witch?" Harry asked, confused.

"Sure. Let's go with that." He leaned back in his seat, drinking from a golden goblet. "So what brings a witch and her shifter lover to my club?"

"Oh, we're not . . ." Harry's denial trailed off as the fae looked her way. "We were looking for someplace to have a good time and was told this was the place to be."

The fae chuckled. "Let me take a wild guess and say that

this is the first time you've encountered someone such as my-self. Uh-uh." He held up a hand when she opened her mouth to speak. "It wasn't a question. Since I haven't had the pleasure of interacting with someone such as you in an age and half, I'd like to offer you one bit of advice."

Harry frowned. That was the second time he'd said that.

Jax's fingers flexed on her hip, a gentle reminder for her not blow this all to hell, or to be closer if this all went to hell and they had to make a quick escape.

"And that would be?" she asked.

"Don't lie to a fae." His smile faded and he snapped his fin-gers, poofing away his drink as he stood and turned toward them. "We can sense a lie better than we can sense a supernat-ural, and in case you were wondering, that's rather well."

He flickered, creating an illusionary effect that had Harry second-guessing everything . . . and that's when she realized he wore a glamour, and it wasn't just on him but their sur-roundings, too.

"Wouldn't you say that pretending to be something you're not is a form of lying?" she asked daringly. "Because unless I'm mistaken, your hair isn't really that sleek and shiny, and we're definitely not standing in the middle of a butterfly garden."

He paused a moment before breaking into peals of laugh-ter, humor lighting up his eyes. "Oh, how I have missed your kind. So abrupt. No filter."

He waved his hand, and in an instant, everything around them disappeared. The lush, vivid colors of the garden turned into a mahogany rich office, complete with bookshelves and a massive desk built for a king. And the fae in front of them defi-nitely wasn't twenty-one years old.

Long gray hair speckled with a dust of pepper hung to his

waist and gone was the silky twinkling suit. He wore jeans and a T-shirt advertising a local rock band. He looked to be in his fifties, but from what she remembered, looks didn't mean much with the fae. Someone who looked twenty could very well be four hundred. If this guy appeared to be in his fifties, she shuddered to think of his age.

"Since we're obviously friendly enough to point out each other's lies," the fae began, "I suppose we should exchange names. I'm Tomlyn. My friends call me Tommy, so you should most definitely call me Tomlyn."

Jax spoke first. "I'm Jaxon Atwood. Alpha to the Rocky Mountain Pack. And this is Harlow Pierce."

"Pierce." Tomlyn rubbed the gray beard covering his jaw. "Interesting . . . any relation to that delightful witch who lives in that little town down the road a ways? Nora?"

Harry narrowed her eyes, taken off guard at the mention of her aunt's name. "Maybe."

The fae smirked. "Definitely interesting. So Alpha Atwood . . . and Harlow. What really brought you into my club tonight?"

Harry exchanged a look with Jax, him giving her a support-ive nod. They'd talked about best approaches with Gavin, but now she was second-guessing everything.

"We're looking for information on a fae shifter, and was hoping that a fae with your status might be able to point us in the right direction." There, flattery initiated . . . without lying.

Tomlyn smirked, basking in the compliment. "And let's just say that I actually do know this shifter for whom you're looking. Why should I tell you anything about them, much less their whereabouts? I shouldn't need to remind you that the fae who remained here after the portal closures did so for a reason. As a whole, they're not people who want to be found."

"I understand that, but I've also read that the fae value family, both blood and found."

Tomlyn's eyes widened, but he quickly recovered, masking his interest. "Are you saying that you're looking for family, little witch?"

"I'm saying I'm looking for a family member of a member of my family."

He sat at his desk, kicking his booted feet on it. "And I reiterate, the fae who have remained on this side of the portals did so for a reason. It's not my right to expose their whereabouts if they do not wish their whereabouts to be known."

Patience shattered, Harry stepped closer, dropping her hands on Tomlyn's desk and ignored Jax's murmured warning. "I'm not really up to playing games, Tommy. It's been a really long couple of years. I need to find someone, and I think you have the knowledge to, at the very least, point me in the right direction."

Tomlyn stared at her, face devoid of emotion. "I like you, Harlow Pierce. That doesn't mean I can help you, but I like you. And because I like you, I will give you one more little nugget of information."

"Which is?"

"There are no documented fae shifters this side of the portals."

Harry digested the information before swallowing a string of curses. "There are no fae shifters."

"None. And as you pointed out, I am fairly in the know when it comes to this realm's fae population."

"Is it possible that—"

"No. No shifter remained, because to do so would risk their second self becoming unstable and unpredictable. *Uncontrollable.* For a shifter to be cut off from the land would be a fate worse than death. So, no, little witch. No shifters remained behind after the closures."

Harry sent a frustrated look toward Jax, feeling all her earlier hope melt away. They'd been so damn sure . . .

"But"—Tomlyn paused for dramatic effect—" you should know that the fae are a very resilient bunch."

"What the hell does that mean?" Jax asked tersely.

"It means, Alpha Atwood, that there is always a workaround when it comes to dealing with a fae."

Harry's hope resurfaced. "So you're saying that maybe one stayed?"

"No. I'm saying that I wouldn't put it past a fae to find a way to return. But as I said before, it couldn't be for long periods. They would need to return to Faerie or risk losing themselves. What is the name of this shifter for whom you search?"

"Luke."

He drilled her with an expectant look.

Harry sighed. "Yeah, I know. It's not a lot to go on, but that's all I have. *Luke.*"

"Not a very fae name, no doubt an alias or a very simplified version of their real name. You know not of what kind of fae shifter he is?"

"Honestly? We don't even know if we're looking for a fae shifter. It's just that we've ruled out everything else."

Tomlyn nodded thoughtfully. "Because of my infatuation with your kind, Harlow Pierce, I will do you another favor, but only if you grant me two in return."

"That seems a little imbalanced don't you think?"

Jax cleared his throat. "Harry, no."

She ignored his warning. "And what are these favors? And what will I get for doing them?"

"I will *lend* you a book in my possession—one to be used to search for the answers to your questions and no others—if you agree to grant me two things. The first, a future favor yet-to-be-named."

"And the second?"

"The two of you participating in a little game for me. Right now."

"Yeah, you can forget that." Jax took hold of Harry's arm, no doubt prepped to carry her from the club if need be.

"What game?" she asked.

"Harry," he warned.

"What game?"

"A simple one that from what I hear, many in this realm play at some point in their childhood. I believe they call it Two Truths and a Lie."

"And this future favor?"

He shrugged. "There's nothing of which you can do for me right now, but I believe that may at some point in time, change. As for the game, it's a simple one. I've always been fascinated with the inability of people in this realm to pick out a false-hood."

"And this book will give us answers?"

"It will not tell you who it is you're looking for, but perhaps it will guide you in their approximate direction."

Harry digested the information, already knowing she'd do it if it meant getting answers. "Fine. Two Truths and Lie." She turned to Jax. "One: I cry over commercials. Two: I'm mistrustful of anyone who eats ketchup on eggs. And three: *Die Hard* is not a Christmas movie no matter what anyone says."

Jax's lips twitched, but Tomlyn groaned. "Maybe I didn't make myself clear enough. These truths and a lie must be deep, raw, and heartrending. Anything less won't be accepted. Again. And make me feel the angst that has been pouring off the two of you since you stepped into my club."

Deep. Raw. And heartrending.

Jax caught her gaze with his. "You really want to do this?"

"We need answers, Jax. *Grace* needs answers."

He nodded grimly, looking resigned and pissed off as he quickly tossed a smirking Tomlyn a hard glare. "One: after you left Fates Haven, I stopped counting how many times I went looking for you after the tenth failed try. Two: the day you left, you took a piece of me with you and I haven't felt whole since. And three: it may have taken me a while, but I'm finally ready to move on with my life."

Silence blanketed the room, the only sound her own racing heartbeat. Jax kept his gaze fixed on her, his breathing nearly as ragged as her own.

"Jax . . ." she whispered.

"Now that's how you play!" Tomlyn clapped his hands joyously. "I know the lie! Pick one, Harlow Pierce!"

She didn't need to guess. Pain lined every inch of Jax's face, so potent it may as well be her own. "N-number three."

Tomlyn cheered again. "Very well done. Now, it's your turn to list two truths and a lie, Harry. Let's see if your mountain lion is as good at picking out the falsehood as you were."

She winced as she swallowed the lump in her throat. "One: there isn't a day that has gone by in thirteen years that I didn't regret leaving Fates Haven and everyone in it. Two: I left a piece of myself behind when I left Fates Haven, and I also haven't felt whole since. And three: I don't have nightly fantasies about what our lives would be like right now if I'd stayed."

Harry held Jax's gaze and refused to look away. To the

chorus of Tomlyn's chuckles, Jax stepped close, his hand cupping her cheek.

"Number three," he answered in a soft whisper.

"Very well done," Tomlyn complimented. "I suppose that will have to do . . . and now for my end of that bargain."

With a wave of his hand, an old, leather-bound book appeared on his desk. It took Herculean effort for Jax and Harry to part and refocus on the old fae.

"For your fact-finding purposes, my dear." Tomlyn held the thick book out to her and paused before setting it in her hands. "And do I have your promise that in payment for this loan, one future favor yet to be named?"

"As long as that favor doesn't include harming anyone or performing anything illegal in both the supernatural and human worlds, then yes," Harry agreed.

The old fae nodded, gently resting the book in her hands. It was a lot lighter than it looked, something she suspected was magically related. "I should warn . . . keep the knowledge of your possession of that tome to only those who you literally trust with your life. There are those within fae society who would kill to keep the secrets that you may find in that book."

"Noted." Harry nodded to the fae, careful not to thank him as per Gavin's orders. To give thanks implies a debt owed. "Should we bring it back here when we're done?"

He waved his hand in dismissal. "The book will find its way back here once you're finished. No need to physically return it. Now that the business side of things is finished . . . would the two of you like to be my esteemed guests for the evening?"

"That's a generous offer, Tomlyn, but I think we're heading back to Fates Haven for some light reading . . . and answer finding."

"Then be gone with you, Harlow Pierce and Alpha Jaxon Atwood. I sincerely hope you find the answers to your questions and find your elusive fae shifter."

The elevator doors opened. On their way down, Harry was a blended mix of an entirely different set of emotions and only fraction of them had to do with the book in her hands.

That game . . .

Or more specifically, Jax's choices for his truths and lie . . .

Her first instinct was to dismiss them, but the fae would've easily—and gladly—called out any additional lies had he sensed them, which meant that every syllable had been true. Just like the words she repeated back to him.

The closer they got to Jax's truck, the more the nerves won out, exacerbated by the silence. When Jax opened the passenger side door, she dropped her hand on top of his.

They both looked where they touched. Neither spoke or moved for what felt like a million heartbeats.

Embarrassment flooded her, and she pulled back, but Jax's fingers caught hers and her gaze snapped to his.

The heat in his eyes nearly melted her right on the spot, imprisoning her right on the spot. "Did you mean it? Did you mean what you said during that damn game?"

Harry swallowed a large lump in her throat. "Pretty sure Tomlyn would've called me out on it if I didn't, don't you think?"

"You spent thirteen years thinking that Elodie and I were Fated . . ." Jax's chest heaved.

"And . . . ?"

"And you still dreamed about a future in Fates Haven? *Our* future?" He eased her back against the side of his truck, one large hand propped by her head. "Answer me, sweet pea. No bullshit. No runaround."

"Every night," she admitted breathlessly. "It was the one constant in my life after leaving."

Jax's gaze drifted all over her face, dropping to her mouth, where she unconsciously licked her lips. "Every night."

"Without fail. You're not the only one who felt like a piece of themselves has been missing, Jax . . . assuming what you said back there was true."

"Pretty sure Tomlyn would've called me out on it if it wasn't, don't you think?" He volleyed her own words back at her, whispering them as his mouth coasted a breath above the shell of her ear.

Harry sighed, eyes closing as she let out an involuntary whimper. "Jax. Please."

"Please what, sweet pea?" His hand cupped her chin, gently steering her face toward his. "I need to hear the words, Harlow. In explicit detail."

"Kiss me." Her need overrode every other thought.

"Do you want me to only kiss you?"

She shook her head.

"What else do you want, baby?" Jax's golden gaze searched hers.

"You. I want *you*."

Harry lost track of time; and for a moment, she thought she'd asked for too much. She wouldn't blame him for keeping his distance, for being unwilling to take that chance.

Jax dipped his head with aching slowness, the anticipation of what was to come killing her in small increments. Afraid to move for fear she'd wake up and find this all a dream, she held her breath until the first tender caress of his lips over hers . . . and then when his mouth came in for a deeper exploration, she could breathe for the first time in forever.

They moved as one, mouths crashing together in a searingly hot give and take, bodies flush together and tongues dancing; it felt like she'd taken her first big gulp of air in thirteen years. Jax pressed her firmer against the side of the truck and Harry angled her body, eagerly dragging him as close as possible. It wasn't close enough, and she signaled her displeasure with a small groan.

"Your place or mine?" Jax temporarily pulled his mouth from hers only to trail it along the length of her neck in a series of nips and caresses.

"Yours." Harry fisted her fingers through his hair and brought his mouth back. "And I'll use my descry magic to make sure there are no speed traps along the way."

Jax's mouth pulled up into a smirk. "Love the way you think."

His big hands gripped her waist and easily deposited her in the passenger seat, and while he made his way around to the driver's side, Harry sent a silent thank you to the goddess that Elodie had forced her into the barely there sexy panties.

16

Boob Tape

With his eyes fastened on the road ahead of them, Jax drove as if the king of hell himself was riding his bumper. He'd anticipated a lot of things happening when Gavin first told them about the fae club, but he hadn't expected *this*.

This errant thought happened when Harry had walked down the newly refurbished Pierce House steps in that sinful dress and fuck-me heels . . . but that's all it had been. A thought. Maybe a wish. One he hadn't anticipated coming true this side of reality.

It didn't go beyond his notice that this was the exact thing he'd told himself over and over again couldn't happen. It wasn't smart for a number of reasons, but hell if he could recall any right now, his brain—and other anatomical parts—too focused on the fact that they'd been without Harlow Pierce for too damn long.

He'd worry about the consequences later. Right now it was all he could do to remain on his side of the lane as he twisted and turned through the mountainous roads back up to his cabin.

Harry's silence from the passenger seat didn't go unnoticed and as he brought the car to a stop right in front of his porch and parked, he took a cleansing breath before sliding his attention toward her.

She nibbled the bottom corner of her lip, her left leg slightly bouncing as it used to do when nerves hit. He slid his palm over her knee, his touch soothing the motion.

Her big purple eyes turned toward him as she settled her hand over his.

That one small point of contact propelled a zap of heat through his entire body that would've brought him to his knees if he'd been standing.

"If you've changed your mind, I can turn this truck right around and take you back to Nora's." He held his breath and hoped like hell she turned down the offer.

"Did you change your mind?"

"Fuck no."

She released a breathless laugh. "Neither did I."

He nodded once, forcing himself to remain in his seat and not haul her over on his lap. "And just so we're perfectly, one-hundred-percent clear with what's about to happen . . ."

"I told you to bring me here so we can have hot, naked fun time in a rustic cabin that may as well have been built specifically for hot, naked fun time in the woods."

"Well, not specifically," Jax teased.

Fuck . . . *this was happening.*

He was out of his seat and at her side of the truck before she fully opened her door. Not waiting for her to navigate the step down, he plucked her off the seat and gently tossed her into a fireman's carry.

With a squeal, she braced her hands on his ass as he bounded up the steps. "Why am I getting a sense of déjà vu? If I didn't know any better, I'd say you have an inner caveman to go along with the cougar, Jaxon Atwood."

"Only a caveman for you, sweetheart." He fumbled with his keys, fighting to open the door one-handed.

"Need some help?" She giggled softly.

"In five minutes, I'll be fucking those giggles out of you, babe." He delivered a playful smack to her ass that had her sucking in a quick breath.

"Promises, promises, Jax. I hope you can deliver."

Finally inside, he kicked the door closed and slowly dragged Harry off his shoulder and against his body. The second her feet touched the floor, he pushed her back against the door. Her mouth was on his in seconds, and he didn't waste a moment.

Running his hands down her hips, he reached the short hem of her dress and gripping the silky fabric, coasted it and his fingers up the sides of her thighs and over her ass. He tore his mouth from hers with a groan and seared a path of hot kisses toward that delicate spot just beneath her ear.

"You're wearing a thong, sweet pea?" He gave her earlobe a playful nip. "It's a damn good thing I didn't know this before walking into that club, or we never would've made it there."

Harry panted with her hands fisted in his hair. "It was deemed necessary and I was outvoted. And, if I'm entirely honest, I'm surprised they haven't melted off me by now. They're pretty fragile."

"Do you like them?"

"Not particularly, no."

"Good. Then you won't yell at me when I do this." With a firm tug, he ripped the delicate sides and tossed the undies somewhere to the side. When he brought his hand back between her legs, the hot, wet heat of her pussy welcomed his fingers.

Eyes closing on a sigh, she tilted her head back against the door. "Oh my goddess, Jax. That feels . . . oh."

He slowly caressed one finger through her wet slit and over the already hard nub of her clit. She sucked in an audible breath as her hips canted forward, silently urging him to do it again. "How does this feel, sweet pea? Tell me."

"Good. So, so good."

"Only good?" He dipped his finger into her snug channel and her body immediately gripped it. "Then I don't think I'm doing this right."

"If this is you doing it wrong, then I don't think I'll survive you doing it right."

He chuckled, adding a second finger and slowly pumping it in time with her hips, using his thumb to brush her clit with every entry. Slow and steady, he savored the feel of her body tightening around his digits.

"Jax." Harry pulled his mouth back to hers with a growl. "I need more. Please."

"Do you want to come?" He nipped her bottom lip, praying like hell she said yes, because, damn it, he wanted to watch her face when he made her fall apart.

"Yes! Goddess, yes."

"Do you want to come on my hand, my tongue, or my cock, baby?"

"All of them."

He could have her coming in two seconds with his fingers, but he wanted to savor this first orgasm, to reacquaint himself with the taste of her. "Tongue first it is."

With a low growl, he guided her legs around his waist and walked them toward his bedroom, never taking his lips off hers until he slowly deposited her in the center of his bed. Chest heaving and skin pink as little blossoms, she stared up at him with heavy need, need he knew was reflected right back.

"Fuck, I can't wait to taste you." He reached for the hem of her dress, ready to toss it aside with the thongs.

"Wait."

"What's wrong?" Her wide, panicked eyes stopped him cold as he studied her face and the sudden uncertainty. "You have to tell me what I—"

"It's nothing you did." She glanced down her body. "It's just . . . it's been thirteen years and a PCOS diagnosis since we've done this. I'm not exactly the same person. Under this scrap of silk, I have tape holding everything in place. Literally."

Jax eased out a relieved breath. Slowly gliding his hand up her torso and toward her breast, he cupped the weight in his palm and left a trail of kisses from her cleavage and up to her waiting mouth.

"Neither of us is the way we were before." He teased her mouth with a slow, exploratory kiss. "But do you know what that means?"

"What?" Her chest rose and fell, voice breathless.

"It means we get the thrill of rediscovering each other all over again." Hands easing her thighs apart, he traveled back down her body, smirking as she released a train of soft curses. "You said something about needing to come."

"Oh, my goddess, yes." With her hand on the back of his head, she guided him exactly where she wanted him.

They had the same destination, and with a slow, soft swipe to her center, her taste burst on his tongue like sweet ambrosia. He wasn't so sure of his thoughts on heaven, but if it existed, Harlow Pierce was his.

* * *

HARRY NEEDLESSLY HELD Jax's head in position because he wasn't going anywhere except driving her quickly toward release. Her other hand, fisted in the sheets, anchored her to the bed. The man took his time, dragging his tongue slowly through her folds only to play with her clit with the tip of his tongue.

Panting, she swiveled her hips in a need to get closer, to urge him a bit faster, but he wasn't having it, continuing at his own torture-tastic pace. He released small growls as he feasted, his tongue slowly bringing her from pleasured hum to bursting rapture.

"Jax . . ." Harry groaned, gently tugging his hair as her body prepped for detonation. "Please."

He simultaneously slid two fingers into her pulsing channel, and gently sucked on her throbbing clit. She erupted, her body bowing, locked in bliss as he alternated between sucks, licks, and deep, hard pumps. Jax stayed with her through it all, never relenting as her body fell apart in the best way possible.

He slowly pulled her back together with soft touches and encouraging murmurs, smirking as her breathing slowly came back to normal. "You taste even better than I remember."

Body practically melting into the mattress, she chuckled.

"Maybe there's something to be said about getting older and wiser."

Grinning, Jax reached for her dress. "Lift your bottom."

Hesitancy made her slow to move, but she relented, watching him eye her breasts as the gravity-defying boob tape came into view. "It's a little tricky to remove. We could leave it."

He shook his head. "I want to see and taste all of you. What do we need to get this off?"

"Do you happen to have coconut oil? It helps soften the adhesive so it's not painful to remove."

Leaning down, he gave her a slow, drugging kiss. "Don't go anywhere. I'll see what I have."

He hustled to the kitchen, opening and closing cabinets in a mad frenzy that made her chuckle. Just as she prepared herself to forego the oil and begin peeling the tape away without, he was back.

"Don't. I don't want you hurting yourself." He tossed a bottle of oil on the mattress, his heated gaze practically devouring the sight of her. "Fuck, you're gorgeous. I can't even tell you how many times I pictured you lying here like this . . . naked in my bed."

"Same . . . except you were always naked, too."

"You want me to level the field a bit?" His lips twitched as he undid the buttons on his black dress shirt one notch at a time.

She nodded, licking her lips. His gaze dropped to action as he popped another button. He did two more before he shrugged out of the thing like a T-shirt, bringing his broad chest and chiseled abs out for her viewing pleasure.

It was like her own personal strip show. A telltale bulge

strained against the fabric of his pants as he reached for his buckle. He unzipped them quickly, dropped them, and kicked them aside.

"Commando?" Harry swallowed a groan. "Always prepared, huh?"

"Just loathe doing laundry, but that seemed to work out in my favor tonight." He slowly slid his hand over his length and it visibly throbbed, the dark red length bouncing from his touch.

He climbed onto the bed, tucking his legs between hers, and reached for the oil. He poured some on his hands before giving her a small dollop, and then they worked together to dissolve the adhesive.

The act shouldn't have felt erotic and yet it did, Jax occasionally leaning in and licking a drop of oil as it rolled over her skin in rivulets. By the time the last of the tape fell away, she was half delirious with the need for another orgasm.

"I need you inside me now, Jax." She ran her hands up his chest and dragged his mouth to hers in a hot, searing kiss.

He rubbed his cock through her dampness, the heat nearly melting them both on contact. "Protection?"

"No unexpected pregnancies anytime soon, and there's nothing healthwise where we'd need a condom."

"Same . . . but are you sure?" He watched her intently for any signs of doubt. "If you'd be more comfortable, it's not a problem to—"

"I'm sure." She guided his mouth down to hers. "We already have a thirteen-year barrier between us, Jaxon Atwood. I don't think we need to add another to the tally."

"Couldn't have said it better myself." He trailed his hand up the inside of her thigh, making her squirm.

Pushing him back until he crouched on his knees, Harry clamped her hands on his shoulders and climbed into his lap, Jax's large hands gripping her waist and guiding the way.

"The time for foreplay is over, Alpha Atwood." She smirked at the arch of his eyebrow and hovered over his hard cock before brushing her mound against it once, then twice. On the third time, the grip on her hips tightened and he slid straight home.

They both groaned, Harry's head dropping back as he stretched her, and then he pulled out and did it over again. It didn't take long to find their rhythm, each working up into a heated frenzy that left them both panting and sweaty.

"Fuck me." Jax growled, his grip tightening as he slammed up into her.

"Pretty sure I already am." Harry rolled her hips faster, falling harder as she tried to get him deeper.

As if sensing what she needed, Jax banded an arm around her waist and flipped them, putting his back on the mattress and her body astride him. Now she felt everything, his cock brushing against that magical spot, and the rub of her mound sensitizing her aching clit.

"That's it, baby." Jax encouraged her hips into movement as he thrust from beneath. "Take it all. Take everything you want. Everything you need. Come on my cock."

"Jax." Her body rippled, pleasure coiling tight in her abdomen.

A strong palm cupped the back of her neck and Jax dragged her mouth to his, tongue spearing past her lips, doing exactly what his cock was doing to her pussy. Harry's fingers latched onto his shoulders as the beginning of her orgasm locked her into place. Beneath her, Jax's thrusts quickened.

They both reached the cliff and jumped off together, Harry's release fueling his own as they plummeted straight into an abyss of pure pleasure . . . and she never wanted to climb back to the surface.

17

Invisible Alien

Harry burrowed into the heated blanket, groaning at the spicy cinnamon scent that tickled her nose. It smelled incredible, a soothing comfort she wanted to wrap herself in and savor until she had no choice but to move, and even then she'd put up a fight.

A pleased hum rolled up her throat as she shifted closer to the intoxicating yummy-smelling source.

Her blanket chuckled, the deep, husky kind that sent a familiar tingle to all her lady bits.

"Well, that's certainly new." A finger slowly skated down her spine and swirled in a delicate pattern just above—and slightly lingering on—the upper half of her left ass cheek.

The tattoo.

Jax, propped up on his side, studied her ink work with his hands as much as he did his gaze. "Is this one of Lenny's?"

"Yeah, but she couldn't—"

"Read it." He transferred his searing gaze to her face, then slowly brought his lips to hers, capturing whatever breath remained in her body in a soft, sensuous kiss. "You good?"

"A pretty significant degree better than good," she hummed.

"No overthinking things?"

"Who can think about anything when your mouth is on me." She pushed him onto his back and followed him down with a kiss when her cell phone rang. She ignored it, and a second later, it beeped with a series of incoming texts.

He chuckled. "Someone's pretty insistent. Sure you don't need to get it?"

"Nope. Whoever it is can wait a few more hours."

Harry's cell went silent only for Jax's to ring, then buzz.

"Oh my goddess, this is not happening." She groaned, reaching for her cell.

Jax chuckled. "What happened to ignoring it for a few more hours?"

"Reality set in and I remembered that's not something the guardian of a teenager can do. You never know if it'll be the police telling you to pick your kid up from the drunk tank."

Behind her, Jax paused. "Tell me that didn't happen."

"Not from the police, but it's no less jarring when it comes from the principal's office and it's because your teenager set fire to an entire chem lab." Harry bypassed the voicemails and went straight to her texts.

> U still w/ Jax? Nora brought
> me to my training sesh at the
> ranch, but he's MIA
> —G

"Crap," Harlow cursed the same time Jax read off his own text, "Shit."

"I have to get up to the main house," Jax added.

They both did, and as Harry searched the floor for her clothes, she remembered her fundamental lack of underpants or bra. Jax came up behind her. Wrapping is arms around her waist, he nuzzled her neck. "You could always stay here naked and wait until I come back."

"While that's a very tempting offer, I'll take the second option."

"And that would be?"

"You don't happen to have something a girl could wear during a walk of unshame, would you?" She cursed herself for asking the moment the words left her lips because she really hoped Jax didn't have some other woman's spare clothes lying around, and then she called herself all kind of names for even thinking it.

It had been thirteen years. She wasn't deluded enough to think there hadn't been anyone since her.

"I could probably find something. Give me a sec." He rummaged through his drawers before pulling out a familiar Fates Haven High T-shirt and a pair of sweatpants. "It's definitely not as flashy as last night's dress, but it should work in a pinch."

"It's perfect." She took his clothes and scurried into the bathroom to freshen up with lightning speed.

As she pulled the T-shirt over her head, she instantly recalled that it had been one of his favorites back in the day, and also one of her favorites to steal. It was soft to the touch, and his pine-fresh scent was practically embedded into the cotton, even still, she noted as she allowed herself a quick sniff.

A small smile worked its way over her lips as she shifted focus to the sweatpants. After rolling up the cuffs and folding down the waist a few times, she drew the drawstring as tight as it went until there was minimal risk of them falling to her ankles. But there was no quick wardrobe fix for shoes, so she regrettably stuffed her feet back into the previous night's heels and called herself fashion forward.

They snuck casual glances back and forth on the quiet drive up to the Alpha House until Nora's yellow hatchback came into view. Two petite forms stood right by the hood and turned their way as he brought the truck to a stop.

Harry didn't know which expression posed the higher risk, Grace's look of cocky assurance or Nora's smirking amusement.

"How do you want to play this?" Jax slid her a questioning look

"No playing." Harry shrugged. "It happened. It's our business. We're both adults, and don't need to explain anything to anyone. You good with that?"

"More than." He nodded.

"Great."

They got out of the truck, Harry clutching Tomlyn's book to her chest and wearing it like a Captain America shield.

Grace, her arms folded over her chest, bounced her gaze from Harry to Jax as he rounded to join them. "Guess we can call off the coast guard search."

Harry lifted her brow. "We're landlocked. There's no coast guard here."

"Fine. Search and Rescue. The Forest Rangers. Smokey Bear. Whoever." Her gaze dropped to the old book in her hands, her sassiness melting away. "Did you get that from the fae guy? He was actually able to help?"

"Yes, and yes and no. According to Tomlyn, no fae shifters remained in this realm after the portals closed."

Grace's shoulders sank. "So that means we're back to square one with knowing absolutely nothing."

"Not necessarily. He was very strategic with what he said and what he didn't say. Just because none stayed, doesn't mean someone or a group of someones didn't return."

"Is that possible?"

Harry held up the old book. "That's what this will hopefully tell us . . . only problem is it's written in Old Fae and that wasn't exactly part of the world languages curriculum at NYU."

"I can help with that," Nora stated proudly.

"You know how to read Old Fae?" Harry asked, surprised. "Since when?"

"No, but I know a spell that might be able to translate it for us, or at least pieces of it. And then you, my dear, can use those descry abilities of yours and possibly locate the information for which we're looking."

"You mean basically search engine the ancient fae book? That almost seems way too easy and I'm not sure I trust it."

"Only way to find out is to try. And there's no time like the present." Nora turned to Jax. "You don't mind if we make use of your glorious porch, do you?"

"Not a bit." He shot a wink Harry's direction before turning toward the teen. "And you and I can work on these super shifter skills you pulled out for Paintball Pandemonium. I'm still not quite sure where you came from. One second you weren't there, and in the next, you were."

Grace shrugged. "I'm not sure why I took you so off guard. I thought I was making a lot of noise."

"Well, let's see if we can replicate it. Devon set up a small obstacle course the other day that would showcase a wide range of shifter abilities."

"Good luck. We'll just be over there." Harry gestured over her shoulder, toward the house.

Harry watched Jax and Grace head toward the field to the right of the horse barn, their heads bent as they talked. When she turned around, she ran into Nora's mischievous smirk.

"Don't," Harry warned, leading the way up.

"Don't what? That's a pretty wide directive. Don't breathe? Don't change my hair color? Don't go out with a former lover to a fae club and appear the next morning wearing said lover's clothing?"

"Can you stop saying *lover*?" Harry grimaced.

"Sweetheart, I didn't get to be my age without knowing my way around a—"

"Stop right there, please and thank you." They settled at the table on the porch, putting the book between them. "So how do we do this?"

"Carefully." Nora hovered her palm over the book, a magical glow slowly trickling down. The book vibrated. "Fae magic isn't always compatible with magic from this realm, so it's always best to tread slowly and lightly and . . ."

Sweat dotted her forehead. Harry nearly told her to stop when she stopped abruptly with a hefty sigh. "There. Take a peek. Let's see if that will make things any easier."

"It worked." Harry carefully flipped page after page, quickly overwhelmed by the amount of information. "Maybe I should've taken this to Gavin."

"Unless Gavin has descry abilities of which I'm not aware, this will actually be the fastest way."

"But I don't even know what I'm looking for."

"Then it's best we get started, don't you think?"

* * *

It was only a matter of time and distance until a smirking Grace opened her mouth. Jax just didn't expect it to be when they were only halfway to the training field.

"Do the two of us need to have a chat, Alpha Atwood?" Grace's tone was as stern as her glare.

"We're about to have quite a few chats, considering I'm ready to put you through the paces. We're seconds away from finding out if all that meditation has been working."

She turned toward him, her arms folded over her chest. "Let's not pretend we don't know what I'm talking about."

"I'm not pretending. I know what you're referring to, but I also know that whatever is or is not happening between Harry and me is just that . . . between *us*." He turned toward her, mimicking her pose. "But I'm glad to see that you have her back. It's admirable. And that protectiveness you're feeling?"

"What about it?"

"Definitely a shifter trait. What do you say about finding out what other shifter traits and abilities you have?"

She narrowed her eyes at him. "You're trying to change the subject."

"And?"

"Fine. It's working. What is it you want me to do, O Master Yoda?"

He chuckled. "Let's start with that popping-up-out-of-thin-air trick, young Padawan."

"I honestly don't know what you're talking about or how

you didn't see me. I was literally like six feet away and practically in your direct sight line. Maybe you were too focused on Harry to see anything else."

"Nice try, but no. My cougar wouldn't have missed you lurking in the wings. He was in prime tracking mode. He would've sensed a second predator if you'd been there."

"Guess your cougar isn't as good at tracking as he thinks," Grace taunted.

Jax's inner mountain lion growled low, not liking the challenge in her tone. He pushed onward, ignoring both him and her smirk. "Let's rewind time back from when you took me off my feet. What were you doing?"

"Following Harry's scent," the teen answered. "I could smell her nerves and her excitement as she worked through the field; and since I wasn't far away from her, I followed."

"And when you found her? What did you notice?"

"She was preoccupied by Maddox and didn't see you coming."

"And?"

"And what?"

"That practically brings us to the moment you took me by surprise. You're leaving something out."

"I don't know what that would be. I found Harry, and almost right away, I saw you stalking toward her. I knew I had to intercept you so she could make it to the flag."

Jax followed her thought train. "And how were you planning on intercepting me?"

"Be quiet. Blend in. Basically, become invisible."

He nodded. "Good. Do it again. Think, feel, and do exactly what you did that day."

He left her in position and drew an *X* in the dirt, marking the approximate location where Harry had stood, and then headed toward his own spot.

"This is ridiculous," Grace complained.

He shot her an Alpha look and she sighed.

"Fine. I'll do it under duress, but it's still ridiculous." She got into position and grumbled again before glancing at the X and back to him. Then, she closed her eyes.

Jax sensed it before his eyes saw it, a shift in the air. Almost a shimmer. It very nearly felt like when Harry or Nora called on their magic, but the two of them were all the way back at the house. This was entirely Grace's doing.

She opened her eyes, staring at him with the gold-flecked eyes belonging to her shifter, and then she shimmered . . .

And disappeared.

Jax's mouth dropped a second before he schooled himself and let his cougar rise closer to the surface.

His animal bristled, sensing something other nearby but unable pin down the trajectory, and neither could he. He glanced left and right, and finally, focused on the ground. There, six feet away and slowly closing the distance between them, *sneaker prints.*

"Stop," Jax directed, and the steps stopped. "Now come closer."

The steps started up again. "Why are you looking at me like that?" Grace's voice drifted in the air.

"Actually, I'm not looking at you like fucking anything because I can't see you," Jax snorted, his amazement rising by the second.

"Excuse me?" The air shimmered, and a moment later, Grace slowly materialized, first, her feet and legs and then her upper body. When her head blinked into existence, her wide eyes stared right at him. "What the hell do you mean you couldn't see me?"

"You shimmered and then suddenly you weren't there, but you were."

"What?" Grace squealed. "Are you telling me I went invisible?"

"I don't think so. I think it was more like a camouflage." He thought hard, not realizing they'd drawn Harry and Nora's attention.

"Is everything okay?" Harry face was etched with worry. "What's wrong? What happened?"

"I turned freaking invisible!" Grace screeched. "I'm a freaking invisible alien!"

"Camouflaged," Jax corrected. "She thought about coming at me and being unseen, and then she shimmered away, coming back again when she lost her focus."

"What the hell is the difference?"

"There's a big difference," Harry added. "Do you think you could do it again?"

"Again? I don't know how I did it in the first place!"

Jax watched a contemplative Harry. "What are you thinking?"

"I'm thinking if she's invisible, my descry magics won't be able to find her, but if it's camouflaged, it will," Harry turned to Grace. "So, do you think you could do it again?"

Grace muttered under her breath but grudgingly got into position. Jax did the same, and a few seconds later, they all watched the teenager slowly slink away. Harry's palm lit up with a little golden compass, and she walked around the spot where Grace had been last seen, a smile on her face.

"She's definitely still there." Harry chuckled. "I have to say, I like this skill a hell of a lot better than the fire one."

Grace shimmered back, a smirk on her own face. "This would've made sneaking out at night so much easier."

Harry's smile vanished along with magical compass. "Still trackable, kiddo."

Grace shrugged. "It's still a cool trick. Do you think this will help you find something in that fae book? I mean, how many fae shifters have the ability to camouflage?"

"I don't know, but I'm about to find out. You keep up the good work and I'll get back to reading."

Harry's gaze caught Jax's right before she turned, and he couldn't help but wink. A pink hue quickly rose high on her cheeks and he grinned, watching her walk away, her hips swaying.

A loud throat clear turned his attention back to a scowling teenager. "I'm thinking maybe we do need to have that talk after all, Alpha Atwood."

"A talk about what exactly?"

"A talk about what will happen if Harry gets hurt with so much as a splinter on your watch . . . because not only can I literally scorch your behind so bad you won't be comfortable sitting for months, but I can now do it without you seeing it coming."

Jax barked out a laugh. "Warning given and received, Sparks. Now let's get back to work and see if there are any other hidden talents buried under all that teenage snark."

18

Supernatural Avengers

Harry could now cross being witchnapped off her bucket list, although Nora, sitting in the passenger seat of Marie's Sugar Tits delivery van, assured them it was for Fates Festival purposes and nothing nefarious.

Her ass disagreed. One more jostle like the one before and she'd either break her tailbone or crack a filling. Blindfolded and without the ability to tell which way the van was about to lurch, she tensed, her muscles already aching.

The van dipped unexpectedly; and with a curse, Harry gripped the closest thing . . . the thigh next to her.

Jax's warm hand slid over hers as he leaned closer, filling her senses with his spicy musk. "Have to say that when I envisioned us using blindfolds, it wasn't in quite this way."

"Jax! We are not alone despite what the sensory deprivation says!"

He chuckled. "Relax. They all can't hear me."

"But enough of us can, thank you very much," Silas volleyed

back. "Listening to your horrid attempts at flirting is excruciating."

"And he can identify horrid flirting attempts because his are even worse," Elodie quipped from Harry's other side.

"You've never been on the receiving end of my flirtation, angel eyes, so how would you know?"

"And that's something I'm thankful for every day of my life."

Harry groaned. "Do you see what you started?"

"Who? Me?" Jax's low chuckle shook his shoulders. Their friends continued their back-and-forth, members from both teams joining the trash talk. "I'm suddenly very thankful that Nora stuffed both our teams in the back of this seatless van because if she hadn't, it would be pretty damn difficult to do this."

Jax's large hand slipped around the back of her head and hauled her lips to his. Fingers flexed in the front of his shirt for support, she held on and enjoyed each and every thrust of his tongue, combining it with her own, and let everything around them melt away into the ether.

She lost track of time, only becoming aware of the abrupt silence when she heard a soft pleasured hum—her own—echo throughout the van.

"Those better be *I'm gonna kick the other team's ass* moans," Elodie warned, "because if they're not, I'll be the one kicking asses."

Harry swallowed a chuckle.

"Worth it," Jax whispered against her mouth, giving her one last hard kiss before pulling away. "Definitely worth it."

"All right, everyone, less smooching and more paying attention," Nora interjected. "We're moments from letting team Big Bads out at their designated drop zone, and soon after, team Fearsome Four. As a reminder, your groups are not to remove your blindfolds or begin your challenge in any way until your beeper alarm sounds. Once it does, your team has until dawn to make it back to the Starlight Gazebo . . . and I stress, your *team*. This isn't a one-for-all scenario. All four team members must be present to consider the challenge complete."

The van came to an abrupt stop and people shuffled.

"We'll try not to embarrass you by being too fast," Jax boasted a second before the brush of his lips feathered along her cheek. "Good luck."

The door closed and they were on the move again. When they came to another stop, a firm touch guided her from the back of the van.

"Good luck, girls." Marie cheered them on. "And don't tell my grandson, but I've got my money—literally—on you four. Don't let an old woman down."

A door closing and engine revving told them Nora and Marie had left them alone in the middle of nowhere.

"I wonder how long until we—" Grace was cut off by the beep of an alarm. "Never mind."

They all shed their blindfolds and immediately scanned their surroundings.

"Any ideas?" Harry tried identifying any landmarks, but every tree looked like the one next to it and what she very loosely considered a trail, which the delivery van must have used, disappeared as if it never existed.

Lenny huffed, catching on to the same thing she did. "Looks like Nora thought of everything. We can't even follow the tire tracks. Anyone have any clue where we are?"

"None. Elodie?" Harry asked.

"On it." The angel shed her backpack, which held the scant few items each were allowed to bring on the drop, and then whipped off her shirt, revealing her sports bra. In another blink, her wings erupted. Nearly eight feet across and a beautiful array of ivory and silver, they were a breathtaking sight every damn time.

Grace's mouth gaped. "That is fucking awesome."

Harry chuckled knowingly. "It never gets old."

"Give me a sec and I'll have a bird's-eye view." Elodie pushed off the ground and shot through the trees. Her curses trickled down from the thick foliage along with a few errant branches. "Shit. That's going to leave a mark."

"Problem up there, El?" Harry glimpsed the angel's wings through the branches, catching a feather as it floated toward them.

"Almost there." Twigs and branches snapped and finally Elodie released an annoyed huff. "We're gonna need that little glowing magical compass because I don't recognize squat. Like not a damn thing. Where the hell did they drop us? Wyoming?"

They'd been afraid of this. Allowing them to use their gifts seemed all too easy for those who could gain an aerial view and quickly spot landmarks. Elodie fought her way back down, sacrificing a few more feathers while Harry heated up her palms and pulled that little thread of magic from her core.

The familiar misty compass pulsed as she turned right and dimmed as she shifted left. "Looks like we're heading right."

With bolstered confidence, Elodie took the lead and set the pace, Harry guiding them into turns as her compass piloted her. Grace hung close to the rear, a contemplative look on her face.

"You doing okay?" Harry sent her a concerned look. She'd been a little quiet since seeing Elodie sprout feathers and take off. "I won't lie. You being quiet is a little eerie. What's up?"

"Just thinking."

"About anything in particular or about everything?"

Grace shrugged. "Why do you think it's so difficult finding out anything about my father?"

"Both from what Gavin said, and then after meeting Tomlyn, the fae have always held their secrets pretty close their hearts. I don't know if that's for any reason other than it's what they've done for thousands of years." Harry studied Grace a little more carefully. "Why?"

"So you don't think it's because I could be something . . . dangerous?"

Harry dragged her to a gentle stop for a moment, letting her compass dissipate. "You are not dangerous, Gracie."

"Except that I kinda am . . . especially when I get angry and my fire gets all temperamental and—"

"And I got pegged in the head with a stuffed pig and Lenny almost had to make an urgent care visit to get a LEGO removed from her nasal cavity when my magic went all wonky. The last time you had problems with your fire was that first day on the ranch, right?"

"Yeah . . . I guess. The meditation seems to help a lot, but you haven't been able to find anything in that fae book and I can't help wondering if there's a reason for it."

"There is a reason," she said seriously. "Because Nora can only keep it translated for so long and I can only read so fast. There's a lot of information in there, and I don't want to miss something important because I'm skim reading."

"So you don't think it's for any other reason?" Grace bit her lower lip.

"Gracie." Harry cupped her cheeks and pulled the teen's attention to her. "I'm going to tell you something that Aunt Nora once told me. A wielded gift is no more dangerous than the wielder who possesses it."

"Meaning?"

"Meaning any gift has both the potential to do good or bad. In which direction it goes relies completely on the gift wielder. Stay true to your heart, and you'll never need to worry."

"You sure about that?"

"Without a doubt. You, my sarcastic, snarky Grace Taylor, have a heart so steeped in goodness that you have nothing to fear."

Tears welled at the corner of the teen's eyes, and before Harry was prepared for it, Grace's arms wrapped tightly around her waist, crushing her in a hug that made breathing challenging. Harry savored the moment and returned the hug.

"Thank you, Harry." Grace's words sounded muffled. "I know I can be a brat a lot of the time, and I don't tell you nearly enough, but thank you. For everything . . . especially for bringing me to Fates Haven."

Harry sucked down her own surge of emotions. "No thanks, needed, kiddo. Although it's nice hearing that you're self-aware enough to call yourself a brat sometimes."

They both chuckled, earning themselves a glare from the angel leading the charge.

"I really hate to break up this touching moment," Elodie interjected, hands on her ample hips, "but we have a team of egotists to beat. Harry . . . light 'em back up, please."

Harry flashed Grace a wink and recalled her magical compass. They got back on track, cursing their drop zone when they trekked up the third steep incline that left even Elodie a little breathless. At the next summit, they stopped for a drink and a quick rest.

Harry took a bite of her power bar when something sucker punched her in the gut. Granola spewed everywhere as she sucked in a breath, doubling over as a secondary wallop of something yanked on her magical core and brought her to her knees.

Grace was at her side in an instant. "Lenny! Elodie! I think Harry's choking or something! What do we do?"

"Not choking." She wheezed, waving off El's Heimlich arms prepped to wrap around her midsection.

"What's happening?" Lenny guided her onto a rock.

Hand clenched to her chest, Harry fought to slow each breath and tried—and probably failed—to keep the panic off her face. "I don't know. It's . . . tugging."

Grace hovered at her side, worried. "What's tugging?"

Lenny's gaze dropped to Harry's pulsing hands. "Magic. *Look.*"

They all glanced at her hands, now alit with twin pulsing orbs. In her right, was the familiar golden compass that directed the way toward Fates Haven and Havenhood Park . . . and in the other was an entirely different glowing compass.

One Harry most definitely had not conjured.

It didn't look like anything she'd ever created before with a brassy antique sheen and a brighter, lighter-blue-tinged glow. It pointed in the exact opposite direction of Fates Haven, and unless she was mistaken, toward Witch's Peak.

Harry shook the hand with the weird compass, but it held on strong, not so much as flickering with the movement. "It won't go away."

Ignoring the pulsing magical waves, Grace clutched her hands. "Close your eyes and take a deep breath. Then slowly picture your special quiet space . . . a place where you feel nothing but peace."

"You think I can meditate the strange away?" Harry quipped wryly.

"Flinging your hands around doesn't seem to be doing the trick. What do you have to lose?"

Point made ... and not without a severely heavy dose of irony.

Following the teen's direction, she focused on soothing her frazzled nerves. It was a lot harder than she anticipated, but eventually her heart rate slowed and a warm cocoon of safety wrapped around her. That safety cocoon slowly transformed into a pair of arms.

Jax's arms.

Jax was her peaceful space. Her safe space. He had been when they'd been teenagers, and there wasn't a doubt in her mind that it would be the same when they were gray haired and zooming around on motorized scooters.

"It's working." Elodie's soft encouragement urged her to keep going.

"Of course it's working," Grace said without a doubt.

Harry took another few breaths before slowly opening her eyes and assessing her magic. Its familiar warmth pulsed like a beacon and was back to where it was supposed to be. Alone. No second strand of mystery magic anywhere in the vicinity.

"That was really fucking weird." Harry's voice shook. "It almost felt like another magical source piggybacking on mine, and it was pretty damn insistent that it wanted me to follow it. Its will was almost all-consuming. It had ... attitude."

"How do you feel now? Do you still have the urge to follow it?" Lenny still looked concerned.

Harry mentally slid her mind down her own cord of magic and felt it vibrate. "No. It's just my magic in there."

"It's probably that general wonkiness that has been going around Fates Haven," Elodie suggested. "Which means maybe we're closer to town than we previously thought."

Harry wasn't sure it was as simple as that, but it did make sense, and she also had the feeling they were closer to the town limits than they'd been earlier. But that remnant sensation of *other* still had a firm hold on her and wouldn't let go.

"I'm sure that's probably it," she heard herself agree.

They all remained huddled around her.

Grace's head snapped left and her eyes flickered gold as she listened to something in the distance. "I hear the Big Bads not that far away . . . and they realize they're not far away from Fates, too."

"Then we better start moving our asses." Harry climbed back to her feet with a groan.

"Are you sure you're okay?"

Harry flicked her familiar golden compass into existence, much faster than she'd been able to before. "Never been better."

She regretted those words an hour later when huffing, puffing, missing a shoe, and dripping with sweat and mud of a questionable origin, they stumbled over the town limits. Starlight Gazebo was lit up with an array of white fairy lights and calling like a gorgeous beacon of hope.

People lined Fates Boulevard, all cheering and waving streamers. A roar erupted in the distance—Jax.

"Let's go!" Harry hobbled as fast as she could, dropping her backpack as Elodie, grabbing Lenny under her arms, went airborne and lifted the screeching seer off the ground.

Harry cursed, shooting a look over her shoulder to see Cougar Jax standing in the middle of the road, Silas, Gavin, and Maddox at his side like the damn supernatural avengers. "We're not making it."

"Hell, yes, we are! We haven't gotten this far to lose now." Grace stopped in front of her and gave her her back. "Hop on!"

"What?" she scoffed. "Honey, no. I have like a hundred pounds on you."

"Trust me, I can do it. And we'll get there before Jax and the others. Just get on." Grace's eyes glinted in the moonlight, that gorgeous golden hue peeking through the brown.

Harry barely had her hand on the teen's shoulders when Grace practically flipped her onto her back with inhuman strength, and then vroom. As if Grace had sprouted wings, she zoomed them past the street-lined crowd and even beat a breathless Elodie and still-screaming Lenny.

Harry and Grace toppled into the gazebo in a gale of laughter with Lenny and Elodie close behind.

"If you ever force my feet to leave the ground, I will pluck all your feathers while you sleep and start calling you Naked Chicken," Lenny threatened the angel.

The seer's stern look vanished and they all broke into fits of giggles. They were still laughing as Jax and the rest of the Big Bad team ambled up the steps, Silas looking highly irritated to have come in second place.

Harry glanced up as a large shadow blocked the glowing moon and looked into Jax's amused expression. He now was on two feet and wore loose gray sweatpants and no shirt. She let her eyes soak in the gorgeousness.

"We won." She grinned.

"Yes, you did." Chuckling, he extended a hand and helped her to her feet in one strong tug. Their bodies collided in a warm, muddy squish. "Please tell me that you just tripped and fell into a vat of mud."

"I *did* trip . . . and I'm pretty sure it's at least seventy-five percent mud."

"And the other twenty-five percent?"

"I prefer to think of it as victory."

19

Are You . . . Chicken?

Hot showers—by definition—should be deemed a miracle because after accepting the Night Drop win, Harry headed back to Pierce House and showered no less than ten times before collapsing on her bed in a haze of exhaustion and sore muscles.

It hadn't been a dreamless sleep, or terribly restful. Instead, her mind replayed the moment back in the woods when her magic surged and picked up a hitchhiker. Every time she found her thoughts wandering to it, she caught herself subconsciously rubbing her sternum, still feeling the occasional shadow tugs.

Witch's Peak was the place that fueled all spooky tales told by the people of Fates Haven.

Have something peculiar happen? Its cause originated at Witch's Peak.

Experience a run of bad luck? The way the moon bounced off Witch's Peak was to blame.

But as far as Harry knew, no one had ever ventured up to Witch's Peak, all the stories and hearsay enough to keep both the superstitious and the not superstitious far, far away.

Eventually giving up on the idea of a nap, she slipped into a breezy sundress and sandals and found a note from Nora telling her that she and Grace had already left for the Midnight Moviethon at Havenhood Park. She briefly considered the merits of skipping the event altogether for an hour of quiet time, but quickly vetoed the idea, already knowing that if she didn't show, it wouldn't be long before someone knocked on the door and dragged her there anyway.

Plus, she'd missed too much of Fates Haven life already and didn't want to miss a second more.

A small smirk on her face, she headed out the front door, momentarily panicked that she'd fall through the rotten beams. But there was no ominous creak, no groan. She glanced down at the fresh boards and even did a little bounce, surprised not to feel even an inch of give.

A deep chuckle turned her toward Jax, leaning casually against a newly built railing. "How did you do this in a day, and how did I not hear you doing it?"

"I had a few extra sets of hands, and Nora placed some kind of silence charm around the house perimeter so you and Grace could rest."

"And you didn't need to rest after all of last night's fun?" Harry teased.

"What can I say? I have great stamina—as you have found out for yourself."

Excited nerves fluttered in her stomach as she slowly descended the new stairs. Jax's gaze slid over her body with each step, warming every inch of skin not already heated by the humid night. "Were you volunteered to make sure I showed up tonight?"

"I actually did volunteer." His lips twitched. "Nora was having such a good time telling Sanjay 'I told you so' about the tourist flow picking up that I didn't want to tear her away. And Grace and Devon were hunting for their perfect movie-watching spot."

Her eyes narrowed at the mention of the teens, making Jax laugh. "He really is a good kid."

"I guess only time will actually tell."

She stopped on the step above him, the position putting them eye level as she fought for something to say. They hadn't spent any time alone since the night they'd gone to Tomlyn's— and back to his cabin. And they sure as hell hadn't talked about what happened, or what it meant.

Not that she knew the answer to that herself, or even what she hoped it meant. Hope led to disappointment, and she wasn't sure she could handle that right now with everything else hovering over their heads like an anvil-weighted question mark.

They followed the trail of music and laughter toward the park. A few people mingled and talked, neighbors with strangers and vice versa. But it being a few minutes until midnight, most already found their perfect viewing spots on the lawn and settled in for a double feature film showing.

Jax hadn't been wrong. The park was packed.

Even more people had showed up to watch the outcome of the Night Drop than there'd been for the Paintball Pandemonium showdown. Shoppers hopped in and out of the boulevard boutiques, open late to take advantage of the bevy of new potential customers. Harry lost count of how many carried the signature pink Sugar Tits boxes. The sight of her hometown flourishing brought a smile to her lips.

"Looks like we're being summoned." Jax touched her elbow and gestured across the street, where Elodie and Lenny waved from the Starlight Gazebo.

Jax and Harry dodged the traffic and headed across the grassy knoll toward her friends, and realized El and Lenny weren't alone. Sitting on a blanket at the bottom of the steps were Grace and Devon, the teens giving them small waves.

Jax chuckled at her sigh of relief.

But what surprised Harry was the presence of a brooding Silas. Sitting opposite Elodie and almost mirroring the angel in stiff posture and painful grimace, the demon stared ahead as if the movie had already started.

Gavin and Maddox sat on the steps, bookends to Lenny, who winked at her. "Evidently the best seats in the house were reserved for the Night Drop's winning team."

Elodie snorted and slid a unsubtle glare toward Silas. "But for some reason they showed up, too."

"And she didn't put up a real big fuss about them sticking around, so . . ." Lenny smirked.

Elodie scoffed but didn't deny it.

The movie screen flickered to life and the rest of the crowd slowly settled in, Harry climbing the steps into the gazebo. She and Jax cozied up on the built-in bench as the first film—a mix between a cartoon and live action—flickered to life.

A few minutes into the movie and her mind wandered to what happened on the mountain.

Jax's arm brushed hers as he stretched his out behind her shoulders. "You've been a little quiet . . . especially for someone who's halfway to securing a win."

Harry smirked. "We may as well have the win in the bag, you know. You and the others should start practicing your dance moves."

"I think we're good to hold off practicing for a bit yet, but seriously. You've got that look in your eye like you're faced with a puzzle that you can't solve as fast as you'd like."

"I guess you could say that. I've been feeling a little off since being back in Fates Haven, but when we were in the middle of the Night Drop, something weird happened."

"What?"

"My magic sensed another's, and it was eerily familiar and yet nothing like mine. I don't know how to explain it."

Jax's brow furrowed. "All the way out there? They dropped us off in the middle of literal nowhere—nothing and no one for miles."

"And yet . . ."

His fingers slid toward the back of her neck, gently massaging the tight muscles. "Did you talk to Nora about it?"

She shook her head. "Not yet. She's been busy making sure Operation Fates Festival is a success. Plus, I don't want to bother her if it turns out to be nothing but my own magical wonkiness."

"Wonkiness?" He chuckled. "Is that an actual term?"

"It is in my world."

"Maybe we should go back there and check it out?"

Harry spun her gaze to his. "You heard the part where I said it was eerie, right? And I had a little time to recover, but in the moment, it nearly scared the piss out of me. That tug and its antique little compass wanted to send me up toward Witch's Peak."

"Are you . . . chicken?" He waggled his eyebrows, looking

so ridiculous she couldn't help but laugh as he quoted a line from what had been one of their favorite movie franchises to binge-watch.

"This isn't *Back to the Future*, and I am not Marty McFly. Calling me chicken will not goad me into doing something potentially stupid."

"So you're saying you don't want me to go with you?"

"I didn't say that at all. I'm saying that we'd both be pretty stupid to go there, alone or together."

"So when are we going?" Jax smirked knowingly.

She swat at his chest playfully and he caught her hand and held it, both their gazes dropping to where his fingers caressed hers. Neither pulled away. Linking their fingers together, he pulled their joined hands into his lap where they stayed for the rest of the first movie.

Harry could honestly say she had no idea what the plot was, because she couldn't tear her gaze or her attention away from the man whose side she was deliciously pressed into.

* * *

MORE DEAD ENDS.

Harry prepped to throw the book in front of her into the nearest trash can when two large hands carefully plucked it from her grasp.

"Let's not take our frustrations out on the ancient fae tome," Gavin admonished, gently placing the book back on Nora's kitchen table.

When more searching and spell casting had wielded nothing in the way of results—or useful information, she'd sent an SOS to the research big guns. For the last two hours while Jax and Grace "'trained" outside in the guise of weeding and landscaping the Pierce House garden, she and Gavin poured over each page of Tomlyn's book.

"I'm starting to think Tomlyn knew we wouldn't find any answers in here and that's why he agreed to let us borrow it." She rubbed her fingers along her temples as if able to will her brewing headache away.

"Tomlyn may be a twisted bastard, but he wouldn't have loaned you the book just to get a few jollies."

"So you think there's something in here we can use?"

"I think that Tomlyn chooses his words extremely carefully, and if he told you that the book would remain in your possession until you found the path to the answers you seek, then, yes, I think the clue is still buried in here. Somewhere."

"And there's no way you think those answers are playing hide-and-seek? Because I feel like the harder I try to find them, the more elusive they get."

Gavin laughed dryly. "Knowing the fae—and Tomlyn—that's exactly what's happening . . . but from everything I've heard about you from Jax and the others, you're not the type to let that deter you."

"You're right. It's not. I just may gripe about it for a bit." The faint sounds of laughter from the backyard garden pulled a small smile to her lips. "And she's the main reason why failure is not an option. Now, if Fate could just give us a damn break. I'm not even talking about a major one. A minor crack would do. I can work with a crack."

Harry stood to refresh her chamomile tea when the floor moved and she tripped over her own two feet.

Gavin zoomed toward her with his vampiric speed and caught her arm before she head-planted on the corner of the kitchen counter. "You good?"

"Sorry. Just . . ." The floor rumbled again, literally shaking the ground beneath their feet. "What the hell is that? Is that an earthquake?"

Panic for Grace washed over her. Grabbing the book from the table, she hightailed it to the back door with the vampire hot on her heels, already calling out Grace's name.

Harry skidded to a stop on the back porch, her eyes wide and book clasped tightly to her chest. Gavin came to an abrupt stop at her side, the vampire's mouth gaping, all his British composure shattered as he babbled, unable to form any actual words.

It wasn't an earthquake that had shaken the ground.

Towering over a slightly bemused, and oddly proud look-ing, Jax, was a massive, winged animal that Harry had only read about in fantasies and seen in her *Game of Thrones* binge watches.

A massive gold-scaled dragon stood in the center of what was once Nora's weed-ridden garden. Very much living. Very, very large. And very much in possession of Grace's golden shifter eyes.

"Holy. Dragon. Tails." Harry clutched the book to her chest like a security blanket.

The golden dragon swung her head toward Harry, her mas-sive mouth dropping open to reveal a double row of gleamingly sharp teeth in what almost constituted a smile. Dragon-Grace released a puff of air, and her tongue lolled out, making her look like an overgrown dragon-esque puppy.

Jax laughed despite being so close that one dragon stomp could crush him into the ground. "Good news! We narrowed down what kind of fae shifter we're looking for!"

Gavin followed on the laughter, and soon enough, Harry

chimed in. Dragon-Grace dropped to the ground as she made a sound that resembled chortling giggles, each one releasing a small puff of minty-smelling smoke.

Drying the tears spilling from her eyes, Harry sighed. "I call not telling Nora that a dragon crushed her azalea bush."

Nora stepped onto the back porch at that very moment, her hands resting on her hips as she gazed at the dragon in her yard as if one happened every damned day. "Oh my."

"Oh my? You come outside and see a dragon sitting on your bushes and all you can say is 'Oh my'?"

"That's not any dragon, that's a Grace." Nora shrugged. "I better head to the grocery store before they close. If dragons are anything like the other shifters in this town, she'll be a very hungry Grace when she manages to shift back. Gavin, sweetheart? Do you think you could give me a hand? I'll need to buy more than my usual this time around because something tells me that she'll be famished."

"It would be my pleasure, Ms. Pierce." Gavin extended his elbow and the two of them disappeared back into the house, leaving Harry alone with Jax and Dragon-Grace, who was busy checking out her wingspan.

Jax joined her on the porch, amazed smile still firmly in place. "She's quite the sight, isn't she?"

"She's a dragon."

He chuckled. "Yes, she is."

"Like a real, winged, fire-breathing *dragon*."

"We haven't tested the fire-breathing part yet, considering we're a bit too close to the house, but I hope to find out sometime soon in an open field. Safe bet would be that she can, considering her fire-prolific abilities in human form. She can probably camouflage, too."

"I really need to call Cassie."

Jax chuckled, slipping an arm around her waist. "How does one tell her best friend that her daughter is a dragon shifter?"

"I have absolutely no fucking idea."

Grace caught a glimpse of something behind her and spun like a puppy chasing its own tail. The ground shook and Dragon-Grace stopped, only to start up again.

"How long before she can shift back to human?" Harry asked, curious.

"I figured I'd let her explore this side of herself for a bit, and then we'll try and get back to two legs, but honestly I don't think it'll take her much. Her transition into the dragon was seamless. Almost mystical, actually. Definitely nothing like my first shift, or the first shift of anyone I know. That fucking shit hurt like hell."

"She didn't have any pain?"

"Like I said, seamless. And her clothes didn't shred, they kind of . . . disappeared with Grace so I'll be curious to see if they reappear the same way. It's quite possibly a fae thing."

"A fae dragon shifter." Harry peered at the book in her hands, the tome warm to touch. "I think I can narrow our focus now . . . but first, I better go call Cassie. You'll stay with Grace?"

"Of course. I'll give her a few more minutes of playtime and then have her go inside, too. I'm sure she'll want to talk to her mother."

Of that she had no doubt.

20

Mother of Dragon

Harry paced in her bedroom, practicing what to say to her best friend—the literal Mother of the Dragon in the backyard. Did Harry just blurt out, "Congrats! It's a dragon!"? Or did she make some inane small talk, give a little dish about Jax, then casually slip it in with, "Oh, by the way, you're the mother of a fae dragon shifter"?

She didn't know if a best way existed in which to break the news that didn't sound far-fetched. She spent so much time deliberating on best tactics that she heard Nora's return; and from the sound of it, she brought a few extra bodies.

Elodie and Lenny's voices laughed downstairs, and the sound of Grace's very human chuckle filled Harry's ears right before the sound of a fast-moving tornado tore up the stairs.

Grace, rosy cheeked and grinning, flew into the room, her happiness pulling a smile to Harry's face. "You're doing okay?"

"Are you freaking kidding me? I'm a fucking dragon, Harry!"

They laughed, falling into each other's arms in a crashing hug.

"But are you okay?" Harry asked, worried.

"I mean, I know this poses a new set of questions and all, but I can't explain it. I feel . . . more at ease. It's almost like I can feel her right there, close enough to talk to and I kinda feel like she's trying to communicate, but I can't really understand her. Yet." Grace flung herself on the bed. "Jax said it's a little different from what he shares with his cougar, so I'm not really sure he understands, but maybe they'll be some information in that fae book."

"This definitely narrows the focus by a lot, so I'm sure we'll be able to find something. But first, we should—"

"Call Mom and then go eat." On cue, her stomach growled, a loud rumble through the room. "Nora wasn't kidding. I could eat about a hundred burgers right now, but I'll start with the lasagna she just put in the oven. And the breadsticks. And anything else she puts in front of me. But first . . . Mom."

"Right. Cassie." Harry glanced at her phone as if her best friend would jump through the screen. "Do you want to do the honors of breaking the news?"

"Nope. All you." Grace beamed. "But put her on video chat because I have got to see her face."

Swearing internally, Harry dialed her friend's number. It took a few rings for Cassie to switch over from regular call to video, and when she did, her friend looked wiped out.

"Hey, you two." Cassie smiled tiredly. "I wasn't expecting a check-in tonight. Is everything okay?"

"You look tired," Harry said, concerned.

"Eh. I'm fine. What's up?"

"So you know how you used to rag on me for enjoying

those dragon-shifter romance novels, and you scoffed, saying I should read something a bit more reality-based and stick to wolves or something?"

Cassie perked up, no longer looking tired as she leaned closer to the screen. "Yeah. Why?"

"Well, it turns out dragons are pretty damn real."

Grace clutched Harry's wrist and pulled the phone toward her. "And I'm one of them! Mom, I'm a freaking dragon shifter! A *dragon*! With a tail and wings—oh my freaking god—you should see my wings! They're fucking *huge*! I mean, all of me was huge. I think I stood at least six feet *over* Jax, and he is one big ass dude!"

Cassie stilled in the screen so abruptly Harry thought the video froze until her friend laughed, and then laughed harder. "Good one, guys. Holy crap. I almost bought that for one split second I'm that tired, but—"

"Mom, we're not kidding."

"Really, it was a good try."

"Mom . . ."

"Maybe if you—"

"Cass," Harry interjected, giving only a slight nod. "You're the mother of a dragon. Surprise!"

Cassie's gaze bounced from one to the other. "Are you fucking serious right now? Swear it to me. Both of you. Right now."

They each held up their right hands.

Harry vowed first. "We're not kidding, Cass."

Cassie didn't speak.

"I think we broke her," Grace whispered.

"Nah. Give her a minute."

Five seconds went by, and then Cassie squealed so loud, Harry ripped the phone away to save their eardrums. Her friend hurled question after question, most which Grace was able to answer as she commandeered Harry's phone, the mother and daughter catching up.

Harry motioned she was headed downstairs, and Grace nodded, indicating she'd be down in a minute. Harry found Jax on the bottom step, prepped to head up.

"There you are." Jax smirked. "I was about to see if you needed some moral support to break the news."

"News broken. Cassie's definitely shocked, but she and Grace are talking right now." Harry glanced around to see that not only had Nora brought Lenny and Elodie back to the house but Gavin, Silas, and Maddox had returned, too. "It's a regular party, huh?"

"You know Nora. We should probably be surprised that the entire town isn't in the backyard right now."

"Very, very true."

"I can't believe it." Elodie approached, pulling Harry into a hug. "Our little Grace? A dragon?"

Harry chuckled. "Looks like it."

"So what does this mean? This should definitely make it easier for her to get a grip on her gifts, right?"

"Hoping that we can find more on fae dragon shifters in that tome Tomlyn lent us, but, yes. Grace discovered a few talents on her own, but we have no clue what others she should be aware of, or anything else that may be different for her with being a fae shifter."

Gavin nodded. "I can take a stab at the book for a while if you'd like. You have a lot on your shoulders right now with Grace and all, and—"

"And it's research," Silas pointed out, "and if it involves an ancient book of any kind, this fella gets a raging boner."

The vampire scowled at his friend but didn't deny. "I wouldn't mind scoping it out."

Harry smiled. "Thank you, Gavin—that would be great. But I should warn you Tomlyn said we'd only have the ability to search for answers to the things directly related to what we needed. I don't really claim to understand what exactly he meant, but I don't know what kind of wide research you'll be able to do."

"I'll be perfectly content finding out what I can for Grace. Thank you for entrusting me with that."

"Thank you for offering, because it was giving me a damn headache."

"So what's next?" Lenny asked.

"Next?" Elodie grinned. "Next, we win Mud Runner, because there's no way we're losing with a dragon on our team."

"No one is to put any additional pressure on Grace because of this. Am I clear?" Harry warned. "She seems to be taking this in stride, but I want to make sure there's no delayed reaction."

"She won't get any pressure from me," Elodie promised.

Harry shot her friend a look.

"What? She won't! I swear!"

"Food's ready," Nora called from the kitchen.

"I better get Grace. Her stomach sounded like it was seconds away from digesting itself." Harry turned, and nearly ran into the teenager herself.

Except this teen didn't look happy.

Or particularly hungry either.

She looked pissed, her eyes a molten gold lava.

"What's wrong?" Harry studied the girl for some sign, her gaze dropping to the phone in Grace's hand. "Is it your mom? What happened?"

"Mom said she's coming to Fates Haven." Grace, her voice

hard, tossed Harry's phone into her hands. "And you may want to check your inbox because someone named Vicky Harting sent you an email. She said they're eager for your return to New York City and can't wait to hear from you."

"Wait. What?" Harry tried connecting the dots. "You read my emails?"

"That's what you have to say? Not a response to the fact that first, you drag me out here without asking my opinion and now that I've learned to love it here just like you told me I would, you want to uproot us all over again?" Pillowy smoke clouds escaped Grace's nostrils. "Well, I'm not going. You can go ahead and leave everything and everyone you care about all over again, but I won't do it."

She turned and stormed out, bursting past a surprised Nora. The loud rolling thunder indicated she'd shed her human suit the second she stepped outside.

A pin could've dropped and echoed like a cannon in the quiet room. All eyes fastened on Harry, but the ones that weighed the heaviest came from Jax. His gray eyes turned stormy as he stared at her.

Everyone's expressions went from shock to hurt, to a wary acceptance, but she went back to Jax.

"Look, I'm not exactly sure what's happening here, but I can explain . . ."

He shook his head, his face impassive. "I better go make sure Grace doesn't burn down the entire town."

"I'll come with you," Silas volunteered, quickly followed by Gavin and Maddox.

Elodie, her face crestfallen, spoke first. "You're leaving Fates Haven? Again?"

"No. I mean . . . I don't know. I'm not sure what this email is but—"

Lenny scoffed. "But Vicky Harting seems to think you're on the way back to New York. Or are you saying you don't know a Vicky?"

"No, I do." Harry slowly connected the dots. "She was on the board of my company, the one that held the vote to give me the boot."

"And now it sounds like they want you back. Congratulations."

"Just because they maybe only now see their mistake doesn't mean I'm heading home."

"So *New York* is home?"

Harry's mouth opened and closed, mentally cursing at her slip. "No. That's not what I meant."

"So you're staying in Fates Haven."

"I want to. I haven't had an opportunity to give what comes next much thought. I've been so focused on Grace and—"

"That's a crock of shit, and you know it," Lenny called her out.

"I—"

"I've heard enough. Thank you for the food, Nora, but I'm calling it a night." Lenny gave the older witch a hug and stormed out.

"Sorry, but she's my ride home." Elodie did a quick, awkward wave, and hightailed it after her.

Soon enough it was just Nora and Harry, the latter sinking onto the couch with a heavy sigh.

Nora followed, taking the seat next to her. "Well, you mucked this one up real good, didn't you, kiddo?"

Harry laughed without a speck of humor. "I wouldn't be me if I didn't, Aunt Nora."

"Do you really have plans to head back to New York?"

"Plans? No. I had no plans that didn't involve finding answers for Grace." She looked at her aunt. "I haven't thought about the city for I don't even know how long. I swear."

"I believe you, sweetheart."

"You do?"

"Absolutely. But even though you had no concrete plans to head back to New York, you also haven't made plans to stay here."

"But—"

"I know." Nora patted her hand. "It's been quite the whirlwind since you returned, but things are shifting—no pun intended. Grace is beginning to find her path, and it's about time that you begin to forge your own. Make those plans. And even more important, make those plans known to those that love you with all their hearts."

Aunt Nora was right, and Harry would kick her own ass if she were that flexible. Hell, everyone probably thought she always had one foot outside Fates Haven, prepped to run. And she couldn't really blame them, considering she'd given them no solid reason to believe otherwise . . . and then came Vicky's out-of-the-blue email, playing right into their fears.

And hers.

The back door opened and slammed closed, a pissed and very human Grace storming through, but not before grabbing the entire lasagna casserole. She paused at the steps to throw Harry a hard glare.

"I am not proud of my outburst, or the way I just scaled out, but I meant what I said, Harry," Grace said, her voice stern and sure. "You dragged me here kicking and screaming, and now, if you think I'm leaving, you'll have to drag out a snarling four-ton dragon. You should probably start some weight training."

She stormed up the stairs, slamming her bedroom door. A second later, a truck engine revved, and Harry knew before she glanced out the front window that she'd see Jax's taillights disappearing down the drive.

Fuck. This night kept getting better and better.

"It'll all be okay." Nora came up behind her and wrapped her in a warm hug. "It's nothing a simple conversation won't fix. For now, I think everyone just needs to clear their heads and cool their tempers."

That sounded good in theory, but she didn't know how well that would translate to reality.

21

Witch's Peak

Hiking boots—check. Bug spray—check. Magical compass—always checked. Confidence and self-assuredness—missing in action.

Maybe Harry would find it in the mountains, although what was more likely was developing a severe case of poison ivy. But threat to her sensitive skin aside, she'd been unable to put what happened during the Night Drop out of her head and enough was enough.

It was time to find out what the hell wanted her to go to Witch's Peak.

Dropping her hiking gear by the front door, Harry did one last check and grabbed another water bottle for good measure. As she turned, Nora stood in the living room, her small body taking up practically the entire room.

"What are you doing?" Nora noticed the equipment. "Are you going alone? Are you going with the girls?"

"Uh, no. I thought I'd do some exploring." Harry paused.

"You'll be okay keeping an eye out for Grace, right? I'm not sure how long it will take Cassie to get here from where she is and—"

"Me and the child will be just fine. My concern is with you."

"I'm fine," Harry lied. "It's been a long time since I've gone on a hike and I figured I could use a little time and space to clear my head. That's all."

"I'm not certain I like this idea."

Harry chuckled. "Did you not just drop me off in the middle of nowhere and tell me to find my way back home? I'll be fine. You forget that I grew up on these mountains, Aunt Nora."

"Yeah, I dropped you off with an entire team at your back, and you know I love you, dear, but you've spent the last thirteen years being citified."

"It's like riding a bike . . . and I have a built-in compass that will direct me home when I'm ready." She pulled her aunt into a firm hug. "I'll be fine. I promise."

"I know you will be eventually, but it's my job to worry about you until you manage to muddle your way there. And don't give me any of that nonsense about being an adult." Nora pulled away gently, shooting her a small smile. "You'll learn soon enough with Grace that worry isn't something you can flip off because someone is technically a grown-up. Adult decisions have the potential for larger, more adultish mistakes."

"Gee. Thanks for the pep talk," Harry joked.

"Just keeping it real, my dear. Be careful."

"Always." Harry collected her gear and tucked everything in the hatchback, and then she was off, armed with both the coordinates of the original drop-off and the general idea of where she'd felt the strange secondary magic.

Unfortunately, she couldn't drive to the exact spot. She had to park a good eight miles away, almost near Rocky Mountain Pack lands, and then hike the rest of the way. It was daylight. She was experienced. She had an actual internal compass. Her hope was to find the magical source, check it out, and get back well before nightfall.

She'd thought about asking Elodie or Lenny to go with her, but replaying their last conversation, she decided against it. She needed to have a much larger one-on-one with her friends, and something in Harry's gut told her whatever lay in wait at the top of Witch's Peak was time sensitive.

She steered Nora's hatchback onto one of the old logging trails, wincing as she bounced, nearly smacking her head on the roof. The twists and turns were almost nauseating and she reduced her speed to a crawl by the time she reached her destination.

A familiar truck sat parked in the small scenic overlook, and as Harry parked alongside it, Jax, his backpack making his broad chest even more impressive, rounded the corner.

Her heart stuttered at the sight of him leaning casually against his tailgate, waiting as she climbed from Nora's car.

"Off for a little daytime excursion?" She kept her tone light, her nerves wreaking havoc on her insides.

"Guess I could ask the same of you." His face was devoid of emotion as he watched her pull out her gear from the hatchback.

She ignored his heated gaze as she ran through her mental checklist one last time, donning her pack like armor as she turned to face him. "Guess I have Nora to thank for your presence."

He didn't confirm nor deny. "I told you I'd go up to Witch's Peak with you, didn't I?"

"Yeah, but that was before Grace went snooping into my

emails and told everyone my personal business, and before everyone held a trial and convicted me before giving me the chance to explain. And in case you're wondering, that everyone includes you, too."

She started walking, not bothering to go around him, and brushed her shoulder against his as she headed toward the tree line.

So maybe Nora's suggestion of giving everyone time to cool tempers only fueled her own. It hurt thinking they'd all thought the worst of her and her ability to stick around, and then not allowed her to explain.

Harry let the hurt spew words from her mouth. "I got this, Jax. Don't feel obligated to stick around after I disappointed everyone once again, in true Harlow Pierce fashion."

"So then why don't you go ahead and explain?" Jax's heavy footsteps followed.

"Nope. The time for that to happen was when everyone jumped to conclusions about my plans and my intentions, and immediately thought the worst of me. Right now, I have other concerns that need addressing."

He grumbled and caught up to her quickly. They hiked in silence for a long time, automatically falling into a rhythm without needing to talk. Despite Harry's speech about not talking about what happened at Pierce House, her anger grew with every mile they hiked.

Was it a bit of a double standard? Yes. Her own mistakes supplied the ammunition for Jax and the others to think her capable of walking away from Fates Haven, and everyone in it, *again*. But that had been in the past. She'd hoped that everything she'd done since returning to Fates Haven had showed them that history wouldn't repeat itself.

It hurt more than anything to think they'd always kept that expectation of her in the back of their minds, and it made her wonder if she'd ever truly get that clean slate they all boasted about, or if she'd always be labeled the Runaway Witch.

Harry plowed through a tight stand of trees, knocking an offending branch away from her face with a magical wave of her hand. She released it just as emphatically, and the sharp pine needles snapped back toward Jax with gusto.

"Fuck." He cursed as it smacked him in the face. "What the hell, Harry?"

"Sorry. You're so quiet with all your cougar stalkiness that I forgot you're back there."

He scoffed. "You're the one that said you don't want to talk. So now you're saying you do? Fuck, you are so frustratingly stubborn, I swear—"

"*I'm* frustratingly stubborn?" She whirled around, nearly headbutting his chin he was so close. "You can look in the mirror and say the same thing to your reflection, buddy. I mean, not now because we're in the middle of nowhere and there are no mirrors around, but later. Later, take a good long look."

He folded his massive arms over his chest, the textbook image of stubborn.

Harry growled. "You want to know why I haven't made any bold, elaborate plans to stay in Fates Haven?"

"That question has run through my mind once or twice."

"Because what if there's not a place here for me anymore?" Harry blurted. She ignored the shocked look on Jax's face and continued before losing her nerve. "Lenny and Maddox have Once Upon a Tattoo, and Elodie and Silas are doing whatever strange mating dance they're doing and about to be business enemies. Nora is on the freaking town council for crying out loud, and Marie is now making penis pastries. And you . . ."

His eyes flashed a gorgeous, liquid silver. "And I what?"

"You're now the head cougar in charge, Jax. You're running both the Rocky Mountain Pack and your business."

"And?" Jax's tone was way too calm.

"I feel like everyone has their solidified, designated roles here. You've all found your thing. Your place. What if I gave mine up permanently thirteen years ago, and Fate doesn't deem me worthy enough of a second chance?"

Jax opened his mouth to counter, but Harry couldn't hear it.

A magical rush surged through her body, igniting her own magic. The dual sensations sucked all the oxygen from her lungs and forced her to her knees. Jax was there in an instant, large hands gently cupping her cheeks.

His mouth moved, but his voice sounded muffled as the unexpected magical presence pulsed through her head and chest. "Harry! Come on, baby. Talk to me."

That secondary magic yanked hard, toppling her into his arms. Time ticked away at a snail's pace until she sucked in a lungful of air, and with painful slowness her other senses gradually returned.

Worry was etched in every line of Jax's face.

"I'm okay." Her voice sounded raspy even to her own ears.

"Baby, you look the exact opposite of okay right now."

"We really need to talk about your flattery skills." She smiled wanly, her hands latching on his shoulders as she used his bulk to return to her feet. She wobbled, but his tightened grip kept her upright and firmly against his chest. "See. All good."

He frowned as he stepped slightly back and studied her

from head to toe, looking for any sign of injury or illness. "Yeah. We're not doing this. I'm taking you back home."

"No. We're on the right track. I can feel it now."

"*It?* Harry, *it* dropped you to your knees and scared about twenty years off my life. I know you think you need to follow this feeling, but it's pretty damn obvious that *it* doesn't want to be found."

"It's not that it doesn't want to be found . . ." Harry tried making sense of that magical signature she could now feel wrapping around her own. "I think it just has rusty people skills . . . like it's been out here by itself for a long time."

"Great. An antisocial *it* feeling hiding in the middle of a mountain. Like that isn't the recipe for some twisted horror flick."

"You and Grace and your horror movies," Harry teased. "The two of you should have a binge watch."

"Sure. I like horror movies . . . when I'm sitting on a comfortable couch, a beautiful brunette tucked tight into my side and her face burrowed in my neck. And locked doors. Locked doors and bright lights are a must."

"And not the beautiful brunette?"

"Right now, that beautiful brunette is hell-bent on sending us up the side of a mountain toward something with antisocial tendencies and rusty interpersonal skills."

Harry's lips twitched. "It's a magical signature, not an ax murderer."

"Guess we'll soon find out if you're insistent on doing this."

"I am. I mean, if *you're* chicken, I can always go it alone from here."

Jax scanned their surroundings and sighed. "Where the witch wanders, the shifter follows. So . . . after you. Lead the way."

This time, they set a new pace, Jax walking at her side as she followed that tug up the side of the mountain; and with each step they took, she became more and more certain that the tug was leading them to Witch's Peak.

Something told her that they'd soon come face-to-face with the fuel of all those Fates Haven stories.

* * *

HARLOW PIERCE WAS literally the only person on this planet for whom Jax would dare hike to Witch's Peak. Even for his mother, he'd give it a hard faux think before shooting the idea down, and that woman had suffered through seventy-two of hours of labor and his nearly sixteen-inch head—if she were to be believed.

Jax scanned the sky and the quickly sinking sun, cursing at the diminishing light. "Harry, we—"

"Just a little farther." She charged ahead as if she'd somehow found a fourth wind.

"You said that at least a half dozen 'little farthers' ago. There's already no hope of getting back to the cars before nightfall, but if we veer left, I'm pretty sure we'll run into at least one of old man Winters's hunting cabins. We can lie low there for the night, and get started again in the morning."

"It's seriously not that farther."

"Harry." He caught her arm and dragged her to a slow stop. "I know you want to see this through, and I want to help you, but we can't do anything if we walk off the face of a damn cliff or into a bear trap. Plus, I don't know if you noticed since you've been practically running up this mountain at inhuman speed, but this fog is getting ridiculous and it's getting cold . . . almost unnaturally so."

As he spoke, his breath clouded around them, making his point.

She nodded, finally relenting. "Fine. We'll call it a night, but I have a better plan than finding one of old man Winters's hunting cabins."

"Yeah? And what's that?"

"That cabin right up there on the summit." She nudged her chin over his shoulder and he turned. The fog obscuring the way slowly parted, and even Jax felt that something else filling the air around them.

"Where the hell did that come from?" he asked warily

"I don't know, but that's where *it* is telling me we should go."

He scanned the log cabin critically, unable to sense anything ominous other than the fact it basically had appeared from thin air. "Let me go first."

She rolled her eyes. "And what will you do if you come across anything of the magical persuasion? Hiss at it?"

"Humor me, will you?"

"Fine." She gestured for him to take the lead. "But you're being ridiculous."

"You can call me ridiculous after we get inside and there isn't an ax murderer about to dismember us and make us the main ingredient in their stew."

Taking her hand, he took the lead up the steep slope. The closer they got to the cabin, the colder the air got, freezing his cheeks by the time they reached the front steps.

"Hello?" he called out, repeating himself a few times before peering through each frosted window. "Is anyone in there? We were hiking and lost track of time. Do you think we can come in and get a little warm?"

No one answered despite the gleaming light coming from inside.

"Stay behind me," Jax directed Harry as they slowly climbed the stairs. He glanced around at their surroundings, hopefully avoiding a rifle barrel aimed at their heads, and knocked on the front door.

A second knock and the door slipped open . . .

He shared a look with Harry, who shrugged, looking woefully unconcerned. "You don't find this the least bit fucking weird?"

"There's nothing about this entire thing that isn't fucking weird, Jax. I'm just finally accepting that just because something is weird, doesn't mean it's dangerous." She tapped her chest. "I don't know how I know, but we're meant to go inside. Trust me."

When she put it that way . . .

He turned to the open door and, ready for anything, called his cougar close to the surface as a second set of senses. "We're coming in, so don't shoot."

He could practically hear Harry's eye-roll.

The inside of the cabin definitely didn't look like the home of an ax murderer. A welcoming fire was ablaze in the massive stone fireplace, and a small army of oil lanterns created a golden glow in the large single room. In the corner, a full-size bed, adorned with patchwork quilts and fluffy pillows, looked as inviting as the plush couch catty-corner to the fireplace.

It looked like a hunter's cabin, but chic, straight out of some country living magazine. Hell, it looked a lot like his own cabin.

"Ooh, hot chocolate." Harry scurried toward a small kitchen counter with two mugs, a boxed mix, and a kettle. "And there's even marshmallows. You want some?"

"Do I want to drink mysterious hot chocolate in the cabin in the woods that appeared out of thin air?" Jax asked, incredulous.

"Well? Do you?" Harry smirked, waiting for his answer. "You're the one who wanted to find somewhere to lie low until the morning. Well, it found us. So what will it be? Hot chocolate? Or whatever sour drink you're currently tasting right now, judging by the look on your face."

Fuck it.

"Sure. I'll take some if you're making it," he grumbled, ignoring her soft chuckles.

He slipped off his backpack and checked the windows and door before heading toward the fireplace and adding a few more logs. Summer shouldn't be this damn cold, even here on Witch's Peak, and yet it wouldn't surprise him if they woke up to a few inches of snow.

"Here. All warmed up and ready to drink." Harry handed him a mug that was emblazoned with the Fates Haven logo: Become Fated in Fates.

"Guess there's no point in being surprised, is there?" he asked, bemused.

"At this point, I would say no." She kicked off her boots with a wince and curled up on the couch. "I don't know what it is about this place, but it feels familiar and yet I know I've never been here. It almost reminds me . . ."

"Reminds you of what?"

She shook her head, chuckling, a pink hue rising on her cheeks. "Never mind. It's silly."

He sat next to her and forced himself to get comfortable. It didn't take much, the cushions molding to his body.

"Silly or not, we've obviously got some time to kill here." Jax grabbed one of the throws behind his head and draped it over her lap. "It reminds you of what?"

"A long time ago, I used to dream about having a cabin high in the mountains, one that only"—she cleared her throat—"one that only you and I knew about. It had a large stone fireplace and a simple bed covered in handmade quilts. This place really could've stepped right out of my imagination."

"You never told me that you pictured a place like that for us." Jax studied her as she gazed into her mug and shrugged.

"It was one of those things that I thought about but didn't think would ever really happen."

"And now?" Jax teased, glancing around.

She chuckled. "Now I'm really not sure what's happening, but I know it's something that needs to. And, yes, I know that's oddly cryptic, and I'm not trying to do it on purpose. It's like my descry abilities have been given a boost. Normally, I have to know exactly what I'm searching for in order to find it, but this time? Not so much. *It's* finding me. Here."

"Then I guess we'll be staying here for the time being, huh?"

Harry's eyes widened. "Shit. Nora! I have to let her know I'm not making it back tonight so she doesn't call out the rescue squad."

"Wouldn't want a rescue squad interrupting our peaceful solitude." He pulled out the satellite phone from his bag and tossed it to her with a smirk. "Glad one of us remembered the hiking essentials."

She grinned but rolled her eyes. "Okay, so I'm a little rusty . . ."

He nursed his hot chocolate while she spoke to Nora, reassuring her aunt that all was well. By the time she coaxed the older witch off the phone, he'd gone from feeling as though he'd hiked an entire mountain to being wired and on edge.

With not a lot of options of things to do.

"Your peaceful wooded wonderland doesn't happen to include a treasure trove of board games or something, does it?" he joked.

"Can't say it did, but I wonder . . ." A warm breeze swept through the room—her magic—and it turned her toward the antique chest at the foot of the bed. Grinning, she pulled out a small rectangular box. "Feel like Jenga?"

"Jenga."

"I mean, unless you're afraid your skills are a little rusty and you can't take the pressure." She obviously referred to the Jenga challenges they had as kids, and the all-night tournaments.

"You're on, Pierce. Set it up, and I'll let you knock 'em down."

She snorted, settling on the rug right in front of the fireplace. "Sorry, buddy, but this witch has nerves of steel. If anyone is knocking over the blocks, it'll be you."

They got comfortable, and after a round of rock, paper, scissors to see who drew first, they worked into a rhythm, each plucking a log from the tower before the next turn started.

About four turns in, Harry's gaze dropped to her block and she chuckled. "Um . . . I'm not so sure this is regular Jenga."

"What do you mean?"

"Check your blocks, Jax."

He glanced at his first two blocks he'd pulled, both blank. Next, he glanced at the third: **Pick one article of clothing to come off—both yours and your partner's.**

Jax plucked his fourth block: **Stand behind your partner and get handsy for 30 seconds.** "What the hell kind of Jenga game is this?"

Harry picked up the box and laughed, turning the front cover toward him. "Jenga for Couples. Well, I guess this was a bust."

"Hold on now." He stopped her from cleaning up. "What was on your block?"

"Mine?" She inspected her latest pull and read: "Sit in your partner's lap for the rest of the game."

Their gazes stumbled together, and suddenly the chill in the air disappeared entirely and the room got really, really warm.

"What do you say, sweet pea?" Jax flickered his gaze to her mouth. "Want to play the mysteriously appearing adult Jenga you found in an old chest in your mysteriously appearing cabin in the woods? I should warn you that I still plan on winning."

Harry's lips twitched as humor danced in her eyes. "Something tells me that if we play this, we'll both end up winning."

He sure as hell hoped so.

22

Winner! Winner!

This escalated quickly, and Harry wasn't all that sorry about it. Never in her wildest dreams would she have thought her magically created cabin in the woods would come complete with adult Jenga.

Okay, so maybe in her *wildest* dreams.

Yet she stared from her block to the ones in front of Jax, her heart thumping wildly at the thought of seeing where this all went.

"We should probably do this in the order they were pulled, right?" Harry fought to keep a straight face. "To keep things all aboveboard and all."

"Seems like the responsible thing to do . . . which means my lap is your new seat." He patted his legs, his lips twitching as he dared her into movement.

His heated gaze remained locked on her as she crawled over to his side of the block tower and settled ono his lap, her back against his chest.

"We have to still be able to play, right?" She shifted in her new seat, instantly feeling the not-so-subtle firmness of his growing erection. "My next two blocks were blank, so that leaves yours next. Something about each of us losing an article of clothing? What do you say? Socks?"

The sound of his chuckle vibrated through her body as his mouth brushed over the nape of her neck. "Nice try, but I think since it's my block, it's my choice."

"So what's your choice?"

His hands slid from her hips and inched beneath the hem of her shirt. "I'm thinking shirts. Yours looks awfully warm and I wouldn't want you to get overheated sitting this close to the fire."

"It is pretty warm." Harry bit her lip to keep from laughing and shifted on his lap, chuckling when she heard his corresponding groan. "Mind helping me?"

She lifted her arms and her coy plan backfired when his hands slowly—and very deliberately—raised her top an inch at a time. The backs of his knuckles brushed her bra-covered nipples, but he may as well have pinched them directly. They hardened, making her suck in a series of slow, even breaths as he slipped the fabric over her head and tossed it to the side.

"One down . . ." A subtle shift later and Jax reached behind his neck and yanked his T-shirt off and away.

Harry thought she'd been warm before, but the heat in the room flushing her skin was nothing compared to now, even with only the fabric of her bra between them.

Jax slipped her hair over one shoulder and bared the other.

"I'm pretty sure there was also something about getting 'handsy.'" Jax, with his mouth scant inches from her skin, ran the backs of his fingers along her shoulder and down her arm, the touch leaving behind a goose bump trail that sent a shiver through her entire body.

It was the barest touch and yet it felt as if he stroked her everywhere; and when he ran the backs of his hands over her breasts, she sucked in a moan and pushed into the touch.

He chuckled behind her, slowly settling his hands on her upper thighs. "I think it's your turn to pull a block."

"Was that thirty seconds already?"

He chuckled. With slightly unsteady hands, she pushed her bottom deeper against his lap and leaned toward the tower. The smart thing would be to pick the easiest block and add it to the top of the tower, and yet her eyes passed over the blank block practically sticking halfway out and landed on the one with writing.

As if sensing her train of thought, Jax's grip on her thighs flexed. She carefully pushed and prodded and plucked another instructional block. "Identify your favorite spot to be kissed."

"That one's easy . . . and we're in the perfect position," Jax teased.

"Oh yeah? Where's my favorite spot?" She peered smugly over her shoulder at him.

"One can only assume it's the same spot that makes you go absolutely boneless." Hand gently tilting her head to the side, he brushed his nose over the smooth column of her neck until his mouth hovered over that delicate spot beneath her ear.

She sucked in a quick breath before his lips even touched, and when they did, her eyes fluttered closed, head tilting to give him easier access. Jax nibbled and flicked the site with his tongue, sending her heart into an unsteady gallop.

She sighed, breathless.

"Well, was I right?" He placed another teasing kiss that she felt straight in her core.

"Damn it, you know you are."

He chuckled and leaned toward the tower to complete his turn, his mouth never leaving her skin until he turned his block for them both to read: Use your mouth—and only your mouth—for at least thirty seconds.

They both froze, the crackling fire sounding like cannon fire in the suddenly silent room.

Jax slowly returned the block to the top of the tower as the weight of those instructions dangled heavy in the air. "It doesn't really go into detail, does it? Kinda leaves it open for interpretation."

"Maybe it's dealer's choice."

His hands glided from her thighs to her torso, his palms like heated brands on her flushed skin. "Is that what you want it to be, sweet pea? Do you want me to pick where I put my mouth on you? Because I should probably give you fair warning, I wouldn't be picking any single spot, and it definitely wouldn't be for only thirty sec—"

"Yes." She turned slightly to lock her heated gaze with his over her shoulder. "I think I'm done playing Jenga."

For two quick heartbeats, neither of them moved—and then they both did.

Harry shifted her weight off his lap while he effortlessly flipped her toward him, banding an arm tightly around her waist, and guided them into a gentle fall, his arm shoving the block game to the side.

A small squeal ended in a low groan as Jax's mouth fused to hers, sending her head into an oxygen-deprived tailspin, before dragging along her neck. His lips and tongue soothed the slight abrasions caused by the stubble peppering his jaw, and as if by magic, both the stubble and the lips captured her bare nipple.

She didn't even ask where her bra went, or comment on how, as she fisted Jax's hair and savored the sensation of every nip and lick, her body heating up from way more than just the fireplace. Harry couldn't believe her panties hadn't melted off her body, but Jax effortlessly unbuttoned her jeans and tugged them—and her panties—down and off in one strong tug.

Her ass barely hit the soft rug again when his talented mouth zoned in on its new target between her legs.

Harry's head thunked to the floor with the first swipe of his tongue over her clit. "Holy. Shit."

He chuckled against her pussy. "Baby, there is nothing holy about what I want to do to you right now."

She was inclined to agree, lifting her hips to push her pussy to his eager mouth. It was the sweetest torture, one that escalated with every swipe of his tongue. He didn't lick her any single way, instead, alternating between slow, delicious swipes and soft, intent sucks. His tactics had her writhing on the floor within seconds.

"Jax." Harry buried her hand in his hair and clamped her knees around his head as he brought her right over the cliff in a pleasure-filled freefall.

Her body bowed and quaked, taking any kind of control away from her as she experienced the sweetest and most all-consuming orgasm of her life.

Golden eyes locked on hers from over her mound, Jax rode out her pleasure with her, only pulling away when she tugged on his hair. Her body still hummed with the aftereffects, but she already couldn't wait for more.

Smug smile in place, Jax climbed over her body and stole her breath all over again with a searing kiss. They worked in tandem to get rid of his pants, and then Harry climbed back onto his lap, this time facing him.

His hands settling on her hips. "You want to ride me, baby?"

She sunk onto his engorged cock with a throaty, delicious groan. "Pretty sure I already am."

* * *

JUST WHEN JAX didn't think it could get better than having Harry's sweet taste on his tongue, her body wrapped around his cock like a tight, wet fist.

Fuck, it was better than a fist. It was *Harry*.

One hand gripped tight on her hip and the other fisted in her hair, he trapped her body flush against his and let her set the pace. She rose and fell, grinding her clit against his lower abdomen on every drop and quickly found a rhythm that had them both panting and sweaty in no time.

He captured a rose-tipped nipple with his mouth and alternated slow licks and gentle scrapes of his teeth. His ministrations had her arching her chest closer, and so he alternated his attention, switching from one breast to the other until her pussy fluttered around his cock in a telltale sign of impending release.

"Jax." Her fingers bit into his shoulders as her hot gaze found his.

"What do you need, baby?" He tilted his hips, thrusting up and relishing the feel of his cock sinking into her body again and again. "Tell me what you need, Harry. Tell me and it's yours."

"I need you deeper. I need . . . fuck. I don't know."

"Do you trust me?" He groaned from the effort to hold back his release.

"Yes. Please."

Desperate to give her what she needed, he lifted her off his cock, turned her around, and immediately slammed back home. Both of them on their knees, he pulled her back against his chest and slid his other hand to that sweet spot between her legs.

"Look in the window, baby." Jax dragged his mouth over that spot behind her ear that they both loved. "Look up and watch us together."

Harry's periwinkle gaze, hooded heavily in lust, found his in the window's reflection. They watched themselves move together, her body pulsing around his the longer they stared.

"That's right." He growled into her ear. "Watch us. See how right we are together. How perfectly synched. Feel it. Feel *us*."

A magical mist permeated the air, bringing a small breeze strong enough to send the fireplace flames into a full roar.

Her eyes drifted closed. "Jax . . ."

"Eyes up, baby." Her gaze snapped back to his, rewarding him when the gorgeous sight of her flushed skin. "Do you see this? Even your magic recognizes what this is . . . what we are."

"What are we, Jax?" Harry's arm lifted, her hand wrapping tight into his hair and holding him even closer.

"Each other's." He felt the rightness in his words the moment they left his lips, his cougar roaring in agreement. "You're mine, Harlow Pierce . . . and I, forever and always, will be yours. Do you understand me? There is no way in hell I'm letting you go ever again."

With a cry, Harry detonated, the thick magical swell igniting the room just as her pussy fisted him with her orgasm. Her pleasure-drenched cries conjured his own, their bodies working in tandem to ride the waves of bliss together.

Jax didn't know where her body stopped and his began. They were fused, in more ways that he could ever really understand.

Hours could've passed before they both slumped back onto the soft, fuzzy rug, their ragged, breathless pants loud as a Mack truck.

Jax slipped from her body with a groan and eagerly pulled her tight against his side.

"Now that is the way to break in a mysteriously appearing magical cabin in the woods." Harry huffed breathlessly before breaking into a stream of soft giggles, her leg lifting over his hip and tangling with his as she nestled into the dip of his shoulder.

"In total agreement with you there, babe." He caressed his hand down the length of her spine and over her tattoo. "Wonder if there's any magical rule of threes when it comes to that, though."

Harry picked her chin off his chest, smirking. "Ooh, you're right. We should probably be diligent and cover all our bases just in case. I mean, it would be the magically responsible thing to do, right?"

Before he opened his mouth to agree, the front door burst open with a flourish, crashing into the wall. Jax reacted instantly. On his feet, he put himself between a naked Harry and the door right as a vaguely familiar man sauntered into the cabin as if making a grand entrance at the Met Gala.

Dressed in expensively tailored pants and a silver-sequined

shirt, a slightly older doppelgänger of Harry Styles glanced around the room before catching sight of the two of them.

"Finally." The Styles look-alike waved a hand and magically shut the door behind him, blocking out a gust of frigid air. "Not that that wasn't necessary, or long overdue, but, yikes. I thought the two of you would never finish. Magical heater or not, it's fucking colder than a witch's tit out there. Pun intended."

Clutching one of the couch's throw blankets to her naked chest, Harry peeked from over the back of the sofa, her wide eyes fastened on their visitor. "*Remus?*"

The supernatural's gaze fastened on her and flashed a genuine, softening smile. "And there is the witch of the hour. How are you doing, darling? Although, based off the fireworks shooting out of the chimney Sleeping Beauty–style, I'd imagine you're pretty damn good, yeah?"

Jax growled low in warning, earning the arrival's attention.

The man's grin widened. "If it isn't the elusive Alpha Jaxon Atwood. Nice to see you again, too." His gaze dropped momentarily before lifting as he smiled. "*All* of you. Now, as much as I hate to ask this, I'll need you both to cover all that gorgeous flesh. We have a lot of shit to discuss."

Remus's gaze fell intently on Harry. "Hope you brought your learning hat, darling. Because you're about to have a cramming session unlike any cramming you've ever experienced. And, yes, I did mean that to sound a bit dirty."

Jax's shock wore away enough that he quickly connected the dots and slowly formed a slightly unfocused picture.

Remus.

Magic.

"*You.*" Jax took a menacing step forward. "You're the asshole who fucked everything up. Fates Haven. The Fate Finding

Ceremony. Because of you, I lost thirteen years with the woman I—"

"Now, now." Remus held up his hand, looking nervous for the first time. "I come in peace."

"Yeah, well. I don't." Ignoring Harry's soft pleas, Jax swung, fist connecting loudly with Remus Chardonnay's jaw.

A supernatural well of bottomless magic or not, Fates Haven's one-time Fate Witch sank to the cabin floor with a heavy thud, his eyes closed and mouth silent for the first time since walking unexpectedly through the door.

"What did you do?" Harry scurried around the couch and knelt to check the pulse of the unconscious witch.

"Something I and every citizen in Fates Haven have wanted to do for thirteen years," he growled out unapologetically. "The second he comes to, I fully intend on doing it again."

"You will not, Jaxon Atwood."

"Like hell I won't."

Harry glanced from Remus and back to him, concern and curiosity filling her eyes, and Jax already knew.

"Fuck." He dragged his hand roughly through his hair. "He's what you felt calling you here to Witch's Peak, wasn't it?"

She sighed, nodding.

"Why the hell would the Fate Witch that literally fucked with the world's Fate Matches have called you up the side of the mountain?"

"I don't know." She stood, giving him a resigned look as she headed toward the kitchen. "And now we have to wait for Sleeping Beauty to wake up from being cougar clobbered in order to find out."

23

Down, Kitty

Saying Harry was confused was a bit like saying Cher is just a singer or the World Series is just a string of baseball games. Still, no other word made sense for the questions currently revolving on the lazy Susan in her head.

The last time she laid eyes on Remus Chardonnay had quite literally been more than a decade ago, when the spell he performed at the Fates Finding Ceremony sent her on a thirteen-year-long self-exile.

She still couldn't believe he was here, unconscious on the couch an hour after Jax knocked him out.

Time hadn't changed him much, the witch possessing that same flair that more than once made him the life of every party he attended . . . and he attended a lot, his social calendar almost always full. It was one reason why his disappearance from Fates Haven—and from supernatural society in general—had created such an uproar.

Well, both his disappearance and the fact he'd botched shit up real good.

"I say we throw a bucket of water over his head." Jax, now fully dressed and leaning against the wall, glared at the witch as if that alone had the power to wake him.

Harry cocked an eyebrow.

"What? It would probably work. Just saying."

"You know what else would've worked? Not coldcocking him to start with."

"Come on. Tell me you didn't want to punch him in the face . . . at least a little bit."

He had her there, because she'd definitely gone through an entire army of emotions when Remus burst through the door. At least one had been a strong desire to magically blast him right back into the cold.

Now, reality and levelheadedness slowly sank in and she wanted answers more than a brief moment of satisfaction.

"I'm getting the bucket." Jax pushed off the wall and headed toward the small kitchen when Remus groaned from the couch, mumbling a string of nonsensical words.

He shot upright in an instant, eyes wide and head swinging around until he saw both Jax and Harry. "You're both fully clothed. That's a little disappointing."

At Jax's low growl, Remus whipped up his hands. "Down, kitty. I tease. I'm teasing." He shot Harry a worried look. "Does he not know the art of a good tease?"

She shrugged. "If you know the art of survival, I would probably stop."

"Noted and suggestion taken under advisement." He threw his legs over the side of the couch and took another glance around the cabin. "Cozy. I probably would've conjured something with a little more space and modern amenities, but it's . . . cute."

"Remus," Harry said sternly.

"Yes, darling?" He glanced from her to a glaring Jax, shifting a little closer to her.

"I don't even know where to begin, honestly. I'm a bit overwhelmed," she said truthfully, sitting heavily on the seat next to him.

"Oh, I can imagine." He patted her hand. "It was a bit much for me in the beginning, too, but trust me, it won't be long before you become an old hand at it."

She mentally replayed the witch's words. "I have no idea what you're talking about."

"Being the Fate Witch."

"The Fate Witch."

Remus rolled his eyes. "If you repeat everything I say, we'll be here even longer than I anticipated, and I found a few shows on one of the streaming services that I'd like to binge-watch this weekend."

"Pause, rewind, and let's start over," Harry directed, trying to bring him around again. "Let's start with—"

"With how the fuck you screwed up thirteen years ago, and then hid in the damn mountains under folklore and bedtime stories like a damn coward," Jax growled.

Remus fidgeted awkwardly. "Yes, well . . . that wasn't my finest moment, I agree, but it's not quite what you both are thinking."

"So you didn't fuck over the town, everyone in it, and anyone hoping to ever find their Fated without dumb luck?"

"Okay, so maybe it's a little like you're thinking."

Jax took a threatening step forward, his fists flexing at his side.

Remus squeaked and jumped up off the couch.

"Stop." Harry leapt up and stepped in the way. "This won't get us the answers we need, and it definitely won't tell me why my magic dragged me up here."

She turned to the witch. "You said it's not like we think. So what really happened thirteen years ago, Remus?"

The older magic wielder kept a wary eye on Jax as he re-claimed his seat. "Okay. So . . . you know how being the Fate Witch is a bit like being Buffy, right? With a little less ass kick-ing. 'One in the all the world' and all that."

"Yeah. And I'm looking at him."

Remus shook his head. "Wrong."

"You're not the Fate Witch."

"Nope." He popped is *P*.

"But you've been the Fate Witch for longer than I've been alive," Harry said, confused. "You've helped hundreds of Fated find one another, the most of any other Fate Witch who came before you."

Remus looked smug, smoothing the wrinkles of his wrinkle-free shirt. "I did, didn't I? You know they even did a spread about me in *Supernatural Weekly*? Made it on the world's Top Fifty Most Influential Supernaturals for ten years in a row— the most any supernatural has made it on the list to date."

Jax scoffed. "You should've created a large magical castle instead of a cabin. I'm not sure his head will fit indoors pretty soon."

Remus scowled at him, unfazed. "It's a good thing you're good-looking, Jaxon Atwood."

"Remus," Harry warned. "Explain. Please."

"I'm not sure there is an explanation. Some people just exude brood through their pores and—"

"Remus! Not Jax, about you *not* being the Fate witch."

"Oh. That. Well, like I said, there can be only one and around thirteen years ago, Fate decided there should be a shifting of the guard. They called in Faith. No, wait. Kendra. Kendra was next, called after that whole Master thing."

Harry pinched the bridge of her nose, trying—and failing—to stave off a migraine. "Can you explain things without using *Buffy the Vampire Slayer* references?"

"I could, but it wouldn't be nearly as fun."

"Rem—"

"Okay, okay. Thirteen years ago, roughly around the time of my last Fates Festival, Fate gave my abilities to another."

"There's another Fate Witch out there?"

"Wait. *Roughly* around the time of your last Fates Festival? How roughly are we talking about." Jax's eyes narrowed into a hard glare, the gold of his cougar shining through the gray.

Remus fidgeted. "Roughly an hour or so before the Finding Ceremony . . ."

"I'm gonna—"

Remus leaped from the couch, keeping it between him and the growling shifter. Harry grabbed Jax's arm, pulling him away from the other witch, who was now very literally sweating magic.

"Sit," Harry ordered Jax with a stern glare before shooting an equally hard look at Remus. "Explain."

"There's not much to explain. My magic had been acting up for a few months before that Fates Festival, and as I consumed my plate of deep-fried Oreos, Fate selected another." He shrugged like it was the simplest thing in the world.

"And yet you performed the Finding Ceremony anyway?"

"Did you see how many people were in attendance that year? If I had backed out, I would've found myself in the middle of a mob worse than one from a last-minute-canceled T-Swift concert."

"So you faked it? Do you have any idea how many lives you affected? Remus! People could've ended up with someone completely and totally wrong for them! Or . . . not be linked to their Fated at all!"

"I didn't fake *all of it*. There was a residual well of Fate magic in there, which was why I was able to summon the Blue Willow Wisps. I just didn't have enough to control them. They went a little . . . rogue. As I'm sure you've figured out."

Jax's jaw clenched. "So if you haven't been the Fate Witch for thirteen years, then who has? You said Fate called in a Kenda, so where are they?"

Remus grinned maniacally. "Seriously? You two haven't . . . put your finger on it?"

"You're saying we know who it is?"

"I would think so." The witch chuckled.

"Then why haven't they stepped up? Do they have any idea what's been happening in Fates Haven through the years? All the wonkiness. All the odd magical shifts. And no Fate Matches?" Her anger grew with every unanswered addition. "Where the hell have they been this whole time?"

Remus smirked. "I don't know. Where is it that you've been again, darling? I heard whispers in the wind that it was New York?"

Harry froze.

Jax froze.

Remus's grin widened to the point it rivaled that of every Joker character ever played.

"Excuse the fuck out of me?" Harry squealed, her voice rising a few octaves.

* * *

THANKS TO JAX'S cougar, he anticipated a lot of things—weather patterns, punches. Hell, even punch lines to jokes. He didn't possess Lenny's seer abilities, but he did okay.

He didn't see this one coming, or the fact that he'd gone from wanting to pummel the former Fate Witch to protecting him from one very pissed curvy brunette.

Harry lurched forward and Jax intercepted. Wrapping his arms tightly around her waist, he pulled her against him and off her feet.

"Let me go, Jax!" She squirmed against him, kicking his shins. "Let me go! You were right. He has a very punchable face. I'd like to experience it for myself firsthand."

"Love the bloodthirstiness, sweet pea," Jax said, chuckling, "but you and your big heart will probably regret it afterward."

"Not likely."

"Babe."

"Fine." Breathless and panting, she went limp in his arms, her hands settling over his. "I'm good."

"You sure? Because I'm not beyond burying bodies in the woods for you, but I forgot my body-burying boots."

"Yeah, I'm sure. No body burying tonight."

He loosened his hold a fraction at a time. When she made

no sudden moves toward the cowering magic wielder, he dropped his arms at his sides but stayed on alert.

"You think I'm a Fate Witch." Harry stared down Remus as she plopped on the couch.

"Not *a*. You're *the*." Treading carefully, he propped his ass on the armrest. "And I don't think. I know. Is it really that far-fetched? You have some pretty fierce descry abilities, do you not?"

Harry scoffed. "Finding lost keys is slightly different from finding someone's Fated match."

Remus wrinkled his nose. "Eh. Not as different as you think."

"I am a horrible matchmaker. Trust me, I tried with Cassie once and it did not go well. I'm not so sure she's ever forgiven me."

"You're not making the match, silly. You're locating them."

Jax sat and took Harry's hand in his, giving it a gentle squeeze.

She held on tightly, her face paling. "And all the wonkiness happening in Fates Haven since the last Fates Festival is because—"

"The town's Fate Witch hasn't been in residence." Remus nodded. "Yep. But now you *are* in residence."

"So that will set everything back to rights?" Harry looked so damn hopeful.

"Sorry, darling. I wish it were that simple. No, I'm afraid when I tried to perform the Finding Ceremony without Fate flying as my wing witch, it kinda got pissed."

"What do I have to do to correct it and . . . make it happy again?"

"You have to perform a successful Finding Ceremony. A real one."

Harry's face paled even further. "Finding lost keys, remember? How the hell am I supposed to perform a Finding Ceremony? Is there a Fate Witch handbook? *Fate Witch for Dummies* or something?"

Remus shrugged. "No clue. No. And definitely not, although I'd read that in a heartbeat."

"You're not being very helpful. You know that, right?"

"I know, which means I'm passing the torch just as I should be. All I can tell you is that when the time comes, you will know."

That bloodthirsty look slipped back into Harry's eyes as she glared at the other witch. "Gee, that's not cryptic or anything. Especially not helpful."

"I aim to please." Remus opened the front door with a magical wave of his hand and paused, looking over his shoulder. "Oh. Another whisper on the wind told me that a certain Fate Witch was in the market to find an elusive fae dragon shifter who may or may not currently be in this realm. That true?"

Jax stared hard at the older witch. "These whispers on the wind seem to know a hell of a lot."

"If it is? Why?" Harry asked, curious.

"Seems like something a Fate Witch might be good for."

"I find lost necklaces. Objects. I'm just not strong enough to find living, breathing people. Especially when those people happen to be in another realm."

"But you hadn't been back to Fates Haven and hadn't jump-started your Fate Witch abilities. And realms? Realms can't compete with Fate." With a wink and magical flash, Remus was gone and the door slammed closed behind him.

Jax gave Harry a moment to collect her thoughts. "Asking if you're okay seems a little redundant right now, but *are you*?"

"I'll let you know when everything processes in about another ten years or so." She dropped her head against the back of the couch. "Do you think Remus is right?"

"About which parts?"

"All of it. The Fate Witch thing. The Fates Haven thing. The fae-finding thing."

Cupping her cheek, he let his thumb trail over her bottom lip. "Yeah, sweet pea. I think he is . . . and I think you're going to kick ass at it, too."

"Which part?"

"All of them." Jax brought his mouth to hers and savored the soft little sigh she emitted as she sank into the kiss, her hand tangling in the back of his hair. "But there's not much you can do about any of it at this exact moment, and, I don't know about you, but I'd kinda like to get back to what we were doing before we were so rudely interrupted. Actually, I want to get back to what we were doing a few minutes before."

The sound of Harry's giggle was sweeter than music to his ears. "I think I can be persuaded. It would be shameful to waste this mysteriously appearing magical cabin in the woods."

"Good. This time, though, we're testing the bed's sturdiness." He stood, hoisting her over his shoulder, and feasted on the sound of her giggles as he carried her across the room.

24

Magical Mojo

Harry glanced in the hatchback's rearview mirror and couldn't prevent the smile that automatically bloomed on her face at the sight of Jax's truck following closely. To say it had been a whirlwind twenty-four hours was an understatement. To say it had been life altering was a bit more on track, but a track she had no clue how to navigate.

A Fate Witch. A Finding Ceremony. And a fae.

It sounded like the setup for a joke and she really didn't relish the idea of being the punch line.

All Harry's festering worries came to an instant halt when she turned down Nora's drive and saw the figure sitting on the new steps. Fifteen yards away from the house, she slammed on the accelerator and ripped up the rest of the driveway before coming to a screeching halt.

Harry flung herself out the car the second she slid it into park. "Cassie!"

Her friend stood up, laughing. "Slow down, you klutzy bitch.

This town of yours is so small, I'm not sure there's a hospital around here to take you to if you fall and break something."

They hugged, both laughing and crying at the same time.

"It was way too long this time, Cass," Harry admonished slightly, hesitant to pull away.

"I know. I just hated to drop back in when I had even less to go on than when I left before." Cassie ran her critical gaze over her. "You doing okay? Grace hasn't been giving you too much trouble, has she?"

"No more than usual." Harry grinned coyly. "So . . . you're the mother of a dragon."

Cassie shook her head in disbelief. "I'm still not so sure I can believe it until I see it for myself."

"You haven't seen Gracie yet?"

"No, your aunt Nora said she went to some kind of flea market with a Devon?" Cassie smirked when Harry released a groan. "Do I need to get all mother on her ass?"

"No, he's a good kid," Harry reluctantly admitted. "And he's completely smitten with her, and her with him. It's actually kinda cute."

Cassie's gaze drifted over Harry's shoulder and her eyes widened. "Speaking of cute . . ."

Jax's hand slid to Harry's waist, his other reaching out to shake her best friend's hand. "You must be Cassie. I've heard a lot about you, from both Harry and Grace. Your daughter is quite the force of nature."

"Don't I know it . . . ?"

"Jax. I'm—"

"Oh, I know who you are, too, Alpha Jaxon Atwood." Cassie's red lips slid into a mischievous smirk. Her gaze momentarily flickered toward his hand still secured around Harry's waist. "You're at the root of most of my conversations with my daughter lately. I can't thank you enough for helping her through this."

"It wasn't all me." He smiled down at Harry. "It was very much a team effort."

"Sure. Sure. I've heard a lot about these efforts."

"Cassie," Harry warned, barely withholding a smirk. "Behave."

"I'm behaving. I mean, I haven't mentioned that fucked-through-the-night skin glow you're sporting this morning, or the fact that Nora told me the two of you were stuck in some secluded mountain cabin all night with nothing to do but each other."

Jax chuckled.

Harry elbowed him, the move making him chuckle harder. "Do not encourage her."

"Well, Cassie, it was great to meet you in person, but I have to make sure that both my business and my pack haven't burned to the ground while I've left both unsupervised." Jax gently spun Harry and pulled her into a kiss that brought the tips of her toes to within an inch of leaving the ground. "I'll drop by later, okay?"

"Hmm-mhm." She peered up at him, a lust-drunk smile on her face. "I need to call a team Fearsome Four meeting. Make some things clear with Lenny and Elodie, and then I should probably start figuring things out."

"You got this, babe."

"I got something, but right now it feels more like heartburn." She patted his chest in an attempt to sooth his worry. "Go and make sure you still have a pack to Alpha, Alpha Atwood. I'll be here trying to figure out how the hell I'm supposed to bring

Fates Haven's magic back into line, perform a ceremony I have no earthly idea how to perform, and find a fae dragon shifter that very well may not be in this realm."

He cupped her jaw, thumb running over the curve of her bottom lip. "See. Easy. Like I said, you got this."

With a parting kiss and a wave for Cassie, Jax got back in his truck and headed out toward the pack ranch. Harry watched him go until his taillights disappeared from view.

"Start talking, witch, or my imagination will start filling in the blanks." Cassie's arm dropped over Harry's shoulder as they headed up the steps.

"There's honestly so much, I don't even know where to begin." Harry sighed. "My head feels like it's exploding."

"From the sheer amount of information or from the intensity of last night's orgasms?"

Harry shot her a look.

"What? It could be either, and I wasn't kidding about that fucked-through-the-night glow. The last time I felt that glow—"

"Was with the fae dragon shifter you picked to be your one and only one-night stand?" Harry shot back with a smirk.

"That would be it." Cassie paused, incredulity passing over her face. "She seriously turned into a fucking dragon? Like with scales and a tail?"

"And beautiful wings, but she hasn't figured out how to use them simultaneously yet, so she's all little-fawn awkward and it's super adorable. I wouldn't tell that to her face though. She's huge. She could swallow Nora's hatchback in one gulp if she wanted."

A mother's pride shone in Cassie's eyes. "Let's go call the others so you can start divulging everything you learned on that mountain—especially the stuff you learned while naked."

"I was fully clothed when the Fate Witch bomb of knowledge was dropped."

"Okay. But I still meant what I said."

*　*　*

"Why is no one saying anything?" Harry asked two hours later, after a full hour assuring everyone that she had no intention of leaving Fates Haven. *Ever.* "Seriously. Anything."

"Well," Nora said first, sitting calmly in her favorite reclining chair, "that makes sense."

"What makes sense?"

"All of it. I had an inkling."

"An inkling?" Harry gawked at her aunt. "About anything particular or *all of it.*"

Cassie raised her hand. "Let's go back to what you learned while naked."

Lenny and Elodie snickered. They'd been a handful while on FaceTime with Cassie, and now they'd officially met in person? An octopus couldn't handle all the snark.

"My sex life is the least concerning thing right now." Harry plopped heavily onto the spare chair. "But, like I said before, there was naked skin, orgasming, and then a witch with a *Buffy the Vampire* obsession literally came bursting through the door."

Nora chuckled. "Remus always did like making an entrance."

"Thank god he didn't enter five minutes earlier or I'm pretty certain Jax's cougar would've used him as a cat toy."

Elodie chuckled. "It's a lot, I agree. So let's think about this logically."

"I'm all ears."

"You're the new Fate Witch."

She nodded. "So Remus claims."

"But you can't fix the magical mojo in Fates Haven until you embrace your cool new powers and perform a fully functioning Finding Ceremony."

"Correct."

"So you need to become one with your cool new powers first. You need to practice. And what better way to practice than seeing if you can find an elusive fae shifter—and not the one who's upstairs in her bedroom right now."

Harry turned her attention to Cassie, whose face slowly slid into an emotionless mask. "Cass? What do you think? We were looking for Luke to get answers, but now that we know what kind of shifter Grace is, do you still want to track him down?"

Cassie nibbled her thumbnail before stopping herself. "That is a *really* difficult question to answer. Part of me wants to keep it all tucked away in the past, because what if the reality isn't quite what I remembered? What if I imagined the connection we had, or the type of person he was? Then bringing him into Grace's life could implode it."

Harry let her friend work through her thought process. "It could, but . . ."

"But it could also be the best thing for her," Cassie finished. "If Luke is the guy I've always thought him to be, finding him could be good for Cassie. And not to mention that, yes, we know she dragons out, but do we really know everything that entails? There's just so much that's still unknown."

"That's also true."

Cassie sighed. "I think I should talk to Grace and see what she wants to do. She's sixteen, and old enough to make these kinds of life-changing decisions. I have an suspicion I know which direction she'll want to go, but I don't want to assume."

"Great." Elodie clapped her hands. "While Cassie does the

mother thing with Grace, we'll start prepping for the monster of all descry spells. What do you need? Incense? Chalk? A Ouija board?"

Harry shot her a funny look. "What the hell are you talking about?"

"You don't think you're leaving us out of this, do you? I want to help hunt down a dragon. Do you have any idea how fucking awesome that would be to put on my résumé?"

Nora chuckled. "Actually, the extra help couldn't hurt."

"See!"

"I don't even know how to do a spell of this magnitude," Harry admitted. "I usually just light up my magical compass and have it point the way. Pretty sure that won't work with inter-realm *Where's Waldo*, and before anyone asks, Remus is not an option. He's probably lying in a lounger on one of those floating Caribbean cruise getaways."

"Then perhaps we should round up the basics." Nora headed toward the back of the house. "I'll gather the typical herbs. You all work on the rest."

"So what else do you need, Miss Fate Witch?" Elodie asked eagerly.

"Candles?" Harry shrugged. "Lots and lots of candles because I'll need a hell of a lot of concentration . . . and space. We'll need a shit ton of space for all the candles."

"We'll do it at the defense studio. There's plenty of room."

Everyone dispersed eagerly.

"Wait!" Harry cried out. "We don't even know if this is what Grace wants!"

"It is." The teen stepped off the stairs, obviously having been sitting there the entire time, *camouflaged*, and sent her mom a strong nod. "I want to find him. If he doesn't want to be involved or have a relationship with me, that's fine. But I'd at least like to know more about who I am and what I can do."

Cassie pulled her daughter into her arms. "We already know who you are, Gracie Lou. You're my sweet, intelligent, and brave no-longer-little girl. We'll do this, but only if you're one hundred percent sure it's what you want."

"Will *you* be okay if we find him?" Grace asked her mother. "If you're not, I'm sure Gavin can help us find all the information there is on dragons. It's what he does."

"You don't worry about me, sweetheart. I'll be more than fine."

Cassie waited a moment before glancing around, her gaze falling on Harry. "So when do you want to do this?"

"In two days? It'll be a witcher moon, and while I'm not one to really believe magical superstitions, something's telling me that that would be the best time."

"And that's the night before the Mud Runner," Elodie added. "So we can work in some last-minute training while we're at it."

Harry, Lenny, and Grace all groaned simultaneously.

"Hey!" Elodie propped her hands on her hips. "There will be none of that! We are tied with those egotists. *Tied!* That event will either make us or break us." She whipped around toward Harry, her finger wagging. "And so help me, Harlow Pierce, if you even for one second think about taking it easy on Jax because he's been your orgasm donor for the last twenty-four hours, I will completely wing out on you."

Harry held her hands up in surrender. "I wouldn't even dream of it."

"Good. Now let's go get our hands on enough candles to melt an entire wax emporium."

Harry couldn't help but laugh, thankful to be surrounded by this kick-ass, supportive group of women. Even if this failed spectacularly, they'd at least have enough people to have one hell of a midnight margarita party.

25

Then. Now. Always.

Harry gawked around Havenhood Park, the entire grassy knoll and Starlight Gazebo lit up with hundreds of flickering flames, making it look like predawn instead of near midnight on the night of the witcher moon.

"This is a lot of candles," she stated obviously. "And has to be breaching some sort of fire code or something."

"If we were indoors, definitely." Elodie beamed proudly. "Which is why we abandoned the idea of doing it at Angel Defense. Then Grace suggested here because . . . well . . . we're not exactly sure how things will go and this is the most open spot in town."

Harry snorted but understood. This was uncharted territory for them all. "This is perfect. Hopefully all of Fates Haven will remain safely tucked in their beds through this entire process. It's a small miracle that this place is as empty as it is."

"I may have had something to do with that." Jax swaggered

across the knoll, a coy smirk on his face. Gavin, Silas, and Maddox trailed behind, taking in the sights of all the candles.

"And how is that?" Harry asked, curious.

He wrapped her up in a hug that instantly soothed her rampaging jitters. They were definitely doing this public thing, and the knowledge sent a flutter of butterflies through her stomach.

She failed to fight off a grin, cocking up an eyebrow in a copy of his signature move. "What did you do? Because I can't imagine the people of Fates Haven sitting tight in their rooms while something potentially big was about to go down."

He shrugged, smirking. "I may have passed it around that tonight was the Ass Bite Moon, the once in five-hundred-year phenomenon when shifters are overcome with the urge to bite any ass that comes into their line of sight. And bites received on such a night are a real bitch to heal. Not really something someone wants to experience when the bite is on their ass."

"I've never in my life heard of an Ass Bite Moon."

"Neither did I until I thought it up." His smirk widened into a full-blown grin. "And before you ask, no. None of the pack will breathe a word of it to anyone who doesn't sprout a tail, or else they'll be on shit-shovel duty for the next month."

"My hero," she said wryly.

"All right, everyone." Nora clapped her hands, gaining everyone's attention. "Let's all get into our places, and by that, I mean anyone without a magical affinity needs to get off my lawn." She chuckled. "I've always wanted to say that. . . . Now scoot."

Elodie and Lenny gave Harry supportive hugs before following Maddox and the guys into the gazebo. Cassie went next, looking a bit more than nervous, and then Jax took Harry's face in his hands and guided her attention to him.

"You got this."

"I got this," she repeated.

"You are *the* Fate Witch."

"I am."

"Now track down that dragon shifter so I can start calling you my little dragon hunter." He hauled her into a hot, hard kiss and slapped her ass before joining the others.

And then there were two . . .

Grace nibbled her thumbnail, her gaze flicking to the magical infinity symbol that Nora had created with wildflowers.

"Have you changed your mind about wanting to try this?" Harry gently saved Grace's nail from further harm and held her hand.

"No. I want to do this. I *need* to do this."

Nora joined them, holding a silken length of fabric in her hand. "Are you two ready?"

"Are you sure we have to involve Grace in this?" Harry asked. "I don't like her being so close in case things go wonky."

"You're trying to find someone with whom she shares DNA. Having her be part of the searching process will hopefully put a bit more oomph behind the spell."

Harry squeezed the teen's hand and then Nora wrapped the golden fabric around their wrists, linking them physically moments before Harry herself would link them magically. They stepped onto the flowery infinity symbol together, one in each loop, and then Nora, too, joined the others in the gazebo.

"Just hold on tight," Harry instructed after a slow breath. "And don't leave the circle unless I tell you to run and duck. Okay?"

Grace nodded, took a deep breath, and held Harry's hand tightly. "Let's do this."

Closing her eyes, Harry tilted her free hand palm up toward the brightly lit moon, and called on her magic. She'd called on it countless times through her life, used to the warm, slow spread of magic through her veins.

But this felt different.

It felt like . . . more.

More magic. More strength. More everything.

She sucked in a quick breath as she attempted to draw the magic into a tight ball in the center of her magical core. She let it build, one second at a time, and invited more magic to join the party. Sweat dotted her forehead, and her heart beat like a drum in her chest.

"Harry . . ." Grace's softly murmured voice squeezed through her concentration.

"It's okay. I'm okay." Once she hit a certain point, all her uncertainty shifted and she knew it was time.

She called on her descry magic and, still gripping Grace's hand, released that magical ball concentrated in her center. Her face automatically tilted toward the sky as it released in a rush of bright, hot, pulsing golden waves.

Soft gasps sounded around them, but Harry concentrated, directing the magic to search. To find. To locate and call.

A massive golden cloud formed in the sky.

Grace sucked in a sharp breath, her eyes locked on the formation. "It looks like a *dragon*. It looks like *my* dragon."

A slow smile spread on Harry's lips.

It did . . . and it was gorgeous.

Cassie reached them first; and not long after, everyone swarmed, taking turns with hugs and keeping an eye on the sky. The magical sky-dragon slowly dissipated, melting into the dark backdrop of the star-laden heavens.

"Did it work?" Cassie asked first. "Do you know where Luke is?"

"I couldn't latch on to a location." Harry pulled her friend into a tight hug at the sight of her disappointed look. "But if he's looking even the slightest bit, he'll be able to latch on to ours. I know it's not exactly what we ho—"

"Thank you so much, Harry." Grace flung herself into her arms, squeezing her into the tightest hug she'd ever given her. "I know it worked. He'll find us. I don't know how I know, but I do."

With a hopeful smile, Harry patted the teen and held her until Grace pulled away and leaped into her mother's arms. Everyone talked excitedly, divvying up the task of packing up Elodie's hundreds of candles while Harry stayed back, watching her friends and family.

Jax's arms slipped around her waist from behind, his mouth coasting over her ear. "You did it, and you looked fucking amazing."

"He's in the fae realm. Luke." She turned in Jax's arms and sighed. "I don't know where, but I could tell that he's not *here*, and if the portals are closed . . ."

He studied her carefully. "You're afraid he won't be able to cross over."

"According to Tomlyn, inter-realm travel abilities are the exception, not the norm. If Luke isn't one of those exceptions, he could theoretically hear and see the Call but not be able to do anything about it."

Jax cupped her cheek. "If Luke is even half as resourceful as his daughter, he'll find a way."

Harry hoped so. She couldn't withstand disappointing anyone else she cared about . . . especially Grace.

Hearing laughter in the background, she glanced at everyone she called family and couldn't help but smile. Without help from Remus, she didn't know how the hell she was supposed to go about getting the magic of Fates Haven back on track, but one thing she did know was that she wouldn't rest until she did.

* * *

AN HOUR AGO, Jax had thought this was a good idea. Now, faced with the actual implementation of this genius plan, he questioned his judgment. Did that mean he wouldn't go through with it?

Nope.

He wasn't leaving until he got what he came for, and that meant he needed to figure this out. It had been so damn easy when all he'd had to do was climb a damn tree.

He cracked his neck and rolled his shoulders, limbering up before he called on his mountain lion. The bastard rushed to the surface, eager to stretch his legs, and Jax let him, pulling the shift to the surface. In a few blinks, he stood on four paws, his night vision spot-on and locked on its target about twelve feet above.

Cougar Jax dropped to the ground, tension coiling in his bottom half as it prepped to pounced . . . and then he leaped, clearing the distance easily.

His paws slipped on the awning's tin tile before he found traction and bumped his head against the bedroom window. He did it a second time, and then did he same with his paw, sans claws.

A light flicked on in the room and then Harry stared at him from the other side, her mouth agape as she opened the window for him to enter. He hopped into her room and shifted back, sheepish smirk in place.

"Were you sleeping?" he asked coyly.

"Honestly? No. I've been trying for about two hours now with no luck. Too much going through my head. You?" Her gaze dropped to his naked form, lips twitching. "Never mind. Unless you sleepwalk naked and while in cougar form, I guess you weren't sleeping either."

"I was too busy planning your kidnapping to go to sleep." He guided her into his arms and she melted instantly. Fuck, he loved how her body responded to his. "Escape with me."

She giggled as he ran a series of kisses over her jaw and down her neck. "I seriously can't believe you stripped naked to shift and sneak into my room. We aren't sixteen anymore, Jax. You could've used the front door."

"And lose some of the excitement? Nah. Plus, I was afraid I'd get a lecture from the current sixteen-year-old in the house. Someone told me she's a dragon. I definitely don't want to fuck with her. Now, about that escape . . ." He nipped her bottom lip. "Let's go on an adventure."

Her eyes heated. "Fine. But I am not jumping off the roof."

"Catlike agility. No jumping needed." He swept her legs up into his arms and easily climbed through the open window.

"Oh my god. Oh my god." Harry buried her face in his neck with a squeal, not able to watch as he dropped them effortlessly to the ground.

He hustled them to his truck. Before getting behind the wheel, he slipped back into his jeans and boots, forgoing his shirt altogether.

"Escape time." Jax hauled her right next to him as he drove down the Pierce House drive and headed toward Mystic Lake.

"And where are we escaping to?" Harry snuggled close.

"It wouldn't be a kidnapping if I told you," he teased back.

Less than a few minutes later, and it wouldn't be much of a surprise. They both knew the way toward Mystic Lake better than the back of their hands. In the winter, it was quite the ordeal to navigate the back roads, but this time of year the route was damn near scenic, not a single cloud in the sky.

Harry played with his fingers as they held hands on the quiet drive, but it wasn't an awkward quiet. It was a comforting silence, and while neither of them talked, he could almost hear the million and one thoughts whirring through her head.

She needed this getaway as much as he did, and he was ten types of thrilled he could be the one to give it to her.

He made the last turn and backed up the truck, pointing its bed toward the lake. She followed him out of the cab and watched as he jumped into the back, where he pulled out a bevy of pillows and blankets from the storage box. Once everything was in its place, he gave the setup a critical eye and turned to see her amusement.

"What? I wanted to make sure we were comfortable." Heat crept into his cheeks.

"Did you steal every pillow and blanket from every house in Fates Haven? Because it sure looks like you did."

"You won't be complaining when you feel like your ass is sitting on a cloud, baby. Now get it up here and tell me I'm right." He grabbed her hands and hauled her up for a quick kiss before sitting and bringing her between the vee of his legs, her back facing his chest.

She emitted a soft sigh and looked out over the crystal lake, the moon's bright reflection a gorgeous mirror across the glassy surface. Combined with the abundant stars and the army of fireflies skimming over the water like mobile stars themselves, the view was almost ethereal.

"I will never get used this kind of beauty." Harry settled against him, her head drifting to his shoulder as she dropped her arms to rest on his around her waist. "If anyone ever doubts the presence of magic in this world, all they have to do is see this view and they'll be firm believers. I don't think I've ever seen anything more magically beautiful."

"I have." He brushed his mouth over her ear. "I'm holding her right now."

She snortled, craning her neck to look at him. "You really need to work on your pickup lines, Jaxon Atwood. Any person with a shred of common sense would see that line coming from a mile away."

"Pickup lines are for those trying to rope themselves a Mate." He paused, sucking in a slow breath. "I already have mine."

Harry froze except for the heavy rise and fall of her chest.

Shit. He hadn't expected to just hurl it out there with all the finesse of a linebacker, but he couldn't take it back. He didn't want to take it back. Harlow Pierce was his Mate in every sense of the word. His one love. His world. There was no use pretending otherwise.

"Harry . . ." Jax trailed one hand over her shoulder to sweep her hair back from her face. "Did you hear what I said?"

"Yes." He could barely hear her, even with his shifter hearing . . . but he could sure as hell hear the fast gallop of her heart.

"And?" He held his breath, his own heart pounding against his chest.

Harry moved slowly from his arms as she turned around, now kneeling between his legs. Her gorgeous purple eyes twinkled in the moonlight as she studied him.

He mentally kicked himself for not being more suave about this. He should've tossed out a few feelers to test the metaphorical waters instead of just throwing them both in the deep end like a frat boy doing a cannonball.

"Jax, I—"

"Wait." He cupped her cheek, placing his thumb over her lush lips. "Let me get everything out before I fucking implode."

She removed his hand and held it, her fingers squeezing his. "Okay. I'm listening."

Jax racked his brain in an attempt to find something that didn't sound clichéd, since everything he'd practiced in the truck on the way to Pierce House abruptly disappeared from his memory vault.

"There's probably a million and one more romantic ways to go about this, but fuck it all if I can think of them right now," he said honestly.

Harry gently stroked his hand with her thumb. "I don't need romantic, Jax. I just need the truth."

"Truth, huh? Okay." He took a deep breath and nearly puked. "I've loved one person in my entire life, Harlow Pierce. I've been *in* love with that person, even before I really knew what that entire concept meant. From the moment I first laid eyes on you over that purple crayon, I knew you were mine. And when I thought I lost you . . ."

Tears welled Harry's eyes. "Jax, I am so, so sorry for leaving the way I did. Those words seem so inadequate, but they're the truth, and there isn't a second that goes by that I don't wish

I could rewind time and do it differently. I should've stayed. I should have fought for us."

Jax fought through his own rush of emotions, the brutal honesty surging forward. "I actually think that maybe things played out the exact way in which they were meant to."

Harry's mouth opened, a tinge of hurt on her face that he quickly wanted to extinguish.

"As much as I would've cherished having thirteen additional years with you, that time apart has made one thing crystal fucking clear to me." His gaze locked on hers, he purged *everything*. "I don't need some fucking Blue Willow Wisp to tell me what I already know straight to my soul. You're *mine*. You're my *Mate*. My world. My heart. My . . . *everything*. And every surly, broody inch of me is *yours*. It always has been, and it always will be. From now and for eternity."

Heat spread high on his cheeks as he studied her contemplative expression, his stomach a ball of nerves. Maybe he'd said too much, laid it on a little too thick, but damn it . . . it was true.

All of it.

"You don't have to—"

She shushed him with a palm to his cheek. "My turn now, Alpha Atwood."

His lips twitched. "You have my undivided attention, my little Fate Witch."

"First of all, it was a blue crayon." Harry grinned coyly. "I remember it distinctly because I wanted to color my rabbit's dress blue, but you hogged it for what felt like a million years."

"Well then, I stand corrected." Grinning, he chuckled nervously.

"But you were right about a few other things."

"What things would those be?" He ran his hand down her arm, unable to keep from touching some part of her.

She leaned close. "I *am* yours, forever and always. Just as much as you're mine. You're mine to argue with. To climb out of bedroom windows with. You're mine to have secret rendezvous by the lake with. And you're mine to love with every inch of heart, body, and soul. I would love nothing more than to be your Mate. I love you, Jaxon Atwood. Then. Now. And always."

With a low, erupting growl, he hauled her onto his lap and crushed his mouth to hers in a needy attempt to feel every single piece of her, to leave an imprint on her as permanent and all-consuming as the one she'd left on him years ago.

Harlow Pierce may be Fates Haven's new Fate Witch, but she was something else, too.

His Fated . . . with or without that damn Blue Willow Wisp telling him so.

26

Tits Up

It was game day, and in more ways than just being minutes away from the final Fates Festival competition and finding out which team's fate included being part of the Gargoyle Girls reunion performance.

Today, there'd be a Finding Ceremony.

Harry hoped.

She just had to survive until then, and at this point she'd give herself a fifty-fifty shot.

"Nope. Buck up, buttercup." Elodie's stern voice snapped her out of her doom-and-gloom mental spiral. "We have no time for imposter syndrome right now. It's time to pick the tits up."

People lined both side of Mud Runner obstacle course, their cheers and excitement rivaling an NFL Monday night football game. Hell, three guys in the front row with their faces and chests painted, screamed their unwavering support, albeit for the Big Bads, in bold colors of gold and purple.

"At least those guys are siding with the right horse." Silas, Jax, and the other two guys joined them, Silas pointing a heated gaze in Elodie's direction. "But I wouldn't worry about it, angel eyes. I'm sure you have your cheerleader in the crowd somewhere. Deep, deep in the crowd."

As if they conjured her up, Cassie pushed her way to the barrier rope, a little pom-pom in her hand and Nora at her side. They both shot them big grins and thumbs-ups.

"I'm feeling pretty good about our chances." Harry smirked at Silas. "Feeling even better since you felt the need to come over here and try to psyche us out."

"Psyche you out? Nah. Came over cuz this one wouldn't stop sending you goo-goo eyes through the crowd; and if bringing him over here was the only way to get his head on straight, then so be it." He nudged his chin toward Jax, who didn't seem the least bit worried. "Don't know what spell you wove on my man here, but, damn, it's lethal."

"It's called love, Si. You should try it sometime." Jax came up to Harry's side, kissing the side of her head. "I highly recommend."

"No, thank you. I'll leave that shit to you all while I stay as far away as possible."

Elodie muttered, "Chicken," under a cough.

Silas bristled. "So then where's the love of your life? Hiding them under that halo of yours?"

"I don't know, but I hope they're a long way off. I have things I want to do before"—she waved her hands in Jax and Harry's direction—"that happens."

Harry rolled her eyes and looked up at a smirking Jax. "Something tells me our friends are happy for us, but happy to not *be* us."

"I'm good with that," Jax teased. "It's their loss anyway. They're totally missing out."

The overhead speakers squawked to life, sounding like the muffled teacher from a *Charlie Brown* cartoon, but the gist was received loud and clear. It was time to take positions.

"Good luck." Jax pulled her into a swoon-worthy kiss, dipping her for dramatic flair. "I'll be waiting for you on the other side of the finish line."

"Or I'll be waiting for you." Harry swatted his ass as he walked away with a smirk.

Every team would leave its starting line spot at staggered times, the clock stopping only when all team members crossed the finish line after completing all ten obstacles. Earlier that morning, Harry had picked her team's fourth-spot start time, and Jax's team had the sixth, with ten minutes between them.

"What do you think the obstacles are?" At Harry's side, Grace looked eager and excited, bouncing on the balls of her feet.

"I don't know, but I'm sure they'll all have a common theme."

"Mud," they said in unison, chuckling.

The first buzzer sounded and the first team took off, running up the steep embankment at a fast clip. Before the Fearsome Four realized, it was time for the second, then the third. . . .

They were up next.

"Remind me never to do this again, okay?" Harry quipped, slipping the teen at her side a wink as they got into position.

"And here I was thinking we should make this an annual thing."

Harry loved the sound of Grace planning for things in the future, and a future that included both her and Fates Haven.

Their team buzzer sounded and they took off, Elodie taking

the lead and drill sergeanting the way up the steep hill. The embankment was slick, Harry's sneakers slipping countless times on the way to the top. When they got there, she wasn't the only one who cursed.

From there they had to descend on their asses on a mud slide, at the bottom of which stood at least twelve massive steps. And not any regular ones. *Mud* steps, each higher than Harry was tall. The three teams before them were in varying locations, struggling their way up and over and in some cases, sliding all the way back to the bottom.

Lenny cursed. "We have two people with wings. What are they chances you can fly us over this monstrosity?"

"If I do it now, I might not have enough strength to do it later, and something tells me that this won't be the most challenging obstacle we face," Elodie reluctantly admitted.

"And don't look at me," Grace added. "I can barely keep myself airborne for longer than thirty seconds much less carry anyone."

Harry lifted her chin and straightened her back. "Then let's do this, Fearsome Four. We won't get up this hell climb by sitting here gabbing about it."

Each eight-foot magically made monster-step had no handles or grips, no indentation in which to fit the tip of your shoe or squeeze in so much as a finger-grip. And as if that wasn't challenging enough, each step exuded a steady flow of slick, muddy goo.

Whichever supernatural designed this particular obstacle definitely didn't want anyone finishing it easily.

Sidling up next to the other struggling teams, Harry hoped for the best, which as it turned out, did not produce results.

Ten minutes of struggling and mud in the mouth later, and an idea hit Harry.

Dropping to her hands and knees, she tapped Grace's leg. "Use me as a stool and hoist yourself up."

"You're a fucking genius," Elodie quipped, quickly getting on board.

They worked together to elevate, hoist, and help Grace up and over the first monster step. They let themselves have a little victory cheer, and then they tackled it again, next with Lenny, then Elodie. The other teams, seeing their success, quickly mimicked their tactics.

"Come on, Harry." Grace leaned over the ledge, her arm extended. "Run and we'll grab you and haul you up."

"Here goes nothing." With a warrior cry, she ran for the mud wall and reached as high as she could. Three sets of mud-covered hands latched on to some part of her arms, but it was the grip fastened around her wrists that hauled her up so fast and high Harry came crashing down in a muddy skid.

Grace glanced at her palms, shock widening her eyes. "Holy shit."

Harry broke out into laughter, and so did the others. "I think you mean holy dragon grip. Remind me to never challenge you to an arm wrestling match."

Elodie's eyes lit up at the mention. "But she should totally challenge Silas . . . and let me record it."

They broke out into laughter again, and a moment later, she stared up at Jax's grinning face.

"Lying down on the job?" He helped haul her to her feet. "One down. Only nine more to go. You feeling up to it?"

Silas shouted at them both before leaping the next wall like he was a fucking gazelle.

"Sorry, babe. Gotta go." Jax winked and then he quickly followed the rest of his team.

The game was on.

By the time they reached the top of the hell climb and officially put the first obstacle behind them, Harry was already winded, dirty, and determined. Not only were they finishing this freaking course, but they'd have the fastest time doing it.

Or she wasn't the damn Fate Witch.

* * *

JAX ATE MUD for the sixth time in as many minutes and it didn't taste any better than the first. Next to him, Maddox commando crawled through the muck and grime, interspersing grunts with high-pitched squeals as the dangling electrified wires zapped him yet again.

Jax released a cougar-like guffaw, laughing at his friend.

"Fuck you, Atwood. Some of us don't have a thick hide to hide behind." Maddox spasmed again when another wire hit him. "Shit. Shit."

"You two are too slow," Silas bellowed from the end of the obstacle, Gavin next to him. "Pick up the pace, fellas, or Elodie et al. will actually give us a run for our money and I refuse to dance backup for the Gargoyle Girls. *Hustle!*"

They plowed through. Six feet. Then four. A foot away from freedom, Gavin grabbed them each by an appendage and pulled them free from both the wires and mud.

Maddox recited a trail of curses as he shook off the effects of the last twenty minutes. "Whoever thought up that damn challenge is fucking evil."

Jax shifted back to two feet with chuckle and accepted the shorts Gavin handed him. Pretty sure the answer to that was

Nora Pierce. "Only one more to go, right? We got this in the bag."

They didn't have it anywhere even remotely near *the bag.*

They jogged up the next steep incline to the final obstacle. It didn't look like much. A slick incline with no footholds. There was no electrocution. No mud pits except for the one at the base. No swinging or slippy bars to grip.

Nothing.

Except a fuck ton of people practically lying in one big muddy heap, and the few stragglers actually *on* the obstacle who slipped and joined the party. They looked like worms on a hook, climbing and falling, making themselves and the wall even slicker than before.

He spotted Harry and the girls easily and pride stirred deep as he watched them systematically create a human ladder, one crawling up and over the body of the others in an attempt to build their human ladder higher.

"Looks like they got the right idea." Jax nudged his chin proudly toward his Mate. "Let's get to it."

Jax stopped alongside Harry as Silas went first to climb on his shoulders.

"Fancy meeting you here, sweet pea." He grinned as Silas stepped on his ear, nearly taking the damn thing off the side of his head.

"Couldn't find another way to get up and over? You have to copy us?"

"Seems like you have a good plan in theory. It's the execution that's a little muddled."

"Shit. This won't work," Elodie called from the top of their ladder. "There's still a good ten feet to go and Grace is how tall?"

"Five feet at best," Grace answered, hands on Harry's hips as she paused her climb. "There has to be something we can do to make up for that amount of distance."

"I'm all ears if you have any ideas."

"And quickly"—Harry's breath shuddered along with her legs—"before we all go tumbling as if the big bad wolf blew the house down."

A slow, satisfied smile slid over the teenager's face. "I have an idea, but I don't know if it'll work."

"As long as it's something more than what we're currently doing, I say go for it." Harry's left foot slipped in the mud before she brought it back, knees buckling.

"Elodie, be prepared to grab me and everyone else. . . . Don't let go of the person above you."

Harry chuckled warily. "Why does that not give me the warm fuzzies?"

"I can't fly us all up and over, but that doesn't mean I can't drag, right?" The teen stepped back and much faster than she'd done before, transformed into her gorgeous golden dragon, her clothes vanishing with whatever magic that allowed them to disappear and reappear with each shift.

A handful of people fell where they stood, taking in the sight of the large reptile, and others who didn't see it at first were knocked over with one flap of her powerful wings. Dragon Grace went airborne, and people ducked and dodged. Jax chuckled as a talon nearly knocked Silas on the side of the head, the tough demon letting out an unexpected squeal.

Grace perched on the top of the wall like a dragon on a castle, and lowered one massive wing with a soft chuff.

"No fucking way," Silas grumbled as Elodie, Lenny, and

Harry worked their way onto Grace's wing. "That should be fucking cheating."

Jax chuckled. "That is fucking genius."

Harry walloped him with a broad smile and waved. "See you when you cross the finish line, Alpha Atwood. *After* us."

They disappeared from view on their very own dragon slide. Harry's throaty chuckles, mixed with the sounds of the surprised crowd on the other side, slowly melted away. Time moved at a snail's pace after that, team after team gradually making their way up and over. By the time Jax and the rest of the Big Bads stumbled over the finish line, it was clear they hadn't won the bet.

Not even close.

Harry waited for him with a clean towel and a smirk. "The Gargoyle Girls take the stage in thirty minutes, so you may want to clean up a bit and get those stretches in. You don't want to pull a hamstring or something."

Emitting a low, playful growl, he hauled her into a muddy hug, their bodies squishing. "Enjoying yourself?"

"Immensely. I'll be enjoying myself even more when you're shaking your hips to the Gargoyle Girls greatest hits."

A faraway commotion rippled through the crowd of spectators. Murmurs and questions. Bodies shifted, creating space as the people parted for something . . . or someone.

The air shifted, and Jax wasn't the only one who felt it. Harry stilled next to him as she turned toward the new arrival who was stepping out from the mass.

A tall, broad-shouldered man strode into the small winner's clearing, his long dark hair and obsidian eyes raking over everyone until they paused on Harry. Jax stepped protectively in front of his Mate.

"Seriously?" she griped, her annoyance palpable.

A small gasp broke the sudden silence and Cassie took a step forward, her eyes wide and mouth agape. "L-L-Luke?"

A slow smile bloomed on the man's face, immediately transforming his stern look to one of pure longing. "*Cassandra.*"

He closed the distance between them in three strides, his large hand cupping her cheeks as he stared at her adoringly. "I'm here. I'm not sure how you were able to locate me, but I heard your Call and there was no keeping me away."

"It worked." Harry heaved a heavy sigh, leaning into Jax's side. "It actually fucking worked."

Luke's gaze slid to her. "You're the one who sent the Call?"

"If you mean the large golden dragon in the sky? Then yeah." She nodded. "I was."

"I'm not sure how you managed it, but I am thankful that you did." He settled one hand over his heart as he glanced back into Cassie's tearstained face. "So very thankful. You have no idea how often I've fantasized about coming back to you."

"Why didn't you?" Cassie asked. "You crossed realms once before. You did now. Why didn't you come back sooner?"

Luke smiled wanly. "*That* is a much longer story, and one that I don't wish to taint this magical moment with. But it's our memories together that have kept me warm on frigid, lonely nights, and I am forever in debt to your friend for signaling for me."

Cassie nibbled nervously on her bottom lip. "Harry didn't do it alone. She used a little piece of you to help direct her Call a little better."

"A piece of me? I wasn't aware that I left anything behind."

"Well, you did." Cassie shot a quick glance to the left where

Grace stepped forward looking a perfect blend of Cassie and her father. "This is Grace. She's your—"

"Daughter." An amazed look slid over the dragon shifter's face as he glanced between the teen and Cassie. "I didn't even know this was possible. It *shouldn't* be possible. My kind . . ." His head snapped back to Grace as he studied her from head to toe, soaking in her existence. "You have a dragon."

It wasn't a question.

He knew, his eyes flashing gold and in answer, so did Grace's.

Cassie blinked through fresh tears and nodded. "I do. She's—"

"Magnificent. I can see her within you. You're both absolutely stunning. I . . . don't even know where to begin." Luke looked back to Cassie, tears in his eyes. "We should probably find somewhere to talk . . . all three of us?"

Cassie nodded immediately, reaching out for Grace. "I know the perfect spot."

Harry and Jax watched as the reunited family headed toward Starlight Gazebo, Cassie's hand firmly encasing her daughter's. The fae's eyes bounced from mother to daughter, pure amazement still lighting up every inch of his face.

Jax planted a kiss on Harry's head. "You did that, Harlow Pierce. You brought a family together, and I have no doubt that you're about to do even more miraculous things. How's that for finding out where and how you belong?"

Harry smacked his chest playfully. "Throwing my words back at me isn't very nice."

"Who said I'm nice?" He emitted a low, playful growl as gently nipped her earlobe. She squirmed and released a stream of giggles.

Silas groaned somewhere to his right. "We're being summoned to the musical stage area, Jax. Let's get this the fuck over with."

Harry smiled against Jax's mouth as she gave him another kiss. "Now go swivel those hips."

27

Fated in Fates

Harry couldn't take her eyes off Jax, memorizing every hip sway and finger snap as he, Silas, Maddox, and Gavin stood behind the octogenarian pop-folk band, the Gargoyle Girls. Next to Harry, Elodie howled in laughter, her phone recording Silas's awkward grimace and each of the demon's froglike oohs and aahs.

It wouldn't be a sight any of them forgot any time soon . . . especially not with the abundant amount of video evidence.

The wind ruffled a strand of Harry's mud-matted hair across her face, temporarily obscuring her vision. As she tucked it behind her ear, movement on her left caught her attention.

Remus leaned his back against Starlight Gazebo, his face pointed toward the full moon a second before their gazes locked. He wiggled his fingers at her, rings sparkling . . . and nodded.

It was time.

Lenny shot her a look of concern. "Hey. You okay?"

"Yeah." She took a slow, steadying breath. "It's time."

The seer's eyes widened as she exchanged looks with Elodie. "It's time? Like, *now* is the time? For that other thing . . . the ceremony thing?"

Harry nodded, sending a momentarily panicked look toward Cassie. Her friend temporarily left Luke's side and wrapped her in a hug. "You can do this, Harry. You just did the impossible. There's not a doubt in my mind that you can do this, too."

Elodie nodded. "We believe in you."

Grace reciprocated with a meaningful, "It's time you believe in yourself as much as we do."

Harry chuckled. "Then I guess everyone should buckle in for the ride."

With the Gargoyle Girls winding down their final set, Harry let the fate magic wash over her. Much like when she'd combined her descry powers to send the call to Luke, her powers merged and rolled around, playing together before slowly spreading like a warm blanket through every inch of her body.

She tingled from head to toe, her breath quickening.

Find the Fated.

With that one simple declaration, Harry released the swell of magic. Every twinkle light throughout the grassy knoll flickered with the power surge, and somewhere in the distance, a car alarm blared. A second later, one by one, they arrived.

The Blue Willow Wisps.

Soft gasps fluttered through the crowd as the first slowly shimmered into focus, and then a second. A third. Harry opened her eyes to find an entire field lit up with dozens of magical blue flames . . . including the ones hovering in front of her three best friends.

More purple than blue, Lenny's Wisp highlighted the pure shock on the seer's face, and Elodie's glowed a brilliant, twinkling sapphire. Cassie's flame flickered between a gorgeous blue and purple and was already on the move.

"What do I do?" Eyes wide, Cassie looked panic-stricken.

"Follow it to your Fated." Harry smiled warmly, watching as her best friend hustled to catch up to her Blue Willow Wisp and followed it right to the matching flame hovering in front of Luke. The fae grinned broadly, not looking the least surprised to realize that Cassie was his perfect other half.

"Not again." Elodie groaned, looking as if she wanted the earth to swallow her whole. "I refuse. Make it go away."

"This can't be right." Lenny's head swiveled. Terror widened her eyes as she scanned their surroundings as though looking for Freddy Krueger. "I think something went wrong. I do not have a—a Fated."

"You and me both," Elodie quipped.

"Nothing's broken." Harry was 100 percent certain even as she slowly registered the fact that there were only three Blue Willow Wisps.

The spot in front of her remained empty . . . and that was okay.

To quote a certain sexy shifter, she didn't need a Blue Willow Wisp to tell her that Jaxon Atwood was hers in heart, body, and soul, and vice versa. He *was* her Fate. Her love. Her world. And knowing that made her the luckiest person in this realm and the next.

"Hey there, sweet pea. You'll never guess what happened to the guys." Jax appeared on her left, his arm wrapping tightly around her waist.

"Oh, fuck to the no!" Elodie squawked loudly, glaring at

Silas as he approached, his footsteps heavy. "What the hell did you do?"

"Me? I think I should be asking that of you, angel eyes," Silas growled.

It took a moment for Harry to connect the dots . . . and the identical Blue Willow Wisps hovering in front of them before the two slowly—and beautifully—merged into one.

As Fated.

"Nope. Nope, nope, nope." Lenny shook her head, her stare transfixed as the twin flame to her own slowly connected to Gavin's. "This is so fucked up."

Jax finally registered what was happening around them and flickered concerned eyes to her. "Babe . . ."

"It's okay." With a genuine smile, Harry cupped his chin and brought his mouth to hers. "We don't need any Blue Willow Wisps to tell us our destiny, right?"

"Damn right." He pulled her close and took her mouth in a hot, searing kiss that left her breathless and her soul melting right there on the spot.

They barely parted long enough to suck in a quick breath when a searing zing of white-hot pain shot through her left ass cheek. She howled and cupped her butt, momentarily distracted from the fact that Jax, too, released a low shriek.

"I think something just bit me." He rubbed his left ass cheek. "Like a prehistoric mosquito or something. Fuck, that hurt."

All their friends temporarily froze, turning their attention to them.

"You got a pain in your ass?" Harry felt weird asking the question.

"Not in my ass, but on it? Definitely." His eyes snapped to hers. "You did, too?"

She nodded, nibbling her bottom lip. "Can I . . . see?"

Jax cocked up an eyebrow but shrugged. "Not like people around here haven't seen my ass pre-and post-shift, so sure."

Harry slowly made her way around him and dipped the waistband of his shorts an inch at a time . . . and sucked in a stunned breath. It was impossible . . . and yet . . .

"You haven't gone to Once Upon a Tattoo recently, have you?" Harry already knew the answer but needed to ask anyway.

"Uh, no. Why? What's on my ass? Is it a rash or something?"

A heady giggle slipped through her lips. "Definitely not a rash."

Everyone made their way around to stare at Jax's revealed left butt cheek, but it was Lenny's gasp that was the loudest of all.

"I can Read it!" the seer shouted, equal parts stunned and relieved. "Holy shit, I can Read it!"

Elodie chuckled. "I think all of us can read it, Len. We don't have to be a seer to know what this means."

Jax growled. "Would someone kindly tell me what the hell is engraved on my ass?"

Harry let his waistband snap into place as she grinned coyly up at the man she loved. "It's just a Blue Willow Wisp. The exact replica of *my* Blue Willow Wisp. The same one that's etched on *my* ass."

Jax blinked twice as his brain slowly computed. "We have matching tattoos."

"Matching magical tattoos."

"Matching magical *Fated* tattoos," Lenny added. "You know . . . just in case anyone forgot that I can Read now."

They all chuckled, Harry and Jax included.

"Guess a Fate Witch's own Fated doesn't show up the same way as everyone else's," Harry teased. "But you know we don't need matching magical tattoos to tell me that you're my destiny, right, Alpha Atwood?"

Jax pulled her into his arm. "Damn right, my little Fate Witch. I was yours the moment we reached for the same purple crayon."

"Blue."

"Nope. Purple . . . because I remember vividly that it was the same color as your eyes. That's why I was hogging it. It reminded me of you."

People all around them shouted and cheered, some while crying. Nora came up to Harry and Jax, a grinning Remus in tow.

"I knew you could do it, my dear." Nora pulled her into a tight hug before doing the same to Jax. "And I couldn't be any happier for the two of you."

Harry slid a look to her friends, Cassie the only one looking even remotely ecstatic about finding her soul mate. "Wish that happiness could be shared among everyone."

Remus chuckled. "Oh, they'll get with the program eventually, don't worry. There's always a handful like them every year. Now that that little Fate seed is planted, it'll eventually grow into what it was always meant to be. Kinda like you . . . a little nurturing, a little water, some orgasms, and, poof! Fate Witch!

"Massive turnout, by the way," Remus added, glancing around at all the Blue Willow Wisps. "We'd have to take an official tally, but I dare say, you may have broken my record. If this is your success rate in your inaugural year, I can't wait to see what you do in the upcoming ones."

Harry blanched, her head snapping toward him. "I have to do this again?"

Remus chuckled. "And again. And again. *Each* year. That's what the Fates Haven Fate Witch does, my dear."

"Oh, my goddess. I'm actually the Fate Witch. Like . . . *the* one." The true scope of the situation was slowly sinking in.

Jax chuckled, tucking a strand of loose hair behind her ear. "Yes, you are, babe. And just like everything else, you'll rock at it. Think of all the people you're about to help find their Fated."

Elodie's and Silas's shouting drew their attention toward the angel-demon duo, their hands flailing and tempers rising.

Harry grimaced. "Not so sure all our friends think this is a good thing."

Remus waved off her sentiment with a decorated hand. "Nurture. Water. Orgasms. Poof. They'll come around. They always do."

Somehow, Harry knew the former Fate Witch spoke the truth.

"So, what's next, Harlow Pierce?" Jax's arms tightened around her, and she not only felt the warmth of his love but saw it in his eyes as he stared down at her. "Where do we go from here?"

She shrugged. "It doesn't matter as long as we do it side by side. How does that sound to you, Alpha Atwood."

He brushed his mouth over hers in painfully soft kiss. "Sounds like heaven."

"Sounds like our forever."

"Sounds like a simple twist of Fate."

ACKNOWLEDGMENTS

With every book that comes into the world, there are people to thank, and as always, the first round always goes to my family. While writing Fates, our family experienced immense change, some that challenged us like nothing has before, and it wasn't without your support and guidance that I was able to get this book written. Your patience and support warm my heart, always.

Tif Marcelo, Bestie and Critique Partner: Your guidance—and ass-kickery—has become one of my greatest companions. Now, let's go write all those words . . .

Sarah E. Younger, Agent of Awesome: I know I've said it before, but I really won the agent jackpot with you! I can't imagine anyone standing in my corner the way that you do.

Tiffany, Editor Extraordinaire: Thank you for helping me bring Fates Haven and all its supernatural citizens to life! I'm so lucky to have an editor such as you in my corner (and deleting all my typos, lol).

Thank you to the entire team at Griffin for giving *A Simple Twist of Fate* a strikingly magical cover, and helping get this book out in the eyes of readers everywhere.

Kristin and Molly, LEO PR: You both are rock stars, and I

definitely wouldn't remember half the things I've put on my calendar if I didn't have the two of you by my side and giving me those nudges (lol).

April's Angels: Thank you for your enthusiasm for my books! Your excitement and enthusiasm have kept me going on trying days, and I love waking up to messages and pictures from all of you!

And thank you to all my readers. You're amazing. You're magical. You matter. And you're Fated for great things.

ABOUT THE AUTHOR

Amie Otto

USA Today bestselling author **April Asher** was hooked on romantic stories from the time she first snuck a bodice ripper from her mom's bedside table. By day, April dons dark-blue nurse's scrubs and drinks way too much caffeine. By night, she still consumes too much caffeine, but she does it with a laptop in hand. She pens rom-coms with a paranormal twist but also writes high-octane romantic suspense as April Hunt. She lives out her own happily ever after in Virginia with her college sweetheart husband and their two children.